N. G. OSBORNE

REFUGE

N. G. Osborne grew up in Angus, Scotland and graduated in 1995 from Oxford University with a B.A. in Politics, Philosophy & Economics. At the age of eighteen, Osborne spent twelve months as a volunteer for Project Trust working in a school and the Afghan refugee camps of Peshawar, Pakistan. This experience was the inspiration for this novel.

Refuge

A Novel by

N. G. Osborne

Cranham & Keith Books

FIRST EDITION, OCTOBER 2012

Copyright © 2012 by N. G. Osborne

ISBN-13: 978-0-6156954-0-2

For Clarke

*For your love, for your wisdom, for your support,
and most of all, for being my light.*

How can one take delight in the world unless one flees to it for refuge

Frank Kafka

PROLOGUE

escape

Kabul – February 1981

ONE

"NOOR—NOOR, MY love, please get up."

Noor opens her eyes to find her mother crouched over her, her mother's lantern just bright enough to bathe her face in a warm glow. Noor fights the urge to go back to sleep.

"The Russians are coming," her mother says.

Noor's eyes snap open, and she swings her feet onto the cold stone floor.

"Wait," her mother says. "Put these on first."

Her mother holds out a set of clothes. It's only now that Noor realizes her mother is wearing a shalwar kameez.

"Mamaan, do I have to?"

"Think of it as a disguise."

That at least makes it palatable.

"Now quick," her mother says, "we've no time to waste."

Her mother hastens away. Noor pulls her pajamas off and grabs the first article of clothing, a pale green kameez.

"You ready?" a voice hisses.

Noor clutches her kameez to her chest. Her brother, Tariq, stands in the doorway, holding a lamp of his own, his shadow looming behind him.

"Get out, I'm dressing," she says.

"Nothing to see," Tariq smirks.

"Not the point."

"Well hurry up."

Noor waits for Tariq to leave before slipping on the kameez and the baggy shalwar pants. She shoves her feet into her tennis shoes and takes off at full tilt. She finds everyone in the kitchen, their faces lit by the flickering light of the stove. Her Aunt Sabha is crying, and her sobs only intensify upon seeing Noor.

"Oh my sweet, sweet girl. When will we see you again?"

"You'll come and see us in America," Noor says.

"That's right, that's exactly what we'll do."

Aunt Sabha sweeps Noor into her ample bosom.

"Do you have the letter from Doctor Abdullah?" her Uncle Aasif asks her father.

"The letter?" her father says.

"Good God, Aamir," her mother snaps, "the introduction to the American Ambassador."

Her father searches his jacket pockets and emerges with a crumpled envelope.

"Give it to me," her mother says snatching it away.

Her mother looks around.

"Where's Bushra?"

"She's awake," her father says.

"But was she out of bed when you left her?"

It's clear from her father's expression that Bushra wasn't.

"Noor, go and get your sister now," her mother says.

Noor grabs a lantern and sprints back upstairs. She finds her older sister asleep, her shalwar kameez lying undisturbed beside her. Noor shakes her.

"Bushra, you've got to get up."

Bushra groans and draws her covers close. Noor rips them off and yanks Bushra out of the bed.

"The Russians are coming to arrest Baba," Noor says.

Bushra yelps and jumps to her feet.

"We've got to go," Bushra says

"That's what I've been trying to tell you."

Bushra scrambles into her shalwar kameez, and the two of them run out the room. Noor halts outside her bedroom.

"Keep going, I'll be right there."

Noor enters her room and takes one last look around; at the doll's house her father built last Eid and which, to her eternal guilt, she hasn't played with once; her posters of Chris Evert and Martina Navratilova; her pet rabbit Bjorn, sitting up in his cage, his nose twitching. She thinks about setting him loose but knows he wouldn't last more than a day before becoming someone's dinner. She puts a finger through the mesh and rubs his forehead.

"I've got to go, Bjorn. A long way away, but I'll always love you, remember that."

Bjorn's ears prick up; outside some cars screech to a halt. Doors open, and a man yells out commands in Russian. Noor sprints out of the room and back downstairs.

"They're here," she screams.

Aunt Sabha lets out a shriek. Booming thuds reverberate from the front door.

"I'll delay them," Uncle Aasif says. "Now go, go."

Noor's mother grabs Noor's hand, and they run out of the kitchen across the snow covered courtyard, past the ancient apricot tree that, to Noor's eternal triumph, she climbed higher than Tariq the week before. Her mother tugs her into the dusty old servants' quarters past the laundry room with its wooden washboards and iron ringer and up to a large metal door. Her mother yanks it open and pulls Noor into an alley where a donkey and cart await.

"Why aren't we taking the Oldsmobile?" Noor says.

"It's too conspicuous."

Her mother grabs Noor by the waist and throws her up onto the straw. Tariq and Bushra bundle in beside her while her parents sit up front. Her father clicks his tongue, and the donkey starts plodding forward.

"Put this on, Bushra," her mother says.

She holds out another article of clothing: it's a burqa. Bushra complies, and her mother puts on one of her own. Noor shivers. They look like jinns sent to steal her soul. Tariq nudges her.

"You scared?" he says.

"Course not."

"Liar."

Her mother hisses at them to be quiet. Noor looks towards the end of the alley. Despite the early hour, the street beyond is already bustling with traffic.

"Faster," her mother says.

Her father urges the donkey on, but if anything the donkey seems to slow.

"We're a simple peasant family from Aynak," her mother says. "If we're stopped let your father do the talking."

"But what if they ask us questions?" Noor says.

"They won't."

"But what if they do?"

"Then only speak Pashtu. If they speak to you in English pretend you don't understand."

A car pulls into the alley its round headlamps lighting the morning mist a garish yellow.

Her father and mother stiffen.

Noor squints; in the glare it's impossible to tell who's inside. The car honks and she senses her parents relax; she assumes if it were Russians they'd have gotten out by now. Her father looks over his shoulder to see if he can back up.

"Don't you dare," her mother says.

The car nudges forward, but for once the donkey's obstinacy works to their advantage. After some virulent honking the driver puts the car into reverse. The donkey keeps pace, as if galvanized by its victory.

Noor hears shouts behind them and twists around to see four men emerging from the back of their house.

"Stop," one shouts.

Her mother grabs the reins from her father and whacks the donkey as hard as she can.

"Stop right now, or we'll shoot," another yells.

The men pull guns from their holsters.

"Children, get down," her mother shouts.

Her mother grabs a hold of Noor and shoves her into the straw. Shots ring out, and Noor clenches her eyes shut.

Her mother yells at the donkey to keep going, there's another crackle of gunfire. The din of traffic and the sweet scent of petroleum fumes engulfs them.

Noor opens her eyes; her brother's crotch is inches from her, a dark urine stain smearing the front of his pants. She rises up onto her elbows and sees the owner of the car shake his fist at them before accelerating back down the alley. Her mother hands the reins to Noor's father.

"Turn right on Chicken Street," she says panting.

She looks back at her children.

"Is everyone alright?"

Tariq sits up doing his best to hide his piss stain with a handful of straw. He catches Noor looking at him and reddens. They turn down Chicken Street with its souvenir shops and restaurants. Bushra lies on the straw moaning.

"Bushra, are you alright?" her mother says.

"Yes, Mamaan."

"Then sit up."

They come to the end of the street and merge onto another bustling thoroughfare. A convoy of Soviet armored personnel carriers rumbles towards them. Noor holds her breath. One of the helmeted gunners stares at her: the days of the soldiers pretending to be their friends are long gone. The final personnel carrier passes by, and Noor thinks it permissible to breathe. She looks at Zarnegar Park, the Mir Abdul Rahman Tomb's dull, copper dome framed by the snow covered mountains. She wonders if she'll ever see it again.

The cart hits a pothole. It sends Noor tumbling forward and elicits a pained groan from her mother. Noor puts a hand on the floor and feels something damp. At first she assumes it's Tariq's urine, but when she brings her hand up she sees it's stained with blood. She notices her mother is bent over.

"Mamaan."

"Yes, my love."

"Are you alright?"

Her mother doesn't answer. Her father looks across.

"What's the matter?" he says.

Her mother pulls up the front of her burqa. Even in the pale light of dawn Noor can see her mother's kameez is soaked in blood. Noor cries out.

"Shh," her mother says, "don't draw attention to us."

Up ahead, just before the turn for the river, a group of Russian soldiers have set up a checkpoint. The traffic slows. Her father yanks on the reins and tries to turn the cart around. It's impossible, a bus is right behind them.

"They'll see me," her mother says to her father.

"No, just stay where you are. We will be past this at any moment, and we will go find a doctor."

"Aamir, it's too late for that."

"Nonsense."

The cart edges forward, and her mother rests her burqa on top of her head. Her cheeks, so rosy even in the coldest weather, are drained. She looks at each of her children as though she wants to burn their images into her soul.

"I love you all," she says, "more than you'll ever know."

"No," Tariq screams.

Up ahead a soldier looks in their direction. Tariq wraps his arms around his mother.

"Don't go, don't go," he says.

Her mother strokes his hair and whispers into his ear. The cart trundles forward again; they're now only three vehicles away from the checkpoint.

"Please, Aamir," her mother says.

Her father stares at her, unwilling to grasp what's unfolding in front of him.

"For their sake," she says.

Somehow he manages to nod. Her mother leans forward and kisses her father on the forehead.

"I love you, Aamir," she says. "Look after them for me."

She extricates herself from her son's grasp, and Noor's father wraps his arms around Tariq. Tariq fights back, his legs kicking out, his arms flailing.

"Take the reins," her mother says to Noor.

Noor scrambles into the front seat. Her mother grabs her by shoulders.

"Never compromise who you are. You hear me?"

Her mother places the reins in Noor's hand and pushes herself off the cart. Noor looks back. Her mother lies there in the street, blood already staining the snow around her. With whatever life she has left she struggles back up onto her feet. Tariq breaks free and crawls to the back of the cart.

"Mamaan," he screams. "Mamaan."

Her mother looks stricken. From beneath her burqa she pulls out the envelope containing Dr. Abdullah's letter. She collapses on the ground, and a woman in the bus behind lets out a piercing shriek. Soon soldiers are running past them until her mother's body is lost amidst a sea of green uniforms. With the checkpoint no longer manned the donkey picks up its pace. The road bends to the left, and soon the checkpoint is out of sight.

Noor turns back and sees her father's eyes are brimming with tears. In the back her brother lies on the straw sobbing while her sister sits immobile as a statue. Noor takes her father's hand in hers, gives the donkey a whack with the reins, and they continue on out of the city

PART I

encounter

Peshawar, September 1991

10 years later

TWO

CHARLIE MATTHEWS WALKS into the arrivals hall, his head already spinning. It's got to be the jetlag, he tells himself, but the longer he looks around the less sure he is. The hall is chaotic, packed with men wearing what look like long-shirted pajamas, passengers pushing over laden carts, and groups of veiled women being shepherded through the throng like livestock at a county fair. And then there's the smell; it's been there ever since he stepped off the plane, a sweet and overpowering combination of b.o. and mothballs.

He drops his holdall and lights a cigarette. A sea of expectant faces stare back at him—all mustached, all with wavy black hair, all wearing shalwar kameez. They all fit the description of the man who's picking him up.

Which one is he?

"Taxi, sir, need taxi—best prices in town," one says.

"Not today thanks," Charlie says.

"Sir, sir, nicest ride in Islamabad," another says, pushing the first man aside. "Please I am showing you, you most impressed."

"It's okay, I got a ride lined up."

The man grabs his arm, and Charlie has to jerk it away. He spots a man coming towards him; unlike everyone else his mustache is pencil thin, his hair spiked and his smile wide.

"I am Wali," he says, "you are Mr. Charlie Matthews, I presume."

"The one and only," Charlie says.

"The one and only, oh, that is quite fabulous, I must use that myself some time. Pardon me while I write it down."

Wali pulls out a notepad and pen from inside his waist-coat. Another taxi driver grabs Charlie from behind.

"Sir, this man no good driver. Me, I assuredly most excellent."

Wali sends a barrage of Urdu in the man's direction. The man shrinks backwards, and Wali goes back to writing. He finishes and puts the pen and pad away.

"Like your technique," Charlie says.

"Forgive me but I don't understand," Wali says

"The way you handled that guy."

"Oh that is most kind, but you have to, I'm afraid. Now please, let me take your bag."

"I got it."

"But I insist."

"It's no big deal."

"It's a very big deal to me, Mr. Matthews."

"Call me Charlie."

"Please, Mr. Matthews, for my honor please let me take your bag."

"Really? For your honor?"

"Most assuredly."

"Well in that case," Charlie grins.

Charlie hands over his stained army-issue duffle bag.

"I am most obliged," Wali says. "Now what do you say to leaving this terminal?"

"Lead the way."

Wali guides Charlie through the seething morass as if he's cutting a path through the jungle, and they burst out the main entrance. Despite only the barest whiffs of orange streaking the dawn sky, it is already sweltering. Wali leads Charlie towards a silver SUV idling by the curb. A grubby kid leans against it munching on a samosa. Wali hands the kid a couple of bills and throws Charlie's bag in the trunk. Charlie goes to get in only for a bearded man to barrel past. A burqaed woman trailing in the man's wake, trips and tumbles to the ground. Charlie kneels down beside her.

"You alright there?" he says.

The woman turns her masked face in his direction. She looks like she's wearing a Darth Vadar costume.

Jesus, who'd put a woman in such a thing?

Charlie offers her his hand only for the bearded man to grab him by the collar and jerk him up. He shouts at Charlie in a strange, guttural language.

"Hey, what the hell?" Charlie says.

The man pokes Charlie in the chest. Charlie pokes him back. Wali slides in between them.

"Please, Mr. Matthews, it is best if you come with me."

He places Charlie inside the SUV, all the while uttering apologies to the man, before jumping in and taking off. Charlie looks back. The bearded man is slapping the woman about the head.

"What was that guy's problem?"

"My advice to you Mr. Matthews, do not attempt to help another woman the rest of the time you are here. The men do not take kindly to it."

Charlie pulls out his Lonely Planet guide.

"I read something about that, but I didn't think it was that serious."

"I would not concern yourself with that book, Mr. Matthews."

"You're right. My mom always said you could never understand a country from one."

"And all you must understand about Pakistan is that it's a crazy place filled with crazy people."

"That's it?"

"The other day the United Nations publishes a list of the world's most corrupt countries, and Pakistan is number two. 'Why', everyone asks, 'did we not bribe them more so we could be number one?'"

Charlie laughs and fishes a pen from his pocket. He scribbles on the guide book's inside cover.

"Okay. One—never help women. Two—crazy place filled with crazy people."

"You need know nothing more."

Wali merges onto a four-lane highway without a second glance.

"So how's Skeppar doing?" Charlie says.

"Not well, I'm afraid."

"Still laid up, huh?"

"He flew back to Stockholm two days since. I am telling you, he looked like a Chinaman he was so yellow."

"You're shitting me.".

"I'm not familiar with this expression."

"Same as you're kidding me."

Wali gets out his notepad and begins writing. The SUV veers towards the opposing lanes. Charlie leans in and corrects the wheel. Wali puts his notepad away and grins.

"Oh, Mr. Matthews, this is most marvelous. You must know, it is my first and most important endeavor to speak like an American."

"Then don't say 'it is my endeavor' just say 'I want to speak like an American'."

"Understood."

Charlie floats his pack of Marlboros in Wali's direction. Wali takes a cigarette. Charlie lights it and one for himself.

"So who's in charge?" Charlie says.

"You are, of course."

"I mean who's running the office?"

"You are."

"Don't think so; not what I was contracted to do."

"Mr. Skeppar explained everything in his letter to you."

"You read it?"

"Mr. Skeppar did me the greatest honor of promoting me on his final day, and as your deputy I presumed it my duty. He says it will be three months before a replacement arrives."

"You're kidding me."

"I am not shitting you in the slightest."

Wali grins at Charlie.

"This is great news no? For now you can live in his house."

Charlie ruminates on this new piece of information. Responsibility is the last thing he's looking for.

"So I'm guessing you've got a ton of experience with mines?" Charlie says.

"Most definitely."

"Where'd you get your training?"

"Interesting you should ask. I'm not certain if you're aware of this, Mr. Matthews—"

"Charlie—"

"But my sister, she was killed by a mine in Afghanistan."

"Shit, I'm so sorry."

"She was coming to visit me; took a wrong step, that's the expression, am I not correct?"

"Yeah, just never heard it used so literally."

"That's the Afghans for you, you'll see; everything and anything terrible that could happen to a people has happened to us—quite literally."

For a moment Wali appears almost tranquil, and Charlie takes the opportunity to stare out the window. The land is green and flat, dotted with one-story mud homes. They remind him of the adobe huts in Peru—just these ones don't have windows. Shoeless kids toss balls at each other, women in scarves balance large ceramic jars on their heads, and old men plow their fields with horned cows.

A smattering of rain drops patter on the windshield and then, just like that, the heavens open. Wali turns on the wipers and leans closer to the windshield. The one thing he doesn't do is slow down. Outside the highway begins to resemble the surface of a lake.

They come upon a couple of trucks whose gaudy murals look like they were created for a seventh grade art project. Wali honks at them to make way. The trucks belch out clouds of soot. Wali spits out a Pashtun curse and swings the SUV into the first of the opposing lanes. A car's heading right for them.

Charlie grabs his seatbelt; the buckle fails to click.

Fuck.

Wali wrenches the wheel to the right and they slide into the next lane. No better luck. A white mini-van's fifty feet away.

Wali pulls the SUV onto the side of the road sending brown water cascading down onto the windscreen. For a second they are blind. When the wipers swipe it away they see the rear-end of an emaciated cow in front of them. Wali swings the SUV back across the two opposing lanes until they're on their side of the road, the trucks now behind them.

Charlie lights another cigarette and takes a deep drag.

"Wali," he says.

"Yes, Mr. Matthews."

"You probably should get my seatbelt fixed."

"It's not necessary, see I don't wear one."

"You probably should get it fixed all the same."

"You're the boss."

That sounds strange. I've never been the boss of anyone before.

Outside the rain stops as quickly as it began. Wali searches the floor beneath him and comes up with a cassette. He pops it into the player.

"I have a feeling you are not a fan of Indian music so I have something I am absolutely certain you'll relish."

The opening of *Like A Virgin* blasts from the speakers, and Wali sings along with the gusto of a backing singer. On '*I didn't know how lost I was until I met you,*' he points at Charlie with a gargantuan grin on his face.

Shit, the guy's hitting on me.

Charlie decides it's best not to encourage him.

"I'm beat," he says, "You mind if I get some shut-eye."

"Shut-eye?" Wali says.

"Sleep."

"Of course, of course. Now shuteye is that one word or two?"

"One I think."

Wali retrieves his notepad.

"Do not worry yourself," he says, "you're in a most safe pair of hands."

"Don't doubt it."

Charlie closes his eyes and is soon out for the count.

***

CHARLIE AWAKES TO find Wali's face mere inches from his own. He jerks back.

"Mr. Matthews, we're here."

Charlie realizes that Wali is standing outside the car. He wipes away the drool from his mouth and climbs out. For a moment he thinks his jetlag's playing tricks. A mansion fit for an ambassador stands in front of him.

"May I present your house." Wali says.

"You're kidding?"

"I do not shit you. Mr. Skeppar called it his 'precious gem'."

"I bet he did."

"Come, come, let me show you inside."

Wali sweeps open the front door and guides Charlie through the house's domed hall and up its sweeping staircase to his bedroom. With its four poster bed, large Afghan rug and antique writing table it looks like it hasn't been redecorated since the days of the Raj, and nor do any of the other bedrooms that Wali leads him through. Charlie loses count of how many there are; at least five on the top floor, another on the ground floor to go along with a book laden room that Wali calls the library, and a slightly less book laden room which he calls the sitting room. There's a study with mounted heads of exotic animals and a vast kitchen straight from the 1930s. Standing in its center are two men; the younger, a rail-thin man with a sporadic beard, keeps nodding his head, while the older one stares at the black-and-white tiled floor, all the while sweeping a twig brush back and forth.

"Who're these guys?" Charlie says.

"Your servants," Wali says.

Charlie retreats to the other end of the room and gestures for Wali to join him.

"Is there an issue, Mr. Matthews?"

"I don't need servants."

"There's no need to whisper, I promise you neither of these men understand a jot of English."

"I don't need servants."

"But all aid workers have servants."

"You're telling me there's not a single aid worker out here that doesn't have a servant?"

"Not one I know, and besides without their jobs these men will be homeless."

"They live here?"

"In a hut at the bottom of the garden."

Stumped, Charlie walks back to the men.

"Okay, what are their names?"

"This is Mukhtar, your cook and housekeeper."

"Good to meet you, Mukhtar."

Charlie sticks out his hand. Mukhtar shakes it vigorously.

"Yes sir, yes sir," Mukhtar says.

"I like that," Charlie smiles. "A firm handshake."

"And this is Rasul your gardener."

"Good to meet you, Rasul."

Charlie sticks out his hand. Rasul continues sweeping.

"He is not much one for pleasantries," Wali says.

They go out onto a verandah and into a garden filled with flowering bushes. Jasmine vines run up the side of the house and a big oak tree stands tall in the center of a well-kept lawn. Wali and Charlie sit down in a couple of rockers. Mukhtar soon arrives with tea.

"So I will come by after lunch to drive you to the office?" Wali says.

"Don't think that's a good idea," Charlie says. "I need a day to recharge."

"Recharge?"

"You know, get my strength back."

Wali takes out his pad and pen.

"But everyone is most eager to meet you."

"Please, Wali, just one day; it took me almost two to get here from New York."

Wali stops writing.

"New York! You are from New York. Oh, you are a most lucky man, Mr. Matthews. Am I not correct in saying that New York has the most sexy women in the whole world?"

"You've obviously not been to Brazil—"

"And most of the time they wear almost nothing on their bodies?"

"That's not really true."

"Never, they never wear almost nothing?"

"I guess when they're in the Hamptons."

"Hamptons?"

"On the beach."

"And when they're on the beach, they let you have sex with them?"

"No."

"Afterwards then?"

"No."

"You mean to tell me you have never been to the beach with a young lady friend who let you have sex with her afterwards?"

Charlie can't help but smile. Wali jumps out of his chair.

"Oh, I knew it! Mr. Matthews may I be so bold as to enquire how many females you've had the good fortune of having sexual intercourse with."

"It's tough to count."

Wali lets out a groan.

I guess he's not gay after all.

"Oh you do not understand, Mr. Matthews, the most dreadful conditions sexy young men like myself must endure. I am more likely to have sexual intercourse with a goat than a woman."

"You're kidding."

"Why? It's not like you can make idle chit chat with women."

"You mean there's no way you could date someone?"

"Date?"

"You know, go to dinner, a movie, that kind of thing."

Wali starts laughing so hard that Charlie grows uncomfortable.

"Oh, Mr. Matthews, you are quite the comedian. No, once in my village, there was this girl and boy who fell in love. So the boy goes to her father and begs to marry her. Of course, the girl's father would not hear of it: he looked down upon this boy's family. So one day they decide to run away to Kabul, but the girl's family soon catch up with them, and they dragged them into the hills and buried them up to their waists. Now tradition is they always start with the small stones so as not to kill you too quickly. It goes on for hours, I tell you. The boy and girl were in agony, their bones broken, blood pouring from their faces, and then the girl watched as her father and uncle carried over a large stone and dropped it on her lover's head. After that, her father turned to her and said, 'You know I only did this because I love you'."

"And then what did he do?" Charlie says.

"He shot her in the head of course."

Jesus, Wali wasn't kidding. This place is crazy.

"But you are fortunate," Wali says. "You can go to the American Club. It's where the foreigners go to drink. The foreign women too. It's no more than a five minute drive."

Charlie looks out into the expansive garden and leans back in his chair.

Okay, maybe living here won't be so bad after all.

THREE

NOOR CROUCHES OVER her fire and tends the few sticks of kindling she was able to scavenge the night before. She hopes they'll burn long enough for her water to boil. She's never understood the logic of drinking tea on a hot day. Her mother never did either, but her father hasn't gone a day in his life without a morning cup and, despite their circumstances, this is one indulgence she has no intention of depriving him of.

The water begins to boil, and she chastises herself for letting her mind wander. She focuses once more on the Dutch phrases she's learnt.

Goedemorgen—Angenaam kennis te maken—Hoe gaat het met u? Goed dankuwel—Tot ziens.

Noor lifts the pot away from the fire and the kindling disintegrates into a pile of ash. She pours the water into their chipped teapot. The corrugated door of their mud hut creaks open, and her father emerges. He runs a hand through his straggly, gray hair.

"You are up early," he says.

"It's like an oven in there. I don't know how Bushra can stand it."

"Quite comfortably it seems."

Her father picks up the teapot, leaving the cups and saucers for Noor.

"Care to join me in my study?" he says.

His joke lost its power to amuse years ago, but for her father's benefit Noor forces a smile. They head along a dusty path until they come upon a bedraggled eucalyptus tree and a carved bench that her father constructed some years back. They sit down and stare out at the barren graveyard. A rabbit pops up from behind a nearby grave and sniffs the air. Noor thinks she's hallucinating. She shakes her head only to see it still there.

How have you managed to survive in a place like this?

The rabbit stares right at her, its ears twitching and makes a couple of hops in her direction. Noor holds her breath. The rabbit hops closer.

"It should be ready by now," her father says.

The rabbit bounds away over the endless earthen mounds towards the crimson Khyber Mountains in the distance. Noor sighs and pours the tea. There's no milk to go with it; that's a luxury they'd had to forego a long time ago.

"So, do you have a busy day ahead of you?" her father says.

"The administrator's visiting."

"That is a rarity."

"The headmistress wants each class to perform a song. I suggested one from *The King and I.*"

"Ambitious."

"She deemed it too provocative and said we had to do *Watan Rana Kawoo* instead."

"Ah, that familiar favorite."

"She thinks the lyrics are inspirational."

"'*We are the army of education and bring light in the darkness.*' You must admit that tugs on the old heart strings."

"If you understand Pashtu."

"Maybe your fearless administrator does."

"I doubt it. None of them do."

Noor's stomach rumbles. She figures if she gets to school early enough she might be able to scrounge some naan from the kitchen.

"Do you think she might know the status of that scholarship?" her father says.

"I'm trying not to think about it."

"And failing, it would seem; you were tossing and turning all night."

"That had everything to do with this damn heat."

Her father takes a sip of his tea. She knows he isn't buying her explanation.

Why should he? I don't buy it either.

"I had the strangest dream last night," her father says.

Noor waits patiently. Listening to her father's dreams is another indulgence she's never deprived him of.

"It was raining, in a manner you could not imagine, and there we were, you, Bushra and I huddled up inside the hut. Water started seeping under the door, and soon it was so high that we resolved to flee. We waded outside to discover the whole camp engulfed by a flood and everything and everyone being swept away. At that moment all seemed lost, but then, right ahead of us, was a boat with your mother at the helm. It was so tiny she only had room for one of us, and do you know whom she chose to go with her? She chose you."

"I wouldn't have left you."

"But you did, and as I watched the two of you drift away, I do not think I have ever felt happier. It is a sign, my love, I think your time in this camp is coming to an end."

"You always dream of Mamaan around her birthday."

"I do not deny that, but this felt different. Truly it did."

Noor kisses her father on the cheek.

"I love you, Baba."

"I love you too, my dear."

Noor pulls her headscarf over her hair and heads for a nearby alley. Noor read once that the Eskimos had twenty words to describe snow, and she wonders why the Afghans haven't come up with a similar number for mud. Everything in the refugee camp seems to be made of it; the huts, the walls, the alleys, even the latrines. She comes to a wider lane already crowded with men making their way towards Jamrud Road, and crosses over the footbridge that spans the concrete storm channel. Shirtless boys are cooling off in its sewage-filled waters. She enters a ramshackle market.

"Water, miss," a boy, standing next to a melting block of ice, calls out.

He thrusts a metal cup in her direction.

"Most refreshing, one rupee only."

Noor puts her head down. She passes the kebab cooks twirling their skewers in the air like swashbuckling swordsmen, and the barbers shaving their early morning customers on the sidewalk, and joins the throng of refugees at the bus stop. She is the only woman. A Pakistani policeman lounges against the side of his rusted pick-up, smoking a cigarette. She catches his gaze and turns away.

"Hey. You," she hears him say.

She squeezes past a one-legged man and strains up onto her toes. The next bus is a hundred yards away.

"Woman, I'm talking to you."

A hand tugs on Noor's sleeve. Noor swings around to find the policeman staring at her like a lascivious uncle.

"You traveling alone?" he says.

"I'm with my husband."

"Where is he?"

Noor looks around as though he might be in the crowd.

"He was here a minute ago," she says.

"You can wait with me."

The bus pulls up, and the crowd begins to surge.

"There he is," she says pointing behind the policeman.

The policeman turns, and she rips her arm away. She uses her slender frame to squeeze through the throng and onto the bus. She hears the policeman blow his whistle, but it's to little effect. The bus pulls away, and Noor looks for an open seat. There are none to be had, and all she gets for her efforts are a couple of goons wiggling their tongues at her. She fixes them with a cold stare, and they turn away. She pulls her headscarf tighter and looks out of the window at a sparkling Land Cruiser ferrying a Western aid worker across town.

What I'd give to experience air-conditioning. Just once.

The bus arrives at her stop, and she wriggles her way off. The school is no more than a two hundred yard walk. In the courtyard the janitors are assembling the stage for the day's performance. She slips into the kitchen and searches for some naan: she finds none. The janitors must have eaten it all. She closes her eyes.

"O Allah," she says, "You have power, and I have none. You know all, and I know not. On this day I ask that you give me strength and kindly look upon me so that I may finally escape my present circumstances. Ameen."

Noor opens her eyes. A janitor stands in the doorway ogling her. She gathers her books and pushes past him. She looks up at the heavens.

Surely, Allah has to be listening to me.

***

THE CLASSROOM DOOR creaks open, and Miss Suha's wrinkled face cranes around it.

"The headmistress and the administrator want to see you."

Noor looks at Miss Suha, not sure if she heard her right.

"Well hurry up girl, they haven't got all day."

Noor puts her chalk down and turns to her students. All thirty girls are staring at her.

"Please continue with the exercise we were working on yesterday," Noor says.

Kamila, a bright-eyed student with a dime-sized birthmark on her forehead sticks her hand in the air.

"Is anything wrong, Miss Noor?"

"Kamila, when teachers go and see the headmistress it's not because we've misbehaved, it's because we have important things to discuss. Now I want you all to have finished the exercise by the time I get back."

"I finished it earlier," Kamila says.

"Do the next one then."

"I've—"

"Enough," Miss Suha says.

Kamila clamps her mouth shut. The girls all believe Miss Suha to be a witch and the last thing any of them want is to be the subject of one of her spells.

Miss Suha leads Noor out of the classroom and hobbles down the corridor at her usual tortoise pace. All Noor wants to do is run ahead and leave her behind, but she is no more inclined to get on Miss Suha's bad side than the girls.

"So what is she like?" Noor says.

"A whore," Miss Suha says.

Noor doesn't take the bait. Miss Suha holds that opinion of all Western women.

"They're a promiscuous race those Dutch. She even brought a man with her. A reporter; probably someone she's—well I'll stop there, don't want to offend your innocent ears."

A reporter. The administrator asking to see me personally.

Noor's heart beats ever faster.

Why else would he be here other than to record the first time a Dutch Aid teacher received a foreign scholarship?

They pass Miss Layla's class. One of her students is attempting to recite an Arabic verse while holding a couple of dictionaries above her head. The student gives Noor an imploring look. Noor looks away.

Not now. Not when I'm so close.

They arrive at the headmistress's anteroom.

"Wait here," Miss Suha says.

She shambles into the headmistress's office. Noor stares at a poster of the Kaaba on the wall and closes her eyes.

Our Lord! Bestow on us mercy from Your presence and dispose of our affairs for us in the right way.

She opens her eyes and gasps. Miss Suha is standing in front of her.

"In you go," she says.

Noor enters the office to find the headmistress behind her desk. The pretty, blonde administrator perches on the couch, while the balding reporter sits on a chair off to the side. The administrator bounces to her feet.

"It's so nice to meet you, Noor. I'm Elma."

Noor is drawn in by Elma's shining eyes and unwavering gaze. Elma takes Noor's right hand in hers.

"Come, sit with me."

Noor allows herself to be led to the couch. She comes out of her daze just enough to remember her Dutch phrases.

"Goedemorgen," Noor says. "Angenaam kennis te maken."

Elma's face lights up.

"You speak Dutch?"

"I learnt a few phrases."

"Oh, how wonderful. Really, I'm very honored."

Noor looks over at the reporter. He smiles at her. Noor reddens.

"Now I'm sure you're wondering why I'm taking the time to meet with you personally," Elma says.

Noor can do no more than nod.

"First and foremost, I want to thank you for the job you're doing. I'm so proud of this school, how it's blossomed in the two years I've been in Pakistan. When I was last in Holland, I had the opportunity to talk with Ruud Lubbers—"

"The Dutch Prime Minister," the headmistress interjects.

"That's right, and he was so proud of how we've been able to give hope and opportunity to so many Afghan girls."

Noor holds her breath.

Here it comes. Finally, after all this time.

"That's why this is so difficult for me, why I insisted I be the one to tell you. Now, as you may be aware, there's a recession in Europe and every department's being asked to make sacrifices."

Noor glances at the headmistress who averts her gaze. Noor notices a box of tissues sitting next to Elma.

Oh God, she's here to sack me.

"I want you to know I fought, harder than at any time in my life. I mean the last thing I want is to destroy what we've all worked so hard to build, but I was told if I don't find the savings, the Hague will impose cuts unilaterally."

Noor's throat constricts.

"I'm sorry to inform you that we're cutting the salaries of the married teachers by twenty percent and the unmarried ones by a third."

Elma pushes the box of tissues towards Noor. Noor doesn't know whether to laugh or cry. Her job is safe, but in one fell swoop her weekly paycheck has been cut to six-hundred-and-sixty-six rupees. If she goes to the moneychangers' bazaar she'll be lucky to get fourteen dollars in return.

"It was agreed," Elma says, "that the unmarried women have fewer dependents and thus require less to live on."

"I understand," Noor finds herself saying.

Elma exhales as if relieved to have come through the ordeal unscathed. She smiles at Noor.

"So, I'm interested to know more about you—you teach the twelve-year-olds, correct?"

Noor doesn't answer; she's too busy trying to work out how she, Baba and Bushra will live off her reduced wage.

We can no longer have meat once a week.

"That is correct," the headmistress says, "she teaches form eight"

"And where do you live?" Elma says.

And we'll have to cut back on the gas lamp at night, just when the nights are getting longer, and we'll need it more.

"She lives in Kacha Gari," the headmistress says, "the refugee camp."

"Have you been there, Rod?" Elma asks the reporter.

"Never been," the reporter says.

"I'll take you around, we have a couple of amazing projects there."

"Perhaps Noor could be your guide," the headmistress says.

"I may take you up on that," Elma says.

Oh no, the British Council library fee is due this week. I'll have to dip into the emergency fund. I can't deprive Baba of his books.

"So, Noor, is there any reason why you're not married?" Elma says.

The mention of marriage jars Noor out of her thoughts.

"Excuse me?" she says.

"You're not engaged are you?"

"No, I live with my father and sister."

"Salman, my driver, isn't married either."

Noor is speechless.

Can this woman really be trying to marry me off?

"He's looking for a wife," Elma says.

"As is every other unmarried man in Peshawar."

Out the corner of her eye, Noor catches the headmistress eyeballing her.

"He has many admirable qualities," Elma says, "he's ambitious, handsome. I think he has a great future ahead of him."

"Then maybe you should marry him," Noor says.

Elma lets go of Noor's hand as if jolted by an electric shock. She busies herself with the stack of papers beside her.

"You can go now, Noor," the headmistress says.

Noor remains in her seat.

"You wouldn't have any information about the Netherlands Fellowship Programme, would you?"

Elma looks up.

"The Netherlands Fellowship Programme," Noor repeats. "I applied for a scholarship six months ago."

"NFP's for mid-career professionals," Elma says. "It's not right for you."

"Of course. I told my father that when we applied."

Elma returns to her paperwork. Noor stands.

"Tot ziens," Noor says.

Elma doesn't reply. Noor catches the eye of the reporter. He is staring at her with a look of amazement.

Amazed that I'd so humiliate the head of the agency that employs me. Oh Lord, what have I done?

Noor feels nauseous yet she straightens her shoulders as her mother taught her and walks to the door. On the other side she finds Miss Raza waiting there, wiping away tears. It's clear the news has begun to spread throughout the school.

"Compose yourself, woman, and get in there," Miss Suha says. "And you, get back to class."

Noor heads down the corridor and remembers the performance they have to give at lunch. Her stomach turns.

It's too late to change it but under these circumstances ...

Outside Miss Layla's classroom she sees a student squatting against the wall with her head in her hands. Noor crouches down beside her.

"It's Haifa, right?"

Haifa nods. Noor lifts her chin up. Haifa's cheeks are wet with tears, her right marked with a fresh crimson welt.

"It's my fault," Haifa says, "I couldn't remember the surah."

Noor knows there's no point in confronting Miss Layla. It'd only make Haifa's life more miserable.

"Has she asked you to learn another?" Noor says.

"Two by tomorrow. There's no way I can do it."

"Come and see me after class, and we'll practice them. You'll memorize them in no time, I promise."

Haifa smiles.

"Thank you, Miss Noor."

"It's what I'm here for."

Noor carries on to her classroom. Kamila is the first to see her and sticks up her hand.

"Yes, Kamila."

"I heard that woman's here to close the school?"

The girls look nervously at Noor.

"Let me be the first to reassure you all that rumor's not true," Noor says. "None of us are going anywhere."

***

ELMA SITS ON the dais and broods. When they'd arrived this morning it had seemed a perfect opportunity to show Rod her human side; how as a dedicated, fast-rising agency head, she dealt hands-on with ruthless diktats from back home with grace and compassion. Now that was all lost because of one comment.

'Maybe you should marry him then.'

Elma can just imagine the opening paragraph of the New Yorker article; the whole episode described in excruciating detail. A single, career-driven Dutch woman asking a beautiful, young Afghan teacher about her marriage prospects. The irony.

How could you be such an idiot?

The seven-year-old girl at the lectern finishes reading her poem, and Elma applauds along with everyone else. The headmistress stands up and takes the girl's place.

"Now form eight will sing Watan Rana Kawoo," the headmistress says.

Elma does her best not to grimace. She's lost count of how many times she's been forced to listen to this turgid song. Three rows of twelve-year-old girls stand up, and along with Noor make their way up onto the stage. Noor catches Elma's gaze and turns her eyes away.

God, she's stunning.

In fact Elma can't think of another Afghan woman she's met who's better looking, and that's saying something considering how attractive Afghan women are. That is before the toils of the camps transform them at warp speed into wizened, dull-eyed automatons.

The girls line up in three rows behind a pretty girl with an unfortunate birthmark on her forehead. Noor nods at the girl. The girl starts singing. Her rendition, while in Pashtu, is more in keeping with a 1950s Broadway musical. Elma senses the headmistress bristle beside her.

"Isn't that from *The King and I*?" Rod says.

"The words are from a popular Afghan song," Elma says.

"Yeah but that tune's *'Getting To Know You'*. I'm sure of it."

The other girls join in and sing the chorus. Their tone is pitch perfect. Elma remembers the film now. Deborah Kerr in her billowing grey dress introducing herself to each of the Thai King's children. She never cared for it; she always felt it had a patronizing, Western-centric air.

And yet here you are guilty of a similar sensibility.

Elma can't help but shudder. She glances at Rod. He is staring entranced at Noor and the girls. The Sun Tzu quote *'keep your friends close, and your enemies closer'* pops into her mind. This impoverished refugee could hardly be considered an enemy, but somehow the quote makes sense. She leans in as if bringing Rod into her confidence.

"We're trying everything we can to get her a scholarship," Elma says.

Rod gives her a quizzical look.

"NFP is the last thing she needs, stuck in some dreary college in the sticks with a bunch of jaded thirty and forty some things."

"So what's the plan?" Rod says.

"An undergraduate program, something which will allow her to blossom among students her own age. We're thinking the University of Amsterdam, maybe Maastricht or Leiden."

"Did you notice she was the only teacher that didn't cry when you broke the news?"

Elma hadn't. Her mind had been too preoccupied at the time, but now thinking back, she realizes Rod's right.

"She's everything we hope these girls can be," Elma says. "Strong, independent leaders in a free and prosperous Afghanistan."

"Well I have to say, you're doing a fantastic job."

Elma feels the day's equilibrium shift back in her direction. The song finishes, and the headmistress stands, ready to hustle Noor and her class off the stage. Elma jumps up and starts applauding wildly. Rod joins her. Both the headmistress and Noor turn and stare at them in shock. Elma flashes Noor a glowing smile.

Keep her close. Yes, keep this one as close as you can.

FOUR

"LOOK, THERE'S A spot on it, you idiot," Tariq says, pointing to a faint dot on his kameez's cuff. "Quick go fetch me another."

His wife scurries from the room, and he breathes a little easier. Using his one arm, he struggles out of his kameez. He stares at the mottled stump of his right arm.

I look like one of those wretched beggars on Jamrud Road.

He curses his father-in-law again for sending him on that ill-fated mission. As far as he's concerned it achieved nothing. The Prince didn't even visit him in the hospital.

Well, you have another opportunity to make an impression tonight. The question is, how? The most words the Prince has ever spoken to you were when he asked you to fetch a glass of water.

His wife waddles into the room with a fresh kameez.

"Help me into it," he says.

His wife pulls the kameez over his head and lifts his stump into its right sleeve.

"Careful," he winces.

She uses a pin to secure his right cuff. He tries his best not to stare at the pelt of fur above her lip and the folds of skin beneath her chin.

"Did you talk to Nawaz's wife?" he says.

"She said there were bruises all over the Princess's body and both her wrists were bandaged."

So the Princess committed suicide. It makes sense considering the Prince treated her like his personal punching bag.

There's a knock. He takes one last look at himself in the mirror and opens the door to find his father-in-law snorting up a glob of phlegm. It takes all the self-control he's mustered over the years not to cringe.

"As-salaam Alaykum, Salim Afridi."

"Let's go," his father-in-law says.

They head across a courtyard cluttered with bales of straw, ducks, chickens, and a couple of donkeys. In one corner, his father-in-law's third wife is milking a cow.

It's like we live in a village.

"How's the arm?" his father-in-law says.

"Painful," Tariq says.

"Come, it's nothing but a contact wound."

If Tariq had two hands he'd throttle the man.

"And my daughter?" his father-in-law continues.

Ugly, fat and an imbecile, .

"She's good," Tariq says.

His father-in-law lets fly with another globule of phlegm.

Tariq remembers his wedding day, and the excitement of it all. Not only had he managed to marry into the family of one of the mujahideen's finest guerilla warfare tacticians, but Badia, Salim Afridi's sixteen-year-old daughter, had a reputation for being as beautiful as any princess. Yet when the veil was pulled back, Tariq found himself staring at a pig of a woman in her mid-twenties. This daughter's name was Badria, and to this day Tariq is convinced his father-in-law tricked him.

It's gotten you closer to the Prince, but still not close enough, and now the war's nearly over.

Once the Communists in Kabul are defeated, the Prince will return to Saudi Arabia with only a trusted few, and

Tariq's father-in-law won't be one of them. 'Who'd want to
live in an oven like Saudi Arabia,' the fool had said to him,
not having a clue that even the cattle there bask in air
conditioning.

"Now you remember how to act around the Prince?" his
father-in-law says.

"Don't stare, don't interrupt, and don't touch him unless
he touches you," Tariq says by rote.

"I'm serious, he's in a foul mood."

*Who wouldn't be if your favorite wife preferred eternal hell to living
one more day with you?*

They come upon the floodlit main building. A hundred
years ago the British had built it to house a boarding school
for the sons of the Indian elite, and it wouldn't look out of
place if it were set down in the English countryside. A line of
dignitaries stand at the bottom of its sweeping steps and
submit themselves to a weapons search. The mujahideen
guard see Salim Afridi and Tariq, and gesture them through.
They make their way down a long set of corridors until they
arrive at the door to the Prince's quarters. A couple of the
Prince's elite Arab guard stand in front of it, and here even
Salim Afridi must submit to a pat down.

Once through, they enter a luxurious reception room. On
either side of the room are two elongated couches on which
forty Pakistani and Afghan dignitaries sit. Tariq and Salim
Afridi find a space. The Prince sits at the far end in traditional
Saudi robes. A man is standing in front of him, and every
time the Prince speaks the man has to lean down to catch
whatever the Prince is saying. The man retreats, and everyone
but Salim Afridi sits up hoping it's their turn. The Prince
speaks to the retainer beside him. The retainer comes over
and informs them that the Prince will receive them. They
walk over and the Prince takes Salim Afridi's hand. Salim
Afridi leans in and the Prince kisses him on both cheeks.

"As-salaam Alaykum," his father-in-law says. "My condolences. May Allah have mercy upon us all. From Him we come, and to Him we all return."

"Ameen," the Prince says.

Tariq waits for the Prince to acknowledge him. He doesn't even look his way.

"I want to start planning the next offensive" the Prince says.

"We have plenty of time till spring, your Highness," his father-in-law says.

"But I don't want to wait until spring."

"Your Highness, no one fights in Afghanistan in the winter."

"I'm not just anyone—"

"Of course, your Highness—"

"I hear Massoud is making moves from the North."

"My sources aren't telling me that."

"Well mine are," the Prince shouts. "The CIA not least."

His father-in-law takes a step backwards. Tariq wonders how he could be so foolish as not to take his own advice. The Prince's hands shake, and he has to grip the arms of his chair in order to control them. The Prince raises a hand and his retainer hands him a handkerchief. He wipes his brow.

"I apologize. I will start putting plans together straight away," his father-in-law says.

The Prince waves his hand to dismiss them. Tariq's heart sinks. They turn and head for the door.

"What happened to you?" the Prince says.

Tariq keeps walking.

"You, the son-in-law."

Tariq stops dead. He looks back to see the Prince staring right at him.

"It's nothing but a contact wound, your Highness," Tariq says.

The Prince frowns, and Tariq senses his father-in-law bristle beside him.

Dear God, what have I just said?

The Prince starts laughing so hard that he doubles over in his chair.

"You hear that?" the Prince says. "Just a contact wound."

He laughs once again, and this time the room joins in.

"Come—what's your name?"

"Tariq, your Highness."

"Yes of course, now tell me how it really happened."

"Salim Afridi sent a small group of us into Afghanistan a couple of months ago, and we set up on a hill above the Jalalabad highway. Three days and nights we waited, and then on the fourth we saw an Afghan Army convoy coming down the road. We fired on them with everything we had, but to our amazement our shots flew wide, and it looked as if they were going to get away. I decided to give it one last go, so I scrambled down the hillside onto the road just as the last personnel carrier was about to pass. The machine gunner was so surprised his first shots spat wide. I got on one knee and fired my RPG. It went straight through the driver's window, and the carrier blew up."

"All praise is due to Allah," the Prince says.

Everyone in the room repeats the phrase. Tariq waits. The Prince nods for him to continue.

"When I woke, I found myself on a stretcher and my arm … truly, it is nothing but a contact wound when you think of the greater jihad."

The Prince ponders Tariq's words. He stands and opens his arms.

"Come here," he says.

He kisses Tariq on both cheeks.

"This here is a pious young man, the kind of man who represents the future of an Islamic Afghanistan."

Tariq does his damnedest not to break into a grin.

"You should be very proud to have such a son-in-law," the Prince says.

"I am," Salim Afridi says.

"I hope to see you again soon, Tariq."

"Thank you, your Highness."

The Prince sits, and Tariq and his father-in-law head for the door. Tariq knows he's the envy of every man in the room.

FIVE

"I'M SORRY, SIR," the manager says, "but this club is only for members and their guests."

"That's cool. How much to join?" Charlie says.

"You need to be proposed by a member, and then your application goes before the committee."

Charlie winces.

"You see that's a problem, I really could do with a drink tonight."

A patron comes through a set of double doors, and Charlie catches a glimpse of a smoky, raucous bar.

"Night, Nawaz," the man says as he stumbles down the foyer's stairs.

"A wonderful evening to you too, Mr. Wigram."

The manager looks back at Charlie as though surprised he's still there.

"There's no such thing as a temporary membership?" Charlie says.

"No."

"Please I'm begging you."

"I'm sorry, sir, but I must ask you to leave."

Charlie sighs.

"Fine. You mind getting me a membership form?"

The manager trudges back to his office. His phone rings, and he picks it up. Charlie waits. From the animated nature of the conversation, it doesn't seem like it's going to end anytime soon.

Screw it.

Charlie heads for the double doors and pushes them open. To call the place a club is a stretch—it's not much better than a dive bar with its mismatched chairs and scuffed wooden floor. He approaches some well-built men sitting around a table littered with empty glasses.

"Hey, one of you guys mind making me your guest for the night?" he says.

"Oh, piss off," a bald-headed brute in a Manchester United t-shirt says.

"Easy buddy."

"Sorry, how about fuck off. That better?"

The other guys laugh like it's the best joke they've heard all night. A hand tugs on Charlie's sleeve. It's the manager.

"Sir, I must ask you to come with me."

Charlie turns back to the table.

"Come on guys, it's no skin off your backs."

"Tourists aren't allowed in here," the Brit says.

"I'm not a tourist."

"Or assholes."

The Brits burst out laughing, and the manager pulls Charlie back into the foyer.

"Okay, okay, I'm going," Charlie says.

Charlie heads for the front door.

"It's okay, Nawaz," someone says, "he's with me."

Charlie turns to see a greasy-haired American standing at the top of the stairs. His collared shirt is tucked into a pair of creased khakis that are so short you can see his white socks.

"I'm sorry, Mr. Gardener, but you are familiar with this man?" the manager says.

"We met a couple of days back."

Charlie grins.

"Come on," the man says. "I'm three drinks ahead of you."

They enter the bar. The table of Brits shoot Charlie a collection of foul looks.

"Don't let em bother you," the man says, "they're just drowning their sorrows."

"Why's that?"

"War's nearly over, least the good part."

"That's a bad thing?"

"It is when there's no other conflict to move on to."

They reach the bar.

"What you drinking?" the man says.

"Bud would be awesome."

The man orders one and a Coke for himself. He sticks out his hand.

"Ivor Gardener."

"Charlie Matthews."

"So what you doing out here, Charlie? You're kind of young for this scene."

"Got a job working for Mine Aware.

"Ah, Skeppar's outfit."

Ivor spies the red "1" tattoo on Charlie's forearm.

"You in the First Infantry Division?"

"Three years. Got out right after Desert Storm."

"That where you get your scar?"

Charlie traces the three inch blemish that curves down his left cheek.

"Yeah, totally heroic. Tripped coming down the back of the transport plane. Was the war's first confirmed casualty."

Ivor laughs. Their drinks arrive and Charlie takes a swig.

Shit, that tastes good.

"Please tell me you're not another of those do-gooder types who think they can save the world?" Ivor says.

"Once upon a time I might've been, but not after what I saw in Kuwait."

"Yeah, war has a way of making you realize all that good intention stuff is utter bullshit."

Ivor surveys the inhabitants of the bar.

"Take this crowd. Nothing they like more than going back home and waxing lyrical about all the lives they've saved. But if it weren't for their tax free salaries and endless servants, ninety percent of em would be lawyers or bankers."

"I just want to open up a dive shop in Belize."

"Well then Pakistan makes total sense."

"It's not going to be cheap and demining's one of my few marketable skills. Figured I could bank my salary and be there in a year, diving the Blue Hole in the morning and sketching in the afternoon."

"Fuck me, an artist and a vet. Could you be any more pathetic?"

Charlie laughs.

"Hey, Gauguin was in the navy, and he seemed to have a pretty good time afterwards in Polynesia."

Ivor raises his Coke.

"Well here's to Charlie Matthew's Dive Shop."

"Free lessons on me."

"Watch out, just might take you up on that."

Charlie downs his beer and orders another.

"So how about you?" Charlie says.

"With the Consulate," Ivor says. "Been here three years."

"Like it?"

"This is what they call a hardship posting."

"What do you mean by that?"

"When they dump you in a city where the ninety percent of the locals hate America despite the billions we've spent, and none of the Afghans credit us with winning the war despite the fact they'd still be fighting the Russians with swords if it wasn't for us, where every man feels like it's his divine right to kill anyone he thinks has offended him, where there are only two places to get a drink, and there's almost zero chance of getting laid, be it paid or free, that my friend is considered a hardship posting."

"Not exactly Paris."

"Fuck, most of us would take Luanda over this shithole."

Charlie's second beer arrives. He takes a swig and notices a long haired blonde in tight pants and a slim white shirt enter the bar. His eyes aren't the only ones to track her curvaceous figure as she slips through the throng.

"Well the place doesn't seem totally devoid of prospects."

"Forget it. Elma Kuyt's vagina is reserved solely for those who can advance her career."

"That's pretty harsh."

"Only if you think it normal to be screwing the Interior Minister within a week of getting here."

"What could he do for her?"

"Let's just say permits that take other agencies months to get approved, Dutch Aid gets in days. From there she moved onto the French Ambassador. He used to come up almost every weekend, tell his wife how important it was to see the jihad close at hand. Might have continued like that forever, but someone gave his wife the location of their little love nest, and four months ago, he and Elma woke to find her standing over them with a pen gun."

"Where she get one of those?"

"It's the souvenir of choice out here. I have a bowl of them in my office for visiting Congressmen. I'll messenger one over if you promise never to use it."

"Why's that?"

"Thing's as likely to blow off your hand as it is the person in front of you, and that's what France's petrified ambassador managed to explain to his wife of thirty years. Needless to say that was the end of the affair. Now every idiot in town thinks he has a shot."

"Any have a chance?"

"Just the one she's talking to. He's writing a big article on the refugee situation out here, and Elma's wormed her way into being its focus. Nothing like a puff piece in the New Yorker to get that UN job you've always dreamed of."

Over by the booth, Elma leans back and laughs at something the reporter's just said. The reporter looks smitten. She glances in their direction and catches Charlie's gaze. She turns back to the conversation.

Maybe she's not as in to the reporter as Ivor thinks.

Charlie orders a Heineken and jumps off his stool.

"Might as well throw my hat in the ring," he grins.

"This should be fun."

"Fortune favors the brave, that's what my mother always used to say."

"So did Saddam Hussein and look where that got him."

"Come on, be my wingman."

"I prefer to watch explosions from afar."

"That's why I'm a deminer, I don't."

The Heineken arrives. Charlie winks at Ivor and winds his way over to Elma's table.

"You guys mind if I join you?"

"I don't," the reporter says. "Jurgen, Elma?"

It's clear neither of them are thrilled, but they don't object. Charlie squeezes in next to the reporter, and places the Heineken in front of Elma.

"Thought I'd bring something over to remind you of home."

"I don't drink beer," Elma says.

"Then maybe one of you guys would like it."

The reporter swipes it.

"One lesson I've learned in life—never turn down a free beer."

Charlie sticks out his hand.

"Charlie Matthews."

"Rod Baylor."

"You were embedded with the Fifth Cav, right?"

"A New Yorker reader," Rod grins. "I'm impressed."

"My mom was an addict."

"Were you out there?"

"Was with the First Infantry Division."

"The Fighting First. What you doing here?"

"Heading up a demining outfit called Mine Aware. Least temporarily."

Jurgen laughs.

"What are you eighteen?" he says in a German accent.

"Twenty-four."

Jurgen turns to Elma.

"This is a joke, no?"

"I have no reason to disbelieve him," Elma says.

"Going to meet my first group of recruits tomorrow," Charlie says. "Should have them up and ready in a couple of months."

Jurgen laughs.

"Oh, dear boy, if you'd said six months I'd have thought you impossibly naïve. I was just telling Rod here that the thing about Afghans is they have absolutely no ability to stick to a plan. It makes them a devil to fight, especially when you combine it with that idiotic bravery of theirs. But these qualities, well let's just say they make for pitiful deminers."

"And what makes you such an expert?" Charlie says.

An awkward silence hangs over the table.

"Jurgen heads up UNMAPA," Elma says.

"So?"

"The United Nations Mine Action Program for Afghanistan."

"Without my permission, dear boy," Jurgen smiles, "you'll never get into Afghanistan let alone demine a field out there."

Charlie glances at Ivor. Ivor raises his Coke in mock salute. Charlie turns back.

"Hey, Jurgen," he says.

Jurgen looks at Charlie like he's a child he's tired of humoring.

"I know you have your fancy job and all, but have you ever actually taken a mine out of the ground? You know picked one up, knowing that despite having done everything right, that bastard could blow your dick off and lodge it in the back of your throat."

Jurgen goes beet red. Elma and Rod stare at Charlie in disbelief.

"Thought not."

Charlie stalks away only to discover Ivor's gone. His business card sits on the bar. Charlie turns it over; on the back Ivor has scrawled his home phone number and a short note:

Warned you it'd blow up in your face!!! Stay safe sapper.

Charlie climbs up onto the stool and orders a Jack Daniels from the bartender. He cranes his neck back and looks around the bar for a set of friendly faces. He sees none.

Strange. I've never had a problem making friends in the past.

His drink comes and he downs it. He slaps a twenty dollar on the bar and orders another.

Screw it. I'll drink by myself.

SIX

"MR. MATTHEWS, MR. Matthews, it is I, Wali, I am here to take you to the office."

Charlie forces his eyes open. Wali comes into focus. He's standing over the bed beaming.

"What time is it?" Charlie says.

"Ten o'clock," Wali says.

Charlie groans.

"I think you had a late night, Mr. Matthews"

"No, no, it's just jet lag. Just give me five will you."

"Five what?"

"Minutes."

"Oh, most certainly."

Charlie stumbles to the bathroom. In the shower he tries to recollect the night before. He remembers meeting a couple of Canadian aid workers, and doing a round of shots with them, but after that nothing. How he got to his bed, he has no clue.

He comes down to the kitchen to find Wali chattering away to Mukhtar and a breakfast of freshly squeezed orange juice and scrambled eggs awaiting him. He sits down at the table and begins scarfing down the eggs.

"Now that's a good breakfast, no?" Wali says.

"Great."

Wali translates for Mukhtar, and Mukhtar grins.

"Thank you, sir, thank you," Mukhtar says.

Wali slaps Charlie on the back, and Charlie feels his brain shatter into a million pieces.

"Did I not tell you it was a good thing to have a cook?"

"You sure this can't wait until tomorrow?" Charlie says.

"I wish it could, Mr. Matthews, but everyone is waiting for you."

"I know but—"

"I mean literally waiting for you; in a line since eight o'clock this morning."

Charlie stands and has to put a hand on the table to steady himself. Wali continues talking to Mukhtar jabbing him in the shoulder to make his point. Finally he engulfs Mukhtar in a warm embrace and turns towards Charlie.

"Mukhtar says he is going to make you the finest dinner you can imagine. Sheep's eyeballs; it's a local delicacy."

Charlie feels the urge to vomit. Wali giggles hysterically.

"I'm joking. Now come, we must go."

Wali leads Charlie out to the driveway where his Pajero is parked. The broiling heat hits Charlie, and he sways. Wali opens the passenger door for him and runs around the car to get in his side. He turns the ignition and the chorus of *Material Girl* erupts from the speakers. Cold air blasts from the AC. Charlie thinks his head is going to explode. He lunges for the cassette player and turns it off.

"Would I be right in thinking that you're not a fan of Miss Madonna?"

"It's just Madonna, Wali."

"You positive?"

"Positive."

Wali gets out his pad and records this new piece of information. He takes off down the driveway and accelerates down a tree-lined street. Up ahead Charlie can see a main road; blue exhaust fumes hang over it like mist over a lake.

"Jamrud Road," Wali says.

Wali slips into a gap in the traffic. A barrage of horns blast away at them. Charlie's never seen such chaos. Rickshaws, mini-vans, cheap Japanese cars, Mercedes buses, motorcycles, bicycles, horse-drawn carts, even man-drawn carts are all fighting for their piece of the road.

Charlie looks out his window at the open-fronted stores. There's one with blocks of candy in every shape, size and color; a tea shop with a vast cauldron of boiling tea up front; shop after shop selling swirls of bright fabric; open air restaurants with what look like hamburgers frying in cylindrical pans the size of paddling pools. After that come the butchers, first the chicken sellers; their live merchandise cooped up front in rope cages while their unlucky brethren are behind having their necks chopped off on benches awash with blood; then the sheep shops, with whole carcasses hanging on hooks in the morning heat while young boys with swatters fight a losing battle against the endless swarms of flies; and then the beef sellers, their upfront displays dominated by cow hooves and calves' heads, the calves' eyes glazed over, their tongues hanging out as though they've had one drink too many.

I know how you feel.

Eventually the shops peter out and are soon replaced with mud huts stretching as far as the eye can see.

"Kacha Gari refugee camp," Wali says.

To Charlie, the huts look like something a child might conjure up in a sandbox; single storey, misshapen, no windows, some with crooked doors, others with just cloth hanging in their entrances. On the side of the road, refugees in turbans and rolled up caps swarm around wooden stalls. Some are missing an arm, some a leg, and an unfortunate few have lost both legs and are getting around on what look like skateboards. Bony dogs wander amongst them, trash swirls in the dirt and streams of putrid green water meander from the camp's alleys and down the side of the road. Boys are everywhere, shirtless ones pushing tires, others shoving long sticks of sugarcane into juicers, while others wait by the edge of the road holding cigarettes, candy, bottles of soda, nuts and fruit. The traffic snarls up, and they dive into it, a swarm surrounding the car, begging Charlie to buy their wares.

"Do not say a word," Wali says, "it only encourages them."

He edges forward seemingly oblivious to whether he might run over their feet.

"This where Mine Aware is?" Charlie says.

"Oh no, Mr. Matthews, our office is in Hayatabad."

The traffic picks up. Charlie looks back at the camp.

"Jesus, what a shithole."

Wali's pen and notepad come out.

"Shithole?"

"You know awful place to live"

"It is where I live."

Charlie looks at Wali. For once Wali has a straight face.

"I'm sorry, I didn't—"

"Trust me, it's quite alright, Mr. Matthews, you are most correct, it truly is a shithole."

Charlie notices a woman wearing a billowing, green burqa. He finds it the strangest thing; it's impossible not to miss these women yet they might as well not exist at all.

"Most women round here wear burqas?" he says.

"In the camps and villages, yes. Amongst wealthier families not so much unless the husband is a very religious man."

Wali turns left and drives down a wide, four-lane avenue. Half-a-mile down they come upon a grid of recently laid streets, dotted with two-storey houses sitting behind high outer walls. They drive up to a small compound of red brick buildings that remind Charlie of his old barracks. Out front, three men are waiting for them in the late morning sun.

Jesus, Wali wasn't joking.

"Come, come," Wali says, "let me introduce you."

They get out, and Wali takes Charlie down the line as though he were a visiting head of state. First up is a man with a trim beard and movie star looks.

"This is Mocam," Wali says. "He is in charge of all equipment."

"As-salaam Alaykum," Mocam says.

"That means 'peace be upon you'," Wali says.

"How'd you say it again?" Charlie says.

"As-salaam Alaykum."

"Well as-salaam Alaykum to you, Mocam."

Mocam grins. Wali moves onto a man with a skull cap on his head and a beard so long that it looks like a child's bib.

"This is Qasim, our accountant and office manager."

Charlie exchanges greetings with Qasim, and they move on to a bearded man who's curiously shaved his mustache.

"And this is Fahran, our esteemed cook and driver."

They exchange greetings. Charlie breathes a sigh of relief.

That wasn't too hard.

He spies a building with AC units and starts towards it.

"Mr. Matthews, wait," Wali says.

Charlie turns back to see Mocam holding a piece of paper.

"Mocam has a speech."

Mocam steps forward.

"It is utter pleasure to meet you, Mr. Matthews, and may I take liberty of saying we thank Allah for your presence here to help us, and our glorious nation, Afghanistan, and inshallah we do most wonderful things together and take out many mines from ground."

Mocam folds the paper and steps back.

"Thanks," Charlie says, "good to be here too."

The men all stare at Charlie. Charlie looks over at Wali.

"We done?" Charlie says.

"Where is your speech?" Wali says.

"I'm meant to have one?"

"It is customary on such occasions."

"Why didn't you tell me?"

"I thought you knew such things."

"Why would I? I'm new here."

"Well you should make one anyway."

The front of Charlie's head begins to pound. He closes his eyes. It doesn't help.

"Mocam, Qasim, Farhad," he says. "I'm excited to be here ... to help Afghanistan ... and together we're going to do great ... that's it."

The men applaud.

"Oh, a most wonderful speech, Mr. Matthews," Wali says. "Now let me show you your office."

Wali guides Charlie through a glass set of doors and a lobby with black-and-white posters of limbless refugees to an office in the back. The furniture is rudimentary, but all Charlie cares about is that it has a couch.

On top of a filing cabinet a photo frame is propped up for all to see. It's of a stout, bearded man and Wali; Wali's smile is as wide as the Suez Canal; the man's is forced to say the least.

"Skeppar?" Charlie says.

"The one and only," Wali says. "Now come sit, sit."

Wali shepherds Charlie around the desk and into his office chair. He picks up a sheet of paper.

"This is the letter I was telling you about?"

Charlie spies a phone on his desk.

"Hey, could you do me a favor?" he says.

"Most certainly," Wali says.

"You mind finding me up the number for Dutch Aid."

"Of course. Qasim should have it."

Wali heads out of the room. Charlie picks up the letter.

Dear Charlie:

I apologize for the circumstances of your arrival, but unfortunately my condition's become chronic and I'm flying home for further treatment.

All is not lost. We've found a replacement for me in Stephen Adams, an Australian who heads up a demining project in Mozambique. The only downside is that he's unable to arrive until December.

This means that, for now, you are nominally in charge. I am confident you'll do fine if you follow one simple rule — "first, do no harm." In the months I've been here I've built up a solid Afghan staff. All you need do is keep an eye on them and make sure they are faxing their cost reports and approvals to Stockholm.

You, of course, were part of the second phase; the training of our demining teams. Wali, who you'll find is most eager, has assured me that he's identified thirty capable recruits and for the next three months it will be your job to bring them along as much as you can.

Remember my admonition — "first, do no harm". You may conduct practical exercises, but under no circumstances should anything more than inactive mines be used. I also ask that you keep all training within the confines of our compound. Coming from the US Army, I suspect you'll have a certain confidence as to how quickly you can train these men. Let me assure you nothing comes easy around here. If they know how to identify basic mines and operate a metal detector by the time Stephen arrives you'll be ahead of the game.

So good luck, be sensible and stay well.

Yours truly,

Johan Skeppar

Charlie puts the letter down.

Doesn't sound too hard. Not too hard at all.

There's a knock on the door.

"I apologize for the delay," Wali says, "I had trouble finding Qasim. He was taking crap."

"A crap."

"Good to know."

He hands Charlie a scrap of paper with the number on it. Charlie picks up the receiver. He's about to dial when he sees Wali still standing there.

"Do you mind? It's a private call."

"Oh, I see. Just so you know I have told the recruits to be here at four o'clock."

"Great."

"A most wonderful and dedicated group of men."

"I believe you."

Wali backs away and closes the door behind him. Charlie dials the number.

"Dutch Aid," a voice on the other end of the line says.

"Yeah, I was looking for Elma Kuyt," he says.

"I'm sorry, sir, but she is out in the field right now."

"Any idea when she's going to be back."

"Two, three hours, I believe. May I take a message?"

"Sure. Tell her Charlie Matthews from Mine Aware called."

"Certainly."

Charlie replaces the receiver.

Three hours. Perfect.

He draws the blinds and lies down on the couch.

***

"MR. MATTHEWS, MR. Matthews."

Charlie struggles to open his eyes. Wali is standing over him beaming.

"The recruits are here," Wali says.

"I thought you said they were coming at four."

"It is four-thirty now."

"You're kidding."

"Why would I shit you about such a thing?"

Charlie struggles to sit up. His mouth is dry and his head woozy. Wali holds out a glass of water.

"Here, this will help," he says.

Charlie drains the glass.

"Thanks, you're a life saver," Charlie says. "By the way did anyone from Dutch Aid call back?"

"I do not believe so. Why? Was it important?"

"Not really. Come on, let's go meet the guys."

Wali leads Charlie outside where a group of men are standing in two ragged lines. Charlie takes them in; half of them look like the residents of an old folks home, the other half like the inhabitants of an insane asylum.

"How you pick these guys?" Charlie says.

"By an utmost rigorous selection process."

"Right, well I might as well introduce myself."

Charlie walks up to the first man in line. The man's face is bathed in sweat. Charlie decides not to shake his hand.

"As-salaam Alaykum," Charlie says.

"Wa-alaykum asalaam," the man says.

"I'm Charlie. What's your name?"

"Please meet a you."

"No your name?"

"It is Zulfikar Mohammad," Wali says.

"Yes, yes, Zulfikar Mohammad," the man says. "Please meet a you."

Charlie turns to Wali.

"He okay?"

"I do not understand."

"His eyes are kind of yellow, don't you think?"

Wali peers at the man.

"He's Hazara, they all have yellow eyes."

Charlie shakes his head and moves on to the next man. There's no mistaking the defects in his eyes. The pupil in his right is milky white while the one in his left zigzags like an out of control cue ball. Charlie exchanges salaams with the man and does the same with the next, an old man leaning on a cane. He comes to the fourth in line, and his hopes rise. Here, at last, is someone young and fit.

"As-salaam Alaykum," he says.

"Wa-alaykum asalaam," the man says.

"My name's Charlie, what's yours?"

The man smiles at him.

"I said my name's Charlie, what's yours?"

The man continues to smile. Charlie turns to Wali.

"What's wrong with this one?"

"Oh, he's just a little deaf. He can read lips most excellently however."

"In English?"

"No, that he cannot accomplish."

Charlie looks down the line and sees no better prospects.

"Mind coming with me?" he says to Wali.

"Is there a problem?"

"Just need to chat, that's all."

Wali shrugs. They walk back to Charlie's office. Charlie closes the door.

"Okay, cards on the table time. How many of these guys are your relatives?"

"I do not understand, Mr. Matthews, not one of these men is my brother."

"I didn't ask if they were your brother, I asked if you were related to any of them."

"I do not understand the difference."

"Okay, how many of them are cousins?"

"Mother or father's side?"

"Both."

Wali counts them out on his right hand.

"No more than four and may I tell you I personally vouch for them; if they fail you I will undoubtedly resign."

"You related to any of the four I met?"

Wali doesn't say anything.

"It's not a hard question, Wali."

"Two of them."

"Which ones?"

"The second and the third."

"The old man and the blind dude."

"He isn't blind."

"In one eye he is."

"Which leaves the other."

"Which seems pretty fucked up as well."

"It's not his fault he stepped on a mine."

"You telling me he's only got one leg?"

"No, he has two legs."

"Does he have two feet?"

"Unfortunately not."

Outside the wails of first one then dozens of muezzins pierce the air.

"Okay, we got to find some new guys."

"Mr. Matthews, if you are accusing me—"

"Listen, I couldn't give a shit about that."

"About what?"

"Nepotism."

Wali gives Charlie a blank stare.

"You know giving friends and relatives jobs—"

Wali gets out his pad.

"—but I've got to train these guys. Please, I beg you, make this easy for me. Find me a bunch of guys who can see, hear, speak English and run a mile in less than ten minutes."

"But this would mean I would have to replace all of them."

"I'm sorry but that's the way it is."

Wali pouts as if he is on the verge of tears.

"Now do you mind giving me the keys to the car?" Charlie says. "I mean that is my car you've driving, right?"

"Where are you going?"

"Home."

"If you could give me some time—"

"It's okay, I can drive."

"But you will get lost."

"Sometimes getting lost is the best way to get to know a city."

Wali looks at Charlie as if he's now officially lost his mind.

"The keys, Wali."

Wali reaches into his pocket and retrieves the keys.

"This is not a good idea, Mr. Matthews."

"Send out a search party if I don't turn up tomorrow," Charlie grins.

Charlie jumps in his Pajero and heads to Jamrud Road. He finds it no less mad than earlier that day. Buses, coming in the opposite direction, drift onto his side of the road and play chicken with him. Rickshaws dart in and out of traffic as if their very intent is to cause a pile up. Donkey drawn carts plod along as if it's their God given right to hold everyone else up. Everyone honks, no one brakes unless they are truly forced to, while random animals and humans cross his path as though they're playing Frogger and have more than one life to give.

By the time he reaches the refugee camp, his nerves are frayed. He wasn't thinking of going back to the American Club so soon, but now he's desperate for a drink.

He looks at the clock. Five-thirty.

As long as you survive, you'll be drinking a beer by six.

He hears a wrenching sound and plumes of smoke start pouring from the hood. He pulls the car over and the engine takes a final gasp. Charlie gets out and goes to pop the hood. The latch scalds his fingers and he jumps back.

"Fuck, fuck, fuck."

He stuffs his fingers into his mouth. An old man squatting nearby looks up at him with a vacant expression. It takes Charlie a moment to realize that the man's pants are around his ankles, and he's taking a shit.

"Jesus," Charlie says.

Across the road he sees a group of refugees standing around. He knows there's only one thing to do. He's got to go back to Mine Aware and get some help. He waits for a gap in the traffic and joins them.

"Evening," he says.

They all look his way.

"Guessing there's no triple A around here."

No one says a thing.

"Guess not."

A packed bus pulls up. Four of the refugees try to get on. Only three make it. Five buses later, Charlie is the only person left at the side of the road. By now the sun has dropped below the Khyber Mountains, and the wind's picked up. Charlie shields his eyes from the dust and sees a couple more buses approaching. Charlie waves his hands in the air but neither of them stop.

"Ah, this is bullshit," he shouts.

Fifty yards out, he makes out the headlamps of another bus. He steps into its path. The driver leans on his horn. Charlie doesn't budge. The bus's brakes squeal, and at the last moment Charlie jumps out of the way. Charlie runs up to the door and grabs a hold of the handle.

"Oh come on, let me in."

The driver shakes his head. Charlie grabs a ten dollar bill from his wallet and sticks it against the glass. The doors hiss open. Charlie clambers on board and hands the money over. He looks up the bus. It's crammed tighter than a cattle trailer. A wizened old man is picking himself up off the floor. He jabbers away at Charlie in Pashtu.

"Sorry about that," Charlie says.

The man starts poking Charlie with his cane.

"Hey, I said I was sorry."

The bus lurches forward, and Charlie and the old man end up on the floor. The man brings his cane up and catches

Charlie in the balls. Charlie rolls over gasping. The man clambers to his feet and jabs him from above. Charlie scrambles down the aisle on his knees until he's out of range.

He raises his head and finds himself staring up at the most beautiful woman he's ever seen in his life. The woman looks down at him with the hint of a smile and then drops her eyes to the books in her lap. He clambers to his feet and tries to catch her gaze again. Her head remains stubbornly bowed, her threadbare, red scarf hiding the top of her head.

Charlie senses others staring at him. He looks around and finds that in fact every passenger is. He glances up at the ceiling; someone has painted a landscape on it dotted with burning tanks and Soviet soldiers dying in pools of blood.

If that isn't a warning, what is?

Charlie lowers his gaze; most of the passengers have turned their eyes away. He glances at the girl; her head's still down.

Damn.

The bus slows, and she gets up, her eyes fixed to the floor.

"Excuse me," she says.

Charlie doesn't budge.

Please, just one last look.

She raises her chin and stares at him. There's not a hint of make-up on her face and he wouldn't want there to be; nothing could improve her beauty.

"Please," she says.

"My bad," Charlie says.

He pushes himself up against the refugee next to him, and she slides past. He scrambles into her seat and through the window watches her walk past the glowing cooking pits, and the ramshackle stalls at the side of the road. She crouches down, and Charlie thinks she must have dropped something. He squints into the darkness and discovers she's stopped to give money to a legless young girl who's propped against a stack of used tires.

My God. She's an angel.

The bus drives forward. Charlie jumps up.

"Stop," he shouts.

The bus lurches to a halt, and the old man goes sprawling. Charlie clambers over him and scrambles off the bus. He navigates his way through the throng and sees the young girl. He feels an obligation to give her something and hunts in his wallet. All he has are one hundred rupee bills.

"Here," he says shoving one of them into the girl's out-stretched hands.

He hurries on and spies the red headscarf. The young woman is standing at a stall stacked high with mangoes. She picks up a couple and asks the price. When the owner gives it to her, she puts one back, hands him some coins and keeps on walking.

Shit, what now?

A young kid comes up to him. His nose is running and he keeps wiping away rivulets of goo with his sleeve.

"You want Coke, mister?" the kid says.

"You got a pen," Charlie says.

The boy gives him a blank stare. Charlie writes in the air.

"Pen, pen," Charlie says.

The kid rushes off. Charlie catches a glimpse of the girl's red headscarf just before she turns down an alley next to a bicycle repair shack. The kid returns with a chewed up ballpoint pen. Charlie hands him one of the hundred dollar bills

"Here," he says.

The kid grins like he's won the lottery. Charlie takes out another and starts scribbling on it

***

NOOR HURRIES DOWN the claustrophobic alleys of the camp, her notebooks held tight to her chest. With each gust of wind ever more dust coats her face and her headscarf edges further back until her hair billows behind her like laundry on a line. Noor prays she can get to their hut without running into a fanatic. There have been more and more attacks on 'loose women' of late.

My bad, my bad.

She can't get the expression out of her head. She's never heard it before. She assumes it's an American way of saying 'I'm sorry'.

What an odious man.

The American had amused her at first, but the way he had stared at her, blocked her path ...

Noor hears someone running towards her. Her heart quickens. She turns just as they come around the bend. A man bowls in to her, and she tumbles to the ground. The man comes to a rest on top of her.

Her hands search for her assailant's face. She scratches at his eyes, cheeks, nose, whatever she can dig her nails into. The man screams in pain. She shoves him off of her and clambers to her feet. She makes sure her weekly wage is still secure in her pocket.

"Stop, please stop," the man says in an American accent.

The man raises his head, his face smeared with dirt and blood. He recognizes her.

"I'm sorry," he says. "I didn't mean to scare you."

"You didn't," she says.

She gathers up her fallen books. The man tries to help her.

"Don't," she says.

She gets up and sees him standing there with the mango in his hand.

"I just had to find you," he says. "You're the most beautiful woman I've ever laid eyes on."

Noor gives him a withering glare and turns for home.

"Wait, you forgot something," he says.

"Keep the mango," she says.

"No, something else."

Noor looks back. The American is holding out a piece of paper. Down the way she hears some men approaching. She edges over to him and snatches the piece of paper. She hurries away and doesn't stop until she's outside their hut. She stands there with her back against the wall and gathers herself. If it wasn't for the paper in her hand she could be convinced that she'd just had an hallucinatory experience.

She pushes open the corrugated metal door and steps inside. It's hotter in the hut than it is outside. Her father sits on a stool reading by the light of a flickering lamp. Bushra squats nearby stirring daal in a blackened pot.

"Evening my love," her father says.

Noor nods a greeting, and her father rises.

"We'll leave you to bathe. Come on Bushra"

He opens the door and a gust of wind rushes in. Noor places the books on the floor and unfolds the crumpled piece of paper. It's a hundred rupee bill. She turns it over and sees the man has written on it.

'If you're married or engaged—'

Those words alone make her shiver.

'Please throw this away.'

It's what I should've done. In fact I should've never taken it in the first place.

'But if you aren't, maybe we could meet tomorrow at 5PM in the lobby of the Pearl Continental.'

Of course, the Pearl Continental; the greatest den of inequity in the whole of Peshawar.

"Noor, you done yet?" Bushra shouts.

"Nearly," she shouts back.

At the bottom he's scrawled his name. Charlie Matthews.

Noor stuffs the bill in her pocket with her wage. She glances at the circular metal tub in the corner, the soap scum on its surface evidence that Bushra and her father have already used it. Noor undresses and hangs her clothes on a nail on the wall. She steps into the tub and using a thin bar of soap scrubs her body as hard as she can.

Was this Charlie Matthews trying to buy my services? Does he really think an Afghan girl's honor can be bought so cheap?

She shudders knowing that many are. She dries herself with a towel and puts on her nighttime shalwar kameez. She retrieves the bills and puts them in her pocket.

"I'm done," she shouts.

Her father and sister waste little time in coming inside. They sit down on the floor mat, and Bushra doles out the daal. They each say a short prayer. Noor places a spoonful in her mouth and chews it over and over. She learned long ago that it makes the dish seem more substantial than it truly is.

"Are you unwell my love?" her father says.

Noor continues to stare at her food.

"Noor."

She looks up. Her father is peering over his reading glasses at her.

"You seem out of sorts, my dear."

"No. A little tired perhaps, but I'm otherwise fine."

Making sure not to hand over the bill the American gave her, she gives four hundred rupees to her father and one hundred to her sister.

"Here," she says.

"You have given me too much," her father says.

"Your British Council library fee is due this week."

"Given our changed circumstances, I don't need to—"

"Baba, you know you'd be lost without your books."

He doesn't argue. She returns to her daal.

"I finished Midnight's Children," her father says.

"That's good," Noor says.

"I did not care for it much. This man Rushdie, his storytelling is too convoluted for my taste."

Noor doesn't say anything.

"I do not mean to denigrate his writing ability, his characters are marvelous; I just think he digresses too much."

"Fine, he's not for you," Noor says.

Silence returns to their dinner.

"That's it," her father says. "You told me you loved it."

"I did, you didn't, what else is there to say?"

"I don't know how either of you can read that man's books," Bushra says. "He's an enemy of Islam?"

Noor can't help but be drawn to Bushra's plate. Bushra never fails to give herself the largest portion.

"Why do you say that?" Noor says.

"Mullah Razzaq says so," Bushra says.

"Mullah Razzaq is illiterate. He hasn't read The Quran let alone The Satanic Verses?"

"Have you?"

"No. Hence why I have no way of knowing if Salman Rushdie is an apostate or not."

Noor picks up her plate and places it in the tub. She lays out her prayer mat and performs the Isha prayer. She feels her irritation seep away. By the time she finishes, Bushra is in the midst of her own set of rakkahs. Noor retrieves her mattress from against the wall and lies down. It's so thin she often wonders why she doesn't just sleep on the earthen floor. Noor looks at her father; he's pretending to read, but she knows he's watching her.

"Night, Baba," she says.

"Night, my love."

He returns to his book. She turns her back on him and slips her hand into her pocket and pulls out the hundred-rupee bill. She stuffs it into a slit in her mattress. It can stay there with the other three hundred and twenty seven rupees in her emergency fund. She closes her eyes and tries her best to go to sleep, but soon images of the American infect her mind. She sits up and searches for her shoes.

"I'm going for a walk."

"On tonight of all nights?" her father says.

"It's just wind, Baba, nothing more."

Noor shoves the door open and heads out into the grave-yard. The eucalyptus trees' leaves rustle in the wind, and the flags that mark the graves flap like sails in a storm. Her eyes adjust to the dark, and she notices a pack of dogs coming her way. They alter their course and go around her. She prays they stay away from the rabbit. For her part, she has no worries about her own safety. Muslims may not believe in ghosts, but she hasn't come across one yet who would willingly go into a graveyard at night.

Except you, a voice in her head says.

Yes, except me.

She comes upon a crude headstone and kneels in front of it. Carved into its face in childish lettering is her mother's name—Mariam Khan. Noor closes her eyes and searches for her mother's face. Of late it's become harder to recall, as if all memory of her mother is seeping away. Back in the camp a corrugated roof comes loose and clatters to the ground.

"Mamaan, I think I'm starting to lose my mind. I feel the world encroaching upon me from every angle. There are times recently when I feel like I can't breathe, worse yet I no longer know where to look, for fear of attracting trouble. I've lost all patience. I mean look how I lashed out at Bushra just now, at the administrator this morning."

The American's face appears front and center in her brain, and she squeezes her eyes tight.

"What's going on, Mamaan? Please tell me. What did we do to bring this on ourselves? How much longer can I be expected to hang on?"

There is no answer. She pushes herself back up and stares at the gravestone. She's always wondered what happened to her mother's body. She assumes she was dumped in an unmarked grave, perhaps into the same one they tossed Aunt Sabha and Uncle Aasif.

"I love you, Mamaan," she says.

Noor stands and comes upon a worn path. The American's image once again appears. She quickens her pace.

Forget about him. He's not worth it.

She breathes in through her nose and lengthens her stride. Her arms swing back and forth, and the graves fly past her like ships in the night. The American recedes further from her consciousness until at last, to her relief, he's forgotten altogether.

SEVEN

CHARLIE AND WALI stand inside the lobby and observe the new recruits. Charlie glances at his watch—four ten; still plenty of time before he has to head off to the Pearl Continental. He has a good feeling the girl will come.

After all she didn't say no.

"Admit it," he says to Wali, "this is a better bunch of guys."

"In all honesty I do not detect any difference, but if you're satisfied I suppose I am too."

"Well their average age is below ninety-five, that's got to be a plus."

"Mr. Matthews I understand that in America youth is prized, but we, Afghans, like to honor our elders."

"Jesus, what crawled up your butt?"

Wali stares straight ahead.

"It's because you had to spend the night in the Pajero, isn't it?" Charlie says.

"That has nothing to do with it."

"I offered to keep you company."

"I would not have heard of such a thing."

"Then get that smile back on your face. I mean you still managed to get three of your relatives on the payroll."

"Two," Wali says before catching himself.

Charlie grins and slaps Wali on the back.

"Gotcha. Now come on, let's do this."

Charlie pushes open the doors, and they walk outside.

"Oh yeah, one other thing, I'm looking for a motorcycle," he says.

"The Pajero is fixed."

"Appreciate that, but it's just not my style, that's all. Shit find me a decent one for under a thousand bucks and the Pajero's yours."

For the first time that day a smile graces Wali's face.

"Oh, Mr. Matthews, you need not worry, I will find you the best motorbike in the whole of Peshawar."

"Counting on it."

The recruits see them coming and jump to their feet.

"As-salaam Alaykum," Charlie says.

A chorus of wa-alaykum asalaams come back his way.

"Good to have you all here, my name's Charlie Matthews and I'm going to be your instructor these next few months. Now what I thought we'd do is just chat a little, you know introduce ourselves, that kind of thing, and then tomorrow at ten we can start on the training; nothing too strenuous, just a basic orientation. What do you say?"

Most of the recruits nod. Charlie turns to Wali.

"They really speak English?"

"I assure you they do."

Charlie looks at his watch again. Four fifteen.

"By the way, how long does it take to get to the Pearl Continental from here."

"Forty-five minutes, maybe fifty. Why?"

Shit, I got to get out of here.

Charlie turns back to the recruits.

"Okay, we'll just do names today, and then we're done."

He points at a fat, Chinese-looking recruit on the far left of the first row.

"What's your name?"

"Shafiq, sir."

He points at the man beside him, a recruit with an un-canny resemblance to Abraham Lincoln.

"And you?"

"My name is Najib, sir, and I sincerely want to thank you for the opportunity you've given us."

"No problem."

Charlie points at a teddy bear of a man.

"You?"

"Bakri, sir."

He nods at a scrawny, young man with round glasses and a desperate wisp of a moustache.

"Obaidullah, sir, and may I, on behalf of all recruits, assure you we will not let you down in this endeavor."

"Good to hear."

Obaidullah raises his hand.

"We're just doing names right now, Obaidullah," Charlie says.

"I understand, Mr. Matthews, but as our most esteemed instructor and out of my fervent admiration and worry of you I desire that you believe that there is no God but God, and Mohammed, upon him be peace and blessings, is Messenger of God."

"Again?" Charlie says.

"I wish you become Muslim, sir."

The other recruits nod.

"You're kidding, right?" Charlie says.

"Most sincerely no," Obaidullah says.

"Why would I want to become a Muslim?"

Obaidullah gasps. A number of the recruits shift positions.

"Sorry," Charlie says, "I didn't mean it like that—"

"No, no," Obaidullah says, "I understand, you Christian."

"Nope."

"You Jew?"

"No, I just don't believe in God."

The whole class gasps. Wali slides up beside Charlie.

"Mr. Matthews, may I have a word?"

"Wali, really not got the time for—"

"I think now would be most appropriate."

Wali grips Charlie's arm and leads him into the lobby.

"This is very bad, Mr. Matthews. Very, very bad."

"I'm sorry, I don't want to become a Muslim."

"I understand, but you should never have told them that you don't believe in God. To most Afghans, that is crazy talk, and they will not be able to accept you as their instructor."

"So we'll find another thirty guys."

"They won't accept you either. Word will spread."

"Amongst three million refugees?"

"Mr. Matthews, believe me, this is not good."

Charlie looks out the window. The recruits are on their feet, a couple gesticulating towards them as if they want to burn down the building.

"Okay, what do I do?" Charlie says.

"Go back out and say you are Christian."

"Why'd that be any better?"

"Because the Quran states that the people most affectionate to Muslims are those who say they are Christians."

"Seriously?"

Wali looks as serious as he's ever looked. Charlie sighs and heads outside.

"Guys, guys, guys," he shouts.

The recruits continue to argue amongst themselves. Charlie puts his fingers in his mouth and lets out a piercing whistle. Everyone falls silent and looks in his direction.

"I want to clear something up. I didn't hear Obaidullah right. Just so you know, I'm a Christian, and a big one at that."

"But you said you were not," Obaidullah says.

"No, I thought you asked whether I was Catholic; that I'm definitely not. I'm a ... Methodist."

"It's like we have Sunni and Shia in Islam," Wali says.

"Couldn't have put it better myself."

Charlie looks at the class. He feels as if the odds of being stoned have lessened.

"So we cool?" he says.

"Why then say that you do not believe in God?" Obaidullah says.

"Because I thought you meant your God, Allah."

"They are the same; Allah is God."

"And that's what Wali just explained to me."

Tears spring in Obaidullah's eyes.

"Oh, Mr. Matthews, please forgive me. I have most truly dishonored you."

Obaidullah begins sobbing.

"Don't be stupid; now come here."

Charlie goes over and hugs Obaidullah. Over Obaidullah's shoulder, he glances at his watch. Four twenty-five.

Shit.

Charlie pats Obaidullah on the back and pries his hands off of him.

"Okay, we'll finish with names tomorrow."

Charlie turns tail and heads for the Pajero. Wali shouts out after him but he ignores him. He is soon speeding towards Jamrud Road. The traffic is as insane as the previous night, but tonight he has more of a handle on it. He thinks about the girl and what he's going to do.

She probably doesn't drink.

It's a shame; he'd been told that the Pearl Continental was the only other place in town that served alcohol.

Maybe we could have a meal, chat a while. It's not like I'm going to put a move on her or anything. Not tonight at least.

Forty minutes later he arrives at the hotel; a white, five storey building with a red neon sign up top and billowing fountains in front. A bell boy runs up, and Charlie throws him the keys. He hurries inside. The lobby's unlike any other place he's been in Peshawar. With its marble floors, vast displays of fresh flowers and smartly dressed managers it's almost five star.

Charlie scans the guests in the adjacent lounge; there isn't a woman amongst them. Over by the front desk he sees a couple of ex-pats and by the concierge desk a veiled woman in a red and gold shalwar-kameez.

Oh my God, she's come.

Charlie edges around the lobby until he is standing right behind her. He breathes in her sweet rose water perfume. His pulse quickens.

"Hi," he says.

The woman turns. His heart sinks.

"Sorry, thought you were someone else."

He looks around the lobby. A woman in a green burqa is sitting in the corner. He hadn't seen her on his first sweep; it's as if the burqa had acted like camouflage. The empty chair next to her begs for him to sit in it.

Wouldn't a burqa be the perfect disguise if she wanted to meet me?

The woman looks in his direction. He turns around; there's nothing but the elevator bank behind him. He turns back. She's still looking at him.

It's got to be her.

He walks over and sits down in the empty chair.

"Hi," he says. "I'm so glad you made it."

The elevator dings, and a gorilla of an Afghan steps out with four AK-47 toting bodyguards. The Afghan strides towards them like a prizefighter heading towards the ring. Charlie snaps his head back towards the woman. She continues to stare straight ahead.

Oh shit, she set me up.

As the group gets closer, he remembers what Wali told him in the car.

They always start with the small stones so as not to kill you too quickly.

He thinks of fleeing, but by now it's too late. The group stops in front of them. Charlie attempts a smile and the leader glowers back at him. The woman stands up and for the first time Charlie notices her hands. They're covered in age spots; she must be at least seventy. With the woman in tow the group head for the door. Charlie sighs with relief.

That's it. Only Western women from now on.

"I apologize for troubling you?" someone says.

Charlie turns to find a man in a faded blazer and threadbare shalwar kameez sitting in the vacated seat. He has a thin film of sweat on his brow and is tugging on his sleeves.

"Your name would not be Charlie Matthews by any chance?"

"Sorry, do I know you?" Charlie says.

"No, but I believe you are friendly with my daughter."

Charlie's slowing heart begins to race once more. He watches a bead of sweat wind its way down the man's brow and along the ridge of his nose.

"My name is Aamir Khan. It's my desire to have a conversation with you."

"Look I'd love to, Aamir, but I'm late for my friend—"

"Perhaps you could call him and say you have been detained."

Charlie detects a bulge beneath Aamir Khan's breast pocket. It's just where a holstered gun would sit.

"Maybe we could have some tea in the lounge," Aamir Khan says.

Charlie sees no other option.

"Sure. After you."

"No, after you. I insist."

Charlie stands up and walks through the lobby.

He wouldn't shoot me in the back, would he? Not in front of all these people.

They enter the lounge, and Charlie sits down at a free
table. Aamir Khan takes the chair opposite him. A waiter
approaches, and Aamir Khan orders two cups of tea. He pulls
at his sleeves once again.

Is this how they do it? Stare into your eyes before they kill you.

Aamir Khan dabs at his brow with a handkerchief. The
waiter comes back with a tray and pours each of them a cup.

"Do you have sugar with your tea, Mr. Matthews?"

"No thanks."

"I am wicked, when I am afforded the chance I tend to
overindulge."

Aamir Khan plops two sugar cubes into his cup and then
goes back for a third. His hand is shaking.

Maybe he won't be able to shoot straight.

"Have you known my daughter long, Mr. Matthews?"

"No, just stood next to her on the bus."

Aamir Khan's cup hangs in the air. Tea splatters over its
side and into the saucer.

"That is all?"

"Well I suppose I chased after her last night. She's so
beautiful ..."

Charlie clamps his mouth shut.

Shit, why did you say that? To her psychotic father of all people.

Aamir Khan's cup and saucer slip from his grasp and crash
onto the table. Charlie jolts back in his chair.

Run!

Aamir Khan reaches inside his jacket. Charlie flings out a
hand.

"Don't shoot."

The lounge goes quiet. Heads turn in their direction.
Aamir Khan's hand returns with a handkerchief and he
begins mopping up the spill. Charlie flops back into his seat.

"Mr. Matthews, were you under the impression that I
came here to kill you?" Aamir Khan says.

"Kind of."

Aamir Khan laughs.

"Oh, Mr. Matthews, you have already spent far too long in this city."

"So that's a no?"

"No."

"That's a relief."

The waiter returns with another cup, and this time when Aamir Khan brings it to his lips, his hands tremble less. Charlie realizes that Aamir Khan was as nervous as he was.

"My daughter, you maybe intrigued to know, considers her beauty a curse," Aamir Khan says. "She's remarked more than once that she would exchange looks with the ugliest woman in Peshawar if offered the chance."

"That's crazy."

"Trust me your reaction on seeing her is not uncommon. I have received over thirty proposals of marriage, once I even had two on the same day."

"Any you liked?"

"I do not know if liked is the word I would use, but there have been a number that would have been advantageous."

"Well she's still got plenty of time."

"Noor's twenty-one, in Afghanistan that practically makes her an old maid."

Charlie says Noor's name over and over in his head.

It's as beautiful as she is.

"So what's her deal?" he says.

"She wants to go to university."

"That's not possible here?"

"Not for an impoverished female refugee. No, it is perverse, but she has more hope of obtaining a scholarship to an American or European institution than one in this country."

"And how's that going?"

"In the last four years we have applied to thirty-one institutions and fourteen so far have sent back rejection letters."

"So she's still in the game with the other seventeen."

"No, they just never bothered to reply. There is an old Afghan proverb, Mr. Matthews, that says a river is not contaminated by having a dog drink from it. No, the river's greatest danger comes from its source, for if that dries up a river becomes no more than a ditch."

"I'm sorry, but I'm not following you, Aamir."

"Hope is the source for all human endeavor, Mr. Matthews, for without hope no one would embark on anything. I fear Noor is losing all hope."

Aamir Khan pulls on his sleeves and forces a smile.

"I have a simple request, Mr. Matthews. Meet with my daughter."

Charlie is so surprised that he doesn't answer.

"I have done all I can, taught her everything I know, but I am a relic of the past. I do not know the current trends, the new ways of thinking, I am not aware of the latest technologies or the modern day vernacular. These are things you could imbue her with and in the process help her escape her present situation."

"Hate to break this to you, Aamir, but I don't think talking to me is going to get her very far."

"You would be surprised. If there is one thing I have learnt it is that Westerners like to be around Afghans who speak and act just like them. Those are the ones who get ahead and get out. I have accepted my fate, Mr. Matthews. I am going to live out my days in these camps, but I will not accept that fate for my youngest daughter."

"Where would we do this?"

"Your house if that is not too much trouble. I will bring her by next Friday at noon when your servants are at prayers."

"How do you know I have servants?"

"Oh come, Mr. Matthews, all aid workers have servants."

Charlie smiles.

"Okay, noon it is."

Aamir Khan stands.

"I thank you for you time," he says.

"Wait, one last thing," Charlie says. "What's in your jacket pocket?"

Aamir Khan pulls out a faded paperback.

"*Arabian Sands*," Aamir Khan says. "Have you read it?"

Charlie laughs.

"It's one of my favorite books."

"Then may I recommend *A Short Walk In The Hindu Kush*. It is a similar tale but more lighthearted. I will see you next Friday, Mr. Matthews. I am a certain it will be a most delightful occasion."

EIGHT

NOOR CHEWS ON a stale piece of naan and stares out at the graveyard; the harsh sun is encrusting its soil in what seems like a permanent glaze. Aamir Khan sits next to her reading. She sees the rabbit pop its head out of a hole and clicks her tongue. The rabbit's ears prick up, and it swivels its head in her direction. She holds out the naan. The rabbit hops over a burial mound and makes its way towards her. Noor holds her breath.

Come on, you're nearly there.

Her father snaps his book closed, and the rabbit takes off.

Not again.

"Well that was a most wonderful read," Aamir Khan says. "When Naipaul writes that men who allow themselves to become nothing have no place in this world, I think it's his way of saying that we must always strive to be something. It is why God put us here. We must never give up hope."

Noor lets the comment pass. For a month now her father has been doing this, making what he considers to be subtle asides in an attempt to keep her spirits up. If she were crueler she would tell him it isn't working.

No, better to let his exhortations just evaporate alongside everything else in this intolerable heat.

"Do you want to go to the British Council?" she says.

"I wish we could, but we have another engagement. A certain young man whom you met on the bus has invited us for lunch."

Noor sits there speechless. She jumps up and starts towards the hut.

"Noor," her father says.

Noor twists around.

"When did you start rummaging through my things?" she says.

"When did you start lying to me?"

"I didn't lie to you."

"You withheld the truth."

"It was an unpleasant incident, no more than that. Do you inform me every time you stub your toe?"

"I would suggest, my dear, that this incident was a little more exceptional than stubbing one's toe."

Noor stares off into the distance as if that might put an end to the discussion.

"I met this Charlie Matthews in your stead and made a proposal; that henceforth you and I will go over to his house every Friday at noon."

"No."

"He is expecting us."

"He's an odious, obnoxious fool."

"And how have you ascertained that? From what he relayed to me the two of you hardly spoke."

"I refuse to go."

"And as your father I request you do."

"So what, you're procuring me out now?"

Aamir Khan's face reddens.

"Stop this petulant indignation right now," he says. "Are you really accusing me of losing all moral fiber?"

Noor shakes her head and sits back down.

"Forgive me," she says.

Aamir Khan looks out over the graveyard. Noor inspects her father's worn, wrinkled face. He's forty-eight, but he looks closer to sixty; his eyes glassy, his cheeks hollow, his thin hair gone grey years ago.

"Tell me, how many Westerners do we have the opportunity of interacting with?" he says.

"Baba, these aid workers, they all say they want to help but none of them ever do."

"How would we know? We are not friends with any."

"So that's the plan? We become his friends?"

"You know better than I how many scholarship committees have rejected you, even though there isn't a soul on this planet who is more deserving."

"You think they care about people like Charlie Matthews?"

"If he recommends you, they will at least give you serious consideration."

Aamir Khan grabs a hold of Noor's hands.

"I have a feeling about him. He's not a bad man."

"Forgive me for not sharing your confidence."

"Please, my love."

Noor bites her lip.

To think I'd forgotten all about him.

"Alright," she says, "just for you."

They walk through the camp, and Noor can't help but feel a new spring in her father's step. They take a bus to University Town, and head on foot into a part of the city Noor's had no reason to visit before. Ancient Sheesham trees provide shade from the scorching sun, and on both sides of the street grand colonial mansions loom, their ground floors hidden by walls covered in all shades of bougainvillea.

Everything's so different here. Kacha Gari might as well be on another planet.

Aamir Khan reads off the numbers of the houses and stops in front of a large, ornate gate.

"Ah, here we are," he says.

He pushes the gate open, and they walk up the gravel driveway. In front of them stands what Noor considers a palace.

"This can't be right," she says.

"This is the address he gave me."

They climb the steps, and Aamir Khan rings the doorbell. Noor prays her father has made a mistake. Moments later Charlie opens the door, his hair still damp from showering.

Oh no.

"Great to see you guys," he grins.

"And it is a delight to see you," Aamir Khan says.

"Come in, come in."

Noor follows her father into a vast vaulted hall. She stares up at the skylight fifty feet above her.

"Can I take your jacket, Aamir?" Charlie says.

"That would be most kind."

Aamir Khan hands Charlie his blazer. Charlie opens a closet door and hangs it up.

"And you, Noor?"

Charlie gives her an eager smile.

Is he really attempting to undress me this early into our visit?

"How about your headscarf, my dear," Aamir Khan says. "I have always believed the veil or worse the burqa, Charlie, to be affectations of the ignorant, and if there is ever an opportunity where Noor is free not to wear one she should seize it with gusto."

"Won't get any argument from me," Charlie says.

Noor decides that now Charlie's in league with her father she despises him all the more. She unties her headscarf, and her long, black hair unfurls. Charlie steps forward to take the scarf, and she recoils at the strong odor of aftershave and cigarettes.

"So I hope you guys are hungry?" Charlie says.

"Oh, you shouldn't have troubled yourself, we had more than a sufficient breakfast," Aamir Khan says.

Half a piece of naan split between the two of us.

"Hate for it go to waste," Charlie says.

"Well if you insist," Aamir Khan says.

"I insist."

Charlie leads them through the hall and down a corridor into a gargantuan room whose four sides are lined with overladen bookshelves. In the center of the room is a neat arrangement of faded sofas, worn leather chairs and lamps. For all intents and purposes it could be a college library.

"I believe I have just died and gone to paradise," Aamir Khan says.

"Pretty impressive, isn't it?" Charlie says.

Aamir Khan scans one of the shelves.

"Walter Scott, William Thackeray, ah even some Joyce."

Aamir Khan moves on to the next shelf. Noor feels an uncomfortable sensation and turns to discover Charlie gaping at her. She twists her head away.

"Well take as many as you want," Charlie says.

"Oh, I could not," Aamir Khan says.

"I insist."

"You are an insistent man today, Mr. Matthews."

"Please you've got to call me Charlie."

"Then Charlie it is."

Noor makes a promise to never call him by that name.

Charlie leads them outside and down a white railed verandah. At the far end is a wrought-iron table. Table settings have been laid out and in the center sit three covered bowls and a dish of homemade yogurt. Noor's nostrils twitch at the panoply of smells. The covers don't need to be removed for her to know that there's orange chicken, rice, beef and something fried in ghee awaiting them. She feels faint with anticipation.

"So I have Coke, Sprite, and Fanta," Charlie says.

"A Sprite would be most lovely thank you," Aamir Khan says.

"And you, Noor?"

Again that smile.

"A Sprite, please."

Charlie snaps the tops off a couple of bottles. He scampers around the table and pulls Noor's chair out. Knowing there's nothing she can do, Noor sits down and lets him push her in. Noor pours her Sprite into a glass and takes a sip. It's ice cold and exquisite.

"So don't kill me if this sucks," Charlie says. "I told Mukhtar I had some guests, well gestured might be a better way of putting it, and this is what he rustled up."

Charlie lifts the covers off the dishes. Noor glances at her father; his eyes have watered over.

"Oh, Charlie, this is some honor. Not just Narenj Palao but Mantu and Bulanni too. In Afghanistan these are served at only the most auspicious of occasions."

"Well let's hope this is one of them. Please, dig in."

Noor watches her father place a modest portion on his plate.

"You too, Noor" Charlie says.

She takes a smaller sized portion. Charlie has no such qualms and piles food on his plate until it's almost falling off the edge. He raises his Coke bottle.

"How about a toast?"

"I think that is an excellent idea," Aamir Khan says.

"To a long and happy friendship."

"Hear, hear."

Noor scoops some Narenj Palao onto her fork and puts it in her mouth. The combined tastes—the saffron, orange peel, pistachios, almonds and chicken—are almost too overwhelming for her simple palate. A moan escapes her lips. She looks up and sees Charlie smiling at her. She can't help but blush.

"So, Noor, how did your English get so good?" he says.

"My father used to teach it at Kabul University."

Noor takes a bite of her Mantu beef dumpling and chews

it over allowing the fat to linger on her tongue. She glances over at her father; he's almost finished what's on his plate.

"So you must be looking forward to going back there?" Charlie says.

"I doubt we will be traveling to Kabul anytime soon," Aamir Khan says.

"I thought the government's about to fall?"

"Despite the mujahideen's exquisite ability at grabbing defeat from the jaws of victory I fear you are correct."

"You not happy to see the Communists go?"

"Once I would have been, but now I would prefer even them over what is to come."

"And what's that?"

"The depths of hell, I am afraid. Our mujahideen has many noble men but I am sorry to say they are overwhelmed by illiterates and radicals who will throttle each other the moment they've taken Kabul. They will fight until not a brick remains."

Charlie holds out the dish of Naranj Palao.

"Please have some more, Aamir."

This time Aamir Khan shows less restraint. Charlie offers Noor more too, but her pride won't allow her to accept.

"So your dad told me you'd applied for a bunch of scholarships in the States."

"I haven't received an offer yet."

"Well you're better than me. I never even went to college."

"Was it too expensive?" Aamir Khan says.

"Oh no, my father would've paid for the whole thing, especially if I'd gone to Duke, his alma mater."

"My word, what a coincidence, that is my alma mater too?"

Charlie looks at Aamir Khan as if he's trying to pull a fast one.

"Duke, as in Blue Devils Duke?"

"I know, it must come as quite a surprise given my present situation, but when I was a little older than you, I spent eight delightful months there completing my post graduate thesis."

"What on?"

"Edith Wharton."

"No way, I read *The Age of Innocence* last summer. Enjoyed it way more than I thought I would."

Noor's convinced Charlie is lying. She doubts he's picked up anything more serious than a comic book since high school. She watches Charlie bite into another dumpling.

"So why didn't you go to university?" she says.

"I joined the army instead."

"From what I have read West Point is as academically rigorous as any university," Aamir Khan says.

"No, I wasn't an officer, just a plain old enlistee. Made a lot of friends, got to see the world. Korea, Germany, Saudi Arabia."

"And now here you are in Pakistan?"

"I know, crazy right?"

"Have you always wanted to be an aid worker?"

"Not really. What I really want to do is open a dive shop—in Belize."

"A dive shop?" Noor says.

"Yeah, you know, go out in the morning with the tourists, show them the best reefs, then in the afternoon—"

Noor pushes her chair back.

"Excuse me," she says.

She hurries down the verandah and sees a set of open doors. She plunges through them into an unused bedroom and slumps onto the bed.

The man's an imbecile, and a frivolous, self-centered imbecile at that. Only an idiot abandons a university education, at Duke of all places, to be a private in the army. And a dive shop!

She feels an overwhelming desire to scream and digs her nails into her thigh in order to suppress it.

One thing's for certain, there's no way he can be of any use to us.

Noor stands up and approximates the direction of Mecca.

"O Lord," she says, "you are my guardian. Forgive me, have mercy on me and pour out on me patience."

She begins her rakahs, and as always the practice calms her. Afterwards she kneels there and reminds herself that nothing has been wasted other than an hour of their lives.

Just get out as quickly as you can.

She takes a deep breath and heads out onto the verandah. with renewed purpose. She finds Charlie smoking at the table.

"Your dad's gone to fetch some books," he says.

Noor heads for her chair; there's nothing else to do. Charlie jumps up to help her.

"Please, I am more than capable," she says.

Charlie retreats and returns to his chair. Noor stares out at the garden.

"I've got ice cream in the cooler."

"Do you think I'm a child, Mr. Matthews?"

"Wish you'd call me Charlie."

She doesn't say anything.

"Well I'm going to have some," he says.

She is soon overcome by the scent of mango and pistachios. She can't help but glance in his direction. He has a quart of Kulfi ice cream in front of him and is scooping it into a bowl.

"Mukhtar turned me on to this stuff," he says. "It's amazing, tasted nothing like it."

Noor remembers the ice cream shop on Chicken Street that they'd walk to every Friday in the summer. She'd always have mango and pistachio flavor, and while Bushra and Tariq would bolt theirs down, she'd take small bites and let the ice cream melt on her tongue. To her mother's chagrin she'd still be eating ten minutes after everyone else had finished.

"Sure you don't want some?" Charlie says.

"I am sure."

She feels him staring at her and focuses on a humming bird zipping in and out of some nearby roses.

"You didn't always live like this, did you?" he says.

"I don't dwell on the past, Mr. Matthews."

"I know, but it must have been difficult, coming here when you were so young, living in that camp. I've never been to a place where women are treated so badly."

She looks back down the verandah.

Where in God's name are you, Baba?

"Look, when it comes to this scholarship thing, if there's anything I can do to help—"

"Thank you but we won't be requiring such assistance."

"Your father said—"

"My father doesn't speak for me, Mr. Matthews."

"It was just a friendly offer."

Noor swivels in her chair and glares at Charlie.

"Oh really, and you won't require anything in return?"

"Course not."

Noor can't help but laugh.

"Forgive me, Mr. Matthews, if I find that answer absurd. I assume you chasing me down a darkened alley wasn't a figment of my imagination?"

"I just I wanted to get to know you."

"'Get to know you', what's that an idiom for?"

"Idiom?"

"If you'd gone to university you might know what that meant. I assume you weren't going to ask my father for my hand in marriage?"

"You're kidding, right?"

"So the only other possible explanation is that you were hoping for an erotic fling with an exotic woman?"

Charlie flushes.

"I thought as much," she says.

Noor stands.

"Mr. Matthews in situations like these I think it important to be clear. I have no interest in getting to know you, not now nor at any time in the future. I may have been stripped of most things in this life, but I still have my honor, and the idea of spending another minute with some warmonger who put killing ahead of learning, a hypocrite who's here to help people but lives like a prince, well to be quite frank, it's utterly noxious to me."

Charlie tries to say something, but Noor cuts him off.

"Thank you for lunch, Mr. Matthews, we will see ourselves out."

And with that Noor turns on her heel and heads down the verandah in search of her father.

NINE

TARIQ SITS ON the floor of the hut and drinks a weak cup of tea. Bushra hovers over him like a bothersome fly.

"Does it hurt?" she says.

"The stump not so much but the arm, there are nights when I think a hundred pound weight is lying on top of it."

"But your arm's gone."

"Yes, but it still feels as if it's there."

Bushra screws up her forehead and tries to comprehend the phenomenon Tariq's just described. Tariq doesn't wait for her thought process to conclude.

"When did they say they'd be back?" he says.

"They didn't."

"And you're sure they were going to the British Council library?"

"That's what they always do on Fridays."

Books, books, books, Tariq thinks, *how I detest books.*

His father had wasted half his life with his nose in them, time which could've been better spent getting them out of this hellhole.

He looks at the earthen walls, the thin bedspreads, their blackened cooking pots. It's an embarrassment that his family lives this way. He's not sure why he even came. Some misplaced sense of familial obligation, he supposes.

Oh well, I guess they lost out on five hundred rupees.

Bushra goes to fill his cup and manages to pour scalding tea down the front of his kameez. Tariq cries out in pain.

"I'm so sorry," she says.

Bushra returns with a rag and dabs at his chest.

"Get away."

He pushes her so hard she falls on her ass.

"You really are good for nothing, aren't you?"

Tariq heads outside. He blinks in the bright light and walks towards the pick-up that Yousef had let him borrow from the fleet.

Shame, I'd loved them to have seen it.

"Tariq."

Tariq turns. His father and sister are walking his direction. His father's face is etched with concern.

"Oh heavens," his father says, "what happened?"

"Nothing but a contact wound, Baba."

"You've lost an arm."

Tariq shrugs as if these kinds of things are to be expected. He looks at his sister; to his dismay her level of concern doesn't seem to have risen. They return to the hut and sit down. Tariq makes sure that the pearl-handled Colt pistol in his holster is on full display.

"When did this happen?" Aamir Khan says.

"A couple of months ago. Four of us slipped into Afghanistan and set up high on a slope overlooking the Jalalabad highway. On the sixth day an army convoy finally appeared. We waited until they were along side us and unleashed everything we had at them. To our amazement nothing hit, it was as if there was a force field surrounding them, so I scrambled down the slope with my—"

"Weren't you high up on the slope?" Noor says.

Tariq looks over at his sister, and she holds his gaze. Bile rises up in his throat. He feels as if she's penetrated his brain and sifted through the reality of what happened that day; how in fact he'd lost his footing and gone tumbling head over heels down the hillside only to find himself sprawled by the side of the road.

He turns back to his father.

"When I arrived at the road, there was only one vehicle left, an armored personnel carrier. The machine gunner was so surprised to see me his shots spat wide. I got down on one knee and fired an RPG through the driver's window—"

"I thought you said you'd already unleashed everything you had at them?" Noor says.

"What's with her?" Tariq says to Aamir Khan.

Tariq points at his missing arm.

"Isn't this enough that she need not challenge the truth of my story."

"Noor," Aamir Khan says.

"I apologize," Noor says, "I took my dear brother's words too literally."

Tariq glances at her and thinks he detects the slightest of smirks. The events of that day replay in his mind; scrambling to his feet to find the personnel carrier bearing down on him, seeing his RPG launcher a couple of feet away only to realize that it was empty, the machine gunner lining him up in his sights, and then a blessed miracle, a massive explosion as the personnel carrier rolled over an anti-tank mine.

Damn her. Nobody else has doubted my story.

"So what happened then?" Aamir Khan says.

"The story's not worth telling," Tariq says.

"No please, for my sake if nothing else."

Tariq sighs.

"I fired my RPG, the carrier blew up and a piece of shrapnel severed my left arm. There you have it. Satisfied."

"Oh my poor, poor boy."

Tariq cringes at his father's words.

"How are you feeling?" Aamir Khan says. "I have read that many amputees feel phantom pain."

"Any pain is but a paltry sacrifice on behalf of the jihad. In fact I'm now in the Prince's office helping prepare our next offensive."

"That is impressive," Aamir Khan says.

And in this case true. Tariq's heroic tale had not only won him a transfer from Yousef's stifling armory but also a gift from the Prince of ten thousand rupees and the Colt. An uncomfortable silence pervades the hut. Tariq notices two books sitting next to his father—*I Claudius* and *Fahrenheit 451*.

"Are these for your consumption or Noor's?" Tariq says.

"That should be no concern of yours," Noor says.

Tariq takes a sip of tea. He won't give her the satisfaction of letting her get to him.

"It's a deep disgrace for any man for his sister to be reading such salacious material."

"These books are hardly salacious," Aamir Khan says.

"Do the characters involve themselves in sexual activity?"

"I dare say somewhere—"

"Then you should be ashamed of yourself for allowing Noor to read them."

"What books would you have me read?" Noor says.

"The Quran is more than sufficient."

"I read it every day."

"Clearly you haven't understood it."

"I understand it more than you ever will."

Tariq pulls on his beard until he feels it might rip from his chin. His eyes are drawn to the scarf resting petulantly on Noor's hair; her come-hither eyes and pouting lips are further advertisement that she's a wanton slut.

If you were my wife, I'd spank your buttocks until I'd beaten the very last bit of disobedience out of you.

He drags his eyes away and focuses on his father.

"I see they still don't wear the burqa."

"You know where I stand on that," Aamir Khan says.

"This only brings further disgrace on our family."

"Our family lives in a mud hut," Noor says. "I doubt we can sink any lower."

"I also see you continue to shave."

"It is my preference," Aamir Khan says.

"We are duty bound to follow the example of the Prophet, peace be upon him."

"Is that a fact?" Noor says.

Tariq rounds on his sister.

"An indisputable one."

"Did the Prophet, peace be upon him, wear a pearl-handled pistol and drive a Japanese four-by-four?" Noor says.

Tariq's eyes twitch.

"These matters have been decided upon by the ulema. You have neither the wisdom nor education to understand such things."

"I thought you just said we're duty bound to follow the Prophet's example. Sounds to me like you should be riding a camel, and fighting the Communists with a sword."

Tariq leaps across the rug and grabs Noor around the neck. He lifts her up and pins her against the wall. Noor kicks back, but Tariq is too close for them to have any effect.

"I can strangle you as surely with one hand, sister, as I could with two."

Tariq stares into her eyes. All he detects is mocking derision staring back.

"Tariq," Aamir Khan says.

Tariq squeezes harder.

"As your father, I beg you, put her down."

Tariq releases her. Noor collapses onto her knees, her lungs clamoring for air.

Tariq stands there a moment, catching his breath. He looks down at the three of them.

"To think I had two thousand rupees to give to you. But I forgot you're not worth it; none of you are."

Tariq spits on the floor and strides outside. He promises himself that this will be the last time he'll ever visit them.

TEN

CHARLIE SITS IN the shade sketching the recruits in their long protection aprons and visored helmets. They are waddling around the yard swinging their metal detectors back and forth. Wali comes up behind him and scrutinizes his drawing.

"A most accurate representation, I must say."

Shafiq trips and falls to the ground.

"Can't say they're not protected," Charlie says.

Wali laughs, and Charlie puts his sketch pad to the side.

"I trust you had a productive day," Wali says.

"Wouldn't categorize it that way. None of these guys seem to listen."

"I hate to say this but if you'd only kept the first men—"

"Yeah then I wouldn't have to worry because they'd all be deaf."

Charlie sticks his fingers in his mouth and whistles. Half the recruits stop and look his way. The other half keep walking around like drones.

"Hey guys," he shouts. "Guys."

Everyone stops.

"We're done for the day. Give your equipment back to Mocam and I'll see you tomorrow."

Everyone makes for the storeroom except for one recruit

who shuffles their way. He doesn't need to pull off his helmet for Charlie to know who it is.

"Yes, Obaidullah," Charlie says.

"Sir, I was wondering if you have given more thought to become Muslim, sir, it would most warm our hearts."

"Actually Obaidullah, now you mention it, I have. I've prayed for many hours and asked God for guidance."

"And what was His answer, sir?"

"For now I'm going to stick with Jesus."

Obaidullah deflates.

"I ask that you continue to pray most hard, sir."

"Will do."

Obaidullah trudges off.

"I almost feel sorry for him," Charlie says.

"Mark my word," Wali says, "he won't give up until you are a full fledged Muslim."

"Then I guess he'll make a great deminer."

Wali gives Charlie a confused look.

"You need a lot of patience in this job," Charlie says.

"Yes, of course."

They head towards the main gate.

"I need a favor," Charlie says.

"Please name it."

"I want to go into Afghanistan."

"So soon?"

"Yeah why not?"

Wali shrugs.

"Whatever floats your ship," he says.

"Your boat, Wali, not ship."

Wali gets out his notepad and writes down the correction.

"I will ask my friend at the UN. They have survey expeditions that go all the time."

"Yeah that may not work. Kind of rubbed that Jurgen fella up the wrong way."

"Jurgen Kaymer. Oh, he's not important."

"He runs the organization."

"Yes, but he's not responsible for the list."

"What list?"

"The list of who goes on the expedition and who doesn't. My friend is."

"And Jurgen can't put someone on it?"

"Of course, but it's up to my friend to actually do it—if he doesn't, you won't have the appropriate permits."

Charlie reaches the Pajero. He puts his hand on the hood and yanks it away. He can't decide if it's scorching hot due to the sun or because Wali's been driving it all day.

"Anything else?" Wali says.

"Yeah, be around a little more when I'm teaching. I'm stretched man, it's tough keeping my eye on thirty guys."

"Mr. Matthews, I most sincerely wish I could, but as your deputy, the number of tasks I have to undertake are so numerous that your request is impossible I'm afraid."

"Like what?"

"Like finding you a super hot, sexy motorbike."

"You found one?"

Wali gives Charlie a gargantuan smile.

"Oh, Mr. Matthews, I am telling you it is a beauty."

Charlie opens his door.

"Well what are we waiting for?"

"The seller is all the way in the Old City."

"I don't care."

Wali jumps in and they speed off.

"Okay, out with it," Charlie says as they pass by the stone walls of the old British cemetery. "What demining experience do you really have?"

"You have asked me this before."

"And you never told me."

"I most assuredly did. My sister was killed by a mine. I think of her every day."

"But what other experience?"

"You don't think that is sufficient?"

"No."

"Mr. Skeppar was most moved when I told him my sister's harrowing tale. You should turn right here."

Charlie makes the turn and swerves to avoid a goat.

"Okay humor me," Charlie says, "what's a Claymore?"

Wali stares out the window.

"Wali?"

"I'm thinking."

"Shouldn't need to."

"You see that Naz cinema? You can park right there."

Charlie pulls up in front of a movie theater with a giant billboard of Rambo above its doors.

"Are you acquainted with the Rambo movies, Mr. Matthews?"

"Course."

"Rambo Three is by far the best, don't you agree?"

"Pretty certain that isn't a commonly held view."

"For the Afghan people it is the greatest movie ever made. He kills many, many Russians. He even plays buzkashi."

Charlie cuts the ignition.

"A Claymore is a directional anti-personnel mine. It fires steel balls out a hundred yards within a circular radius and is used primarily in ambushes and as an anti-infiltration device."

"I could not have put it better myself."

"You don't get it, Wali, I don't give a shit what experience you have. I'm not going to fire you, I just want to know that's all."

"I assure you, you won't find a better deputy in the whole of Peshawar."

"Never in doubt, just admit—"

"In the whole of Pakistan, I would suggest."

"Goddamn it, Wali, admit it, just admit it."

Charlie looks past Wali. A group of grubby street boys are pressing their noses up against the glass.

"I admit it," Wali says.

"There that wasn't so hard, was it?"

"Do you think less of me now, Mr. Matthews?"

"Hell no."

"Really?"

"You got a lot of other talents, finding mines just isn't one of them."

"You won't tell Mr. Skeppar."

"Who do you think I am? Now come on, let's go."

They get out and the boys crowd around them jabbering away at Wali. Wali picks the wiriest of the bunch and hands him a five-rupee note.

"What did you say to him?" Charlie says.

"If the car is in the same condition when we return he gets another ten rupees. Trust me, he will fight with his life to protect it."

They turn off the main street and enter the tight alleys of the Old City. They're heaving with men and a mixture of shawled and burqaed women. It's a frenetic, upbeat maze with smoke from open fronted restaurants wafting down the alleys like evil spirits searching for victims. A schizophrenic fusion of smells assaults Charlie's nose. One moment it's sweet cinnamon and nutmeg from the spice stores, the next it's the putrid stench of chicken entrails from the butchers'. Wali barrels forward ignoring the sales pitches of the store-owners and the pleas of the deformed beggars, and by necessity Charlie has to as well. They plunge into the shimmering jewelry bazaar, its stores heaving with bronze ornaments and gaudy jewelry, and burst out into a large square, teeming with hundreds of turbaned men sitting on their haunches.

"This is Sarafa, the moneychangers' bazaar," Wali says.

Charlie looks in one of the stores. A money-counting machine whirs its way through a large stack of bills. They leave the square and head down an alley filled with stationers and booksellers, the books piled high like they're part of some ancient library. Wali leads Charlie down a couple of passageways so dark and narrow Charlie half-expects to be knifed. They emerge into an area that is split between pharmacies and motorcycle garages. Above each of the pharmacies a neon half crescent shines, and combined they bathe the area in a pale green light. They enter an open garage that seems to be more a repository of spare parts than actual motorcycles.

"You sure this is the right place?"

Wali calls out, and a grease-stained mechanic emerges from the back with a gleaming black and chrome motorcycle.

"Honda Rebel," the man grins at Charlie.

Charlie inspects it. It's in good shape.

"You won't believe this but this was my first bike. Bought it with my army signing bonus."

"Ah, there's nothing like a man's first love," Wali says.

The mechanic comes over and points at the chain.

"He says he changed the rear sprocket from thirty-three tooth to thirty. Says it can go at least eighty miles an hour."

"What's he want?"

Wali asks the mechanic.

"He says one thousand five hundred dollars."

"Forget it, I could buy a new one for that price back home."

Wali translates and the man replies.

"He asks what's your price?"

"I don't know. Seven. It's in good condition but it's been driven a lot."

Wali gives the mechanic Charlie's offer, and the man cries out.

"He says why do you want his children to starve?" Wali says.

"Tell me you're kidding?"

"Oh no, he's very upset."

"So what's his price?"

Wali turns to the mechanic who goes into a sales pitch full of gesticulations and hair pulling.

"He says one thousand three hundred dollars but only because you are friend."

"I just met him."

"Still he considers you a friend."

"Seven hundred."

Wali goes back again. The man raises his fist.

"He says you are cruel, cruel man, why do you torment him so?"

"Screw this," Charlie says, "He can keep it."

Charlie turns. The mechanic runs over and tugs him on his arm. He launches into another impassioned diatribe.

"He says the price is one thousand one hundred," Wali says, "but he will make no money from the sale."

"One thousand and we're done."

Wali tells the mechanic, and the mechanic, wiping tears from his eyes, nods.

"He says okay for you he'll do it."

Charlie counts out ten one hundred dollar bills.

"Please tell me he's making some money?" Charlie says.

"Oh, I suspect at least three hundred dollars," Wali says.

Charlie stares at Wali.

"You tell me that now?"

"If you had wanted me to bargain for you, you should have said."

Charlie sighs. He hands the bills to the mechanic whose mood has transformed markedly. Charlie suspects Wali's getting a hefty commission.

Charlie wheels the bike outside.

"Want to give it a spin?" he says to Wali.

"Would you mind if I visited one of these chemists first."

"Go for it."

Wali enters the nearest pharmacy. Charlie turns the ignition and the engine purrs.

A thirty tooth rear-sprocket. Who'd have thought?

He looks through the pharmacy window. Wali is haggling with the storeowner. Wali throws up his hands and storms out of the shop.

"You didn't get anything?" Charlie says.

"He charges too much."

"What for?"

"It is of no importance."

"No, tell me."

"Morphine. My mother has cancer, she needs it otherwise the pain is too much."

For the first time Wali seems worn down and vulnerable. Charlie looks down and notices how tattered Wali's shoes are.

If he's into all these side businesses he's sure not spending the money on himself.

"Is she getting treatment?" Charlie says.

"There are no cancer hospitals for refugees."

"I'll get her into one."

"That's most kind but I'm afraid she is beyond help."

"Then let me pay for the morphine."

"I could not ask you to do that."

"Why not? I'm your friend."

"You are?"

"Course I am."

Wali's smile returns. Charlie heads into the store, and triples Wali's orders. He comes out with the pills and hands them to Wali.

"I don't know how to thank you," Wali says.

"I've been there. It's the least I can do."

"I don't understand."

"My mom, she died of cancer when I was fourteen."

"Oh, I am so sorry."

"I wouldn't wish cancer on my worst enemy."

"On that I am in utmost agreement with you."

Charlie smiles.

"Now come on, jump on."

Charlie revs the bike, and they take off on a twisting journey through the darkened alleys of Old City Peshawar. At each intersection Wali taps on either Charlie's right or left shoulder to tell him which way he should turn, and ten minutes later they find themselves back in front of the cinema. The boy is there standing guard over the Pajero. Charlie throws Wali the keys.

"It's yours."

Charlie winks at Wali and takes off. He threads his way through the late night traffic until he's on an open stretch of road. He opens the throttle, and when he looks down at his speedometer he sees he's going eighty-five miles an hour. He whoops with delight.

ELEVEN

NOOR HEARS A knock and turns to find Elma standing in her classroom doorway.

Oh Lord, is she here to deliver more bad news?

"I'm sorry, I can come back later," Elma says.

"No," Noor says, "we're almost finished."

Elma comes in, and the girls' eyes follow her as though she's some sort of exotic animal. She leans up against the wall in an attempt to make herself inconspicuous, but, in so doing, her pert breasts push up against the fabric of her starch white shirt. Both Noor and the class look at them goggled eyed.

"Miss Noor, don't mind me," Elma says.

Noor jerks out of her trance and blushes.

"Girls," Noor says, "this is Elma Kuyt. She's in charge of the aid agency that funds this school."

"Good morning, Mrs. Kuyt," the girls says.

"It is Miss," Elma says, "but thank you for your welcome."

Kamila makes a face at Noor as if to wonder what woman would still be unmarried at Elma's age. Noor ignores her and finishes writing the quote from *Anne of Green Gables* on the chalkboard. Noor turns back to the class. She does everything she can to avoid Elma's gaze.

"So tell me, like Anne, what are each of you interested in finding out about the world?"

She turns to a plump girl at the end of the front row.

"Hila?"

"I don't know," Hila says.

"Oh come on, there must be something that you wish you knew more about?"

Hila's face lights up.

"Watermelons," Hila says. "Why do they grow so big?"

The class cracks up. Noor shushes them and writes watermelons on the chalkboard.

"I'm curious about that too," Noor says. "I mean why aren't they just the size of mangos, for instance? Let me do some research and we can it discuss it more on Sunday."

Noor turns to a sparrow-like girl next to Hila.

"Rashida?"

Rashida blushes.

"I do not know if this is rightful," Rashida says.

"Rashida, how many times have I told you there's no such thing as a wrong question."

"I do wonder who my husband is going to be."

"That's a totally legitimate query. How many of you also think about that?"

Every hand in the room goes up.

"Well here's the good news, whoever he is, it will never change what you know up here," Noor says. "No one can take that away from you."

A girl near the back raises her hand.

"Yes, Gulpira."

"Miss Noor, do you think about who your husband's going to be?"

No, because I never intend on having one.

Noor glances at Elma. Elma is staring at her intently.

"In such matters, I trust in Allah's providence."

The girls nod as if that makes total sense. Noor turns next to Kamila.

"How about you, Kamila? What are you interested in finding out?"

"I want to know why Miss Kuyt cut your wage so much."

Noor stands there with her mouth agape.

"I am so sorry, Miss Kuyt," she says, recovering. "I don't know why Kamila would ask such a question."

"You just said there's no such thing as a wrong question?" Kamila says.

"That's true but—"

"How can there be a 'but'. Either there is no such thing as a wrong question or there isn't."

"Kamila, enough," Noor hisses.

Elma wanders into the center of the room.

"No, it's alright, Miss Noor, I'm not offended by Kamila's question. Actually I'm proud we're teaching the girls to not be afraid of authority figures.

"So why did you do it?" Kamila says.

Noor stares at Kamila in an attempt to quiet her, but Kamila has all her attention focused on Elma.

"Because if we hadn't cut costs across the board," Elma says, "we'd have had to close the school entirely."

"Did you cut your own wage?" Kamila says.

"I cut mine first, and I cut it the most."

Kamila sits there, her righteous fury doused.

"Now does anyone else have any questions?" Elma says.

Elma glances around the room; the girls shake their heads. Kamila raises her hand.

Oh Lord, what now?

"Yes, Kamila," Elma says.

"You should know that Miss Noor is the best teacher we've ever had. Before I go to sleep at night I thank Allah that she is my teacher."

Elma smiles.

"Trust me, we feel very blessed to have her."

Out in the courtyard Miss Suha rings the bell for recess. Noor sighs with relief and excuses the class. The girls grab their books and rush out the door.

"She's feisty that Kamila," Elma says.

"She's the brightest student I've ever taught."

"Maybe she'll be a teacher like you one day."

"That'll depend on her husband."

"Well let's pray he's as educated and enlightened as she is."

"I fear that won't be the case. She tells me her father's adamant she marry when she's fourteen."

"That isn't legal."

"No, but you know how it is, the authorities don't care. There are some days when I think about going on the run with her."

Elma doesn't saying anything.

Oh my Lord, what have I said?

"I would never do that of course, it's just a silly fantasy, I mean where would we go?"

"I know that, Noor," Elma smiles. "Though I have to say you and Kamila would make a unique Thelma and Louise."

"I'm sorry, I don't understand the reference."

"It's a movie about two American women who go on the run."

"Why do they do that?"

"One of them killed a man who was raping her friend."

"And they didn't go to the police?"

"They should have, but they panicked."

Neither needs to tell the other that in Pakistan a woman never would. Without four male witnesses to a rape the authorities would charge her with adultery, and once convicted, hang her for her trouble.

The thought darkens Noor's mood, and she starts gathering her books.

"I want to apologize for the other day," Elma says. "I can't believe I was so insensitive, I mean to be talking to you about Salman in that way, I'm still mortified."

"I overreacted."

"No, you stood your ground, just like Kamila did, and I appreciate that. What do you say, can we start afresh?"

"Of course," Noor says.

Elma sticks out her hand, and Noor shakes it.

"So tell me, how good are you at learning languages?"

"I speak English, Pashtu, Arabic and a little Farsi."

"What do you say to learning a fifth?"

Elma opens her leather folder and hands some fax pages to Noor. At the top in large letters are the words *Universiteit von Amsterdam.*

"My friend works in the admissions office; she suggested a scholarship that might be right for you."

The pages tremble in Noor's hands.

"The only catch is you have to be proficient in Dutch. I can translate your application and essay, but if you get to the second round there's a telephone interview in late January."

"That's only four months away," Noor says.

"That's why I asked you how good you were."

Noor looks up at Elma with tears in her eyes.

"I can do it."

Elma smiles.

"Then I have but one request in return. This Friday I'd love you to take me and Rod on a tour of Kacha Gari."

"It'd be my honor."

"Perfect, we'll meet you here at ten."

Elma heads for the door.

"Miss Kuyt," Noor says. "Can you play tennis at this university?"

"If you're successful I'll introduce you to Betty Stove when you get there."

Elma leaves. Noor sits down at her desk. She tries to read the application but the text is obscured by her tears.

TWELVE

TARIQ STARES ACROSS the rug at his father-in-law.

"He wants what?"

"A new fourth wife," his father-in-law says. "He feels he's mourned enough."

"Does he have anyone in mind?"

"No, but the Prince wants her to be Afghan, he thinks it would be a way to honor the jihad."

Why haven't I heard of this? No one mentioned it in the office.

Tariq's father-in-law tears a wing off the chicken and proceeds to gnaw it until it's mere bones.

"I suggested Badia to him," his father-in-law says, using his sleeve to wipe the grease off his hands.

Of course you did. You were clever to hold Badia back all this time.

"It would be a great honor for our family," his father-in-law says.

For you, you mean. It gets me nothing but having to listen to you wax lyrical every night about your royal son-in-law.

"How did he respond?" Tariq says.

"He said he'd heard how beautiful she was and asked to see her."

"That's good."

"I said 'no'. It's not Pashtun custom, he should take my word."

You idiot. The Prince surely knows there's a vast disparity in this world between the number of women who're beautiful and the number whose fathers think they are.

"You made the right decision," Tariq says, "nothing's more important than your honor."

"He's still interested—"

Maybe the Prince is a bigger fool than I imagined.

"—but it would help matters if someone else spoke favorably about her."

"Who do you have in mind?"

"You. He'll consider you more impartial than her brothers."

"But I've never met her."

His father-in-law shouts out Badia's name, and a teenage girl enters. Her eyes remain fixed on the floor.

"Look at your brother-in-law," Salim Afridi commands.

Badia does as she's told. She's as beautiful as any virgin a martyr might meet in paradise.

If only I had this delight to come home to rather than that swine of a wife.

There's only one woman Tariq knows who surpasses her beauty.

Noor.

An idea forms in his mind.

"You can go," his father-in-law says.

Badia scurries away.

"I've arranged for you to sit down with the Prince tomorrow," his father-in-law says. "I told him you had some excellent thoughts regarding the coming offensive."

Tariq tries his best to contain his growing excitement. He looks over the empty dishes; there's nothing left for his father-in-law to devour. Hopefully he'll dismiss him soon.

"Your wife has mentioned some things to her mother," his

father-in-law says.

What's the bitch been saying?

"She says when you fuck you don't finish inside of her."

"She's mistaken," Tariq says.

"It's been almost two years."

"I'm more aware of that than anyone."

"Maybe stay in there a little longer at the end, eh."

Maybe if you'd married me to your other daughter I would.

"Of course," Tariq says

"You're a good man, Tariq. Things will only grow more concrete between us once you have a child."

"That's all I desire," Tariq says.

His father-in-law grunts. It's his way of telling Tariq he's dismissed. Tariq walks away, his mind working overtime.

THIRTEEN

CHARLIE STUDIES THE pen gun. It looks just like a black, metal, fountain pen. He twists the cap off. It seems simple enough; just place a bullet in the barrel, screw the cap back on, pull back the pen clip, and press.

He hears someone coming down the verandah and turns to find Mukhtar with a dish in his hands.

"Narenj Palau," Mukhtar grins.

"Thanks, but no one's coming to lunch this week."

"My pleasure, sir," Mukhtar says, placing it on the table.

Charlie pulls out his wallet and hands Mukhtar two fifty rupee notes.

"For you and Rasul. Go buy something for yourselves after mosque, okay?"

"Thank you, sir."

Charlie watches Mukhtar head towards his hut. Halfway there he does a little jig. Charlie laughs.

Now what the hell am I going to do?

He's already been for a run, sketched a grinning Mukhtar's portrait and finished *A Short Walk In The Hindu Kush*. One thing's for sure, he isn't going to stay locked up here all day. He sees the Naranj Palau sitting on the table and can't help but think of Aamir Khan, and how he'd devoured his two portions the previous week.

He could use this a hell of a lot more than me.

Charlie grabs the dish and a ball of twine, and goes out front to his motorcycle. With the dish tied down, he speeds towards Jamrud Road. For once it's empty; the whole city seems to be at Friday prayers. At Noor's bus stop, he begins retracing the path he chased her down. A throng of boys trail after him.

"Hello, mister, how are you?" a kid in a Soviet army beret says.

"Good thanks."

"You have dollars?" another in a skull cap asks.

"If you can help me."

The kid in the beret pushes the one in the skull cap to the ground and jumps on the back of the bike.

"Hey, watch the dish," Charlie says.

"Where you go?" the kid says.

"You know a man called Aamir Khan?"

The boy points down the alley.

"This a way," he says.

"You sure?"

"Go."

They hurtle down one mud-walled alley after another, the kid hooting and hollering, until they come to a halt beside a hut the size of a garden shed. A toddler in a grubby pink dress sits out front dipping a bowl into a puddle of green, stagnant water. The kid shouts out a stream of Pashtu and grins at Charlie.

"Aamir Khan," he says.

A hacking cough emanates from within, and a gnarled old man pulls back some sewn-together cloths.

"This isn't Aamir Khan," Charlie says.

"No. Aamir Khan," the kid says pointing at the man.

"Not mine, mine different. This man too old."

The kid's smile disappears. The group of boys come running around the corner, and the boy in the skull cap sucker punches his rival. Before long the two boys are on the ground exchanging blows. The others form a circle around them.

Charlie apologizes to the man and pushes the bike back the way he thinks they came. The kid in the beret comes running up to him, his nose bleeding.

"Please, sir, please, sir, no go," the kid says.

"Sorry buddy, just not my day."

The kid rushes over to a group of young, bearded men exiting a mud walled mosque. He jabbers away while pointing at Charlie.

Shit, where's this going?

A man, who seems to be wearing mascara, walks over.

"As-salaam Alaykum," the man says.

"Wa-alaykum asalaam," Charlie says.

"I hear you're looking for someone."

"Yeah, a friend—Aamir Khan."

"There are many Aamir Khan's in this camp, you'll need to be more specific."

"In his fifties, grey hair, no mustache—was an English professor back in Kabul."

The man turns to his friends and speaks to them in Pashtu.

"My friend knows where this Aamir Khan, you talk about, lives," the man says. "Come I take you."

Charlie goes over to the boys. He pulls out a five dollar bill and holds it up.

"For all of you," he says making a circular gesture.

"Yes, sir, yes, sir," the kid in the beret says. "Understand. Hundred percent."

The kid grabs it and takes off running. The group chases after him. Charlie shakes his head.

The man leads him through the camp, down one mud-walled alley after another. It's as though they've entered a

Byzantine maze, and the deeper they go the more Charlie
wonders if he's being set up.

Shit, maybe he wants to kill me for my bike?

The mud huts fall away, and they come upon an open
expanse of land dotted with fluttering flags. Charlie imagines
the man's compatriots waiting to pummel him to death. The
man stops and points behind Charlie.

"That is where he lives," he says.

Charlie is loathe to turn his back on him. He takes out a
fifty rupee note.

"Please, sir," the man says, "no need."

"I insist."

The man shakes his head.

"When a stranger seeks help, it is a Muslim's duty to be of
service."

The man walks away leaving Charlie feeling like a fool. He
turns to find a row of mud huts. Outside one, he sees Aamir
Khan laying a rug on the ground and a woman in a headscarf
cooking over a small fire. He pushes his motorcycle towards
them. Aamir Khan looks up.

"Charlie?" he says.

"I brought you something."

Charlie unties the dish and hands it to Aamir Khan.

"Oh my, Narenj Palau, you truly did not have to do this."

"It'd have gone to waste otherwise."

"Well that is most kind."

Aamir Khan says something to the woman in Pashtu, and
she stands.

"Charlie, may I introduce to you Bushra, my oldest daughter."

"Good to meet you, Bushra," Charlie says.

The woman gives him a timid nod. Charlie can't help but
think how different she is from her sister. Not in looks so
much, though she's not nearly as beautiful as her sister. It's in
her eyes. Unlike Noor's which burn with such righteous fury,

hers are lifeless, as if she gave up the fight long ago.

Aamir Khan hands Bushra the dish, and she disappears inside the hut. Charlie leans in to see if Noor is in there but the interior is too dim for him to tell.

"I want to apologize for last Friday," Aamir Khan says.

"No big deal. Trust me, I've been in crazier situations."

"I want you to know it is as much my fault as Noor's, after all I am the one who condemned her to this life. It does not excuse her lashing out at you the way she did, but hopefully it makes it understandable."

Bushra comes back out and places some naan and cutlery on the rug.

"Well the offer still stands," Charlie says. "If there's anything I can do to help."

"That is most kind of you, but since we last met I won't say we've experienced a miracle, but there has been a very hopeful development in our lives. Another aid worker, the head of Noor's charity, to be precise, has offered to help her obtain a scholarship."

"That's amazing."

"We expect her here shortly."

Aamir Khan gives Charlie an awkward smile.

"You need me to skedaddle, don't you?" Charlie says.

"Trust me, I would like nothing more than for you to join us, but I fear your presence could have a ruinous effect on Noor and by extension her prospects."

"Totally get it. "

Charlie climbs on his bike.

"How about you come by my place next Friday?" he says. "No Noor, just you by yourself."

"That is most kind but it would not be worth the anguish."

"Oh come on, you're a free man, you can do what you want."

Aamir Khan shakes his head.

"Maybe when you have daughters you will understand."

"Well it was good seeing you again, Aamir."

"And you, Charlie."

Charlie surges forward just as a group of people are emerging from a side alley. He skids to a halt and finds Noor, Elma and Rod standing there in shock.

"Charlie, right?" Rod says.

"Yeah."

"What are you doing here?"

"Oh you know, just visiting one of my recruits. He's been sick as a dog. I got a little lost on the way back, and Aamir Khan here was cool enough to give me directions."

"Yes, yes," Aamir Khan says stepping towards them. "As-salaam Alaykum, I am Aamir Khan, Noor's father, it is an honor to meet you."

Elma and Rod introduce themselves, and while they do Charlie can't help but glance in Noor's direction. Set against the bleakness of the graveyard, her veil loose around her sweeping hair, she resembles an angel sent to destroy him.

"So where's your friend?" Elma says.

Charlie turns to find Elma eyeing him suspiciously.

"Friend?"

"Ivor."

"The guy bought me a drink, hardly call him a bosom buddy"

Elma pauses as if she's reevaluating Charlie in light of this new information.

"Well I guess I'll leave you to your lunch," Charlie says.

"Why don't you join us?" Rod says.

"No, it's okay, look what happened the last time I sat down with you guys."

"I don't think Jurgen's yet recovered," Elma says.

"See what I mean."

"Oh, go on," Rod says. "Be fun to swap war stories. I mean if that's okay by you, Aamir Khan?"

Aamir Khan looks stricken.

"Yes, of course" he says.

***

NOOR SITS ON the rug and does her best to remain calm.

The tour had been going so well. Both Elma and Rod had been attentive, Rod especially so, and as he'd asked her more and more questions she'd felt Elma draw closer to her.

And then he had shown up.

At first she'd thought she was hallucinating, but no there he was, and there he is now, sitting across from her, stealing furtive glances. Since they've sat down she's tried to affect a carefree attitude but then something will throw her off; his incessant chatter, her father's jittery treatment of their guests, Elma remarking on the quality of the Naranj Palau when, to Noor, it seems utterly incongruous amidst the rest of the simple fare. Her opinion of him is unchanged. If anything it's worse for she can't help but think he's part of some elaborate conspiracy to thwart her from ever leaving this camp.

She attempts to focus on the conversation. Charlie is talking to Rod and Elma about the Gulf War.

I can only imagine what a testosterone driven thrill that must've been.

"It was weird," Charlie says, "it was like we were in Saudi Arabia, but we weren't. They kept us so far out in the desert I didn't talk to a single Saudi the whole time I was there. For months we just sat around, a bunch of guys going crazy—no beer, no women, no outlet for all those things that ..."

Charlie catches himself too late.

"That men need," Elma smirks.

Charlie blushes. In Noor's mind, Charlie's just confirmed every suspicion she ever had of him.

"And then the bombardment started. We were sent forward to clear a path for our tanks. All day and night artillery would screech over our heads, and in the distance we'd hear these constant, dull booms,"

"Were you scared?" Elma says.

"Definitely, we all thought the Iraqis were going to hit us with nerve gas. Then the order came in to advance. I tell you, it's the closest thing to hell I've ever seen."

"You mean the burning oil wells," Rod says.

"More than anything that highway into Iraq."

"The Highway of Death."

For the first time since they've sat down Charlie falls silent. A woman in a pale blue burqa walks past, her two young sons traipsing behind her.

"What was it about that highway?" Elma asks.

"We were among the first to get there; for miles all we saw were the shells of burned out cars and trucks; there were clothes, TVs, mirrors, even hundred dollar bills fluttering about, but it was the bodies trapped inside the vehicles that I remember most. There was this one guy, the lid had been blown off his truck, and he was sitting at the wheel, his hands resting on the dashboard. He looked like a zombie, his face burned away. On the floor of his truck I saw the remains of his wallet. I opened it up, and inside was a photo of him sitting with two little boys on his knee. I thought of those two boys, how they'd never see their dad again, and I felt responsible."

Charlie looks in Noor's direction and blushes as if embarrassed to have revealed something so personal. Noor looks out over the graveyard. The woman is sitting by a grave in silent contemplation, her burqa billowing around her like a sheet on a clothesline. Her two young children run around her playing a game of tag.

"I guess on that highway it sunk in that we're all just pawns in other people's games," Charlie says.

"But don't you expect that when you join the army?" Elma says. "I mean isn't that your job, to fight your President's wars."

"I guess I didn't really think about that when I enlisted."

"So why did you join?"

"You really want to know. To piss my dad off."

"Did you succeed?"

"We haven't spoken in five years."

Noor sits there, unsure what to make of Charlie's story, worried that her carefully constructed portrait of him has taken a serious hit.

But isn't this what all former soldiers do? Try and excuse their service once the atrocities have been committed. And spurning university out of some adolescent desire to wound his father, could there be a more ridiculous act?

Noor feels the comfort blanket of righteous indignation wrap around her once again.

"I like this spot," Aamir Khan says. "I understand the view is not the most uplifting but at least graveyards are quiet."

He chuckles.

"I sense them, would you believe it?"

Oh no.

"The dead?" Elma says.

"I tell you many an imam would have me strung up for uttering such blasphemy, but I do."

"And how are they?" Rod says.

"Relieved. The next world's a lot easier than this one."

My God, could this lunch get anymore morbid?

"It's late," Noor says to Elma and Rod. "I should walk you back to your car."

She goes to stand.

"Wait," Charlie says.

He puts a hand on Noor's knee. She is so surprised by his touch that she remains where she is.

"See that rabbit," he says.

Everyone turns. The rabbit is standing on a burial mound, its nose twitching, its ears bolt upright.

"What about it?" Elma says.

"I think it's coming in our direction."

Charlie extracts a candy bar and holds it out. The rabbit hops over a couple of mounds and onto the dirt track.

"Come on, little fella," Charlie says.

The rabbit hops to within a foot of them. Noor notices Elma and Rod holding their breath. Charlie edges his hand out, and the rabbit takes one final hop. It starts nibbling on the bar. Noor coughs, and the rabbit takes off.

"Wow," Elma says.

"Never seen that before," Rod says.

"A New Yorker reporter surprised by something," Charlie grins. "That's got to be a first."

Rod laughs.

"This has been really great," Rod says. "Thanks Aamir, the lunch was delicious, especially that chicken dish."

Noor glances at Elma and sees she's smiling.

She's pleased, so I should be too.

Except she isn't. In fact she can't remember the last time she was in this dark a mood. She stands and makes for the alley. When she reaches its opening, she glances back to make sure Rod and Elma are following her. Charlie is staring right at her. She spins away.

Dear God, please let this be the last time I ever lay eyes on that man.

Some way down the alley, Rod has them stop next to an abandoned hut with a caved in wall. He takes photos of Elma and Noor and then of each of them individually. Noor feels awkward, especially when he asks her to push a lock of hair away from her face. The last time she can remember having her photo taken was when her mother took her to get her passport.

What a wasted trip that was.

They continue on and come upon a wider lane. It is swarming with men, the mosques having released them all at the same time. A few stare at Elma and Noor with a toxic mixture of lust and loathing. Noor pulls her headscarf close. Elma puts her arm through Noor's.

"Don't worry," she says, "you won't have to endure this much longer."

Noor feels a tinge of happiness reenter he soul.

They reach Jamrud Road, and to Noor's relief Elma's Land Cruiser is still there, unharmed.

Maybe this wasn't so bad after all.

They hear a series of beeps behind them and see Charlie speeding towards them on his motorcycle. He flies past and turns to wave. His bike heads straight for an oncoming bus.

"Charlie!" Elma shouts.

He twists back around, and weaves out of the bus' path. Elma shakes her head.

"I might just have underestimated that Charlie Matthews," she says. "He's seen more suffering than most people his age ever will. A little like you really."

He's not at all like me.

Rod beeps the horn.

"Sorry guys but I need to get going," he yells.

Elma rolls her eyes.

"So you ready to start on your Dutch lessons?"

"Absolutely," Noor says.

"How about we meet at the school, say five o'clock Monday evening?"

"I can do that."

"Good. Stay safe till then."

Elma climbs in, and she and Rod take off towards the comforts of University Town. Noor waits until they're out of sight and turns for home.

FOURTEEN

TARIQ WAITS ALONE in the vast reception room and wonders if it was designed to remind men like him of their place in this world.

"Remember, always let the Prince talk first," his father-in-law had said just before he headed out, "then count to five after he finishes a sentence just to be sure. And on no account ever disagree with him."

It must be marvelous to be a Prince.

He gazes at the crystal chandelier, it alone has to be worth a thousand times his yearly stipend; at the Chinese vases, the gilt edged mahogany coffee tables, the custom made couches, the gold ashtrays and trinkets scattered around the room like careless afterthoughts, the carpet on the floor, so plush that when you walk on it your feet sink an inch.

Yes indeed, it must be marvelous.

"Ah, there you are."

The Prince and a couple of his Saudi bodyguards enter. The Prince is wearing a t-shirt and sweatpants.

"I apologize," the Prince says. "I was on a call to Riyadh. Come we can talk while I exercise."

The Prince exits. Tariq stumbles to his feet and catches up with the Prince halfway down the corridor. A servant opens a door on their left, and they step into a state of the art gym. The bodyguards stand up against the mirrored wall. The Prince gets up on the treadmill and begins jogging at a moderate pace, his soft belly jiggling up and down.

"I have much respect for Salim Afridi—" the Prince says.

"He's a great man, your Highness."

The Prince stares Tariq down. Tariq castigates himself. It's taken him less than a minute to interrupt him.

"He's taught me much about guerilla warfare," the Prince continues, "but he's also a simple man, his motivations plain to see."

Tariq holds his tongue.

"You don't have any new interesting concepts on fighting this war, or maybe you do, but the point is that isn't why you're here today. You're here to persuade me of the beauty of Salim's daughter, aren't you?"

Tariq waits a moment just to be sure.

"I owe so much to Salim Afridi, your Highness. He has treated me like a son."

"And I appreciate your loyalty, it is an admirable quality."

Tariq counts to five.

"My only true loyalty is to Allah, praise and glory be to Him. My prayer and my sacrifice and my life and my death are all for Him."

The Prince grunts. Despite the moderate pace, he's already bathed in sweat. Tariq notices a pile of fresh white towels on a stand. He retrieves one and gives it to the Prince. The Prince wipes his face and hands it back.

"I'm tired of this charade already," the Prince says. "One loose remark in one meeting, and I have emissaries from every self-important fool in Pakistan knocking on my door extolling the beauty and virtue of their benefactor's daughter. One looks like a willow tree next to a mountain stream, another has the purity of Aisha. This morning the Chief Minister even called and asked me to lunch. From what I'm told he has five unmarried daughters, and I'm sure they will be paraded in front of me like mares at auction. So go on, give it your best shot, wax lyrical about your sister-in-law."

Tariq screws up his forehead as if he's giving the command careful thought rather than preparing the lines he's spent the previous night memorizing.

"Badia is definitely the prettiest of Salim's daughters, I can assure you of that—"

"But I sense hesitation."

"Only because the one other woman I can compare her to is so much more beautiful than she."

The Prince presses a button, and the treadmill slows to a halt. He gestures at Tariq to give him a fresh towel and takes a moment to catch his breath.

"Who's this woman?"

"I feel caught between two masters," Tariq says.

"Let me be clear—your true loyalty may be to Allah, but as long as you're in my employ after that it's to me."

Tariq affects a look of pained confliction.

"My sister, Noor, your Highness."

The Prince heads over to the weight rack and selects a twenty pound dumbbell. He sits down on the bench and begins doing repetitions with his right arm.

"You think you can be an unbiased judge when it comes to your own family?"

"Last year my father received fifty marriage proposals alone."

The Prince pauses.

"I assume that means your sister doesn't wear the burqa."

"To my shame, my father forces her not to, but Noor's a religious woman, literate, reads the Quran in Arabic every day. And strong too. Badia is such a delicate flower, sometimes you fear the wind could snap her in two."

Unlike your deceased wife, Noor will be able to take a beating.

The Prince switches the dumbbell to his left hand.

"How old is your sister?" the Prince says.

"Twenty-one, your Highness."

"This Badia is sixteen, correct?"

"She is."

The Prince grunts, and Tariq castigates himself.

Why didn't you lie, you fool, say Noor was seventeen?

The Prince drops the dumbbell on the floor. A bodyguard returns it to the rack.

"And she lives in a refugee camp?"

"She does. Once my family was of some means, but now they could not be much poorer."

The Prince stands. A guard hands him a glass of water, and he gulps it down.

"Can I see her?" the Prince says.

"I have a photo," Tariq says.

He pulls out a faded photo of he and Noor from when she was twelve. The Prince studies it.

To think we were once friends.

"How do I know she hasn't changed?" the Prince says.

"I assure you she is more beautiful than ever. I could bring her here this Friday."

"No, the refugee camp's fine. It's been a while since I've been to one."

Tariq wills himself to count to ten. On eight the Prince speaks up.

"What's troubling you, Tariq?"

"Salim Afridi will think I betrayed him."

"It's not up to Salim Afridi whom I marry."

"I understand but I hope you realize the delicate nature of the situation."

"Then we'll arrange it so he won't know a thing. First thing Friday you and I will go see her. Understood?"

Tariq nods, and the Prince heads for the door. A servant opens it from the other side, and the Prince turns back.

"It'd be quite something, wouldn't it?" he says. "All these pompous fools throwing their daughters at me, and I go and marry some miserable refugee."

It'd be quite something indeed.

FIFTEEN

"ARE THEY PERFORMING any better?"

Charlie looks up from sketching the recruits to see Wali standing there.

"I must have told them a hundred times to lie on their stomachs."

Wali takes the recruits in. They are on their knees poking the ground with metal probes. The courtyard has so many holes in it a visitor might suspect a rabbit infestation.

"Maybe they need a rest."

"Maybe you're right."

Charlie puts his fingers in his mouth and whistles. The recruits turn in his direction.

"Okay, we're done. See you tomorrow."

The recruits stagger over to a corrugated porch where some water jugs sit. Charlie sees Obaidullah coming in their direction. He grabs Wali's arm.

"Let's get out of here."

They walk towards the main building.

"So what's up?" he says.

"I have good news. My friend was able to place us on the list for the next survey expedition—"

"That's awesome."

"Unfortunately when Mr. Kaymar saw your name on it, he took it off."

"I thought you said your friend had the final say."

"He says in all his years, he has never come across a situation like this. This Mr. Kaymar must really despise you."

Charlie opens the lobby door and shuts it behind them.

"Can your friend do anything?" Charlie says.

"Mr. Kaymar said he'd be sacked if he put that 'cocksucker back on'. You were the cocksucker he was referring to."

Charlie lights a cigarette.

"So what you're saying is I'm blackballed?"

"Blackballed?"

Wali gets out his notepad and pen.

"You know, shut out, excluded, motherfucking banished from these trips."

"If that is the definition then, yes, I'm afraid so."

"Fuck."

Charlie looks across to see Qasim smiling at him from his office. He gives him a weak wave..

"You should buy him a gift?" Wali says.

"He's not some corrupt official, Wali."

"I wasn't suggesting you bribe him."

"A gift's a bribe."

"Or it can be just a gift."

Charlie doesn't have the strength to argue the point.

"Okay, like what?" Charlie says.

"Johnny Walker—that's a favorite of the foreigners."

"Where am I going to find Johnny Walker round here?"

"Don't worry yourself, I have contacts."

"How much?"

"Well in this country if it's a small favor you require you give Red Label, if it's a medium favor Black Label and if you need a big one, well then you must bring Blue Label."

"Pretty much told him to go fuck himself."

"Then I would definitely suggest Blue Label."

Charlie pulls out his wallet.

"How much you need?"

"Two hundred dollars."

Charlie winces and hands Wali two crisp one hundred dollar bills.

"Keep the change," Charlie says.

"I'll go to the smugglers' bazaar Friday and buy your gift."

Charlie pulls out a twenty dollar bill.

"Can you get sneakers in the smuggler's bazaar?" Charlie says.

"Of course, counterfeit naturally, but excellent counterfeits. What size do you require?"

"Not for me, for you. You need a good pair."

Wali grins.

"You know Mr. Matthews you are the very best friend I have ever had."

***

THE BOTTLE OF Blue Label sits on the desk. With the evening sun shining through it, it looks like an ingot of gold.

"I was out of order," Charlie says.

Jurgen sits back in his chair, his lean fingers intertwined.

"Suppose I got defensive," Charlie continues, "I lashed out, no excuse."

"You understand, as an employee of the United Nations, I'm duty bound to report any and all attempts to bribe me."

"It's just a gift."

"So you don't want to go on a survey expedition?"

"I wanted to say sorry."

"You didn't answer my question."

Charlie stares at the whisky.

God I could do with a slug right now.

"You know when you go out with someone—someone you really dig but you've had a shitty day, I don't know, your boss kicked your ass or you and your buddy got in a fight—and instead of treating her right you take it out on her instead. Well the next day you feel bad so you send flowers. Now it's not like you still don't want to get with her, hell that's why you went on the date in the first place, but really at the end of the day you just want to say you're sorry."

"So you're comparing me to some floozy back in the States?" Jurgen says.

"No—yes—maybe that wasn't the best analogy."

"Mr. Matthews, I don't know whether to laugh or cry."

"If I were you, I'd just have a shot of that beauty—it's amazing how it makes everything seem right."

Jurgen stands up and retrieves two glasses from a nearby cabinet.

"My sources tell me your operation is a joke; haphazard training, ineffectual management, substandard protocols."

"Guilty as charged."

"You didn't give it much thought when you applied for your position, did you?"

"Guilty again."

"Well now you're stuck here why don't you try and make something of it?"

Jurgen twists off the top and pours each of them a thimbleful. He hands a glass to Charlie before breathing in the aroma from his own.

"What it remind you of?" Charlie says.

"I was in Geneva; I'd just been offered this job and my partner and I, we went over to the President Wilson and he ordered me a glass. The funny thing is I never drink whisky, actually I've an aversion to it, yet he insisted and, my God, if it wasn't the smoothest drink I've ever tasted."

"Are you still with him?"

Jurgen shakes his head.

"He's an architect back in Munich, and besides the idea of two men living together out here ..."

Jurgen shrugs.

"Maybe him buying you that drink, maybe it was his way of saying goodbye," Charlie says.

Jurgen takes a sip.

"I never thought of that," he says. "Maybe you're right, maybe I was drinking at my own funeral."

Charlie takes the opportunity to take a sip.

Shit, it really is nectar.

"Your friend, Ivor, you are aware he's CIA?"

Charlie's glass hovers mid air.

"Can't be a very good spy if everyone knows," Charlie says.

"Oh, he's very good—there's no one more expert at manipulating the mujahideen groups. Whenever we have an expedition I always call him in advance to make sure we receive safe passage."

"Why you telling me this?"

"Thought you should know."

"Doesn't make me like him any less."

"Given your age I suspect it'll make you like him even more. Just be careful that's all; you may think I was being discourteous when I called you naïve but you are. I look at you and see myself twenty years ago."

"What were you doing twenty years ago?"

"I was marching in the streets of Frankfurt."

"I'm not much of a marcher."

"Maybe you haven't found the right cause yet."

Jurgen brings the glass to his lips and knocks back what remains.

"Thank you for this," Jurgen says, "it was a sweet gesture. I'm sorry I kept you waiting so long."

"No, you're not."

Jurgen smiles.

"I'll say one thing about you, Charlie, like Scotch you're an acquired taste."

"I'll take that as a compliment."

Charlie stands and heads for the door.

"By the way," Jurgen says, "we've an expedition scheduled at the end of the week."

Charlie turns back.

"It might do you some good to have Shamsurahman show you what we're trying to achieve out here."

"Who's Shamsurahman?"

"Oh, you'll see. Have your colleague call his friend over here."

"Thanks, Jurgen."

Jurgen picks up the bottle and pours himself another glass.

"Likewise."

Charlie heads downstairs to the waiting room. Wali is chatting with a group of Afghan employees. He's hiked his shalwar pants up high so no one can fail to miss the bright white Nike Air Max sneakers on his feet.

Wali catches sight of Charlie and excuses himself.

"You're a genius," Charlie says.

SIXTEEN

NOOR HEARS SOMEONE cough and looks up from the assignment she's marking. Miss Suha has somehow crept into the teachers' room without her noticing.

"You have a guest," Miss Suha says.

Elma.

Noor hurries for the door.

"A Mr. Skeppar."

Noor looks back at Miss Suha.

"Young man, Swedish, says your fathers were friends."

None of this makes any sense. Noor's never heard her father mention a man named Skeppar.

A hideous thought strikes her.

"What does he look like?" she says.

"Tall, thin—a scar down his left cheek."

Oh Lord, why am I tormented so?

"Would you please tell him I'm indisposed right now."

"Your father asked that you meet with him."

"I understand—"

"And the headmistress asked me to fetch you."

Noor rubs her temples.

"Don't worry," Miss Suha says, "we'll keep the door open."

Noor nods; that's what worries her. They inch down the hallway, Miss Suha's walking stick making an unnerving clunk with each step she takes. Halfway down Noor hears Charlie's loud, confident voice and shudders. It's followed by laughter from the headmistress, a sound so rare that even Miss Suha frowns.

When they enter the office, the headmistress is in fits, and has the countenance of a teenage girl. Charlie stands by the window with a broad grin on his face.

"Ah, there you are, Noor," the headmistress says. "Mr. Skeppar was telling me how he ate live octopus in Korea."

"The key is to suck it down in one go," Charlie says. "You let it wriggle in your mouth then it's all over."

The headmistress shrieks before descending into a fresh set of giggles. Noor finds it impossible to say anything.

"Well it's been a pleasure meeting you, Mr. Skeppar," the headmistress says. "I wish you the best with the rest of your trade mission."

"Thank you and you with the school."

The headmistress leaves. Miss Suha lingers in the doorway.

"It's alright, Miss Suha," Noor says, "you can return to your work."

Noor waits until she hears Miss Suha sit down at her desk and start typing.

"Your father thought it'd be nice if we met," Charlie says loudly.

Noor ignores him and walks over to the far window. She stares down at the girls playing below in the courtyard. Charlie comes up beside her.

"I didn't think it possible," she says, "but the lengths you have gone to hound me have only increased since I had the misfortune of first meeting you."

"It was the only way I was going to see you."

"Have you never heard of writing a note?"

"You wouldn't have responded."

"What do you expect?"

"That's my point."

Noor spins to face him.

"What is it with you Mr. Matthews? First you chase me down a darkened alley, then you bamboozle my father into making me have lunch with you, then, once I had made it crystal clear that I had no interest in seeing you again, you turn up at our hut and now this. This is Pakistan, not New York. Women here are not objects to be pursued, and the more you do it, the more you put me in danger. Is that what you want? For me to be thrown in jail for impropriety."

"Of course not."

"Then I beg you, leave me alone."

Charlie eyes gesture to the far end of the room. Noor turns to see Miss Suha leaning against the door frame.

"Is everything alright?" Miss Suha says.

"Absolutely," Noor says. "We won't be much longer."

Noor stares Miss Suha down, and Miss Suha retreats to her desk.

"Believe it or not," Charlie hisses, "this isn't about you. It's about your dad. I'm going to Afghanistan for six days. I thought you guys could stay in my house while I'm away."

"Is this a joke?"

"If it is I'm not sure what the punch line is."

"I thought you said this had nothing to do with me."

"It doesn't. Look, I get it, you don't like me, but your father's a good guy, and I've a ridiculous house with a ridiculous amount of books—"

"Then why rent such a place?"

"I didn't. It came with the job. Hell, I'd have been happy with a shack."

Noor is knocked off her stride. Charlie seizes the opportunity.

"Point is, if I can't offer it to him while I'm gone then what kind of friend would I be?"

Noor stares at Charlie.

"This is ludicrous," she says. "This isn't a sincere offer."

"It's the sincerest offer I've ever made in my life."

"Then why not go to my father and make it?"

"Because the only way he'll do it is if you're on board."

"He's a mind of his own."

"Give me a break, he's totally whipped."

Noor reddens.

"That's it," she says. "I've heard enough."

Noor storms for the door. To her astonishment, Charlie grabs her arm.

"Get your hand off me."

Charlie doesn't let go.

"For Christ's sake stop being so obstinate and do it for his sake. Let him sleep under clean sheets, take a hot bath, eat three large meals a day, hell, let him think that his life's back to normal."

"But it won't be, it'd only be an illusion."

"Isn't everything in some way or other."

Charlie releases her arm. Noor is breathing so heavily it's as if she's just finished a run.

"In case you change your mind," Charlie says, "Mukhtar knows you're coming. I told him you're friends of Mine Aware's."

Charlie walks out. Soon after Miss Suha enters the office. Noor forces herself to appear calm.

"That was quick," Miss Suha says.

"There wasn't much to be said," Noor says.

"Strange, he sounded more American than European."

"His mother's American."

"Ah, that must explain it."

Miss Suha wanders over to the window. Noor fumes.

Now he has me lying for him as well.

"I tell you one thing," Miss Suha says, "he definitely has a way with women."

"That's not a quality I've noticed," Noor says.

"Come see."

Noor joins Miss Suha by the window. Down below, Charlie is encircled by a large group of girls, answering questions as best he can. Kamila seems to be the ringleader. Charlie makes a funny face, and the girls all burst out laughing.

He's only doing this in a desperate attempt to impress me.

Kamila tugs on his arm, and Charlie leans down to listen to her. Moments later the girls take off in every direction, their blue headscarves flying behind them. Charlie counts to ten and tears after them. He tags one after another until only Kamila is left. They face each other at opposite ends of the yard.

"You can't catch me," Kamila shouts.

Charlie creeps towards her. When he's halfway down the yard he takes off in a sprint. Kamila feints left before running to her right. Charlie changes direction and reaches out a hand. Kamila arches her back and his fingertips clutch at thin air. His right foot slips from under him, and he finds himself face down in the dirt. The girls howl with laughter.

A janitor rings the bell for the final class of the day, and the girls run inside. Kamila stands over Charlie like a victorious matador. She offers him her hand and pulls him to his feet, before rushing after her friends.

"I pity the man who ends up marrying that one," Miss Suha says.

Noor says nothing. She's waiting for Charlie to look up at the window to confirm her suspicion.

Come on.

Charlie ambles across the courtyard.

Do it.

He continues out the front gate. Noor can't help but feel a little disappointed.

PART II

evolve

SEVENTEEN

CHARLIE AND WALI roar into the UNMAPA compound to find three Land Cruisers and a pick-up waiting for them. Six policemen, each cradling an ancient Lee Enfield rifle, sit in the back of the pick-up. A bearded man wearing a worn camo jacket gets out of the lead Land Cruiser. A black patch covers his right eye giving him the look of a modern day pirate.

"You in that one," he says to Wali indicating the Land Cruiser behind them.

Wali scurries off without a word. Charlie's never seen Wali so intimidated.

"You with me."

Charlie sticks out his hand.

"Guessing you're Shamsurahman. I'm Charlie."

Shamsurahman crushes Charlie's hand. Charlie does his best not to wince. Charlie throws his backpack in the trunk and climbs in. A man in a blue blazer and sits up front. He looks like he's off to a cocktail party.

"Ah, the stragglers," the man says in a posh British accent.

Shamsurahman beeps his horn, and the pick-up drives off. Shamsurahman hugs its bumper.

"Colonel Jack Litchfield," the Brit says.

"Charlie Matthews. You in the British Army?"

"Was. Now with an outfit called The Angel Foundation."

"You run their operation out here?"

"Good heavens no, too much of an old fogey for that. Out here on a little fact-finding jaunt."

"When I hear the word jaunt I think Miami not Peshawar."

"Trust me, once you've been married to the same woman for thirty years, you'll think of this as a jaunt too."

Charlie laughs and looks out the window. By now they're past the refugee camps and are bearing down on a spot-lit archway that looks like it's been transplanted from Disneyland. A large sign at the side of the road proclaims 'No Foreigners Beyond This Point'. They blow past it. On either side of the road storekeepers are opening up their shuttered stores. The stores sell everything from cigarette cartons to televisions, suitcases to washing machines, mattresses to computers.

"Doesn't seem that tribal," Charlie says.

"Smugglers' bazaar," Shamsurahman says.

Ah, so this is where you went, Wali.

Charlie guesses the alcohol isn't on such prominent display.

"So you were in the military as well I gather," the Colonel says.

"First Infantry Division," Charlie says.

"Officer?"

"Just an old fashioned private."

"Army not for you?"

"Can't say it was."

"The two chaps who run our operation were in the Paras. Mike saw action in the Falkland Islands; story goes that his platoon was pinned down by a machine gun placement so he just up and ran at it; killed four Argies in the process."

Charlie knows Mike's type well; curiously none of them tended to be his friends in the army.

The bazaar comes to an end, and they begin racing across a barren plain towards a looming mountain range lit golden by the rising sun. Mud-walled compounds with turrets on every corner dot the landscape. It's as if they've entered some mystical land. The Colonel rubs his hands together.

"Now this is a treat," he says. "I'm told there's nothing quite like your first time up the Khyber Pass."

Charlie rests his head against the window and his eyes droop. It isn't long before he's fast asleep.

He wakes to find the Colonel prodding his arm. The Land Cruiser has come to a halt. He looks out the window to see a swarm of grubby Pakistani kids staring back.

"Where are we?" he says.

"Torkham," the Colonel says. "Shamsurahman's getting our passports stamped."

One of the kids holds up a Coke bottle. Right now there's nothing Charlie wants more. Charlie gets out, and the kids shove their wares in his face. Charlie buys a Coke and wanders over to the SUV behind theirs. The Colonel is standing there with two muscled men in polo shirts. Charlie recognizes them as the Brits from the American Club.

Fuck.

"Charlie, I'd like to introduce you to Derek Simons and Mike Henderson, our chaps out here."

"Good to see you guys again," Charlie says.

"Alright," Derek says.

Mike, the Manchester United supporter, barely nods.

"Can you believe this one slept all the way up the Khyber Pass?" the Colonel says.

Mike and Dave look like they're not surprised.

"We were thinking of doing a quick recce," Mike says to the Colonel. "Care to join?"

"Why not? You alright Charlie?"

Charlie holds up his Coke bottle.

"Got all I need."

They head off down a main drag of decrepit, low strung buildings, and the kids give chase. Charlie catches the eye of a six-year-old boy dragging a bunch of soccer balls in a net.

"Please, sir," the boy says.

"How much?"

The boy flashes his right hand two times. Charlie hands him a twenty rupee bill. The boy grins and tosses Charlie a soccer ball. Charlie sees Wali regaling some Afghan staff members and heads towards him. Wali excuses himself.

"What a marvelous trip that was," Wali says. "The mighty Khyber Pass."

"That the border?" Charlie says, nodding towards an open metal gate.

"You are most correct."

"Well, shit, let's go take a look."

They walk up. A couple of nearby Pakistani soldiers glance at them. Charlie bounces the ball over to a cheap plastic billboard. 'Welcome To The Islamic Republic Of Afghanistan' it proclaims. Charlie turns back. Wali is staring at the far off mountains with tears in his eyes.

"Good to be back?" Charlie says.

"More than you can believe. It's my first time in six years."

They hear Shamsurahman shouting out to them and they trudge back to their vehicles. The expedition carries on without its police escort, and not far beyond the border they turn off the main highway and head down an earthen track. Charlie stares out the window at some abandoned concrete huts in the distance; beside them is a firing range nestled into a barren hillside and an obstacle course with climbing walls and monkey bars. He shivers. It has an eerie feel to it. He assumes it used to be a Soviet base.

An hour later they come upon their first village, a collection of mud homes perched on the side of a wide muddy river. Charlie gets out. The place reminds him of those towns in Westerns from which the inhabitants have all fled. Doors creak back-and-forth, weeds grow against the sides of buildings, and farm equipment lies scattered, broken and rusting. The foreigners gather around Shamsurahman as the Afghan staff set up lunch.

"Soviets attack village six years back. The Nangarhar Province major mujahideen stronghold and they suspect village people of aiding mujahideen. Two platoons Spetsnaz land and round up mans over age of twelve. They take them to the river and gun down. Womans and childrens flee to Pakistan."

Shamsurahman takes them into a grain mill. Its stone grinder lies shattered in pieces.

"Before leave they blow up irrigation systems and plant mines in village and fields so no one think of return."

They go out the other side and gather beside the riverbank. Beyond the river is a jigsaw of overgrown, squiggly shaped fields.

"We clear village already," Shamsurahman says, "but no peoples return until fields cleared also."

Shamsurahman turns to a squirrel-faced man with a salt-and-pepper beard.

"Kenneth, you think your mans do this?"

Kenneth winces.

"Don't know. Fact the fields are waterlogged makes it tricky."

Shamsurahman turns Mike and Derek.

"And you?"

"No problem," Mike says. "Our lads train in this type of environment all the time."

Mike looks over at Charlie.

"Unless you'd like to take it, mate."

Derek and a few others in the group laugh. Charlie feels his face redden.

"No, all yours," he says.

"Thought you might say that," Mike says.

"Marvelous, well that's settled," the Colonel says. "Now

what do you all say to a spot of lunch?"

The group heads back. Wali and Charlie bring up the rear.

"I learnt a most interesting word of slang some months back," Wali says.

"What's that?" Charlie says.

"Douchebag."

Charlie laughs.

"I would assume I would be correct in using it in reference to that man."

"He's the definition."

After lunch they drive on until they come to another village. It's almost a carbon copy of the previous one. By now the sun's beginning to set below the mountains in the west. The Afghan staff put up the group's tents and Charlie pitches in to help. Over to one side, he sees Mike and Derek have somehow got their hands on his soccer ball and are passing it back and forth. He thinks about asking for it back but let's it go. He finishes putting up his tent and drags his backpack inside. When he clambers back out he sees Mike and Derek setting up next door.

Great, they're going to cut my throat in the middle of the night.

Derek sees him.

"Were we using your ball, mate?" he says.

"Totally cool," Charlie says.

"Here you go."

Derek grabs the ball and throws it wide of him.

"Oh shit, sorry about that."

Charlie chases after the ball and grabs it just before it enters a field on the village's perimeter. He looks out over the tall grass and wonders how many mines lie there in wait. He turns to see Mike pantomiming him being blown up. Charlie heads over to a blazing pile of firewood and sits down next to Kenneth. Nearby Shamsurahman is leading the Afghans in prayer. Wali looks over and winks at Charlie. Charlie winks back.

"I don't know if you're aware of this but I'm in the army myself," Kenneth says.

"The Scottish army?"

"God's."

In the flickering orange light Charlie tries to discern whether Kenneth's screwing with him.

"Didn't know God had an army," Charlie says.

"Oh, it spans the globe, made up of billions of Christian souls. Blood and fire, that's our motto, our mission to advance the Christian religion and relieve poverty."

"How's the first one going?"

"Won't lie, ain't easy out here. Got to admire these Afghans, hold fast to their religion they do, tend to get a wee bit tetchy if you push Jesus on them."

Charlie watches the embers drift up into a night sky infested with stars.

"You mind if I ask you a personal question, Charlie?" Kenneth says. "Have you accepted Jesus Christ as your Savior?"

Charlie looks at Kenneth. Kenneth's gaze is unwavering.

"Jesus came into my heart at a young age, Kenneth, and hasn't left since."

"So you believe everything written in the Old and New Testaments?"

"Absolutely. Adam and Eve, Noah's Ark, the guy in the whale, all of it."

On the other side of the fire, Derek and Mike sit down next to the Colonel.

"But you know who's definitely not Christian," Charlie whispers.

"Who?" Kenneth says, his eyes darting about.

"Derek and Mike. Back in Peshawar they live a totally debauched life. Told me their goal was to have sex with a different aid worker every week they're here."

"That's scandalous."

"I tried to talk to them, but you saw what happened earlier. I don't know, maybe it's because I'm American, but they're really hostile towards me. I can't get through to them."

Kenneth pats Charlie on the back.

"Don't you worry, I've got this one covered."

Kenneth prowls over to them and launches into his pitch. Derek tries to get away, but Kenneth puts his hand on Derek's shoulder and pushes him back down. The Colonel excuses himself and comes over.

"Good heavens," the Colonel says, "those boys are in for it."

The Afghans finish up their prayers. Shamsurahman sits across from them. He stares into the distance, his face serene.

"Shamsurahman's not much one for chit chat, is he?" Charlie says.

"I suspect once you've been through what he has, life takes on a whole new light," the Colonel says.

"What do you mean?"

"Was quite the war hero a few year back, his face on posters all over town—right up there with Hekmatyar and Massoud's. Had this blinding reputation; they say the moment a Soviet outpost heard he was in the vicinity they'd flee. Soviets created a special forces unit dedicated to killing him."

"Guess they failed there."

"Oh, it was worse than that. He tricked them into thinking he was hiding out in this village. Over a hundred Spetsnaz poured in and when it was all over only one came out and only because Shamsurahman allowed him to."

"So what happened?"

"Some time later the man he was walking beside stepped on a mine. From all accounts it took him almost a year to walk again and when he reemerged he'd laid down his weapons and dedicated his life to ridding Afghanistan of mines."

An Afghan staff member comes over and places a plate of skewered chicken and rice in front of them. Charlie and the Colonel concentrate on their food. Across the way, Kenneth continues his bombardment of Derek and Mike, and at the first opportunity the two of them flee to their tent. Everyone else retires soon after.

"By the way," Charlie says to Wali in the darkness of their tent, "How's your mom? That medicine helping?"

"It was a most wonderful relief to her, I can't thank you enough."

"Need any more?"

"That is most generous but it won't be necessary."

"Why? What's the rub?"

"The rub?"

"The issue?"

Wali fumbles for his flashlight and proceeds to write the expression down. He turns the flashlight back off.

"Wali?"

"The rub, Mr. Matthews, is she died last week."

"Shit, I'm sorry. Why didn't you tell me?"

"There's no need to burden you with such things, and besides now she's with God."

The two of them lie there in silence. Charlie thinks of his own mother. Of that Saturday morning he'd gone to see her to find her dressed, sitting by the window in her hospital room. For a moment he'd thought she'd been discharged, that somehow she'd beaten her cancer, but instead she'd suggested they go for a walk. There sitting on a bench in Central Park next to the Alice In Wonderland statue, she'd told him that she had a month to live at best, and as she spoke about how her spirit would be in the sun on his face, the sound of birds in the sky, and the wind at his back, he'd crawled up next to her and hugged her, hoping that by doing so he could stop her from ever leaving him. Within a week she was dead.

"How are you doing?" Charlie says. "I mean you must miss her."

"I most assuredly do, she was a fine and good woman."

"And your brothers and sisters."

"I have no more, I'm afraid."

"So you're all alone?"

"Not entirely. I still have you, Mr. Matthews, isn't that correct?"

"Yes, you do."

Charlie senses Wali is smiling.

"Good night, Mr. Matthews."

"Good night, Wali."

EIGHTEEN

NOOR STRUGGLES DOWN the alley, a bucket of water in her hand. An orchestra of muezzins accompanies her, each calling out the azaan in a different style and pitch. Some are hurried as if the imams need to get their prayers over with while others are more measured, even mournful, the imams stretching out the words like opera singers. Noor thinks about Charlie's offer.

Would it be so wrong to take him up on it? After all he won't be there, and Baba would adore it.

However she knows she can't. If she does, she'll always be in Charlie's debt, and that's something she can never allow.

She comes out of the alley, and walks along the side of the graveyard. An SUV and a collection of pick-up trucks are parked out front of their hut. She catches her foot, and the bucket goes tumbling. By the time she sets it straight, only a couple of inches of water lie in its bottom.

What is it with him? Why can't he stay out of our lives?

Noor strides towards the hut determined to put an end to any relationship her family might have with Charlie Matthews. She shoves the door open to find Tariq pacing back and forth. Her father and Bushra sit huddled on the floor.

"So you're not at the market after all," Tariq says.

Noor looks at her father. She's never seen him so disappointed to see her.

"I had to get some water first," she says.

"Well, inshallah, this will be the last time you'll ever do such a task."

"Unless this is a fairytale I highly doubt it."

"It just might be. Now come outside a moment."

"I didn't know you'd softened your views on the burqa."

Tariq lifts up their gas lamp and studies her face. He licks his thumb and wipes away some dirt from her cheek.

"This is a special case," he says.

Tariq holds the door open, and Noor follows.

"Noor," Aamir Khan says.

Her father has risen to his feet.

"It's okay, Baba, I'll be right back."

She and Tariq go outside. In the backs of the pick-ups are a mixture of battle-hardened Arabs and Afghans. It's the first time she can remember not being leered at by a group of men. It unsettles her.

What does he want to show me this time?

Ever since Tariq joined the mujahideen he'd only ever visited them to show off.

You've been nothing but bravado from the earliest age. Yet you never got as high as me on the apricot tree, and neither of us will ever forget it.

He leads her to a gleaming white Range Rover. Tariq touches her arm, and they stand there waiting. The tinted window edges down, and expensive perfume wafts out.

Could this be that prestigious bride of his, the one we've never met?

The window opens fully, and Noor comes face to face with a pudgy man with a trim beard. His bright white thobe and checkered headdress mark him out as an Arab and a rich one at that. The man scrutinizes her like a butcher might a heifer at market, his fleshy eyes traveling up and down the length of her body.

"You weren't lying," the man says in Arabic. "With a little

make-up she'll be stunning."

Noor feels her throat tighten. The man runs his thumb along the length of his lower lip.

"I like her," the man says.

The electric window slides back up, and the Range Rover drives off followed by three of the pick-ups. Noor glances at her brother. His face is so flushed he looks sexually aroused.

"Go and say goodbye to Baba," he says.

"Why?"

"You're going to be his Royal Highness's next wife."

Noor looks around for an escape route. Across the grave-yard would be pointless. She knows she's fast, certainly faster than her brother, but not fast enough to outrun the ten remaining men. The only other option is to lose them in the camp but that requires getting past the two pick-ups and to the alley.

Buy time, a voice inside says.

She starts towards the hut.

"This is an amazing honor," Tariq says. "Do you know how unprecedented this is? The luxury you will be living in; the clothes, the jewelry, the servants at your beck and call, especially when we get to Riyadh."

They enter the hut. Aamir Khan is kneeling on a rug praying. The longer they wait, the more agitated Tariq becomes. He pulls out a set of prayer beads and plays with them in an attempt to control himself. Aamir Khan stands.

"The Prince wants to marry your daughter," Tariq says.

Aamir Khan's gaze shifts to Noor.

"And did you accept?" Aamir Khan says.

"The only permission we need is yours," Tariq says.

"I would still like her answer."

If you refuse, Tariq will have his men drag you away.

"I accept," Noor says.

Aamir Khan looks stunned. Tariq smiles.

"I will arrange for the Prince to pay you a dowry of two thousand dollars," Tariq says to his father. "I think that would be most generous."

"I have but one condition," Noor says.

Her father and her brother look her way.

"You don't make conditions when marrying a Prince," Tariq says.

"I want to spend one more night with Baba and Bushra."

"Fine. You can all share a room in the compound."

"No, here."

Tariq looks around; at the earthen floor, the blackened pots, the battered suitcases stacked in the corner

"You may despise our dwelling," she says, "but for us this has been our home for eight years."

Tariq stares at Noor trying to divine her intentions.

"I also want the dowry increased to ten thousand dollars," she says, "the Prince can more than afford it."

Tariq pulls on his beard.

"He won't accept such a figure."

"Then five thousand, it's only fair. Baba and Bushra will no longer have my teaching income to rely on."

Noor watches Tariq as he weighs the pros and cons. She knows his greed. She prays that it will blind him.

"I'll return at dawn," he says.

Tariq pushes the door open, and soon after they hear the vehicles drive away. Noor looks at her father. He is trembling.

"Why are you doing this?" he says.

"I'm not."

A glint returns to her father's eyes.

"We need to get out of here immediately," he says.

"But where will we go?" Bushra says.

"I have an idea," Noor says.

***

TARIQ WALKS DOWN the long line of vehicles. Yousef hobbles beside him.

"I don't care which one," Tariq says, "I'm only going to be gone an hour."

"Oh no, that wouldn't be right," Yousef says.

Yousef stops in front of a gleaming, black Land Cruiser.

"Was delivered only a couple of days back, you'll be the first to drive it."

Yousef flashes him a smile.

"And may I be the first to offer you my congratulations."

So it's out.

Tariq wonders how. His pulse quickens.

The Prince must have told somebody.

"Who knew when you first came to work for me that you'd end up being the Prince's brother-in-law."

"You were always good to me, Yousef. I won't forget."

Yousef hands him the keys. Tariq climbs in and breathes in the scent of fresh leather. He casts his eyes over the controls and the polished wood trim.

This is how a man should live.

He drives past the rear of the main building. Mujahideen are everywhere, laying out supplies and equipment for their next expedition into Afghanistan. One of them walks in front of his path. Tariq brakes and lays on the horn. The man doesn't move. Tariq gets out and strides up to him. The man turns. It's Salim Afridi.

"I see you're already pretending to be a Prince," his father-in-law says.

"I took what Yousef offered me."

"That's what it means to be a Prince, you get to choose from the best."

Salim Afridi scoops out a wad of chewing tobacco and places it underneath his lower lip.

"This will be good for our family," Tariq says.

Salim Afridi snorts.

"As far as I'm concerned you're no longer part of our family."

"I've done nothing but serve you faithfully."

"You might as well have snuck into my bedroom and slit my throat."

"I pleaded Badia's case, praised her virtues—"

"Yet somehow it's your sister the Prince wants to marry. Curious, huh?"

"He wouldn't take my word. Noor was our best hope of salvaging anything."

Tariq notices that a number of mujahideen have stopped working and are watching them. Salim Afridi lets a huge of glob of brown saliva drip from his mouth. It hangs there a moment before pulling loose and splattering on the ground. He opens his arms.

"Come here," Salim Afridi says.

Tariq steps into his father-in-law's embrace.

Thank God, he bought it.

Salim Afridi puts his wet lips up against Tariq's right ear.

"If there is one thing you can be sure of in this life, Tariq Khan, it's that I'm going to kill you. When, where, how, that will be of my choosing, but it will happen, and when it does, don't fear, I'll be sure to make it as agonizing as possible."

Salim Afridi slaps Tariq on the back and walks over to a couple of mujahideen. They huddle in conversation. Tariq shivers.

Could they already be planning my murder?

Tariq forces himself back into the Land Cruiser and drives away, his hands shaking so badly he finds it almost impossible to grip the wheel.

It's an empty threat. No one would dare kill the Prince's brother-in-law, not even Salim Afridi.

And then he remembers the legend of how Salim Afridi had killed his uncle.

It had been at the wedding of his uncle's favorite daughter; the same uncle who had shot Salim Afridi's father ten years earlier. By tradition every man had had to leave their weapons outside, so Salim Afridi, who was Tariq's age, had pilfered the sharpest knife he could find in the kitchen and waited for his uncle to head to the bathroom. Supposedly Salim Afridi had stuck the knife in his uncle's belly as he was halfway through taking a shit. By the time he was finished, his uncle's balls were in the toilet bowl, and the floor was awash with blood. Salim Afridi had walked calmly out the front gate and fled to the tribal areas for Panjshir. Five years later he joined the insurrection against the Afghan government, and six years after that the Soviets invaded Afghanistan. By the time Salim Afridi arrived in Peshawar he was a venerated guerilla warrior.

Tariq's left leg begins to shake, and he has to grasp it with his hand to bring it under control.

You're going to have to kill him before he kills you.

The question's how?

He comes on Kacha Gari refugee camp and turns down its main drag. In the early dawn, his high beams catch those refugees lucky enough to be heading to work. With their shawls wrapped tight around them they look like phantom spirits fleeing before the sun rises. He beeps his horn and the refugees part. Before long he's outside his family's hut.

He pulls out five thousand dollars from his inside pocket. The previous night he'd told the Prince's accountant that his father had asked for fifteen, and without blinking the accountant had handed him three neat stacks of one hundred dollar bills.

I'm an idiot, I should have asked for fifty.

He stares at the money. There are plenty of people who'd kill his father-in-law for ten thousand dollars.

Perhaps Yousef would do it.

He wonders why no one's come out yet. He gets out and bangs on the corrugated door.

"Baba, Noor, time to go."

He yanks the door open and steps inside. No one's there.

A cold sweat forms on his brow. He scans the room. The pots are still there as are the lamp, the table and the mattresses. He looks in the corner. Something is missing.

The suitcases.

He throws his hand against the wall to steady himself. It's as if the fetid air inside the hut is poisonous. He stumbles outside and sinks to his knees. He gasps in a lungful of air.

How could they do this to me?

Just beyond the path, he sees a rabbit looking his way. He clambers to his feet and withdraws his gun. The rabbit cocks its head and hops onto the track. Tariq points the gun at it.

Come on.

It hops closer until it's only a couple of feet away. Tariq pulls the trigger, and its head explodes in a mist of blood and brain.

NINETEEN

CHARLIE CRAWLS OUT of his tent and draws in a lungful of crisp, chill air. He takes in the gold tipped mountains in the distance.

This is going to be a good day.

They review the village at nine, which Dave and Mike claim for no better reason than to spite Charlie, and arrive at their second just past eleven o'clock. Unlike the other two, the mud homes here are whitewashed and sit perched on a steep hillside overlooking the river. At the bottom lies a flat communal area with broken fields on either side. An ancient truck is parked there with three beleaguered families camped around it. Shamsurahman goes over and talks to them. One of the boys catches Charlie's eye. Charlie grabs his soccer ball.

"You play?" he says.

The boy grins. Charlie kicks it over to him, and the boy kicks it back.

"See you're a natural," Charlie says.

"And you're a regular Bryan Robson," Mike says.

Charlie ignores him. He and the boy continue to pass the ball back and forth. Shamsurahman returns.

"What's their story?" the Colonel says.

"They come two days ago. They want to go back Pakistan;

they remember it differently. I told them we all do."

For a moment no one says anything, the Afghans lost in thoughts of better times.

"Well what do you say we take a look around?" the Colonel says.

Charlie stares up the steep street.

What's the point? It's not like Shamsurahman will give it to us..

"You know what, I'm going to pass on this one," he says.

"Scared you won't make it to the top?" Derek says.

"I think I will join you," Wali says.

No one objects, and Shamsurahman leads the rest of the group up the village's only street.

"Assholes," Charlie says.

"Oh, I would not worry about them, Mr. Matthews," Wali says. "Sticks and stones may break your bones—"

"I know, I know."

"So now that's settled pass me the ball."

Charlie kicks the ball to Wali, and pulls his sketch pad out of his backpack. He sits with his back against a broken cart, the morning sun warming his face, and draws Wali and two of the boys kicking the ball back and forth. The village acts as his backdrop; it looks like a crumbling wedding cake. At its very top the rest of group stands on the roof of a house. Shamsurahman has a map open and is pointing out the minefields.

Maybe I should have gone?

Charlie shakes his head. It's too late now. He looks down at his pad and puts the group in as stick figures. When he looks up again he sees that Wali and the boys have gotten further apart, requiring them to kick the ball ever harder. He gets a queasy feeling, and jumps to his feet.

"Hey guys."

One of the boys kicks the ball to Wali, and Wali takes a wild swing at it. The ball rockets over the boys' heads and into some undergrowth beyond. The two boys turn and race to retrieve it.

"Stop," Charlie shouts. "Wali, stop them."

Wali realizes what Charlie means and screams out in Pashtu. The boys cross into the undergrowth.

"Stop, goddamn it," Charlie shouts.

He spies a mine detector leaning against one of the trucks, and runs over and grabs it. When he turns back he sees Wali racing into the undergrowth. The two boys have reached the ball and are fighting over it.

"Wali," he screams.

Wali tramples through the stalks of wild grass.

"Wali."

There's a bright orange flash, and Wali is flung into the air. Before Wali can even fall back to the ground a cloud of dust obscures him.

And then there's just silence, as if for a moment in time the soundtrack to the world got lost.

The boys begin to wail.

"Stay there," Charlie screams. "Don't fucking move."

Charlie runs to the edge of the undergrowth and turns the mine detector on.

"Wali—you hear me?"

He waves the detector over the ground and hears nothing. He steps forward and waves it again. The detector beeps.

Fuck.

He turns to his right and sweeps again. When he hears no beep he steps forward and turns back in Wali's direction.

"Wali!" he shouts. "Wali!"

He listens, hoping for at least a pained cry. Instead all he hears is the rustle of the wind as it weaves its way through the knee high stalks of grass.

"Oh God, oh God," he says, "please let him be alive."

He continues on, his route beginning to resemble that of a Pac-Man game as he alters his course whenever his detector beeps. By the time he's halfway there, the cloud has dissipated and he can make out Wali lying on the ground like a piece of discarded trash.

"Wali! Wali!"

Charlie carries on sweeping until he comes to a point where there seems to be a mine on all three sides in front of him. He's now so close he can touch Wali with the detector. Charlie looks down; shrapnel litters the ground.

They've got to be the reason.

Charlie places the detector on the ground, and steps forward. Nothing happens.

Thank you, God.

He kneels down beside Wali. Wali's left leg looks like a steak that's been left on the grill too long. Pieces of skin hang off of it and shards of white bone jut through its flesh. Charlie closes his eyes and takes a couple of breaths.

Remember your training.

He opens his eyes and places a finger on Wali's neck. Wali's pulse is weak but constant. He looks back. Shamsurahman is at the edge of the undergrowth, a mine detector in his hand, Derek and Mike behind him.

"He's alive," Charlie shouts.

Charlie sees one of the boys edging his way.

"Don't move."

The boy freezes. Charlie turns back to Wali.

"Hang in there, buddy. Help's on the way."

Charlie puts his hand underneath Wali's right hamstring and finds that most of it's gone. When he brings his hand back up it looks like he's dipped it in paint. He examines the wound. A severed artery is spurting blood.

Remember your training.

He reaches in and pulls on the artery. It stretches like a rubber band and slips from his hand. He tries again and this time manages to keep a hold. With his other hand he fashions a knot and pulls it tight. The blood stops flowing. He looks back. Shamsurahman, Mike and Derek are halfway to him.

What next?

Charlie rips off his shirt. He tears off each of its arms, and stuffs the shirt into the leg's gaping wound. He uses an arm to tie it in place and the other to tourniquet the left leg.

"How is he?" Shamsurahman says.

Charlie turns to find Shamsurahman and Mike at his side. Derek continues on with a second mine detector towards the boys.

"Not good," Charlie says. "The femoral artery on his right leg is severed."

"We gotta tie it off," Mike says.

"Already did."

Mike pulls the t-shirt away and examines the wound. He repacks it and nods at Shamsurahman.

"Lift him under arms," Shamsurahman says. "I take other end."

Charlie gets behind Wali's head.

"One, two, three. Lift."

With Mike guiding them, they carry Wali back to the village. Someone has lain a tarpaulin beside one of the Land Cruisers, and they place Wali on it. Charlie pulls the shirt away. It's sodden with blood. With each of them working on one leg, Charlie and Shamsurahman clean Wali's wounds before packing them with gauze. Charlie looks up and sees Derek reach the edge of the undergrowth with the two trembling boys.

"Ready?" Shamsurahman says.

Charlie nods. Mike opens the Land Cruiser's trunk and drops the back seat. Charlie and Shamsurahman lift Wali up and place him on his side.

"I'll drive," Charlie says.

"No," Mike says, "you get in with him."

Charlie climbs in. He turns to see Kenneth standing there with his hands clasped in prayer.

"Kenneth," he shouts. "I need you."

Kenneth's eyes snap open, and he jumps in beside him. Charlie grabs some sleeping bags and elevates Wali's legs.

"Press on the end of his left leg," Charlie says.

Kenneth does as he's told. Charlie presses down on the wound on Wali's right leg. The engine revs. The Colonel runs over.

"Good luck," he says.

The Colonel slams the trunk door shut. Mike hits the gas, Shamsurahman in the passenger seat beside him. They speed along the dirt road, the speedometer rarely dipping below fifty. Mike does his best to steer around the road's potholes and on the occasions he can't, he shouts a warning, and Charlie and Kenneth hold Wali down as the SUV crashes up into the air. It takes forty minutes to get to the main road. Once on it Mike pushes the Land Cruiser over a hundred miles-an-hour.

Charlie puts a finger on Wali's neck and feels his pulse. It's weaker than before. He looks through the front windshield and sees the border at Torkham approaching.

"Don't stop," Charlie says.

"We have to," Shamsurahman says.

The SUV screeches to a halt, and Mike and Shamsurahman jump out. The startled mujahideen guards wave their guns at them until they recognize Shamsurahman and start running up to the Pakistani side of the border. A group of Khyber police rush towards their pick-up. Mike and Shamsurahman sprint back to the Land Cruiser.

"Still with us?" Mike says.

"Just," Charlie says.

"Do your job and he'll make it."

For the first mile Mike stays behind the police pick-up, but as soon as the climb begins the pick-up starts to labor.

"Fuck this," Mike says and swings into the opposite lane.

The pick-up tries to match their speed. The two vehicles head side-by-side towards a blind corner. A train of camels come around it. Mike swings the wheel left barely missing them and slips in front of the pick-up. The pick-up soon disappears from view. Once past the high point of the pass they hurtle down other side, the bare, ominous Khyber mountains pressing in on them. Kenneth and Charlie do all they can to brace Wali as they careen around the slew of tight corners. And then just like that the road straightens up. If there's a record for getting down the Khyber Pass, Mike has surely broken it.

"Want to take him to Red Crescent?" Mike says.

Shamsurahman nods. Mike cuts in and out of the afternoon traffic. Charlie checks Wali's pulse for the hundredth time. He can't feel one. He tries again. Still nothing. He twists Wali onto his back and puts his ear to Wali's mouth.

"We're losing him," Charlie screams.

Charlie straddles Wali's chest and tilts his head back. He gives him mouth-to-mouth and begins pushing down on his chest.

"You're not dying on me now, motherfucker."

Kenneth places his hand on Wali's forehead.

"Dear Father, we pray that Jesus meets this man, Wali, in his moment of death just as He did the thief on the cross—"

Charlie shoves Kenneth's hand away.

"What the fuck are you doing?" Charlie says.

The Land Cruiser screeches to a halt, and Charlie is flung into the back of the seats. The trunk door opens, and a couple of nurses lift Wali out. Kenneth gazes down at Charlie, his hands and shirt-sleeves drenched in blood.

"If that boy goes to hell he'll have you to blame."

Kenneth staggers away. Charlie stares at the ceiling of the SUV. In the distance a muezzin calls the faithful to prayer.

"You good?" Shamsurahman says.

Charlie gets up on one elbow. Shamsurahman stands there, a red neon crescent flickering behind him.

"Never better."

Shamsurahman lights a cigarette for each of them, and they smoke as the light seeps from the sky. Mike comes out the hospital entrance. Shamsurahman extends his pack. Mike takes one.

"He's a fighter, that's for sure," Mike says.

"He's alive?" Charlie says.

"He's in surgery. Best thing any of us can do is get a good night's sleep and come back in the morning."

"I'm going to wait."

"Maybe hours before he gets out."

Charlie stares at the both of them. Shamsurahman shrugs.

"Then I wait also," Shamsurahman says.

It isn't until nine that Charlie gets in to see Wali. At first glance he looks bizarrely normal with just a cotton wool patch taped over his right eye and some IVs snaking into his arm.

"Hey buddy," Charlie says. "How you doing?"

His words seem ridiculous. Charlie edges closer and pulls back Wali's blanket. Wali's right leg is gone while his left looks like a bandaged baseball bat. Charlie backs out of the room and finds Shamsurahman in the corridor.

"Let's go," Charlie says.

TWENTY

NOOR SITS ON the lowest bough of the oak tree and swings her legs back and forth. Through a gap in the leaves she spies her father in the sitting room. He reads under the warm glow of an antique, brass lamp, his feet resting on a well-worn ottoman, a glass of iced water and a bowl of almonds on the side table next to him. He looks so peaceful, she wishes he could stay there forever. She tiptoes along the bough and shinnies her way down the trunk. She walks across the lawn and into the house. Her father looks up.

"Ah, there you are," he says, "I was wondering where you had gotten to."

"You look so at home."

"And so I am, at least for a couple more nights."

Noor scans the book shelves. She sees a tatty old copy of Jane Eyre and pulls it out. She sits down and tries to focus on it. It's impossible.

"Baba, why aren't you more worried?"

"I think it was my old friend Mark Twain who once said 'I am an old man and have known a great many troubles, but most of them never happened'."

"You can stop trying to shield me from your fears. I saw how scared you were yesterday."

"Is that what you believe I do?"

"I think you believe that if you're endlessly optimistic that it'll improve my life somehow, make everything else we endure seem insubstantial."

"Without hope man has little to live for."

"And without honesty a man is living nothing but a lie."

Noor sees a look of unimaginable hurt in her father's eyes. Aamir Khan picks up his book, but she knows he's just staring at the words. She sits down on the arm of his chair.

"I'm sorry," she says, "I didn't mean—"

"To think that I pride myself on being the most honest man I know."

"You are."

"No, I am no less a hypocrite than any other. You must understand though, my primary concern has always been to protect you and Bushra."

"There's just no need to protect my feelings anymore."

Aamir Khan nods as if acknowledging a whole new chapter in their relationship.

"I'm going to go to Lahore," Noor says. "We have enough for the train fare."

"And then what? How do you expect to survive?"

"Tariq's after me, not you and Bushra."

"No, we stick together. There's a hostel on Ganj Bazar Road, it's cheap and if I recall correctly safe—"

"We only have enough money to stay there a week, two at most."

"And that is all we should need. I have heard talk that the Prince is about to return to Afghanistan. Once they leave we can go home."

"And when they come back?"

"You will have this scholarship, inshallah, and be gone."

"And if I don't."

"There will be nothing to worry about. The Prince has his pick of every unmarried woman in Pakistan. Trust me, he will be looking elsewhere within a fortnight."

"Tariq will be furious."

"Undoubtedly but there is nothing he can do."

The two of them fall into silence. Noor looks around the room; at the ten foot long satin drapes, the stone fireplace, the fine rugs on the floor, the array of cushions and lamps and endless little ornaments. It's almost surreal to be in such surroundings. Aamir Khan takes a sip of his water.

"I forgot how pleasurable a glass of iced water could be."

"We've forgotten a lot of things."

"All the more reason to get reacquainted with them this weekend."

"We're here to hide, Baba."

"Yet that doesn't proscribe us from taking delight in what this house has to offer, now does it? What are you so afraid of Noor? That if you sleep in a bed or have a shower that you will enjoy it too much."

Noor doesn't want to admit to him that the less she takes advantage of this house the less she'll feel in Charlie Matthew's debt.

"Go and have a shower," her father says.

"I washed myself thoroughly this morning."

"It is not the same. Now please, for my sake."

"Only if you insist."

"On this one occasion I do."

Noor sighs and makes her way to the downstairs bedroom. The blankets she slept on the night before are folded on the floor. She goes into its bathroom; it only has a bathtub. She takes a towel off the rack and heads upstairs. She'll use the shower in Bushra's room. When she reaches the landing, she sees Bushra's light is off.

She must be asleep.

Noor continues on down the hallway into her father's room and finds its bathroom only has a tub too. There's only one more option—the bedroom at the far end of the hallway.

Mukhtar had pointed it out on the tour he'd given them. It's the one room, he'd said, that Mr. Charlie didn't like him going into.

Presumably because it's a mess.

Noor can't help but be drawn towards it. She steps inside and is met by the pungent smell of male body odor and cigarettes.

What a surprise.

In the dark she fumbles for the light switch only to discover his sheets at perfect right angles, his shoes lined up by the balcony door, and the floor swept.

She wanders over to his writing desk, and next to some CDs she spies a sketch pad. She picks it up and flicks through it. Most of the sketches are rough, but she cannot deny they have a real sense of life to them; a man pushing a cart stacked high with watermelons, an old man weeding a flower bed, some men in demining outfits waving mine detectors.

At the back she comes across a series of attempts at drawing a woman. It takes her a moment to realize they are of her. Some he's abandoned after completing the outline of her face, in others he's concentrated on her eyes and the bridge of her nose. In some her look is intense as if she's pondering some deeper mystery while in others she stands tall, her hair flowing behind her as if she's in the midst of the monsoon. She stares at the sketches in fascination. As far as she's aware no one's drawn her before.

But then a thought rises up. A thought that grows in fury the more she dwells on it.

This is a violation. No more acceptable than if he'd spied on me. I mean, God knows what he's thinking when he's drawing me.

She looks up and sees a framed drawing on the wall. It's of a woman lying in bed, her head angled towards the sketcher, her eyes closed, the slightest of smiles on her face. The woman seems vulnerable as if the artist has intruded on the most personal of moments.

Was this a lover? Or just another woman he became obsessed with?

She puts the sketch book down and sees a stack of books and magazines on his bedside table. She goes over and picks up the first one. *'Oh The Places You'll Go'* by a Dr. Seuss. On the worn cover is a little boy in yellow pajamas standing on a multi-colored cone. Noor leafs through the eccentric drawings. She can't help but think it odd that a twenty-four year old man would read such a book.

Maybe there's something wrong with him on a psychological level. Some sort of stunted development.

She reaches the inside cover and sees a written inscription.

"To my darling Charlie, may your life be filled with adventure. I know you're going to move mountains. I love you, Mommy."

She looks through the rest of the books. *A Short Walk In The Hindu Kush, One Flew Over The Cuckoo's Nest, The Firm, A Confederacy of Dunces.* She is ashamed to say she hasn't read any of them and from the considered reviews on their back covers it seems like none of them are pulp.

Could he really have read them all?

She begins to feel as if Charlie's set her up. As if he placed them there to play a cruel game on her.

The last book is a *Lonely Planet Guide to Pakistan.* She flips through it; he's written something on the inside cover.

(1) Never help women! (2) Crazy place filled with crazy people!

She feels her righteous indignation return.

Of course, what else should I expect from such a patronizing, egotist.

Galvanized, she picks up the pile of magazines and starts rifling through them. There are a few motorcycle magazines, a couple of New Yorkers, a copy of a magazine called Rolling Stone, and right at the bottom—Playboy.

Noor gasps. On its cover are two identical bronzed blondes, related she assumes given that the caption proclaims them to be the Barbi Twins. As if compelled by some strange force, Noor opens the magazine. It flips to a centerfold of a woman with dark frizzy hair lying on a zebra skin rug with her hips arched upwards. The woman has voluptuous breasts, a tiny stomach, and impossibly long legs, but what Noor can't help but be drawn to is her neat patch of pubic hair and what is the merest hint of her vagina. Noor's face burns up, and she throws the magazine to the floor. She grabs her towel and heads for the bathroom. She's never felt dirtier in her life.

She pulls back the shower curtain and turns the knob. Water shoots from the tap, and after several failed attempts, and with her shalwar kameez now drenched, she manages to get the water to flow out of the shower head. She takes off her shalwar kameez, pulls off her yellowed underwear and steps into the tub. She gasps; the water is freezing. She finds a bar of soap and scrubs her body with it.

Of course he has pornography. Given how he represents every other reprehensible trait of the West, why should I be surprised? God damn him, it's images like these that make men delirious and convince the zealots that the only way to protect women is to cover them from head to toe.

She works her way down her body and by the time she reaches her calloused feet, she has convinced herself that Charlie's responsible for the burqa, arranged marriages and the enforced subservience of all Muslim women.

I wish he'd seen my feet first. Perhaps then we'd never have had to go through this ridiculous charade.

The water warms yet it does little to soothe her temper. She turns the shower off and steps out. It's the cleanest she's been in ten years, and yet she still feels as dirty as when she stepped in. She dries herself with her towel and sees her wet clothes lying on the floor.

It's alright, no one's in the house.

Noor wraps the towel around her chest and opens the bathroom door. She screams. Charlie is standing in the middle of the bedroom. She slams the door shut and looks for a lock. There isn't one. She sees a plunger behind the toilet and grabs it.

He won't have me.

She holds the plunger out as if it were a sword and waits. A horrific thought enters her mind.

Maybe he's flicking through his sex magazine, getting himself worked up before coming for me.

Her arms begin to tire, and she feels her towel slip from around her breasts. She puts the plunger down and spies her shalwar kameez.

Better to fight clothed.

Noor wrestles into it, the damp fabric sticking to her skin. She hears a muffled sob come from his room. She picks up the plunger and edges towards the door.

Is this a trick, a way of enticing me out?

She continues to listen, and the sobs get louder.

If it is, it's an extraordinary performance.

She eases the door open and creeps into the bedroom. Charlie is lying face down on his bed.

He's drunk. Or perhaps on drugs.

Charlie begins breathing so fast she's afraid he's having a seizure.

"Mr. Matthews?" she says.

He doesn't respond.

She inches up to the bed. For the first time she sees his t-shirt's stained with blood.

He must have been in a brawl.

She bends over him.

"Mr. Matthews?"

He turns his head to the side, his eyes bloodshot, his cheeks streaked with tears.

"It's all my fault," he says. "It's all my fault."

He turns his head away as if he's too ashamed to look at her and is wracked once more by sobs. Noor unfolds his blanket and lays it on top of him. She turns out the light and heads downstairs. Her father has already gone to bed.

In the morning we'll leave. There's no way we can live under the same roof as this man.

She heads to her bedroom and locks the door for good measure. She puts on her one other shalwar kameez and slips into the bed. Enveloped by a set of clean sheets and with her head resting on a firm pillow, she lies there and wonders what could've happened to provoke such distress.

Forget about him.

It's not easy, but eventually she does, and she slips into a deep and wondrous sleep.

TWENTY-ONE

TARIQ SITS IN the reception room, consumed by his father and sister's treachery and wearied by his search for them.

He'd concluded that they couldn't have gone far—they didn't have the money to—so he'd driven to Jalozai and Baghbanan refugee camps, and enquired as to whether a middle aged man and his two daughters had sought shelter there. They hadn't, so he had moved onto the hostels, especially the flea bitten ones he knew they'd be able to afford. He'd turned up a couple of leads, but in each case they'd proven false. He'd moved onto the streets, and, at night, he'd driven around the city. He'd stopped every time he'd seen a cluster of three bodies lying on the sidewalk, and shined his flashlight into their startled upturned faces. Again nothing. Every time he'd returned to the group's HQ he'd run across Salim Afridi supervising preparations. He had begun to wonder whether he should flee just as his father-in-law had years earlier.

And then this morning after another unsuccessful night's search, he'd been told that the Prince wanted to see him. Any hope of escaping was now gone.

He can't know. Can he?

He decides to tell the Prince that he'd taken Noor for some tests, and she'd been diagnosed with hepatitis C. It will put pay to any marriage but it will at least explain her absence. 'Nothing your Highness is of greater concern to me than your well being', he'll say and perhaps the Prince will even thank him.

The door opens, and the Prince enters in camo gear and a checkered ghutra. Tariq leaps to his feet.

"So—" the Prince says.

Tariq readies Noor's pitiful story.

"—we leave today."

It takes a moment for Tariq to process what the Prince has just said.

"The timetable's been moved up?" Tariq says.

"Massoud's making moves," the Prince says. "When I last saw my uncle, the King, I promised him that, God willing, it would be a Saudi who first raised the jihadi flag over the Presidential Palace. I intend on keeping that promise."

The Prince sits and takes a sip of tea.

"I want you to be one of my bodyguards."

"It would be an honor, your Highness."

The Prince studies him.

"You don't seem very excited."

If only you knew how jubilant I am.

"I beg your forgiveness," Tariq says. "I am, it's just—"

"Just what?"

"I'm ready to take the fight elsewhere, your Highness. God willing we will be victorious in Afghanistan, but now I believe it is our duty to establish the Caliphate worldwide."

The Prince smiles.

"This is why I like you, Tariq, your ambition is boundless."

"I am but a poor servant of Allah."

"Then allow me to counsel patience. A wise general knows you can only fight one battle at a time. What I require from you now is your vigilance and service."

"And you have it."

"Good, go get ready. We leave in ten minutes."

Tariq heads for the door.

"Oh and Tariq," the Prince says.

Tariq turns back.

"Your sister, how is she?"

Tariq finds himself unable to speak.

"I understand," the Prince says, "you're disappointed that the wedding will have to be postponed."

"Nothing is more important than the jihad, your Highness."

"Don't be. Once this is over I'm sure I'll be even more eager to make your sister my wife."

Tariq strides down the corridors of the grand old house, a man reborn. Allah has given him the one thing he'd been praying for—time. He walks out the front door. The Prince's force of a thousand men await his inspection. A number of them look in Tariq's direction and nod.

I'm somebody.

Tariq heads around back to the old stables. How he despises this place, the endless hours he'd had to spend disassembling weapons piece-by-piece before cleaning them and reassembling them once more. The smell of gun oil makes him want to vomit. Yet it was here that he'd first met his father-in-law. It had been an inauspicious first meeting. Salim Afridi had berated him for being too slow in retrieving a box of bullets. Afterwards, however, Yousef had told him about Salim Afridi's influence with the Prince, and Tariq had hatched his plan to get in the man's good graces.

Oh, how times change.

"Yousef," he shouts.

"What now?" he hears Yousef shout back.

Tariq makes his way down a metal shelved aisle and finds Yousef sitting beside a workbench picking his nose.

"Long night?" Tariq says.

"Screw em all, coming in here, trying to snatch things when my back's turned."

"I'm sure Salim Afridi was pleasant."

"He's in the worst of moods, but I don't have to tell you that."

Tariq picks up a Beretta pistol lying on the workbench. He checks the chamber is empty and begins twirling it around his finger.

"What are people saying?" Tariq says.

"That you're a dead man."

"Then why are they treating me differently? With respect?"

"For now you have the ear of the Prince. But they still think you'll end up in the ground."

"We all go there some day."

"Yeah, but you lad are headed there sooner than most."

Tariq stops twirling the gun.

"Trust me, Salim Afridi's bones will turn to dust many years before mine."

"Those are fighting words."

"He's no different than the Soviets. From the outside he seems invincible but all it will take is a smaller, nimbler opponent to bring him to his knees."

"And you're that man?"

"You've known me longer than most. You think I'm going to let a dinosaur like Salim Afridi stop me."

Yousef goes over to a shelf and returns with two boxes of 9mm bullets.

"You didn't come here for a Beretta," Yousef says. "What do you need?"

"My sister."

Yousef's face floods with realization.

"Oh, you're up shit creek, my friend."

"No, she can be found."

"She could be in Karachi by now."

"I doubt it; in fact I suspect she'll surface once we're back in Afghanistan."

Yousef hobbles towards the front of the armory.

"Sorry, but you're on your own on this one."

Tariq grabs the bullets and chases after him.

"Help me. Please. No one need know a thing. If you don't find her all you'll have lost is time you'd have spent sitting around here on your fat ass."

"And if I do?"

"I hear in Saudi Arabia the taps are made from gold."

Outside a roar of 'Allah Akbar' rises up, and the convoy's engines start turning over

"You got a photo?" Yousef says.

Tariq pulls it from inside his jacket and hands it to Yousef. Yousef whistles.

"Our beloved Prince is a lucky man."

"She's twenty-one now but she doesn't look so different. Her face is a little leaner, her hair longer."

Tariq takes out a pad and pencil and scribbles on it. He rips the page off and hands it to Yousef.

"Places you should look," he says.

Yousef scans the list.

"I'll send word if I find her."

"I'm forever in your debt."

Tariq hurries for the door.

"Oh and Tariq."

Tariq turns to find Yousef holding out a couple of grenades.

"I rejigged these—have ten second fuses. You never know, may come in useful."

Tariq shoves the grenades into his pockets and takes off. By the time he arrives at the front of the building, the convoy's already halfway down the driveway. He sees the Prince's Range Rover and runs in his lopsided way to the pick-up behind it. A Saudi bodyguard spots him and reaches out a hand. Tariq grabs it and the Saudi pulls him up. Tariq looks at the other men. They're all Saudis. The Prince's closest protectors.

I'm one of you now.

TWENTY-TWO

"GOEDE MORGEN," THE woman on the tape says. "Ik spreek maar een klein beetje Nederlands."

Noor hears the floorboards creek behind her. She turns expecting it to be her father. Instead it's Mukhtar. He gives her a warm and gracious smile.

"May I make you some tea, memsahib?" he says in Pashtu.

"There's no need to call me memsahib, Mukhtar, I'm only a guest in this house."

"What should I call you then?"

"Noor, Miss Noor would be fine."

"Well may I make you some tea, Miss Noor?"

Noor is about to decline but thinks better of it. She sees how much Mukhtar wants to do it.

"That would be lovely thank you."

"I will return with it shortly," he grins.

Noor looks up at the carriage clock on the mantelpiece. It's seven o'clock. She turns off the tape machine and wonders where her father is. She'd like them to be packed and gone before Charlie wakes up. She heads to the study and puts her Dutch books down on the desk. She picks up the phone and, on hearing the dial tone, realizes this is the first time she's used one since they fled Afghanistan. She dials the school's number. Miss Suha picks up on the third ring.

"As-salaam Alaykum, it's Noor."

"What you doing calling at this hour?"

"I'm not going to be able to make it in today, most likely all week I'm afraid, my father has fallen ill."

"Uh-huh and why can't your sister deal with it?"

"It's serious, I need to make sure he sees a doctor. She's not good at getting people to do things."

"Not a problem you've ever had. Hold on a moment."

Noor hears Miss Suha repeat a more dramatic rendition to the headmistress. The headmistress's replies are too muted to discern. Miss Suha returns to the phone, breathing heavily as if Noor had forced her to go to the other side of the school.

"She's not happy, it's going to cause a lot of complications, but I guess we'll do our best to cope," Miss Suha says.

"Could you do me a favor and give me Miss Kuyt's phone number?"

"Have time for her but not us, do you?"

"We were going to meet this week, and I don't want her to think I was being rude."

"I'll leave her a message."

"That's kind of you, but if it's all the same I'd like to call her myself."

Miss Suha sighs and flicks through her index cards. She gives Noor the number, and Noor hangs up before Miss Suha can interrogate her further. Noor dials the number, and asks for Elma. A minute later Elma comes on the line, and Noor explains her predicament.

"Oh, I'm sorry to hear that," Elma says. "Anything I can do to help?"

"No, I have it all in hand."

"You have the books and tapes, right?"

"Yes, I'm studying them—"

"Then all I need is your essay by the end of the week."

Noor's essay is already done but she isn't going to let on. Despite having rewritten it ten times she's still not satisfied with it. The doorbell rings, and she hears Mukhtar make his way towards the front door.

"I just heard the craziest story," Elma says.

The door opens, and a man talks to Mukhtar in Pashtu. Noor strains to hear what they're saying.

"Noor, you there?"

"Yes, I'm sorry."

"You won't believe it, but one of Charlie Matthew's employees was blown up in Afghanistan yesterday. Supposedly Charlie ran into the minefield and saved the man's life."

Suddenly it all makes sense. Charlie's demeanor, his clothes, the reason he came home early.

"Well it's the talk of the town, that's for sure," Elma says.

Noor hears Mukhtar and the man head upstairs.

Where are they going?

"I'm so sorry, Elma, but—"

"No, I understand. Get back to your father, I'll see you next week."

Elma hangs up. Noor stands there motionless, every sense of hers directed towards this mysterious visitor.

Who could it be?

It wasn't Tariq. She'd have recognized his voice.

Could it be someone who works with him? But then why's Mukhtar taking him upstairs?

She relaxes. It has to be a friend of Charlie's. She decides to just stay put and wait them out. To the side of the desk she spots a large globe; half the land is in pink, depicting a time when the British Empire stretched around the world. She twirls the globe until her finger lands on Holland.

She hears someone come back down the stairs and head towards the study.

Oh, no.

Noor searches for a place to hide. The footsteps get closer. She drops onto the floor and crawls under the desk. The door swings open, and she sees a pair of scuffed, black leather shoes approach the desk. Their wearer stops inches from her face and dials a number.

"Hi, it's Ivor," he says. "Yeah, yeah I'm at his house—like shit—how do you think you'd look if you saw someone blown up in front of your eyes?"

The man picks something up off the desk and begins leafing through it.

The Dutch books.

"So I'm thinking of going on a trip next week to visit our friend. Any interest?—No, I get it, I can do it on my own— every day that goes by I'm trusting this fuck less and less— he's up to something with this Al Qaeda group, I'm telling you—I know it's all fucking rumors but hasn't it always been?—Hey, just because I'm paranoid doesn't mean I'm wrong—"

Noor hears the globe whir around and around, and a long, plaintive fart. She covers her mouth to stop herself from giggling.

"Trust me, I know it's not a priority for Langley but it should be—anyway we can talk about it later—by the way I hear he's found his next punching bag, fucking refugee if you can believe it."

Noor freezes.

"He probably thinks an illiterate bitch can take a left hook better than some spoilt princess—no, no clue who she is but we'll find out soon enough."

The man laughs.

"Yeah, see you tonight."

The man puts down the receiver and knocks one of Noor's Dutch books on the ground.

"Fuck," he says.

Noor holds her breath. The man's baseball capped head comes into view. He picks up the book and straightens up without looking in her direction. He tosses it back on the desk, and exits the room.

***

CHARLIE STARES UP at the wooden ceiling fan and listens to two birds calling back and forth. All night grim images had punctuated his sleep—the fiery explosion, the splintered bone jutting out the end of Wali's leg, the tear-streaked children in the weeds, Wali's muddied and bloodied face. Despite their brutish quality Charlie had clung to them hoping that was all they'd remain. Then Ivor had woken him, and he'd had to face reality. His dreams weren't fevered imaginations. All of them had occurred—except for one that is. Intermixed with all the other images was one of Noor standing in his room with a towel wrapped around her. It makes no sense, and he convinces himself that it couldn't have happened.

What is it with this girl? She infects my mind even in times like this.

He stumbles into the bathroom and looks in the mirror. His face is as muddy and bloodied as Wali's was.

He steps in the tub not waiting for the water to warm. The water spatters his face, and the grime and blood swirl around the drain. He stares at his feet and realizes they've taken on a significance he'd never afforded them before. Once out he puts on a t-shirt and a pair of cargo pants and plods downstairs to find Ivor waiting in the hall.

"Want breakfast?" Ivor says.

"Just want to get going if that's cool."

"Suits me."

They climb into Ivor's Bronco and head down the driveway.

"So everyone's calling you a hero," Ivor says.

"Trust me that's the last thing I am."

"Well Shamsurahman says you are and coming from him's a bit like Greg Maddux saying you can throw a ball."

"Why you talking to Shamsurahman?"

"An American, namely you, was involved in an incident over the border—it's my job."

"Got nothing to do with the fact you're CIA?"

Ivor glares at him.

"That fag, Jurgen, tell you that."

"Says everyone knows you are."

"Some fucking spy that'd make me. Sorry to dispel the fantasy, buddy, but my job's a lot less glamorous. I just look out for Americans like you when you get in trouble."

"Well like I told you, I'm fine."

"Maybe your body is, but how about up here?"

Charlie looks out the window. At the side of the road a blind boy with deformed feet sits in the dirt selling bottles of soda. He feels a desperate urge for a Coke.

"You mind pulling over?" Charlie says.

Ivor jerks the wheel to the left, and Charlie jumps out. He jogs up to the boy.

"Yo Coke, luftan," he says in pigeon Pashtu.

The boy's hands search the crate in front of him and pick out a Coke bottle. He flips off the cap and stares up at Charlie with his blank eyes.

"Five rupee," the boy says.

Charlie hands him twenty dollars.

"Keep the change."

Charlie gets back in the SUV, and Ivor drives off. Charlie guzzles the Coke down in one go.

"It was all my fault," he says.

"No, it wasn't."

"You weren't there."

"No, but I know two things. You weren't the bastard who laid that mine, and, with all due respect to your employee, you weren't the idiot who ran into a minefield."

"I shouldn't have brought him with me."

"Yeah and I should've taken that gig in Tokyo rather than coming to this gem of a city, but it's all water under the bridge. Once you've visited your guy, you need to write down your version of events and fax it to your boss."

"It won't make a difference. I broke so many rules, I'm sure to be canned."

"I don't give a fuck. Just do it, okay?"

The traffic slows, and Ivor lays on the horn.

"So you see any mujahideen while you were out there?" Ivor says.

"Except for the border guards, nothing."

"How about training camps?"

"What do you mean by that?"

"You know a smaller version of an army base—low slung huts, obstacle courses, shooting ranges that sort of thing."

"There was one a few miles off the main road."

"Anyone there?"

Charlie looks out the window. A gaggle of pedestrians surrounds a young girl lying contorted on the road; blood pools around her head. A woman in a burqa is screaming hysterically, pointing at a car with a bashed in windscreen.

"So was there?" Ivor says.

"No."

"You sure? Nobody?"

"Jesus, Ivor, what did I just say?"

"Cool, just wanted to be sure."

Charlie lights a cigarette, and they drive the rest of the way to the hospital in silence. Ivor pulls up at its front entrance.

"Don't be long," he says, "I gotta be at a meeting across town."

Charlie nods and walks in the main entrance. He finds the nurses' station, and a nurse gives him Wali's room number. Charlie heads down a corridor past an orderly pushing a cart filled with bloody, soiled sheets. The smell of metal and shit lingers in his nostrils. He finds Wali's room and takes a deep breath.

Get it together. This is not about you.

He enters the room and calls out Wali's name. Wali doesn't respond. Charlie walks over and sees Wali's eyes are closed.

"And you are?" a voice says.

Charlie turns to see a young Pakistani doctor standing there.

"Charlie, I'm a friend."

"I'm Doctor Halim, I operated on Wali last night. I wish I could have saved his left foot but there was nothing else to do."

"He in a coma?"

"No, I don't believe so, it's most likely the amount of medication he's under. We will reduce that soon."

"How long will he be here?"

"Four weeks, six at most."

"That all?"

"It never ceases to amaze me how resilient the human body is. There will be complications, of course, but within a month it's more a question of rehabilitation. From there on he'll need his family more than anything else."

"He has no family."

"Well that will certainly make it harder."

Charlie turns. Wali has a contented smile on his lips as if he doesn't have a care in the world.

"I'll make sure he's taken care of," Charlie says.

"That's quite a commitment."

"It's the least I can do."

Charlie lays a hand on Wali's shoulder. He wants to say something profound, something that shows how much he cares but words fail him.

Charlie walks out past a rogue's gallery of limbless patients. They stare at him like zombies in a cheap horror flick. Out front he hears a car horn, and Ivor pulls up beside him. He gets in and asks Ivor to drop him at the UNMAPA offices. When they get there, Ivor scribbles something on a piece of paper and hands it to Charlie.

"There's a party at this general's house tonight," Ivor says.

"Thanks but I'm not up for parties right now."

"Trust me, there's nothing worse you can do than dwell on this shit. Elma will be there."

"So?"

"Come on, buddy, I saw the Dutch books on your desk. Don't think it's gonna work, but I sure as hell respect the enterprise."

"I don't know what you're talking about."

Ivor smirks.

"Sure you don't."

Charlie steps out of the SUV, and Ivor tears out of the compound. Charlie crumples up the piece of paper and tosses it into a nearby trash can.

TWENTY-THREE

NOOR SITS ON the unused bed in Bushra's room and studies her Dutch grammar book. Bushra retreated to the bathroom a couple of hours ago and still hasn't emerged. If it weren't for the occasional turn of the hot water tap Noor might begin to fear she'd drowned.

They hadn't left after all. After her conversation with Elma, Noor's argument for doing so had seemed specious at best, and her father, on learning that Charlie had arrived home early, had felt it best to wait and thank him for his kind hospitality. And wait they had. Past seven in the evening, past eight, past nine, until her father had announced that he was retiring, and they could thank Charlie in the morning. Though Noor would never admit, she'd been relieved. The idea of searching out a cockroach ridden hostel at this late hour filled her with dread.

Noor hears tires crunch on the gravel outside and slips off the bed. She pulls back the curtain and sees the light of a motorcycle extinguish. Noor steps away and catches her reflection in the mahogany standing mirror. In this venerable antique her shalwar kameez seems shabbier than ever.

You know you must go and apologize, a voice inside her says.
For what?

How about your inability to offer Charlie comfort in his time of need.

She grimaces and does up the top button of her kameez. Downstairs she heads through the library into the sitting room. She smells cigarette smoke wafting in through the open verandah doors and makes her way outside. At the far end Charlie is sitting in one of the rocking chairs, a cigarette in one hand, a bottle of beer in the other.

"Mr. Matthews," she says.

He looks up at her as though she were a ghost.

"So you were here," he says.

"We all are."

Charlie goes back to staring out at the garden.

"We can leave if you wish."

"No—just surprised you came that's all."

"We've had a lovely time, thank you."

"Good."

Noor waits for him to say something more, but he ventures nothing further. She sits down in the other rocking chair and looks off into the garden.

Apologize, the voice inside her says, but she finds herself incapable of doing so—at least personally.

"I was sorry to hear what happened to your colleague," she says.

Charlie takes a long swig from his beer bottle.

"I'm not going to soften this for you, his recovery's going to be long and painful. However if I've learnt one thing from living in the camps it's that he can still have a fulfilling life."

"Could you live without your legs?" Charlie says.

"I know I would survive."

Noor feels his eyes fall on her. She continues to peer out into the darkness.

"I don't know if my father mentioned this," she says, "but my mother was killed when I was eleven. One moment she was sitting right there beside me, the next she was gone, gone so quickly that I never even told her how much I loved her.

That's what's so strange about life. You go on these long stretches where nothing extraordinary happens, where each day feels so similar to the last that it's impossible to tell them apart. Then in the blink of an eye your whole universe is turned upside down, and everything you believed in is shaken to its core. I've often wondered why God does this, it seems so cruel, and the only answer I've been able to come up with is that these hardships somehow allow you to have a deeper, more profound sense of yourself."

Charlie puts down his bottle. In the garden hut, Noor can hear Mukhtar and Rasul chatting. Mukhtar lets out a hearty chuckle, and Noor sees it as her cue to leave.

"My mom died when I was fourteen," Charlie says. "Breast cancer."

Noor waits.

"I was at school when the hospital called, they said I should get there as soon as possible. When I did my mom looked fine. I suppose you wouldn't have said that if you were meeting her for the first time, but I guess I'd gotten used to the way she looked. I stopped worrying, but then she got real intense, told me to always lead the life I wanted to live, and I suddenly realized she was about to die.

"She asked me to sing 'My Sweet Lord' - when I was young she'd sing it to me to put me to sleep - and so I started singing it louder and louder, thinking if I didn't stop that she'd never leave me. And then I felt this hand on my shoulder. It was Maggie, one of the nurses. 'I'm sorry Charlie,' she said. 'She's gone'."

Noor looks over at Charlie. A single tear is winding its way down his cheek.

"After they'd done what they had to do, they left me alone with her, and I felt this incredible urge to draw her. It was my last chance. I had a sketch pad in my satchel, and I became so absorbed I had no idea how much time passed. I heard the door open and looked up to see my Dad there, his tie still done up like he was there to meet a client. He stared down at me with disgust. 'Give her some respect, she's dead,' he said. He ripped the pad away, and asked for a moment alone with her. That was it, he didn't hug me or anything like that. So I waited in the corridor, and five minutes later he came out and said we were going. I told him I'd left my homework in the room, and I ran back in and searched for my sketch pad. I found it in the trash. I shoved it in my satchel and went over to my mom. I begged her to tell me what to do, but she said nothing. I've never felt more alone."

Charlie wipes his cheeks with the bottom of his t-shirt. Noor castigates herself for thinking the sketch in his room was of a lover.

Why do I think the worst of people.

"From what my boss told me today," Charlie says, "I'll be on my way home by the end of the week."

"They blame you for what happened?"

"They have every right to. Point is if you want to stay a little longer, you should."

"I don't know if that's a good idea."

"I thought it was part of the Pashtun code not to turn down hospitality."

Or refuge.

"Thank you," she says, "that's very kind of you."

Noor stands.

"Good night, Charlie."

"Night, Noor."

Noor makes her way back down the verandah. She realizes that she just called Charlie by his first name.

TWENTY-FOUR

ELMA CIRCULATES THROUGH the crowded bungalow and feels eyes all over her; the smartly dressed Pakistani officers with their neat mustaches and crisp uniforms, the immaculately dressed Pakistani bureaucrats in their starch white collarless jackets and shalwar kameez, the Western diplomats in their Savile Row suits and ties, and the more slovenly cadre of Western aid workers with their rumpled jackets and scuffed shoes, as if both should be taken as a sign of their altruism. For years she has feasted off such attention, but now she's beginning to feel wearied by it all.

She enters a small sitting room and finds Ivor there, chatting with a group of whisky drinking Pakistani officers. They stop talking and look her way. She recognizes one of them, General Faisal, the commander of the Frontier Force Regiment and a notorious groper. His gaze drifts towards her breasts, and she turns to leave. Ivor's at her side before she's even at the door.

Great.

"Not happy to see me," he says.

"I'm just looking for someone."

"Your new boyfriend from the New Yorker?"

Elma swivels on him. Ivor doesn't bother to wipe the

smirk from his face.

"Why do you persist in spreading malicious rumors about me?" she says.

"Trust me I don't give a fuck how you choose to get ahead, hey we've all got to do what we gotta do, but the truth's a funny thing, Elma, it always gets out in the end."

"I never had an affair with the Interior Minister."

"Yeah, and you weren't banging dear old Raymond either, were you?"

"Fuck you, Ivor."

Elma marches towards the patio doors.

"I read his article, least the preliminary draft," Ivor says. "Those hotel fax machines, they're just too tempting not to bug."

Elma can't help but turn back. Ivor walks up. He gets so close she can feel his warm breath on her cheek.

"I don't know why you never chose to sleep with me," he says. "I could be so much more useful to you than anyone else around here. That job at the UNDP you're so desperate to get, you think the Agency couldn't swing that for you?"

Elma stares Ivor down. The idea of being in this weasel's debt makes her skin crawl. Ivor sighs.

"Fine, do it the hard way."

"The article, Ivor, what did it say?"

Ivor sucks on his straw.

"The guy's got a major hard on for you—made you out to be a cross between Mother Theresa and Margaret Thatcher."

"I'm not sure that's a compliment."

"The way he writes it, it is. Compassion crossed with steely resolve. Hell by the time I finished it I was ready to vote you UN Secretary General."

Despite it all, Elma can't help but feel a visceral thrill. She does her best to maintain a composed demeanor.

"You and me, we're not that different," Ivor says.

Elma snorts.

"You want to save lives, and despite what you might think, so do I."

"American lives," she says.

"Sure, I'll concede the point, but whether you like it or not it's a similar impulse."

"I don't believe in screwing people over to achieve my goals."

"No, but I know you'll pretty much do anything else. I had our European office check you out—where you were born, where you went to school, who your friends were—which teacher was your lover."

Elma feels a chill run up her spine.

He can't know.

"Mr. Hiddink still has no clue he has a son, does he? And from what I can tell your brother, Isaac, doesn't know you're his mother either? Quite the sacrifice your mom made there. Why she do it? My guess is she was damned if some philandering Dutchman was going to screw up your life the way one had screwed hers. Am I close?"

Elma feels dizzy. She looks around and imagines everyone in the room to be looking at her. She staggers towards the patio doors.

"Don't worry," Ivor says, "your secret's safe with me."

She keeps on going. The manicured garden is brimming with guests. She spies an empty bench at the far end and winds her way over to it. She closes her eyes and takes a series of deep breaths.

For the last five months of her pregnancy, her mother had kept Elma home with 'lupus' and had even worn a pillow to work to make her colleagues think it was she who was expecting. Fifteen years ago she'd been petrified that someone would discover her secret, but as the years had passed she'd become less and less concerned. The fabrication had been so complete that of late Elma had even stopped thinking of Isaac as her son.

And now this.

She feels the urge to vomit.

"Elma," she hears someone say.

She opens her eyes to see Rod standing there in a safari jacket. He gives her a concerned look, and she straightens up.

"You okay?" he says.

"Yeah, just one of those days."

"I hear you. You mind if I take a load off?"

She shakes her head, and he sits down beside her. They gaze out at the partygoers.

"I don't know how you can do your job," he says. "I've never come across a bigger group of self-satisfied bastards in my life."

"I guess you just have to remember who you're doing it for. If you don't get this lot on your side you'll achieve nothing."

"No scholarships for Noor."

"Exactly."

She watches Ivor worm his way through the crowd. He looks her way and raises his glass. She turns towards Rod.

"I don't know if you have time, in fact it's probably silly even to ask, but I have to visit one of our projects in the Hunza Valley for a couple of days. It doesn't involve Afghan refugees, but I'm really proud of what we've done up there; it's such a poor area but it's so beautiful especially in the autumn when the leaves are turning. I promise, you've never seen mountains so tall, rivers so blue—"

"Elma, stop, you don't need to sell me. I'd love to come."

Elma blushes. All she wants to do is to wrap her arms around him and sink into his embrace. But she won't. And she won't go home with him tonight either. There's no way she'd want to give Ivor the satisfaction. She looks back out at the party and wishes she was anywhere but here.

Don't worry. In New York, it'll be different.

TWENTY-FIVE

"OKAY, I WANT to start off by offering you all an apology. Ever since I got here I haven't taken this job seriously, so I get why you haven't either."

Charlie looks at the faces of his Afghan recruits. They stare back at him without any hint of emotion.

"But things are going to change from now on. First off, I'm going to be here at eight every morning and I expect you to be too."

Charlie hears a couple of grumbles. The only teenage recruit in the group sticks up his hand.

"Mansoor," Charlie says.

"I live in Baghbanan. Rahmahullah, Mohammad Khan also too."

"That a problem?"

"It long way away."

"I'm sorry but you'll just have to get up earlier."

Mansoor glowers at him.

"Secondly, we're going to stay each day until we've completed whatever task we set out to do, even if that means going home after dark."

Jawad, a refugee in a checkered sweater, raises his hand. Charlie nods at him.

"I have job at night," Jawad says.

"Again I'm sorry, but you've got to choose. It's either this or that."

Charlie knows without a doubt that the Mine Aware job pays way more. Jawad and Mansoor share a look.

"Now can anyone tell me what my main mission is?"

Obaidullah sticks up his hand.

"To teach us to get mines out of the ground, sir."

"Good try but no. Anyone else? No one? Okay, it's simple, to keep you guys safe. Got that; S—A—F—E. Now how many of you know someone who stepped on a mine?"

This time every single hand goes up.

"So I guess you all know what bastards they are."

"Bastards, sir?" Shafiq says.

"Tough, not easy to find, hell most are overgrown with weeds or hidden in scrub."

Yunus raises his hand.

"In Baghran, Russians laid the mines all around the walls of our villages and in fields."

Charlie picks up a circular mine off the table beside him.

"And did they look like this?"

"Exactly, sir."

"What's wrong with Yunus's answer?"

Najib sticks his hand up.

"Go for it, Najib."

"That mine is too clean, sir."

"Right—most look like this bastard."

Charlie picks a rusted mine.

"Sir, I beg your pardon, but why do you insist on calling the mines bastards?" Najib says.

"Because one of them took both of Wali's legs."

"I understand, but still why?"

"Where I'm from a bastard's someone who's got no morals, who doesn't fight fair and this here is the very definition. Corroded, waterlogged and entangled in roots which means?"

"It could explode most easily, sir," Bakri says.

"Got it and to make matters worse, the person who laid it's also a bastard and a crafty bastard at that. For as much as he'd like it to take off some kid's leg or blow off your mother's face, what really gives him a hard on is the idea of blasting your balls to smithereens."

"Sir," Shafiq says, "I am afraid to tell you, I do not understand what you are saying."

The class murmurs their agreement.

"Let me put it another way. There's no one a minelayer would like to kill more than a deminer. You're his greatest enemy, and he'll go to incredible lengths to kill you."

The recruits stare back at Charlie as though he were telling a ghost story around a campfire.

Finally, I've made a connection.

"So what does he do? He attaches the mine to a trip wire hoping you'll snag it. But you're cleverer than that, you've been taught well."

"Not so far," Yunus says.

The recruits laugh. Charlie chuckles.

"Well you're going to be, so you'll find his wire and trace both its ends. Only problem is boom."

The class jerks back as Charlie shouts out the word.

"He's laid anti-personnel mines around it. And boom— they jump in the air and send pieces of metal in all directions. Boom—a metal fragment slices your belly open like a can opener. Boom—another lodges in your brain and makes you a drooling idiot.. And boom—the rest cut your legs into shreds and you get to spend the rest of your life rolling around on those pathetic wooden sleds hoping someone'll take pity on you. Now who wants to be one of those guys?"

"Not me," Najib says.

"Everyone."

A chorus of 'not me' rises up from the group.

"So I'm going to let you in on a secret, tell you how you're going to stop this from happening. First, from now on you do everything I say, even when it sounds dumb. Second, never cut corners. Never. You do these two things and a mine goes off, you'll not only survive but ninety-nine percent of the time you'll suffer only superficial injuries."

"That is it?" Obaidullah says.

"Yes, but it's not as easy as it sounds. You see, demining is one of the most boring jobs known to man. For every mine you find you'll get four-hundred-and-fifty false hits. So guess what? Instead of lying flat on the ground with your balls in a knot, you start squatting. I mean why not, there's only a slim chance the piece of metal in front of you's a mine, and even if it is the odds are it's stable. But if it's not then you're fried."

"Fried, sir?" Yunus says.

"Decapitated."

"I do not understand this word either."

"The blast will pierce the gap between your visor and apron and your head will fall off as surely as if an executioner had sliced it with a sword."

The recruits sit there in silence. Charlie lets them—he wants the message to sink in. He sees Qasim exit the main building and hurry in their direction.

Great, probably Skeppar on the line, wanting to berate me again.

"Mr. Matthews," Najib says.

Charlie looks over at him.

"I know what a brave thing you did for Wali. We all do."

"Thanks, but anyone would have done what I did?"

"No, most people would not, especially for an Afghan."

"In Quran," Obaidullah says, "it says if anyone saves a life, it is as if he saved the lives of all mankind."

Charlie can't help but smile. It's the nicest thing anyone's said to him since the accident.

"Well I appreciate that Obaidullah. Truly, I do."

He points to a neat line of thirty miniature flags.

"Okay, today we're going to do some probing drills."

"We have already done these," Mansoor says.

"Yeah but this time we're going to do them properly. So go get your gear from Mocam and come back here and lie down in front of a flag."

The recruits rise to their feet and head for the storeroom. Qasim reaches him.

"Mr. Matthews, sir, I received call from hospital. Wali has woken up."

Charlie's pulse quickens. He sprints for his bike and makes it to the hospital in record time. Doctor Halim meets him outside Wali's room.

"How's he doing?" Charlie says.

"Remarkably lucid and in good spirits."

"Despite, you know …"

"He's not aware of his misfortune yet."

"Maybe he's not as lucid as you think."

"The lower half of his body is covered, and so, in all frankness, he doesn't realize his legs are gone."

"Apart from the fact he can't feel them anymore."

"On the contrary his nervous system's telling him that they're still attached to his body. In fact he complained just now that his right leg was itchy."

"So why haven't you told him?"

"We find the shock is lessened when the news comes from a friend or a family member. You did say he had no family to speak of, didn't you?"

Charlie nods.

"There is some good news," Doctor Halim says. "The ophthalmologist thinks he'll be able to save his right eye."

"Well, thank God for that."

Charlie glances at the door. All he wants to do is run.

This is not about you.

He takes a deep breath and pushes the door open. A broad grin breaks across Wali's face.

"Mr. Matthews, what a wonderful surprise."

"Good to see you too, buddy. How you feeling?"

"A little woozy but don't worry I'll be up on my feet before you know it."

Charlie does his best not to grimace. He grabs a chair and sits down beside him.

"Wali, do you remember how you got injured?"

"In all honesty, Mr. Matthews, I do not."

"You remember going to Afghanistan?"

"Of course."

"And how about the two boys who ran after the football?"

"Is that something I should remember?"

"Kind of, because you did a very heroic thing. You ran into a minefield to save them."

Wali's smile wavers.

"Was the minefield where I had my accident?"

"Yes."

"And were the two boys also hurt?"

"Because of you they weren't."

"That is a blessing."

They hold each other's gaze.

"Mines do nasty things, don't they?" Wali says.

Charlie nods.

"You're aware a mine killed my younger sister?"

"It was one of the first things you told me."

Wali laughs.

"So I did. If I'm not mistaken I was trying to impress on you my experience with mines, and now I have even more experience, don't I? More experience than I probably would wish for."

"You sustained some injuries," Charlie says.

"My eye is gone, I suspected that was the case."

"Your eye's going to be fine. It's your legs—I'm sorry, but you've lost your right leg and your left foot."

Wali's smile falters, and then he begins laughing.

"Mr. Matthews, I have to tell you that you had me there for a second."

"It's the truth, Wali."

"And what a magnificent job you did at keeping a straight face. But you see all this time I've been wiggling my toes, even now as we speak."

"Your body still thinks they're there but they aren't."

"Then be so kind as to show me."

"I don't think that's a good idea."

"I must insist. Please, show me."

Charlie goes in search of another pillow. He finds one in a metal cabinet and uses it to prop Wali up. Charlie lifts away the blanket and stares at the floor. Anything not to witness Wali's moment of truth.

"Thank you for doing that, Mr. Matthews."

Charlie pulls the blanket back up. He looks over at Wali. Wali is still smiling.

"Well I don't want to be keeping you. Will you give my kind regards to everyone back at Mine Aware?"

"I can stay, I've nowhere to be."

"No, please, it's best if you get back to the office. You're a good friend, Mr. Matthews."

Charlie takes Wali's hand in his and squeezes it. He walks out and looks up and down the corridor. Doctor Halim's nowhere to be seen.

When he returns to Mine Aware he finds the recruits lounging around the yard chatting. He decides to leave them be. In the sanctuary of his office, he calls the hospital and asks for Doctor Halim. A few minutes later he comes on the line.

"How can I help you, Mr. Matthews?" Doctor Halim says.

"Just checking in. See how's he doing?"

"We just gave him a sedative. He's been sobbing ever since you left."

TWENTY-SIX

"HOE GAAT HET met jou," the woman on the tape says. She is fast becoming a familiar acquaintance.

"Goed, en met jou?" Noor replies.

At least I won't make a fool of myself during the first ten seconds of the interview. That is if I get that far.

"Ah, there you are," she hears her father say.

Noor looks up. The last time she'd spied him he'd been reading in the garden.

"Goed, dankjewel," she says.

Aamir Khan smiles.

"You should take a break," he says. "Your brain can only retain so much in one day."

"So what would you have me do?"

"How about relax?"

"I've no interest in becoming a woman of leisure."

"And God forbid you ever become one. But a couple of hours—"

The woman on the tape utters a new phrase.

"What was that she said?" Aamir Khan says.

Noor rewinds the tape and waits for the woman to repeat the phrase.

"Ik ben hier op vakantie," the woman says.

"I am here on holiday," Noor translates.

"Now if that's not a sign from Allah, I don't know what is."

Aamir Khan saunters back in the direction of the garden. Noor sighs and turns off the tape machine. She wanders through the house and into the kitchen. Mukhtar is at the sink cleaning up the breakfast dishes.

"Ah, Miss Noor, would you like me to make you some lunch?"

"It's fine, I can make myself something."

Noor opens the fridge. Its shelves are laden with enough food to feed thirty refugees for a week. She takes out a bottle of milk.

"Mr. Matthews likes my breakfast very much," Mukhtar says. "Every morning he puts his thumb up and smacks my hand. He calls it a 'hifithe'. It is most sad about his friend, is it not?"

"You mean his colleague?"

"Yes, but he and Wali are more like friends. That is most unusual, don't you agree?"

"Yes, I suppose it is."

Noor pours herself a glass and lets the milk slip down her throat.

Oh Lord, that's good.

Noor can't resist pouring herself a second glass.

"What would you like me to cook for this evening?" Mukhtar says.

"If it's alright I'd like to make tonight's meal," she says, "but maybe you could help me obtain the ingredients. Just give me ten minutes and I'll tell you what I need."

Mukhtar leaves, and Noor contemplates what she's going to cook. She draws a blank.

What were you thinking. You haven't cooked in years.

Noor thinks about rushing after Mukhtar and withdrawing her offer.

But wouldn't it be a nice gesture? A way of showing your appreciation to Charlie, a voice says.

She opens the nearest cupboard and scans the first shelf of spice bottles—mango powder, carom seed, green cardamom, cinnamon, kala namak, coriander powder, tamarind, garam masala, tamarind, and nutmeg.

The last thing you want to show any Western man is appreciation, she thinks. *Look how he misinterpreted my smile on the bus.*

She scans the second shelf—shopa aniseed, holy basil, flax seeds, sonth dried ginger powder, mustard seed, methi leaves and zaafraan saffron. She doesn't have a clue what to do with any of them.

And if he hadn't, the voice says, *maybe Tariq would have found you by now.*

Noor shivers at the thought and feels ever more resolved to make the meal. She heads to the library and scans the bookshelves. *Afghan Cooking,* a book published in 1967, is the best she can find. She flips through it and fixes on a recipe for Afghan Kofta. Noor has fond memories of standing on a short stool in their Kabul kitchen and helping her mother knead the mixture of ground beef, onions, pepper and garlic into balls.

I can make this. Better yet I can make it well.

Six hours later she hears the front door slam shut.

Oh no, he's back.

By now she's a frazzled wreck. Mukhtar had returned from the market with sides of beef not ground beef, and by the time she'd realized his mistake he'd already left to go visit a relative. She'd looked in vain for a meat grinder, and in the end had had to settle for cutting up the beef with a knife. However hard she'd tried she couldn't get the meatballs to stick together well. Her mothers' kofta had always had this wonderful symmetrical shape; hers looked like misshapen mud pies and crumbled at the slightest touch. Though she was loathe to waste a single shred of meat, she'd tried a second batch but they'd come out no better. At that point she'd begun cursing the very notion of cooking a meal for Charlie.

It's as if I'm some clichéd housewife trying to impress her husband.

Any hope of returning to her Dutch studies has long been extinguished, and now she's faced with either canceling dinner or going with what she has. She can't countenance the former so with utmost delicacy she places her skewered meatballs in the oven and turns the heat up on the rice. She hears Charlie talking with her father on the verandah and prays he comes no further. The kitchen looks like a battle zone, and she a civilian who's gotten caught in the crossfire. The conversation ends. She waits. Nothing.

Thank God, he's gone upstairs.

"So I hear you're cooking tonight."

Noor whips around to find Charlie standing in the door-way. She attempts to push her disheveled hair off her face.

"Mind if I grab a beer?" he says.

"You don't need my permission."

"Just trying to be sensitive."

Charlie opens the fridge and pulls out a bottle of Murree Beer. Noor glances at the oven and wonders if she should be turning the meatballs by now.

"So how was your day?" she says, catching herself too late.

The clichés only multiply.

"Wali woke up," he says. "I was the one to tell him he'd lost his legs. He's devastated."

"How are you doing?"

"I have both of mine."

"You know what I mean."

"I still have a job."

Noor stops stirring.

"Jurgen called this afternoon. Said he told the folks at Mine Aware it was him who'd ordered me to go on the expedition, and if they fired me they'd never get any cooperation from the UN again. Hate to say it but you're stuck with my sorry ass."

Noor can't explain it but she's relieved. She does her best not to show it.

"I'm sure you'll be able to do a lot of good," she says.

"That's what I'm hoping."

Noor glances at the oven again; she needs to turn over the meatballs.

"I'm sorry, do you mind ..."

"It's okay," he says, "I was off for a shower anyway."

Charlie grabs another bottle and leaves. Noor opens the oven door and winces. The meatballs are burned on top. There's nothing she can do. She twists them around and clumps of meat fall away.

Maybe this is how the Soviets came to think of Afghanistan. A failed venture that could only get worse the longer it went on.

She waits for the other side to cook and tries to dissect her emotions.

Everything I said was true. He can do some good out here, and perhaps in the process he can better himself.

But why are you so happy personally? the voice inside her asks.

I'm not. Next week we'll return to the camp and as far as I'm concerned we'll never see him again.

She bends down and takes the meatballs out of the oven. She strains the rice and goes out onto the verandah. Bushra is reading a 1950s French travel guide while her father is bent over the table carving something into a strip of wood. Aamir Khan covers what he's working on.

"Dinner's ready," she says.

"Oh, how wonderful. I'll be right there."

Noor retrieves the meatballs and rice from the kitchen and places them on the sideboard in the dining room. Her father and sister join her at the table. Ten minutes pass with no sign of Charlie, and with each passing minute Noor's irritation grows.

He may be not as bad as I once thought, but he's not a lot better.

"Let's start," Bushra says.

"No, we'll wait," Noor says.

"I'm hungry."

"I can't see why, you spent the whole day in bed."

Bushra's eyes drop to the table.

"Noor, apologize to your sister," Aamir Khan says, "that was uncalled for."

"I'm sorry, Bushra, I'm a little on edge that's all."

"Why?" Bushra says.

"I just feel cooped up in this house."

"It's huge."

"I guess it's a state of mind, that's all."

They wait five more minutes. Noor fixes her father with a stare.

"You should go get him."

"That would be rude."

"And his tardiness isn't?"

"Did you make clear when dinner was?"

"The meatballs were cooking in the oven."

"That means nothing to a man, he could have thought they would take an hour."

Charlie saunters into the room in a fresh t-shirt and jeans, his hair still wet from his shower.

"Hope you guys weren't waiting for me."

Aamir Khan stands up and pulls Charlie's chair back.

"Please sit, you have had a most stressful day," Aamir Khan says.

My God, we're back in the days of the Raj, and Baba's his butler.

"I'll survive," Charlie says. "Everything okay this end?"

"Oh, most delightful, thank you," Aamir Khan says.

Noor shoves her own chair back and heads to the side-board. She begins doling out the meatballs and rice onto plates.

"So I got a proposal," Charlie says.

Noor looks his way.

"Wali's doctor says he'll be out in a month, and I've decided to look after him."

"That is wonderfully considerate of you," Aamir Khan says.

Noor knows where Charlie is heading but feels powerless to stop what he's about to say.

" So I was wondering if you'd help me, Aamir? Course I'd pay you, and you guys could go on living here, in fact you'd kind of have to if it's going to work."

Noor catches her father's eye and shakes her head. Aamir Khan looks away pretending not to have seen her.

"That is a most generous offer," Aamir Khan says.

"Trust me," Charlie says, "you'd be doing me the favor."

"Baba—" Noor says.

"Wait your turn, Noor, I think it only appropriate to ask your elder sister's opinion first."

Noor is flabbergasted. Not once since they've been in Pakistan has her father not consulted her first.

"So Bushra," Aamir Khan says, "what do you think of Charlie's offer?"

Noor tries to catch Bushra's gaze, but Bushra is staring down at the table cloth.

There's no way she'll agree to live in a house with a strange man.

Bushra mumbles something, but her voice is so quiet that no one can decipher what she said.

"I'm sorry, my dear," Aamir Khan says.

"I like living here," Bushra says.

"Then since I do too, that is settled. Thank you, Charlie, we accept your offer most gratefully."

Noor stands there with her mouth agape. Charlie smiles at her. She twists away and dollops the rest of the food out.

Why didn't he ask my opinion in the kitchen? Obviously because he wanted to set me up.

She plunks everyone's plates in front of them and returns to the sideboard to retrieve her own. She sits down and sees Charlie shoveling up a forkful of rice.

"If you don't mind," Noor says, "we always say a prayer before we start eating."

"My bad," Charlie says.

How I hate that expression.

"Bismillah ar-Rahman, ar-Raheem," the three Afghans say.

Charlie picks up a skewer and brings it up to his mouth.

"I assume you're going to say one too," Noor says.

Charlie looks bewildered by her sudden onslaught.

"Sorry, course."

Charlie closes his eyes.

"Dear God, thank you for this meal, for saving Wali's life, and for keeping everyone in this room safe. Amen."

He opens his eyes.

"Oh, that was most heartfelt," Aamir Khan says.

And you couldn't be more of a sycophant.

Out the corner of her eye, she watches Charlie take a meatball off his skewer and pop it in his mouth. He chews it over and over as if he's having difficulty swallowing it. He reaches for his glass of water and takes a large gulp. The meatball slithers down his throat.

"If you don't like it just say," Noor says.

"What do you mean? It's good."

"Sounds like faint praise to me."

"What? Should I've said that it was awesome?"

"Not if you don't believe that to be true."

Charlie shakes his head and eats some rice.

"Well your rice is awesome, Noor. Thanks for making it."

Noor tries some. It has the texture of daal that's been left in water overnight.

"Have you ever read *On The Road*, Charlie?" Aamir Khan says.

"It's got to be my favorite book," Charlie says.

"I am ashamed to say I had never read it before, but this morning I noticed it in your library—"

"You're lying," Noor says.

Everyone looks in her direction. She stares Charlie down.

"Come on," Charlie says, "every kid in America with half a brain's read Kerouac."

"The rice, you don't think it's awesome. There were no high-fives, no thumbs up. Besides it's cold and sticky."

"Maybe I like it that way."

"No, you don't."

Charlie holds his hands up.

"We really need to fight over this?"

"Just so you're aware," Noor says, "the reason it's the way it is, is because you took so long to join us."

"That's the reason?"

"When someone goes to the trouble of cooking you dinner the least you can do is come down on time."

Charlie picks up his napkin and wipes his hands with it. He fixes Noor with the first cold stare she's ever received from him. It disconcerts her.

"You ever thought that sometimes people say things to be nice?" Charlie says.

"That's what every liar tells himself," Noor says.

Aamir Khan's fork clatters onto his plate.

"Noor."

"No, it's cool, Aamir," Charlie says. "I'm happy to give Noor an honest review if she wants one."

Charlie pops a meatball into his mouth, and takes what seems like an eon to swallow it.

"So?" Noor says.

"If you'd ripped the sole off my shoe and cut it into tiny, little pieces it'd have tasted better."

Bushra gasps.

"Night Aamir," Charlie says. "Night Bushra."

Charlie shoves his chair back and strides from the room.

"I do not know what has gotten into you lately," Aamir Khan says.

He stands up and leaves the room. Bushra follows him.

"I'm not hungry," she says.

Noor sits there at the table, staring at the crumbled meatballs. She wants to cry but refuses to.

TWENTY-SEVEN

NOOR SITS ON the bus, her application essay in her hands. She keeps her head bowed and her eyes on the floor in an attempt to show her face to as few people as possible. She imagines every man that glances in her direction to be one of Tariq's brothers-in-arms.

When Elma had called and suggested meeting at a tea shop in Qissa Khawani bazaar, Noor hadn't protested. How could she? If anything she felt fortunate that Elma hadn't forgotten all about her.

But why here of all places?

At the entrance to the bazaar, she gets off and enters its shadowy warren of alleys. Their very tightness only increases her paranoia. At any moment she fears someone is going to reach out from a doorway and snatch her. She finds the tea shop, squished between a tailor's and a book store. Up front its owner sits on a raised platform in front of two massive brass urns. Blue and beige teapots dangle above him, and each time one of his boy servers races up, he grabs one and fills it with either sweet, milky chai or dark green kahwah. The tea shop is throbbing with customers. Noor looks for Elma but doesn't see her. She does, however, see an empty table towards the back. She threads her way over to it and sits down. A boy comes over, and she orders a cup of kahwah. She glances around the tea shop. Every man in the place, and there are only men here, is staring at her. She turns her head away. 'Never draw attention to yourself,' her father has often counseled her, yet in this establishment it seems impossible not to.

Her thoughts stray to the previous evening. Even now she's baffled as to what came over her.

To get worked up by him of all people.

All night she'd tossed and turned, and that morning her father had insisted she apologize to Charlie. As a child her father had scolded her so rarely that when he had she'd retreat to her room in tears for the rest of the day. She hadn't done that in this instance, but it had shook her up nonetheless. The apology won't be pleasant; in fact just thinking about it makes her queasy.

But better that than having to face Baba's continued displeasure.

A hand rests on her shoulder, and she twists around. She finds Elma standing there in jeans and a jacket, a head scarf draped lazily over her head.

"Sorry, I'm late. I took Rod to get a shalwar kameez next door, and you know how these tailors are; it's like they have to show you every ream of cloth in the store."

Noor nods as if she does.

"So is that the essay?" Elma says noticing the pages in Noor's hands.

"It still needs a lot of work."

"Well let me be the judge of that."

Noor hands the essay over and pulls her head scarf tighter. Elma notices and takes a sweep of the tea shop. She curses the assembled throng in Pashtu, and the men look away, ashamed.

"That's better," she says.

Elma focuses on the essay. Noor knows it by heart, and she can't help but recite it in her head as Elma reads it.

On my twelfth birthday my father gave me Three Guineas by Virginia Woolf. This may strike you as a peculiar gift from a father to a daughter, especially to a daughter so young, but you must understand my father is a peculiar man, peculiar in all the best possible ways.

To say the book had an impact on me would be a gross understatement. I suspect this was because the subjects that preoccupied it were so prominent in my part of the world. There's no better example than Afghanistan of Three Guineas' central message regarding the interconnectedness between male patriarchy, education and war.

I'm an Afghan refugee from a war that's claimed over a million lives, a war that's been raging for a decade now and, despite the imminent fall of the Communist regime, looks likely to continue on in some new and reconstituted form.

I'm also a woman from a society that's never placed any value in women's work, where young girls can be bartered for the misdeeds of their male family members, and which every day finds new ways to restrict what women can do. Here men rule supreme with women unable to make decisions of even the slightest import. Most of us are forced into burqas when we venture outside, and inside we must labor for our menfolk without reward. The greatest insult of all is that our men tell us they do this out of concern for our honor, but there is no honor to be had in this world unless you have freedom and are treated as an equal.

Despite our history, martial qualities are still celebrated by my people as if they're the essence of what it means to be a man. It's ironic that Afghanistan is known for its opium fields, for if anyone is a ruinous addict it's my country that bemoans this war yet continues to instill in our boys a reverence for fighting.

At present the United Nations ranks Afghanistan as the poorest nation on the planet. When you exclude half your population from productive life and only teach the other half how to fight and recite (rather than understand) the Holy Quran how could that not be the case? Given this situation it is understandable that I was seduced by the words of the outsider in Three Guineas who says "As a woman I have no country. As a woman I want no country. As a woman my country is the whole world." And yet as Virginia Woolf predicted I'm unable to *abandon my country, and I hope you'll forgive me if I quote her further with a little artistic license.*

"And if, when reason has said its say, still some obstinate emotion remains, some love of Afghanistan dropped into a child's ear by the cawing of rooks in a mulberry tree, by the hum of a kite overhead, or by Pashtun voices murmuring nursery rhymes, this drop of pure, if irrational, emotion she will make serve her to give to Afghanistan first what she desires of peace and freedom for the whole world."

You see despite the indignities I've experienced and the tragedies I've endured I still love my country and hope to craft a better future for it one day. I fervently believe that if we can promote the education of women we might slowly but surely break our ruinous obsession with war. It should be an education that stresses compassion and non violence to our children because one day that will turn into advice given to imams and tribal leaders, governors and presidents, and aggression and wars over property (or may I be so bold to say human souls) will lessen, and a more peaceful coexistence of humans as equals will result.

This may seem like some fanciful dream but isn't Germany a country that celebrates such values? If the society that gave birth to the holocaust and the blitzkrieg can achieve this, can't we Afghans do so too?

To do my part I need further education, an education in educating so to speak, and that's something I'll never be able to obtain living here in a refugee camp on the outskirts of the most fundamentalist city in Pakistan.

In Virginia Woolf's other great treatise In A Room Of One's Own, she contended that an equally talented sister of Shakespeare's would never have written a word, let alone a play, for all people need a living wage and a private place or else their potential will never be realized. What I humbly ask you to provide me with is just that – an opportunity to broaden my mind at your inspiring university with just enough money that I might live. I might not write Hamlet or Twelfth Night, in fact I can guarantee you I won't, but I know if you are kind enough to afford me this opportunity that I will flourish and maybe, just maybe, I can be part of a wave that will turn my beloved country into a more equitable and peaceful place for all Afghans, and by extension for everyone in the world.

Yours truly, Noor Jehan Khan

Noor watches Elma for a sign. Elma's eyes still haven't left the pages.

She hates it.

"How many words is it?" Elma says.

"Eight hundred and fifty-one," Noor says.

Elma nods.

"It's too long, isn't it?" Noor says. "Too saccharine, too convoluted."

Elma looks up. Her eyes are wet with tears.

"Don't change a thing, it's beautiful."

"You really mean that?"

"There's no way they won't give you a scholarship after reading this."

Noor feels her heart beat fast.

Calm down, you're not there yet.

"Now we just need to get your Dutch up to speed."

"I'm practicing every day."

"Good but you and I need to meet. We start Monday at my house. No excuses anymore. Now how's your father?"

"He's getting better, thank you. And how about you? How are you doing?"

Elma seems surprised that anyone would care to ask.

"Can you keep a secret?" she grins.

"Of course."

"I'm in love."

"With whom?"

"Have you ever been to the Hunza Valley?"

"I've read about it."

"It's like the Gods created it as a garden for themselves. I took Rod there to see a couple of girls schools we started. These girls, they don't even look South Asian. They have fair skin, blue eyes, some even have blonde hair -"

"Alexander's lost battalion."

"Exactly. For two days they took us around, through the harvested fields, up the terraced hillsides, past the baskets of apricots drying in the sun, the snow covered peaks jutting into the sky above us, and I felt a connection to him like I've felt for no man before. I'm not going to lie to you, Noor, I've been with a lot of men, more than I care to remember, but in that valley, amongst those people so cut off from the rest of the world, I felt chaste and pure. It was like I was reborn. We stayed in this hotel overlooking the valley, and each night we'd sit on its balcony, blankets wrapped around us, and stare at the mountains as the sun set."

Elma takes a sip of her tea, and Noor waits, desperate to know what happened.

"The last night he reached out his hand and took mine in his. That was it, nothing more, yet it was the most magical thing I've ever felt in my life."

Elma blushes.

"Look at me, babbling away like a silly teenage girl."

"No, I think it's beautiful," Noor says. "I'm happy for you."

"How about you? Have you ever been in love?"

"Me? No."

"Not even for a moment?"

"Not really."

"Not really's not ever."

"Back in Kabul when I was nine there was a boy, Omar, the son of our cook. I suppose I pined over him for a week."

"Why just a week?"

Noor blushes at the memory.

"Oh come on," Elma says, "you've got to tell me now."

"I caught him defecating into a flower pot."

Elma giggles.

"No way, what was he thinking?"

"It was early, Bjorn, my rabbit had escaped, and I was looking for him. I went into the vegetable garden at the back of the house, and there was Omar with his trousers around his ankles squatting over a flower pot. I don't think he even knew I saw him."

Elma collapses into a laughing fit. The men at the table next to them look in their direction. One of them flashes a lecherous smile at Elma.

"Shit, I woke up the creeps," Elma says. "Come on let's get out of here."

Elma drops some rupees on the table and takes a hold of Noor's hand. She leads her out of the teashop and into the cramped tailor's next door.

"Rod?" Elma says.

"Almost there," Rod shouts out from behind a partition at the back.

Elma and Noor sit down on a big roll of fabric lying on the floor.

"So this Omar," Elma says, "did he put you off boys for life?"

"No, this war did, this situation we find ourselves in."

"As a woman I have no man. As a woman I want no man. As a woman my man is the whole world."

"Is it so bad to think that?"

Elma ponders the question.

"For a long time I thought the same way as you. I enjoyed men, don't get me wrong, but I didn't want to be tied to one, worse yet rely on one. My career is my first love, I suspect it always will be."

"That's why I so admire you."

"But there comes a point that the idea of sharing your life with someone becomes incredibly appealing. 'No man is an island,' who said that?"

"John Donne."

"Right. Well the longer I live, the more I think it's true, not just in the work we do but in our personal lives. I think you're going to be surprised, one day you're going to meet a man and fall in love with him without even realizing it."

Rod jumps out from behind the partition in a lime green shalwar kameez and grey waistcoat. The proud tailor stands behind him beaming.

"What do you think?" Rod says, twirling around and around.

Elma jumps up clapping.

"Oh my God, you look so dashing."

"How about you, Noor? You think I look sufficiently Pakistani."

"You could run for the National Assembly."

"And I just might. From what I hear it's a license to print money."

Rod sits down on one of the fabric rolls, and Elma snuggles up next to him.

"I'm glad you're here," Rod says, "I had a couple more things I wanted to ask you."

"Of course," Noor says, "what do you want to know?"

Rod looks over at the tailor.

"You mind if we hang out here a while?"

The tailor beams at them as if Rod has bestowed on his humble establishment the greatest of honors. He claps his hands, and a young boy comes racing out from the back. The tailor barks at him, and the boy soon returns with cups of steaming kahwah from the shop next door. For the next two hours the three of them talk, not just about life in the camps but the future for Afghans in general and Afghan women in particular. They touch on questions of identity, both cultural and gender, the role of Islam, and the neocolonialism of both the West and Saudi Arabia. Noor feels a visceral thrill.

This is what it will be like in Holland.

She imagines herself in some smoky Amsterdam coffee shop, squeezed in tight with her fellow students, arguing the great topics of the day while outside it snows and boats bob on the icy canals.

At some point Elma insists on buying Noor a couple of new shalwar kameez. They are her first in four years. Finally the tailor mentions that he must close his shop. Noor feels like a child who's been told by her parents that it's time for bed. Rod and Elma offer to drive her back to the camps, but she tells them she is fine taking the bus. For some reason, she thinks it'd only diminish the evening if she were to explain why she and her family are living at Charlie's.

The bus ride is uneventful, and she returns to the house still buzzing. She walks through the sitting room and out onto the verandah. In the fading light, her father and Mukhtar are working on a ramp to place over the steps. Her father sees her and waves. She smiles, relieved. He has no idea she was even gone. She goes back inside, and begins preparing her apology to Charlie.

TWENTY-EIGHT

"YOU SEE THAT man over there with no arms?" Wali says.

Charlie looks over at a scrubby lawn where an impromptu cricket match is underway. It's safe to say there isn't a more bizarre cricket match going on anywhere else in the world. A one armed man bowls the ball to a no legged man. The no-legged man hits it right at the man with no arms, who with no way to catch it, lets the ball smack him in the chest before he kicks it towards a one-legged man, who hops on over and throws it back to the one armed wicketkeeper.

"Most wonderful bowler," Wali says.

"You shitting me?"

"He puts the ball under his neck and bowls it with a little twist of the neck. It gives the ball a most wicked spin."

This time the one armed bowler bowls one with pace. The legless man swings too late, and the balls hits him square on the forehead. The legless man crumples to the ground.

"Jesus, a mine couldn't kill him but a cricket ball just did," Charlie says.

Those that can run over to the man and drag him to his wheelchair. A one legged, one armed man takes his place at the wicket.

"So how you doing?" Charlie says.

"I told you, I'm most well."

"You can't bullshit a bullshitter, Wali."

"Oh, I like that expression."

Wali grabs his pad and pen from a pouch in his wheelchair and writes it down.

"Well?"

"My life is over, Mr. Matthews, is it not?"

"It's going to be tough, no doubt, but over? Far from it."

"I will never have sex now."

Charlie looks at Wali.

"Shit, did something—"

"No, no, it was unharmed by the accident, in fact I've been waking up with the most glorious erections. Doctor Halim's most impressed. But I know of no woman who would want to have sexual intercourse with a man who looks like me."

"Bullshit."

"Don't bullshit a bullshitter, Mr. Matthews."

"I'm not. There was this movie recently, Tom Cruise was in it, where he played this real guy, Ron Kovic. He was shot in Vietnam, paralyzed from the waist down, shit, his dick didn't even work, and women were all over him."

"Maybe he is the exception."

"Look at me, Wali."

Wali turns his way and pouts.

"One of the things I learned long ago is that women don't care what you look like, they care how you treat them. It's all attitude. You come with me to New York, and the girls are going to be all over you."

Wali smiles. Charlie is unsure if he is doing so just to placate him.

"Ah, now take a look," he says.

He gestures towards the field. The man with no arms runs up with the ball under his chin and releases it down the wicket. It bounces in front of the one armed batsman, takes a bamboozling turn and knocks over the stumps. His team-mates run, hobble and drag themselves over to him.

"I'll be damned," Charlie says.

Charlie pulls out his cigarettes and lights one for each of them. The smoke drifts away in the evening breeze.

"So how is everything at Mine Aware?" Wali says.

"I'm trying, but nothing seems to work. They just don't listen. No, that's not right, they listen fine, but the moment you turn your back they totally slack off."

"Slack off?"

Wali sticks the cigarette between his lips and grabs his pad.

"You know, don't try?"

"And how do you know this?'

"I gave them this exercise yesterday. All they had to do was lie on their stomachs and sort through a bag of rice. It's a way to build patience, get in their heads what the prone position is like. So I go around the back of the compound and climb on to the roof of the storeroom to watch. You know how many were still in that position five minutes later?"

"Not many I assume."

"Two."

"Please tell me you didn't say anything."

"Course I did. I mean, why wouldn't I?"

Wali takes a deep drag.

"Mr. Matthews, all aid workers are the same. They come out here and tell us how they want to make a difference. My word if we Afghans were paid one dollar for every time we heard those words we would be a rich nation. But soon they get frustrated, things don't go as expected, and, of course, they cannot blame themselves, as we all know they are perfect, so they blame the Afghans, treat us like we cannot be trusted."

"But most of my guys can't."

"That's not true, it just takes time to build trust, on both sides. Until then they will only do what is necessary to keep their jobs."

"So you're saying they don't trust me?"

Wali laughs.

"For nine years the West tells the Afghans, 'we stand beside you, we are your friends forever', but look what happens, as soon as we defeat the Soviets, your aid agencies start pulling out, and your governments lose interest. Trust me, all these men know someone who lost a job with an agency this year, and they have no reason to think this one will be any different?"

"I just hired them."

"Yes but for how long? Don't think they don't know about the recruits who lost their jobs when you arrived. They say to themselves, 'When the next boss comes in December why will that not happen to us too?' Can you promise it won't?"

Charlie knows he can't.

"So what do I do?" he says.

"Someone very wise once said an Afghan is like a lamb, 'if you pull him by power towards heaven he will resist but if taken with love he will happily go with you even to the depths of hell.' Trust them, Mr. Matthews, in all things, and I promise you, you will see big changes."

Charlie tosses his cigarette away.

"You know something, you lose your legs and you get ten times smarter."

Wali laughs.

"Come on," Charlie says, "I told Doctor Halim we'd only be gone five minutes."

Charlie gets behind Wali's chair and pushes him towards his wing.

"Just so you know, I've hired someone to look after you. He and his two daughters will be staying in the house."

"How old are these daughters?"

"Early twenties."

"And this man has no concerns about you being around them?"

"He's not like your average Afghan."

"You can say that again. Are his daughters attractive?"

"One is, I suppose."

"Yet she's not married?"

"She's impossible. She's turned down over thirty proposals."

"Then she must be much better looking than you're letting on."

And even more impossible.

After Noor's latest outburst Charlie's come to the conclusion that there's nothing he can to do to make her like him.

They reach the door to Wali's wing. Wali sucks on his cigarette like a condemned man, and flicks it away. Charlie pulls him through the door, and a nurse takes command of the chair.

"Ghazal will vouch for my erections, won't you Ghazal?" Wali says.

The nurse rolls his eyes and pushes Wali down the corridor to his room.

"I promise you, Mr. Matthews," Wali shouts, "when I get to New York I will not disappoint your beautiful American women."

"You better not!"

Charlie heads outside into the parking lot. He shivers; the nights are getting colder. He gets on his bike and starts back to the office. Better that than risking another verbal assault from Noor.

***

THE RECRUITS SIT cross-legged on the ground. In front of each of them is a mine detector, a blast helmet, a pair of protective gloves, and a demining vest. Charlie faces them with a sheaf of paper in his hand.

"I want to start by being totally honest with you."

A few of the recruits lean forward intrigued.

"I'm going to be abandoning you in a few months, but before that happens, we're all going to get a new boss, a guy called Stephen Adams. From what everyone tells me he's a good guy, but that's beside the point because, you know what, there'll come a time when he abandons you too, and so will every other Westerner you'll ever meet in your life. It's your history to be abandoned, and I hate to say it's ours to abandon people like you

"I guess what I'm trying to say is that I don't care whether you learn to be deminers or not. I mean on some ego driven level I do, everyone likes to feel they've accomplished something in this life, but at the end of the day, five, ten, twenty years from now I'm not going to be living in Afghanistan, scared shitless every time my child goes out to play that they might step on a mine. So the real question is whether you want to have the capacity to demine your country or not? To learn a skill that when we abandon you, you can still use to better the lives of your family and friends? If you don't, I'll make it easy. Just stand up, right now, and head to Qasim's office. I told him to give you six months wages no questions asked."

The recruits glance at each other.

"Right now?" Jawad says.

"That's right?" Charlie says.

Jawad looks over at Mansoor. Mansoor giggles, and the two young men jump to their feet. Charlie goes over and hugs them.

"Ma'salaam," he says.

They smile back as if they've won the lottery.

"Ma'salaam, Mr. Matthews."

Jawad and Mansoor saunter towards the main building.

"Anyone else?" Charlie says.

It's obvious a few are tempted, but no one else gets up.

"Okay I'm sure you're wondering why all your equipment's in front of you. It's very simple, it's yours now, and I
have a letter here for each of you that confirms that. If you
want you can store it all here, but if you prefer you can take it
home. Hell, if you don't believe in what we're doing you can
go to the bazaar and sell it. I bet you could get one, maybe
two thousand dollars for it all. It's up to you, it's yours now."

The recruits sit in stunned silence.

"Najib?" Charlie says.

"Yes, Mr. Matthews."

"You mind handing these letters out."

"Of course not."

Najib jumps up, and Charlie hands them over.

"Good night guys."

Charlie walks towards the main gate. He makes certain that
he doesn't look back.

TWENTY-NINE

NOOR HEARS THE front door open and feels her heart skip a beat. She knows it's him. She focuses on her Scrabble tiles. The door creaks open.

"As-Salaam Alaykum," she hears him say.

"Wa'alaykum asalaam," Aamir Khan says, "it is most wonderful to see you."

Aamir Khan glares at Noor. Noor turns towards Charlie. He looks warily at her.

"Did you have a good day?" she says.

"Yeah, turned out better than I could've imagined."

"I'm delighted to hear that."

Charlie frowns. Noor attempts a smile to put him at ease but ends up with something that resembles a grimace. From Charlie's expression, it's clear he's now utterly discombobulated.

"I want to apologize for the other night," she says. "I was unnecessarily confrontational."

"Totally cool," he says, "it was childish of me to storm off."

It was.

The two of them stare at each other neither sure what to say next. Noor decides to cut her losses and returns once more to her tiles. Charlie wanders away and starts chatting with Bushra at the other end of the room.

What on earth could they be talking about?

Charlie gets down on his knees and helps Bushra with her puzzle. To Noor's astonishment, Bushra giggles. Noor bristles; if she didn't know better she'd think she was jealous. Charlie looks over and catches her staring. She snaps her head away and stares at her tiles. She hears him approach.

"So everything good with you guys?" Charlie says.

"Apart from my daughter showing me scant mercy everything is most delightful, thank you," Aamir Khan says.

Noor sees a word—vow. She puts her tiles down.

"I'm out," she says.

"You see," Aamir Khan says shaking his head. "Have you played much?"

"My mom and I used to play from time to time," Charlie says.

"Then you must take my place."

"I don't know—"

"Please, you would be doing me a solid favor by allowing me to return to my book."

"Well I guess ..."

Aamir Khan escapes to the leather reading chair. Charlie looks at Noor.

"You cool?" he says.

"Of course," she says.

I might have to be polite, but there's nothing stopping me from eviscerating him.

Charlie sits on the ottoman across from her. Noor scoops the tiles back into the bag and holds them out. Charlie retrieves seven tiles. She takes seven of her own. B—I—I—I—O—O—X. There are way too many vowels, but the X could earn her a decent score. She rearranges her letters. 'Box' seems the best option.

"You go first," Charlie says.

"Any reason?" she says.

"I don't know, ladies first, that kind of thing."

How patronizing.

"No, you go," she smiles.

"Fine, whatever you want."

Charlie lays down "serve".

"What's that?" he says. "Eighteen?"

She writes down his score and scans the board. 'Box' is now available with two double letter scores, and with the 'so' and 'ex' that go with it, it comes to forty-two points.

Look what your sexist attitude got you.

She places her word on the board and looks triumphantly at Charlie only to discover he's looking around the room like a distracted toddler.

"What you reading there, Aamir?" Charlie says.

"Middlemarch," Aamir Khan says.

"Who's it by again?"

"George Eliot."

"He any good?"

"George Eliot was actually a woman."

"It was a pseudonym," Noor says. "She used a man's name because women weren't taken seriously as writers back then."

"Guess you learn something new every day," Charlie says.

"I guess you do if you never went to college."

Aamir Khan peers over the top of his book at Noor. She wonders if she's gone too far. Charlie smiles back at her.

"You think you're going to win this pretty easily, don't you?" he says.

I severely doubt you'll come within a hundred points of me.

"I'm sure you'll provide me with stiff competition," she says.

Charlie leans in.

"Watch out, I just might kick your butt."

Noor can't stop herself from blushing.

Right that's it. No mercy.

Charlie puts 'ad' perpendicular to 'serve' to achieve both 'ad' and 'served'.

Only an amateur puts down the first word that pops into their brain.

She takes three more tiles. I—T—U.

Could I have picked worse?

She stares at her tiles.

"If you're up for it, Aamir," Charlie says, "I was thinking you could come with me to the hospital on Wednesday, you know say 'hi' to Wali, that sort of thing."

"That sounds like a wonderful idea," Aamir Khan says. "In the meantime I have started reading up on rehabilitation methods."

Noor places 'it' on the board.

"'Exit' for eleven," she says.

She takes two more tiles and draws a U and a Z. She lets out an inadvertent sigh.

"Shitty tiles?" Charlie says.

"Of course not."

"You know what they say, a bad workman blames his tools."

"I don't have bad tiles."

Charlie grins; it's clears he doesn't believe her. Charlie puts his word on the board.

"What does 'heir' get me?" he says.

"Are you incapable of adding it up yourself?"

"Okay, chill—seven for 'heir', five for 'ha'—so twelve total."

"Was that so hard?"

"Not as hard as those tiles of yours, I'm guessing."

Noor does everything in her power to concentrate. It's impossible; she knows he's staring at her. She looks up and confirms her suspicion.

"So?" he says.

She's tempted to exchange her tiles but couldn't bear the ridicule he'd fling her way.

"'Our' for five points," she says.

"Thought you said you didn't have bad tiles."

"I didn't."

"Then five's kind of a shitty score, don't you think?"

Noor glances over at her father. His face is hidden by his book. She suspects he's smirking behind it. Charlie places 'quart' off the 't' of 'exit'.

How on earth did he come up with that?

"Twenty-eight, not so bad," Charlie says.

Noor pulls out two more letters. O and T.

Oh dear Lord.

"So did you guys play this a lot back in Kabul?" Charlie says.

"To tell you the truth, we have played it more in recent years," Aamir Khan says. "Soon after we arrived I carved some wooden letters and drew a board on the back of a poster, a Hekmatyar poster to be precise. Given his distaste for girls' education I always thought it fitting that we rubbed his face in the dirt whenever we played."

Charlie laughs.

Good God, what a couple of sycophants.

Noor stares at her tiles. She can't find a spot for her Z.

"So what you got?" Charlie says.

And how I despise his impatience.

"'It' for fifteen," she says laying down her tiles.

Her father comes over and takes a look.

"You could have done 'ziti' off the end of 'quart' for forty-three, my dear."

"Or you could have done zit," Charlie says.

"Zit?" she says.

"You know a pimple, like the one on your chin."

Noor blushes once more. She pushes her chin down into her chest.

"Good night, my love," Aamir Khan says. "I am retiring to bed."

No, don't leave me.

Aamir Khan bends down and kisses her on the cheek before bidding Charlie good night. Noor looks around. Bushra's nowhere to be seen. She must have slunk off too.

"Now your dad's gone there's no shame in quitting," Charlie grins.

Noor doesn't deem his remark worthy of a reply.

"Okay, I guess it's to the death," he says.

"To the death," she says.

Charlie lays down his tiles.

"Quarte and elate," he says. "For twenty-two."

How could he possibly know what quarte means? He can't. It was just a lucky guess.

She pulls another 'O' and a 'G' from the bag.

Finally.

"Zit, that was the word?" she says.

"You got it."

"Zoo and Zit," she says. "Forty eight points."

She looks across at Charlie and gives him the smuggest smile possible.

Two more rounds and it'll be over.

Charlie puts down three tiles.

"Okay," he says, "'Fie' and 'de' with the triple word score makes twenty-one."

"Neither of those are words," Noor says.

"What you talking about? De's the language of a recently discovered Amazonian tribe."

"And how do you know that?"

"My mom took me on a trip up the Amazon."

"And you managed to learn their language?"

"He no ra te la dosaya doda."

"I assume that's your sorry attempt at one of their expressions."

"Means 'my brother likes goats more than girls'."

Noor giggles despite herself.

"And fie?" she says.

"It's a shrub. A Chinese botanist stumbled on it in deepest Congo and named it after a girl he loved. Rumor has it she was so beautiful he thought this gesture might win her over."

"Typical man."

"When he returned, he discovered an astronomer had named a newly-found galaxy after her, and already won her heart."

"I'd prefer to have a shrub named after me than a galaxy. At least a shrub's a part of this world."

"You got a point."

She looks up to see if he's mocking her, but there's nothing in his expression to suggest so.

"So you cool with both of them?" he says.

"Absolutely not, I'm challenging."

Noor grabs the dictionary. She looks up 'de' first. It isn't an Amazonian tribe, but it is a prefix.

How stupid. I was certain I knew all the two letter words.

She flips forward to the f's. She can't believe it. There it is. Fie—an exclamation, Middle English, used to express disgust or outrage.

"Neither of them match your definition," she says.

"But they're in there, aren't they?" Charlie grins.

Noor purses her lips.

"So I get another turn, right?"

"Go."

"Remind me how much do I get if I use all my tiles?"

"Fifty points, why?"

Charlie places 'painted' down the right edge of the board.

"Thirty eight for 'painted' plus the fifty gets me eighty eight. You mind adding up the scores."

Noor scrawls down eighty-eight on Charlie's side of the ledger, the number even more unbelievable now it's there in pencil.

"You're at two-hundred and fifty five," she says.

"And you?"

"Two-hundred and two."

Noor renews her focus but nothing seems to work. The next few rounds pass in a blur with her words routinely coming second best to Charlie's. As she lays each word down her fury mounts, not at Charlie so much but at herself.

How can you be losing to him?

She looks at the score—three-hundred and twenty-three to two-hundred and forty-two—she knows it's impossible to beat him.

"You win," she says.

She glances up expecting him to gloat. Instead he looks at her with sympathy. It infuriates her all the more.

"Want to go again?" he says.

"Of course."

"Great, let me just stretch my legs."

Charlie wanders out onto the verandah. Noor looks at the clock. Nine o'clock. It's late. She wonders if she should've challenged him to another game.

You have to beat him. You won't be able to live with yourself if you don't.

Noor scans the dictionary for words she doesn't know, and when she next looks at the clock it's ten past.

Where the hell is he?

She strides out on the verandah and finds him leaning against the railing, a cigarette in his hand.

"Are you coming?" she says.

"Sorry, thought I'd have a second."

He takes a final drag and flicks the butt over the side. He looks over at the oak tree lit blazing white by the full moon.

"That tree sure is tall."

"I've climbed higher."

Charlie looks across at Noor.

"You don't believe me?" she says.

"No, I'm just amazed that's all."

"I bet I could climb higher in it than you."

"That a challenge?"

"Yes, I suppose it is."

Without waiting, Noor marches over to the tree. She takes off her sandals, tucks her kameez into her pants and starts climbing. When she reaches the first bough, she looks down. Charlie's at the base of the trunk.

"Hey, give me a moment," he shouts.

She doesn't and continues on up past the second and third boughs. Above her the trunk splits two ways. To the left it carries on towards Charlie's balcony. To the right it ascends vertically for fifteen more feet before splitting off again. She grips the right hand trunk and continues her ascent. Halfway up the bark becomes smoother. There are almost no crevasses or cracks to dig her fingers and toes into.

"Still coming," she hears Charlie say.

She grips the trunk and begins thrusting her whole body up, one inch at a time. Her arms ache, her breath gets more ragged. She looks up. She's two feet away from the split.

"Noor," Charlie shouts, "you can stop now—you win."

Noor sees a branch sticking out of the bough above. She grabs it and pulls herself up. The branch breaks, and for a split second she's certain she's going to fall to her death.

And all to impress a boy.

Her other hand flails, and by some miracle her fingertips latch onto another branch. She pulls herself onto the bough. She stands up, her heart beating wildly, and yells out in triumph.

"Noor, please" Charlie shouts. "Come down before you kill yourself."

Noor detects real concern in his voice and finds it strangely comforting. She takes a moment to gaze at the twinkling lights of Peshawar before scooting down the trunk. Charlie is standing in the hollow of the split.

"Unbelievable," he says. "Insane but unbelievable."

Noor grins, her face flushed, her heart still beating madly.

"I could always climb higher than my brother," she says. "It infuriated him."

She waltzes along the lowest bough as if to confirm her fearlessness and sits down. Charlie comes over and plops down beside her.

"So did you really go to the Amazon," she says, "or was that just something you made up?"

"Oh no, my mom was always taking me on trips. Paris, London, Costa Rica, New Zealand. She had this Mark Twain quote she never tired of saying, hell she'd even yell it out to me when she dropped me off at school."

"What was it?"

"'Twenty years from now you will be more disappointed by the things you didn't do than by the ones you did. So throw off your bowlines, sail away from the safe harbor and catch the trade winds in your sails. Explore. Dream! Discover!'"

That is exactly what I am going to do.

"The Amazon had always been a dream of hers, something she'd told me we'd do when I graduated high school, but that spring she was diagnosed with cancer, and she decided to move the trip forward."

"How long did you go for?"

"Ten days. We flew into Lima and took this tiny plane over the Andes to a town called Iquitos where we boarded an old rubber boat. You ever read *Love In The Time of Cholera*?"

"A couple of years ago."

Noor looks away so Charlie can't see she's blushing. What she doesn't mention is that the book both aroused and disgusted her in equal measure, with Florentino Ariza seeming to embody everything she despised in men, and everything she hoped they might be.

"Well remember the boat Florentino and Fermina take when they're really old, that's kind of like the one we were on. Rickety, low to the water, dim cabins, creaking air conditioners, a big smokestack near the back. It was magical. I pretended I was Teddy Roosevelt searching for some undiscovered tribe."

"The De's?"

"Yeah, never did find them, but I saw a bunch of amazing stuff; pink river dolphins, tree frogs, squirrel monkeys, manatees, hell so many different types of birds you lost count, and, of course, and for a thirteen year old boy the coolest thing of all, piranha. They even let me help catch them, and at night we'd grill them under the stars. It was the greatest trip of my life."

"Did your father go too?"

"The only trip he ever went on was to London and that was because he had business there. To be honest he and my mom should have never got married."

"Then why did they?"

"Because for one summer after college my father thought he wanted to live this free spirited, selfless life, and during it my mom got pregnant. After they got married my Dad became a banker instead of an activist, and before my mom knew it, he'd joined all the right clubs, become an elder in the local church and set out on his new life's mission of becoming a respected pillar of the community. To be honest my mom should've left him then and there, but for all her free-spiritedness she believed children needed to grow up in a family."

"Do you have any brothers and sisters?"

"When I was born my mom got an infection, and they had to remove her uterus. It was a serious bummer for my dad, especially when he realized I took after Mom. He was always trying to steer me towards the things he thought important, and like some guerrilla warrior she always tried to counter his influence. The trips were part of that. Though he'd never admit it, I think her death was a relief to him. Eighteen months after she died he married this uptight paralegal in his office, and they had twins. Finally he had the family he'd always dreamed of, yet for some crazy reason he wouldn't let me just do what I wanted."

"And what was that?"

"Be an artist—that was my dream at least. He couldn't understand it. 'Art is something you go to benefits for,' he'd tell me, 'it's no career,' and when it came to choosing a university, he wouldn't let me apply to CUNY and instead used all his influence to get me into Duke. I think deep down he thought that one day I would change just like he had, and thank him. But I was never like him ..."

"You were like your mother."

"I felt paralyzed, like I was heading down some path I'd never be able to get off, and then one night, just before I was about to head down to North Carolina, Beau Geste came on TV, and suddenly I had an idea. I'd enlist in the army—it was the biggest 'F you' I could think of. I called him on the way to boot camp. He was so stunned he could hardly speak, he kind of just sputtered and told me if I got on that bus I'd be dead to him. We haven't spoken since."

"Did you enjoy the army?"

"If I thought my dad's rules were stupid, the army's were insane, but in some ways I didn't mind. In the army, at least, I knew none of it was personal. And I made friends, with the type of people I'd never have come across at Duke—black guys from the Bronx, farm boys from Kansas, high school dropouts from the Jersey Shore. Don't get me wrong, there are times I regret not going to university, there's a lot I wish I knew which I don't, but every time I meet college graduates back home all I see are a bunch of people who're only interested in making money. It's as if college has sucked every ounce of originality out of them. My buddies in the army were different. We may have been the lowest of the low but we were loyal to each other, a brotherhood—it was the first time since my mom died that I felt like I had a family again."

Charlie looks over and gives her a bashful smile.

"Sorry, must be boring you to death," he says.

"Not at all. I'm sure your mother is really proud of you."

"I'd love to think that, but unlike you, I don't believe in an afterlife."

"But she did?"

"What do you mean?"

"That song, *My Sweet Lord*, the one she had you sing."

"She was never religious."

"But it sounds like she was spiritual."

"Yeah, I suppose she was."

"So how does the song go?"

"It's really just the same words repeated over and over."

"Sing it for me."

"Trust me, you don't want to hear me sing."

"I'd love to."

"Well don't say I didn't warn you."

Charlie starts to sing, his voice tentative and strained at first. However the more he loses himself in the song, the more melodic his voice becomes. Noor watches him entranced until eventually he trails off and stares out through the branches as if searching for his mother. Noor fights the urge to reach out and take a hold of his hand. She stands.

"Good night, Charlie."

He looks up.

"Oh, you out of here?" he says.

"It's late."

Charlie nods.

"Well thanks for listening."

"It was my pleasure."

Noor walks back down the bough. When she reaches the trunk she looks back. Charlie is still staring off into the distance mumbling the words to the song. What she sees is a fourteen year old boy holding his dying mother's hand, bringing her untold comfort as she slips into the next life, and it breaks her heart.

***

UP ON THE bough, Charlie watches Noor walk along the verandah, her posture straight, her gait graceful.

I love her. I love her like no other woman I've ever met.

It scares him to death. He remembers what Noor had said the first time she came to the house. *'I assume you weren't going to ask my father for my hand in marriage?'* and when he'd asked her if she was kidding how she'd remarked that the only thing he could thus be hoping for was *'an erotic fling with an exotic woman'.* Charlie can't help but smile; only Noor could come up with such a phrase. At the time he thought she was being ridiculous, but the more he thinks about it the more he realizes she has a point. For a self-respecting Muslim woman the only romantic relationship she can have is a married one.

Could I marry her?

Maybe. No, not maybe. Yes. Absolutely.

So you're certain you love her?

Yes.

Just like Dad was certain he loved Mom?

Charlie would like nothing more than to argue that his father's feelings had been fraudulent, but whenever his mother spoke about their whirlwind love affair, it was always with a sparkle in her eye. It was magical, she'd tell him; the two of them had felt like no one else existed in the world.

So what happened?

They weren't compatible. They had different outlooks on life.

And how can you be so sure you and Noor don't too?

Questions begin to pepper his brain. Will he really be alright with a Muslim wife? What if she wants to raise their children Muslim? Would he be okay walking in the door at night to see them prostrating themselves towards Mecca?

You'd be an alien in your own home.

Unless of course he became a Muslim too. The concept seems absurd, but perhaps Noor would pressure him into becoming one, just as his father had pressured his mother into going to church and joining the Junior League. Noor might deny it now, be as fine with him drinking as his father once was with his mother smoking joints. But it hadn't been long until his father had disapproved. Hell he'd objected right up until the end, even when his mother's doctor said it could help with her nausea.

Will I be sneaking beers on the porch? Chewing gum on the way home after going to a bar with a buddy?

He knows he'd start to resent Noor, just like his mother had come to resent his father.

And then what? Live a sham of a marriage like my parents did? Never. I'd never do that to myself, more importantly I'd never do that to Noor. No one deserves that.

The breeze picks up, and the decaying leaves rustle all around him. He sits rock still and listens for his mother, hoping for some words of wisdom. He hears nothing but the wind.

It must be nice to think like Noor does. To believe your mother's out there looking down on you.

But he knows different. Once you're gone, you're gone, dust at best, lost for eternity. And he knows any hope of him and Noor being together has crumbled as surely as any dead body will.

It will never work, and if I respect her I won't try to make it.

Charlie stands up and makes his way back inside, turning off the lights as he goes. He walks down the upstairs corridor and stops next to the switch outside Noor's and Bushra's room. He stares at their door. To know she's so close is almost unbearable. With a heavy sigh he flicks the light off and continues on.

THIRTY

TARIQ STANDS OUTSIDE the Prince's tent, two Saudi body-guards cradling high-end assault rifles on either side of him. To call it a tent is a gross mischaracterization; it has nothing in common with the miserable canvas dwellings that are spread out in front of them. The Prince's tent could hold a wedding for two hundred, has warm air pumped into it, and its floor is lined with the most sumptuous of rugs.

Now that is living.

A lumbering Ford Bronco appears at the far end of the camp, and he watches it bounce its way towards them. The Saudi bodyguards tense.

"It's fine," Tariq says.

The Prince had told him to expect an American guest, and ever since he's been intrigued to meet him. The Bronco rolls to a stop, and two well built Americans climb out. The passenger door opens, and a weasel of a man steps out. He sniffs the air and takes in the dispirited mujahideen trudging about in the snow.

How he must deride us.

The American catches Tariq staring at him and approaches.

"Ivor Gardener, he's expecting me," he says in Arabic.

"Your men have to stay outside," Tariq says in English.

The man's eyes flicker.

"No problem," he says.

The American spreads his arms and legs wide. One of the Saudi guards comes over and pats him down for weapons. Tariq tells the other to go and inform the Prince that the American has arrived.

"I haven't met you before," the American says.

"My name's Tariq Khan."

"Ah, so you're the one. Congratulations."

Tariq can't help but feel a visceral thrill that the American knows who he is. The guard nods at Tariq. Moments later the other returns and relays that the Prince will see the American immediately. Tariq wishes he could keep the conversation going but knows it'd be unthinkable to keep the Prince waiting. He pulls back the flap.

"Have a good meeting, Mr. Gardener," Tariq says.

"See you around," the American says.

Snow starts to fall, and Tariq stomps his feet to keep them warm. The stump on his right arm throbs as if someone's hitting it with a hammer. One more hour of this guard duty, and they'll rotate, and he'll be inside and beside the Prince once more.

Tariq sees three men walk up the track and recognizes them as Salim Afridi, and his two brutish, oldest sons, Iqbal and Nasir. The three of them stare at Tariq with undisguised malevolence. Iqbal, his nose running, snorts like a farmyard animal and hawks a hefty glob of mucus at Tariq's feet.

"The Prince is expecting us," Salim Afridi says.

"One moment," Tariq says.

He turns for the entrance, and Salim Afridi grabs a hold of his arm.

"Did you hear what I said, boy?"

"I did, but the Prince put this protocol in place, not me."

Tariq stares down his father-in-law. Salim Afridi lets go of his sleeve, and Tariq pulls back the flap. He steps into the interior's warm embrace. Two bodyguards, on the other side, give him the go ahead, and he walks to the far end of the tent where the Prince is conferring with the American. The Prince knows he's there but doesn't acknowledge his presence. Tariq hopes the Prince makes him wait forever just so his father-in-law and his two idiot sons freeze their balls off. Tariq projects an air of studied indifference while listening intently to what the two men are saying.

"So you haven't spoken to bin Laden recently?" the American says.

"You make it seem like we're the best of friends," the Prince laughs.

"You guys hung out all the time."

"We were two Saudis in a foreign land, our paths were bound to cross."

"I went by a couple of his training camps in Nangrahar. They're totally deserted. The Stingers we gave him too."

"I believe he distributed them equally amongst the factions.."

"So he has left?"

"If he gave away his Stingers then one would presume so."

"But you don't know where?"

The Prince stares back at the American.

"No. If I did I would have told you. Now enough about bin Laden, I want to hear more about what your sources in Kabul are telling you? Do you think it is a propitious time to attack"

Please say no, Tariq prays.

The Prince glances up at Tariq.

"Where's Salim Afridi?" he says.

"He's waiting outside." Tariq says.

"Then what are you doing standing there. Show him in."

Damn.

Tariq hurries back outside.

"You're good," he says.

His in-laws barge past him. Tariq zips the entrance shut and pulls out the letter he received from Yousef that morning. He reads it one last time.

Tariq, As-salaam Alaykum. No success yet in finding your package. Are you sure it is still in Peshawar? Yousef.

Tariq pulls a lighter from his pocket and lights the letter. Before the flames can lick his fingers he lets it go, its ashes intermingling with the snow flakes..

He walks over to a nearby tent. Sarosh, one of the Prince's clerks, looks up.

"When's the mail going to Peshawar?" he says.

"End of the day," Sarosh says.

Tariq pulls out an envelope addressed to Yousef and hands it to the clerk. Inside is a simple two word reply.

Keep looking.

THIRTY-ONE

NOOR SITS MEMORIZING a list of Dutch nouns. She glances at the carriage clock on the mantelpiece. It's close to midnight. She wonders if Charlie is ever coming home.

Maybe he's sleeping somewhere else.

It'd certainly solve the mystery of why they hadn't seen him all week. She wonders whether he has a lover, another aid worker perhaps.

Why do you care?

I don't.

She tries concentrating on the words in front of her but instead reminisces about her visit to Elma's earlier that week. Elma's cottage had only been a ten minute walk, so close to Charlie's house it was perturbing. Elma had opened the door with an infectious smile, and swept Noor into the house, and for the next two hours had insisted on only speaking Dutch as she plied Noor with food.

She still thinks I live in the camps, that's why she fed me so much.

As the evening had progressed Noor had become increasingly paralyzed. Elma was speaking so fast that Noor could barely pick out one in twenty words.

There is no way I'll be able to learn this language in time, she'd thought.

Elma had noticed the terror on her face and asked her in English what was troubling her. From then on Elma had spoken at a more deliberate pace, repeating sentences over until Noor understood them, and by the end of the night while Noor was hardly confident in her meager grasp of Dutch, she could at least see a path forward. Elma had insisted on increasing the number of lessons from one night a week to three, and in turn Noor had set herself the goal of studying every night until eleven o'clock.

If he is sleeping with a woman he has to be leaving her bed well before dawn.

When she'd spoken with Mukhtar that morning he'd insisted he'd made Charlie breakfast every day that week.

Noor throws her book down.

This is ridiculous, I'm beginning to act like the wife of a philandering husband.

She walks out onto the verandah and stares up at the tree.

"I'm not scared of you, Tariq," she says. "I never have been and never will be."

Then why are you hiding from me? she hears him reply.

She shivers. Strange as it may sound, she misses the camp, especially the graveyard and her nightly runs. They always allowed her to clear her head.

Then do something about it.

She tucks her kameez inside her shalwar pants and walks onto the lawn. She slips off her sandals and starts doing jumping jacks until she feels her heart beating fast. She gets down onto the grass and does fifteen push ups followed by thirty sit ups. She does this three times until she can no longer push her body up. She sits there gulping for air.

Keep going.

She stands and does squats and after that a set of lunges around the lawn. By now her face is bathed in sweat. In the graveyard there was an abandoned swing set from which she could do pull-ups. She looks up at the great oak.

Surely there must be a branch up there that can carry my weight.

She clambers up the trunk and hops onto the lowest bough. Above her, she sees an L shaped branch so sturdy that a gale couldn't break it loose. Noor grabs a hold of it and starts on her pull-ups. Golden leaves fall all around her as the branch shakes. By her ninth pull up, her legs are jerking like those of a convict at the end of a noose. She forces herself up one last time. Her chin touches the branch, and she drops back down onto the bough, her head light, her muscles aching in the most wondrous way.

Finally, you're relaxed.

She hears the growl of an approaching motorcycle.

Charlie.

She wonders whether she should go down and greet him.

No it's late. And besides, what is there to talk about?

She hears the front door slam shut and can't help but feel a visceral thrill.

Maybe he'll come out onto the verandah and I can spy on him.

She peers down at the darkened porch and waits. Across the way the lights of his room burst on, and through the fragmented canopy she sees Charlie throw his satchel on his bed. He heads over to his desk and selects a CD. Moments later the melodic strumming of a guitar drifts in her direction. Charlie throws open the doors to his balcony and disappears out of view. Noor strains to hear the words of the song. It seems to be about a stranger, battling through a storm, who is given shelter by a woman. Noor can't help but think that shelter is what Charlie has given them.

He's not only given us shelter. He's the only person to have ever given us shelter.

The thought startles her. The song continues. The singer sings about a place where it's always safe and warm. Noor imagines what that place would be for her.

Holland. Only there will I truly be safe.

Noor wonders what her lodgings would look like, what it'd feel like to be sitting surrounded by fellow students in a lecture hall, what friends she'd make.

The song ends and Charlie passes by the open balcony doors. It takes Noor a moment to register he's naked. She gasps, and claps her hands over her eyes. After what seems like an eternity, she decides she can pull them away.

Surely it is safe now.

She has to fling one out so as not to fall off the bough. Charlie is standing on the balcony, a cigarette between his lips. Noor wants to turn away but finds it impossible to. She's never seen a naked man before.

She stares at him; at his toweled, disheveled hair, the scar on his cheek, his robust chest, his slender waist, his vigorous thighs, his circumcised penis topped by a thatch of curly hair. Her face burns. Yet the longer she stares the more entranced she becomes. Charlie's brow furrows, and he looks up into the night sky as if pondering the immensity, or perhaps even the insignificance, of the human condition.

He is the most beautiful thing I've ever seen in my life.

It's as if God is proclaiming the nobility of man in his purest form.

Charlie heads back inside and pulls the drapes shut.

Noor takes a moment to collect herself and then begins edging down the trunk. Near the bottom she loses her grip and falls to the ground. She winces, not daring to cry out. She struggles to her feet and limps inside. In her bedroom, she lays down her prayer rug and begs Allah's forgiveness for not turning her face away. And yet, despite this, when she lies in bed, she continues to see him naked. She feels something stirring deep within.

THIRTY-TWO

CHARLIE AND AAMIR Khan enter Wali's hospital room to find Wali writing in his notepad. Wali flashes them a broad smile.

"Ah, so this is the famous Aamir Khan," he says.

"And you must be the legendary Wali," Aamir Khan says.

"How about that, Mr. Matthews, a more intelligent and handsome man than I imagined."

Charlie looks over at Aamir Khan.

"Get used to this, it never stops."

"And I hope it never does, pronouncements like that only brighten my day."

Wali grins. Aamir Khan drags a chair over to Wali's bedside and opens the binder he's carrying.

"I had the good fortune of meeting with your doctor earlier," Aamir Khan says, "and he is confident that you will be in a position to leave the hospital in a couple of weeks. Now I have taken the liberty of developing a rehabilitation program—"

"You know what," Charlie says, "I'm out of here. Aamir, you okay getting a rickshaw back to the house?"

"Why, most certainly."

Charlie makes for the door.

"Oh, Charlie, a word if I may?" Aamir Khan says.

"What's up?"

Aamir Khan comes over and lowers his voice.

"I am not sure if I mentioned this, but my son, Tariq, is a member of a mujahideen group, Hezb-e-Inqilab-Islami. Well, as you might imagine I am worried for his safety, and I was wondering if you could ascertain whether his group is still in Peshawar, or whether it has already headed to the front lines?"

"You mind writing that down for me, I'm not good with names, especially Arabic ones."

"I took the liberty of doing so already."

Aamir Khan hands Charlie a piece of paper.

"Let me see what I can do," Charlie says.

Charlie drives over to Mine Aware and finds the recruits checking their equipment. He's elated to see that not one has absconded with theirs. He walks over and the men form into two straight lines.

"Okay behind me are fifteen lanes. In each are eight dummy mines at differing depths. You'll be working in teams of two today, fifteen on, fifteen off, and it's your job not only to detect the mines but to excavate them. Once you've cleared the earth away from a mine, you'll shout out 'mine' and I'll come over and take it away. So far so good?"

The recruits all nod. Charlie picks up a dummy mine.

"Now to make it a little harder, I've applied a latex coating to every mine. This is what we call a witness plate. When you're probing if you pierce this coating that's evidence you applied too much pressure. Now what would that mean if this was a real mine?"

A bevy of hands go up. Charlie points at Yunus.

"Boom," Yunus grins.

"Exactly, boom. So go easy, you hear."

The recruits pair off and begin excavating the mines. The air is filled with shouts of encouragement, and every ten minutes or so an excited yell of 'mine' goes up, and Charlie heads over and retrieves it. After two hours only one latex coating has been pierced.

Charlie hears a vehicle pull up and turns to see Shamsurahman and Jurgen getting out of a UN Land Cruiser.

"Thought we'd pay a surprise visit," Jurgen says.

"Must be a slow day at the office for you to be coming out to this far flung outpost."

"We'd heard reports so fantastical we felt compelled to investigate them personally."

"Well here they are, Mine Aware's first class of recruits."

Jurgen and Shamsurahman observe them in silence. From down the way Obaidullah yells out 'mine'.

"Right back," Charlie says.

Charlie goes over to Obaidullah.

Please, don't be scratched.

He picks up the mine. It's clean. Looking as nonchalant as possible, Charlie returns to where Jurgen and Shamsurahman are standing. He tosses the dummy mine to Shamsurahman. From the corner of his eye, he sees Shamsurahman inspecting the witness plate.

"Skeppar just called to tell me Stephen Adams was in a car accident in Mozambique," Jurgen says.

"You kidding me?" Charlie says. "It serious?"

"If shattering your left femur is serious then yes."

"When's he going to get here now?"

"April at the earliest."

"That's cool, we'll cope."

Jurgen smiles and slaps Charlie on the back.

"That's what I told Skeppar."

Charlie walks them back to their SUV. He remembers Aamir Khan's request and pulls out the piece of paper.

"Shit, while I've got you here, you ever heard of a mujahideen group called—Hezb—e—Inqilab—i—Islami? Friend of mine's wondering if they're in Afghanistan."

Jurgen looks over at Shamsurahman.

"What do you hear?"

"I hear they not so far from Kabul itself," Shamsurahman says.

"Fighting?" Charlie says.

"Waiting. Last time they attack big city not go well."

"It going to be any different this time?"

"Maybe, the government's low on supplies," Jurgen says. "This group, you know it's extremely radical. It's run by a Saudi prince and full of Arabs."

Shamsurahman spits on the ground.

"You got something against Arabs?" Charlie says.

"Just ones who come here," Shamsurahman says.

"Tell him about the time you took those four Saudis into Afghanistan," Jurgen says.

Shamsurahman sighs as if Jurgen's forced him to tell this story a thousand times.

"Some years back we about to go into Afghanistan when four Saudis come and say they want to go with us. I do not want them, they Gucci soldiers, want Afghans do all work, like we take them on the safari. But one of them, his father give us much money so we have no choice. All the way they complain, it is too cold, no comfort, bad food. On third night, we meet more mujahideen, they camping, smoking the hashish. They say area has many new mines, they thinking what to do. So Arabs see this, they go crazy. Saying we need to trust Allah and cross minefield. Big argument, guns rise up. I step in and they walk away. Next we see they going into minefield. Believe me, men who smoke the hashish think they smoke too much. Soon mine goes off then three others. Three dead mens and one on ground screaming for mother."

"You go in and get him?"

Shamsurahman looks at Charlie like he's lost his mind.

"We wait for him to die."

"How long did it take?"

"Four, five hours only."

"Jesus."

"After he stop, we say prayer and go back to Peshawar. We think the Saudis be angry to lose all four men, but they so happy, now men most glorious shaheeds."

"You think they were martyrs?"

Shamsurahman shakes his head.

"It is glorious to give your life for Allah, not to waste it."

Jurgen and Shamsurahman drive off. Qasim comes out of the main building and hands Charlie a stiff envelope.

"This came for you," he says.

Charlie rips it open and pulls out an invitation.

The Consul General cordially invites you to a holiday barbecue at 2 PM on Wednesday, December 18th, 1991.

"What's the date today?" Charlie says.

"November twenty-seven," Qasim says.

Jesus, time flies.

THIRTY-THREE

"YOU REALIZE," THE headmistress says, "that without Miss Kuyt's intervention I'd have sacked you."

"I understand," Noor says.

"We all have problems, sick relatives, abusive husbands, my word, Mrs. Nasreen's son was killed by a lorry last month, but three days later there she was back at school."

"I apologize, they were exceptional circumstances."

"Don't you listen? There's no such thing as exceptional circumstances at least if you want to continue teaching here. Now go, before I change my mind."

Noor exits praying that the next time she enters it will be the day she informs the headmistress that she's leaving for Holland. In the anteroom, Miss Suha sits back in her chair.

"Enjoy your flogging?" Miss Suha says.

Noor ignores her and opens the door.

"You know what people are saying, don't you?"

Noor can't help but look back.

"Here's a Dutch woman, still unmarried despite being in her thirties, and here's a poor Afghan girl who turns down every marriage proposal that comes her way. What could they possibly be doing when they get together?"

Noor's face burns up.

"You know full well she's helping me with my scholarship application."

"So that's what they call it nowadays, is it?"

Noor hurries down the corridor. She opens the door to her classroom, and the girls rush in her direction. Each of them has a question, and as a result Noor hears none of them. She shouts at them to sit down, and they retreat to their desks.

"Before we begin, I'd just like to say that I missed you all very much," she says.

A chorus of 'we missed you too' rings out.

"And now I'm back we're going to have to work extra hard to make up for lost time. Now who can tell me what you've been doing in my absence?"

A host of hands go up. Noor glances towards the front row and the second desk on the left. She's surprised to find Sawdah, an intense, snub-nosed Tajik girl sitting there. Noor's eyes dart across the faces of the other girls.

"Where's Kamila?" she says.

"No one told you?" Hila says.

"Why would I be asking the question if they had?"

"She's getting married this Friday."

Noor puts a hand on her desk to steady herself.

"Who to?"

"A cousin, I think, from Jalozai."

Noor sees the same worry writ across every one of her student's faces: 'There but for the grace of Allah go I.' Noor picks up her history textbook and finds her hands are shaking.

"Please read the section on Indira Gandhi in chapter four."

Noor sprints down the corridor, the sound of the Arabic chanting from Miss Layla's class pounding in her ears. She opens the door to the headmistress's anteroom. Miss Suha looks up from typing a letter.

270 N. G. OSBORNE

"Back so soon."

"I need to see the headmistress."

"She's unavailable."

The click clack of Miss Suha's typewriter starts up again.

"Why didn't you tell me Kamila was being married off?" Noor says.

"Oh, that's why you're here?"

Noor stares Miss Suha down.

"It was of no importance, she's no longer a student so she's no longer our problem."

"She's twelve. It's illegal."

"Oh come on, I know you're not that naïve."

"We can't stand around and do nothing."

"No, you're right, we can get off our self-righteous asses and go back to what we're paid to do. Now I know what you're thinking—Suha's the devil—but that's where you're wrong, young lady, because the devil deceives and that's one thing I never do. You, on the other hand, well that's another matter, throwing out concepts in class like freedom and empowerment as frivolously as rice at a wedding. Are you blind when you walk around the camps? We Afghan women are born in shackles and die with them still attached to our ankles. All you create is greater despair in these girls' lives for you can't mourn the loss of something you never knew about in the first place."

"I think the headmistress will disagree."

Noor makes for the headmistress's door.

"Oh my dear, you really are naïve. She may pretend to believe in those things, she couldn't keep her job if she didn't, but she lost any hope long ago."

Noor stops, for once unsure of herself.

"While there's life, there's hope," Noor says.

"Yeah and I bet whoever said that was rich and male. Now away with you."

Noor gladly leaves. How she makes it through the rest of the day she doesn't know. There is the discussion on her return regarding Indira Gandhi in which the girls want to focus less on Gandhi as a woman and more on her being a barbarous Hindu; there is the staff meeting where the news of Kamila's impending marriage is treated as matter of factly as a report of rain on the horizon; then lunch where the chicken seems to have come from hens placed on a starvation diet; there's 'play' to be supervised; and one more session in class, this time English. They're reading *The Secret Garden* right now, and Noor can't help but wish there was such a place for her to hide Kamila in.

The school bell rings and Noor looks up. The girls are leaning forward like runners on their starting blocks.

"You can go," she says.

The girls run out. Noor listens to the wind whistling outside. Winter is late this year but today it's announcing its imminent arrival. The shutters slam against the side of the building, and Noor goes to fasten them. She looks out the window at the deep red sun setting over the Khyber Mountains. Down below students and teachers are streaming out of the school, dust and trash whirling around them. She notices a black SUV parked across the street. It isn't a father waiting to pick up a student; none of the girls have fathers rich enough to buy a car let alone a brand new, Japanese 4x4. No, whoever's inside has to be watching the school for some other reason, and the more Noor thinks about it the only reason that makes any sense is that they're waiting for her.

Noor yanks the shutters closed and stands there, her breathing shallow. Her first instinct is to flee out the back, but only dusty fields surround the school. They'll be able to cut her off. She could wait them out but that leaves open the possibility that they might come inside. And then she fastens on a solution. She runs down the corridor and finds Miss

Layla in her classroom writing Quranic verses on the chalk board.

"As-Salaam Alaykum," Noor says.

Miss Layla turns. Despite her sixty years, her hair is still jet black.

"Wa'alaykum asalaam," Miss Layla says.

"This may be a terrible inconvenience but I was wondering if you had a burqa I might borrow?"

"I thought you deplored their very existence."

"Things have changed lately, I'm getting a lot of unwelcome attention on the buses, I'd feel safer wearing one."

Noor feels like the ground is swallowing her up each time she lies.

"Then why didn't you wear one to school today?" Miss Layla says.

"I'm ashamed to say my father is so ill I cannot afford one right now."

Noor hears a man's voice and edges further into the classroom.

"I don't care what the headmistress told you," Miss Layla says, "you were a good Muslim daughter to stay home with him."

Noor sees a shadow cross the frame of the door and turns her face away.

"Get out of here, Imran," Miss Layla says.

Noor looks over at the gangly old janitor standing there in his grey shalwar kameez. He gives her a toothless smile before scuttling away.

Does Kamila's husband look like him?

"You're in luck," Miss Layla says. "I have an extra."

Miss Layla retrieves a light blue burqa from her cupboard. Noor places it over her head, the garment wrapping around her body like an invisible cloak. Her urgent breathing dominates its interior, but already she feels safer.

"Thank you," Noor says.

Noor makes her way out of the building and crosses the courtyard. She stops short of the school entrance hoping to find a couple of teachers she might accompany. There are none. She takes a deep breath and walks out the entrance and towards the main road.

Don't look back.

The wind gets under the burqa and threatens to rip it off. Noor wrenches it back down. She hears a vehicle approach from behind and stares straight ahead. An old Datsun pick-up passes by.

Thank you, Allah.

She comes to the road and huddles next to a group of burqaed women. She glances back. The SUV is still parked there. A bus pulls up, and she gets on board. As it pulls away, she realizes she's heading the wrong way and towards the refugee camps. An opportunity has presented itself. At the intersection of Jamrud Road and Nasir Bagh Road, Noor struggles off the bus and joins the crowds. Another bus pulls up, and she forces her way on board. The bus soon leaves the city behind and heads down a road lined with sporadic trees and grey tilled fields. None of the men offer her a seat.

Charlie would've offered me his.

The bus comes upon Nasir Bagh refugee camp, and she gets out. She hadn't thought it possible that there could be another place on earth more forlorn than Kacha Gari but here it is, a mixture of poorly constructed katche huts and battered tents. The tents billow in the wind, their guide ropes straining to keep them attached to the hardscrabble ground. Any cart sellers that there might have been have fled, and soon Noor finds herself standing alone, her fellow passengers scurrying into the distance.

Noor remembers Kamila once mentioning that her family's tent was close to the camp's main mosque, but in the fading light, she fails to see it. The muezzins start up, and Noor detects a chant that's louder than the rest.

That has to be it.

Men start coming out of their tents, and she follows them. She stumbles down one path after another until the mosque is right in front of her. It's an unimpressive concrete block with an impressive number of men lined up out front. Noor realizes Kamila's father must be amongst them.

This is your chance.

She hurries down a row of tents and sees a woman tending a pot of boiling water.

"Do you know a young girl by the name of Kamila Samim?" she says.

"What's it to you?" the woman says.

"I'm her teacher."

The woman pulls back the front of the tent.

"Zahara," she says.

A girl, maybe a year younger than Kamila, sticks her head out the tent.

"Show this woman to Kamila's tent."

Zahara crawls out. She reaches out her hand, and Noor takes it. They take off in a zig-zag fashion around the tents.

"Are you here to offer her congratulations?" Zahara says.

"Something like that."

Zahara points at a large, patchwork tent.

"There it is," she says.

Zahara runs away. Noor raises the front of her burqa and stares at it. Inside she can make out five, perhaps six women moving about. Kamila must be one of them.

"Hello," she says.

No one responds. She edges closer and places her lips next to the fabric.

"Excuse me."

The entrance snaps open, and a woman steps out. Noor knows the type well. Her worn face makes her look like she's in her late forties, yet it's doubtful she's even out of her twenties.

"I'm looking for Kamila Samim's mother," Noor says.

"Yes."

"My name's Noor Jehan Khan, I'm her teacher. I thought I'd come by and visit, tell you how well Kamila's doing."

The woman's eyes narrow.

"On a night like this?" she says.

"She's an exceptional student."

"Good to know."

The woman turns to go back inside.

"I think Kamila could really benefit from another year at the school," Noor says. "If you kept her there longer, her marriage prospects would only increase."

The woman turns back.

"So it's you who's been planting all these ideas in her head."

"I have only taught her things that the Prophet, peace be upon him, would approve of."

"I told my husband not to send her there."

"It was a courageous decision, I promise you."

"And now here she is crying so hard even a good beating can't force an end to it."

"I beg you, convince your husband to stop this marriage."

The woman pushes Noor, and Noor staggers backwards.

"You think it's easy feeding six kids," the woman says.

"I'm sure the school can help—"

"You think we can afford to keep a girl around who has her nose stuck in books all day."

"You don't understand—"

"No, it's you who doesn't."

The woman shoves Noor so hard that Noor topples over, her head whiplashing against a guide rope on the way down. Noor struggles back up onto her feet.

"You can't do this," Noor says. "It's not right."

The woman swings her fists at Noor's face. Noor grabs a hold of the woman's wrists and holds her off.

"Please," Noor says.

The woman shrieks, and, out the corner of her eye, Noor sees the tent flap open, and another woman emerge. Kamila's mother breaks Noor's grip and digs her nails into Noor's cheek. Noor cries out. The second woman punches Noor in the stomach. Noor tumbles over and the blows begin raining down. Noor guesses that a third woman, perhaps even a fourth, has joined the fray. Hands punch her in the ears, rip at her breasts, pummel her in the back, pull at her hair, dig their nails into her buttocks.

Oh Lord, I'm going to die right here.

Noor tries to crawl away, however a hand yanks her head up and drives her face into the ground. Her nostrils fill with dirt. She can't breathe.

And then just like that the blows stop.

Noor twists on her back expecting a final coup de grace. It never comes. The women have gone. She looks towards the mosque; the men are returning from evening prayers. She crawls in between two tents and realizes Kamila's mother likely meted out a similar beating on Kamila. Noor begins to cry. Miss Suha was right. She hasn't helped these girls, she's only brought greater despair into their lives.

***

AAMIR KHAN GLANCES at the carriage clock on the mantelpiece. Twenty past ten.

"Where are you?" he mutters.

For the last hour he's told himself that Noor's still at school, forced to work late after her ten day absence, but as the minutes have ticked by that explanation's become ever more fanciful.

"Where are you? Dear God, where are you?"

Scenes play out in his mind, scenes he's had many years to hone. Noor walking home. A car coming up behind her, a couple of young men up front; mustaches, no beards, youthful attempts at looking debonair. They are blasting Indian pop music, passing a cigarette laced with hashish between them. One of them notices Noor and says something to his friend. The car arcs in the road, and Noor stands there frozen in its headlamps. The men throw her in the back. She screams, and the passenger punches her in the head. When she comes to they're dragging her into a room where each has his way with her. Noor begs for mercy, but they don't stop. Finally sated one slits her throat. They throw her back in the trunk and dump her on some waste ground. Another dead Afghan refugee no one will give a damn about.

No one but me.

Aamir Khan swallows, his mouth dry, his breathing labored. He knows there's no point in going to the police. A missing refugee in a city of millions; there could be no lower priority. Worse yet they could be involved. The scenes replay in his mind except this time the car is a police pick-up and the men sweat-stained police officers.

'Look after them for me'—those had been Mariam's final words to him.

"Oh Mariam," he cries out, "how I have failed you."

Aamir Khan forces himself up out of his chair. He spies the wooden frame he's been crafting for Noor to place her university diploma in. On it are scenes of women with their heads gloriously unveiled, in a lecture hall, working alongside men in an architect's office, playing tennis.

"You fool."

He throws the frame against the wall and it shatters. He stretches his hands out in the air.

"O Allah, please spare Noor, place her in your ever merciful embrace and protect her from those who seek to hurt her. I know I have sinned, I know I have spent my life with my head in the clouds, but even I know you are the embodiment of forgiveness and you love to pardon, so pardon me. O Allah, please I beg you, bring home my daughter ..."

Aamir Khan curls up on the floor and sobs. He hears Noor say 'Baba'.

Is she now speaking to me from the grave?

"Baba?"

He looks up. Noor's blurred form stands in the doorway. He laughs. It doesn't seem possible. He uses his sleeve to wipe his eyes, and she comes towards him. He can now make out her face; her right cheek lined with scratches, her left eye half closed, its eyelid purple as if it's been smeared with ink.

"Oh my love," he says.

She kneels down beside him and wraps her arms around him.

"What happened?" he says.

She doesn't reply and squeezes him tighter. He buries his nose in her hair and breathes in her scent. This isn't a dream, Allah has returned her to him.

"I have to get out of here," Noor says.

"You will," Aamir Khan says. "I promise, you will."

THIRTY-FOUR

CHARLIE PULLS UP in the Pajero. He takes a moment to take in his house. It seems strange in the full light of day, its bricks glistening white, the meandering vines a lustrous green, the bougainvillea bright and cheerful.

What was Skeppar thinking when he rented this place?

He glances at the dashboard. Three ten. Noor won't be home yet. He turns to Wali.

"Ready?"

"I was about to ask the same question of you," Wali says.

Charlie gets out and lifts the wheelchair out of the trunk. He staggers backwards, and it clatters to the ground.

"You should feel the weight of this thing."

"That is because it was built in the Soviet Union. It was the Russians' final revenge against the Afghan people."

"Their final revenge against the American people, you mean. You're not the one pushing it."

Charlie places Wali in it and pulls him up the front steps one onerous clunk at a time. The front door opens. Aamir Khan stands there with Bushra.

"Sorry," Charlie says, "took longer than I thought. Wali insisted on thanking every nurse and doctor in the place."

"And so he should," Aamir Khan says. "They are truly the most marvelous of people. Now, Wali, may I introduce to you my daughter, Bushra."

"It's wonderful to meet you," Wali smiles.

"You too," Bushra says blushing.

Charlie starts for the SUV.

"Charlie, I was so hoping to show you the parallel bars," Aamir Khan says. "Mukhtar and I finished them just this morning."

"Well I suppose I got time."

"Marvelous. Bushra, would you please push Wali for me."

Bushra gets behind the chair, and Aamir Khan leads them through the house and out onto the verandah. Down on the lawn below are the freshly painted set of waist-high parallel bars.

"They're awesome," Charlie says.

"They will allow you to build upper body strength," Aamir Khan says to Wali.

"Then I must try them immediately," Wali says.

Wali wheels away from Bushra and flies down the ramp. The chair lurches onto one wheel and for a moment it seems as if Wali is going to tumble onto the lawn. Bushra screams. Just in time the wheelchair restores its balance and comes to a skidding halt right in front of the parallel bars.

"No way you're going on those things," Charlie says.

Wali grabs a hold of one of the bars.

"Please, Mr. Matthews, just one minute on this magnificent contraption."

"No. The only reason you got out early is because you promised to rest up. Aamir Khan? Bushra?"

"Charlie is most correct," Aamir Khan says.

Wali slumps back into his chair.

"Fine, but someone has to try them."

Charlie looks over at Aamir Khan.

"Fancy a spin?"

"Oh, I think that would be most injudicious of me."

"Then it must be you," Wali says.

"I haven't done this stuff since I was in high school," Charlie says.

"Kindly give them a try."

"Okay, just for you."

Charlie places a hand on each of the bars.

"Can you go from one end to the other?" Wali says.

"I'd hope so."

Charlie works his way down the length of the bars and twists around to face them. Wali claps.

"See you're a natural. Now please you must show us some other tricks."

"Like what?"

"Can you walk upside down?"

"When I was seventeen."

Out the corner of his eye, Charlie sees someone coming down the verandah. From her erect, purposeful stride he knows instantly who it is.

Noor.

He feels his pulse quicken. She reaches the ramp and gives him a curious look.

"So are you going to do it?" Wali says.

Charlie jolts out of his trance.

"Yeah, why not."

He makes his way to the center of the bars and begins swinging his legs back and forth. Noor comes up beside her father and sister.

"As-Salaam Alaykum" Noor says.

Wali twists around in his chair, and for one of the few times in his life is struck dumb.

She really is that beautiful.

"Charlie is about to show us a gymnastic trick from his youth," Aamir Khan says.

"Do you think that's a good idea?" she says.

Charlie gives his legs an extra jerk and flips upside down. He has to concentrate so hard on keeping his position that he hears nothing they're saying. His arms begin to shudder.

Noor glances up at him, and for the first time Charlie notices the garish yellow bruise around her right eye and the fading network of scratches across her cheeks. It's as if someone's tried to deface a masterpiece; they have failed miserably. In that moment every reason he's constructed for staying away from her is obliterated.

What the hell was I thinking?

Charlie's left arm wobbles, and he falls, his right shoulder plowing into the ground. A stab of unimaginable pain shoots down his right side.

"Ah, fuck me," he screams.

Noor crouches down beside him.

"Charlie, are you alright?"

He looks up into her eyes, and the agony subsides only for it to return as if some animal is trying to tear his right arm from his body. He roars so loudly that Bushra squeals.

"Did you hear anything crack?" Noor says.

"Think I just dislocated my shoulder," Charlie says.

"I will take him to the hospital," Aamir Khan says.

"No—all I need is a wall. Aamir, help me up."

Aamir Khan puts his arm underneath Charlie's good shoulder and lifts him up. Charlie stands there swaying.

"I advise you to go to the hospital," Noor says.

"Hate hospitals," Charlie says.

He staggers towards the house, his arm hanging limp. Noor runs after him.

"Charlie," Noor says.

"Don't worry I've done this before."

A hot sweat envelops his body. He stumbles into the sitting room but doesn't see a good place for a run up.

"Please, Charlie."

He continues on down the corridor. The wall at the far end is perfect.

"Baba, come stop this madness," Noor shouts.

Charlie grits his teeth and sprints towards it, angling his shoulder upwards.

"Charlie," Noor screams.

A torrent of pain shoots through Charlie's shoulder, and he blacks out.

***

NOOR ENTERS CHARLIE'S bedroom with a tray of food in her hands. Over by the balcony doors, Charlie sits hunched over his desk, sketching in his pad. She stands there and watches him. He looks like an expat from the 1920s. He sees her and smiles. She sets her face in as stern an expression as possible.

"The doctor was clear, you're not to use your arm to do anything."

"One more minute."

"Charlie, you're my patient and you'll do what I say."

"When did we agree on that?"

"When you came back from the hospital."

"I was high on Vicodin."

"You agreed, and that's all that matters."

Charlie slaps his pad shut and turns to face her. His hair is as long as she's ever seen it, hanging over his forehead and curling around the back of his ears.

It suits him.

"I brought you some lunch," she says.

She places the tray on his desk. It's simple, a glass of milk with some grilled chicken breast and rice. She didn't trust herself to make anything more complicated this time around.

"Thanks, you didn't need to do that," he says.

"Is there anything else I can get you?"

"No, all good."

"Then I'll have Mukhtar come back later and collect it."

Noor heads for the door.

"How's it going with Wali and your dad?" Charlie says.

Noor turns back.

"Good, they're already inseparable."

"Knew they'd get along."

"And surprisingly Bushra's helping out too. I think the opportunity to be of use has really galvanized her."

"Well I'm glad it's all working out. You want to sit a moment."

Whenever a man is alone with a woman the Devil makes a third. Wasn't that the Prophet's admonition?

"I don't know—"

"Come on, five minutes, I hate eating alone."

Charlie stares at her with those puppy dog eyes of his.

"Fine, five minutes."

She sits in his armchair, her hands clasped in her lap.

"What happened to your face?" he says.

She touches the bruise over her eye.

"It's of no concern."

"But I am concerned. I mean that's okay, isn't it?"

"Of course, but I'd rather not talk about it if you don't mind."

"Are you in danger?"

She shakes her head.

"Fine. That's all that matters."

Charlie picks up his fork and starts eating the way she assumes most soldiers do; fast and mechanically. She looks at his bedside clock. By this time tomorrow Kamila will be married, and her husband will have had his way with her.

Just like Ameena.

She trembles. She hasn't thought of Ameena in years.

"When I was twelve," she finds herself saying, "a family from Ghazni moved in next door to us."

Charlie stops eating and gives her his full attention.

"At dawn the father and their four children would go to the local dump and sort through the garbage, and every night on their return they'd wash themselves in a tub of warm water their mother had prepared. Their daughter, Ameena, was a year older than me and while she waited for her father and brothers to bathe first, we'd lean against the side of our hut and talk."

"About what?"

"Girl stuff mainly. I loved her, she had this infectious imagination, believed that a couple of princes would come along and whisk us from the camp. Then one day, she whispered to me that she'd ..."

Noor looks down at her hands in her lap.

Oh Lord, why did you start this story?

"What?" Charlie says.

"It's not important."

"You can't stop once you've started."

Noor looks him in the eye.

"She whispered that she'd begun menstruating. Of course she didn't say it like that, at the time she thought she was dying. Anyway I calmed her down, told her what was really going on."

"How did you know?"

"Baba had explained it all to us."

And I'll never forget how mortified he'd been when he did it.

"I told Ameena it was normal, that she should share the news with her mother. I didn't see her the next couple of nights, and so the next day I went over to her hut. Ameena came to the door and explained that her father had ordered her to stay inside until she stopped bleeding. 'And then you'll go back out with them?' I asked. 'Oh no, that'd be impossible,' she replied. She held up a burqa and told me her father was insistent she wear it from now on. I told Baba all this and I'll never forget the blood rushing to his head. 'Believe me, Noor,' he said 'it's not an article of clothing these men make their women wear but a set of chains, and on Judgement Day Allah will ask them what the hell they were thinking'. The next day I returned home early from school and went over to Ameena's hut. She was all alone, and we started chatting, and at some point I asked if I could try on her burqa. She thought it a marvelous idea. 'It'll be good practice for when you have to wear one,' she said. I didn't bother telling her there was little likelihood of that ever happening."

Until now.

"I pulled it down, and giggling, Ameena pushed me out the door. It took me a moment to get my bearings but when I did, to my horror, I saw Baba coming up the path. He looked in my direction, and I thought for certain I'd been caught. But then the most amazing thing happened; he kept walking. I felt giddy, as if I was a spy, but then my foot caught in the burqa's hem and I went sprawling.

"'Noor,' I'll never forget him saying. 'I know it's you.' I scrambled to my feet, and he proceeded to tell me what a disgrace I was. I began sobbing, and for the first time in my life Baba didn't comfort me. He ripped the burqa off my head and told me not to leave the hut until he said so. My father slept outside that night. He was ashamed of me and the more I realized that the more I cried. The next day Tariq and Bushra left for school, and the fact I wasn't going with them spoke to the severity of my crime. Morning stretched into afternoon, and just as I began to fear that I was going to be imprisoned forever he opened the door and told me to come with him to his bench.

"'I thought I'd taught you well,' he said to me, 'but right now I don't even recognize my own daughter.' I began to cry, and once again he failed to comfort me. He told me he was postponing my studies and instead wanted me to read the three books in his hand and write him a five thousand word essay on why women were men's equals."

"What were the books?" Charlie says.

"*The Liberation of Women and the New Woman* by Qasim Amin, *A Room Of One's Own* by Virginia Woolf and *The Life of Indira Gandhi* by someone whose name has escaped me."

"Jesus, how long did it take you?"

"Two weeks. As you may guess none of them are easy reads, especially for a twelve year old, but I soldiered on, reading from dawn until dusk, taking notes as I went. When I wrote the final sentence I went back and counted. I'd written over seven thousand words. I gave Baba the essay and he took it to his bench. Eventually he gestured me over, and I noticed he was crying. 'Do you believe what you've written?' he asked, and I told him I believed every single word. 'Then I guess you truly are my daughter,' he said. He hugged me and never had his embrace felt so good.

"That evening, I knocked on Ameena's door. Her father answered, and I asked to see her. He told me that Ameena no longer lived there, that she had gotten married a week earlier, and I fled back to our hut and once more cried through the night. I never saw Ameena again, and sometime later I heard she'd been married off to a sixty year old cousin. By now I suspect she's widowed with four, perhaps even five children."

"Why are you telling me this?" Charlie says.

"I don't know, you asked about these ..."

Noor touches the fading wounds on her face.

"One of my students, Kamila, the same thing's about to happen to her, so I went to Nasir Bagh camp thinking I could persuade her family to call off the wedding."

"They did that to you?"

"I think deep down I've always felt guilty about Ameena, that there was something I could have done to help her, but now I realize there's nothing I can do, that anyone can do really. I'm starting to believe that our country is a lost cause."

"I don't believe that."

"That's because you're American; you're an optimistic people."

Noor looks at the bedside clock. She's stayed far longer than she intended.

"I have to pray," she says.

"Right now?"

Noor studies the concentric patterns of the rug.

"I believe in God, in Allah," she says, "I believe Mohammed was his final messenger."

"I know."

"My religion, it's the most important thing in my life. Without it I'd be lost."

"Noor, I don't look down on your beliefs."

"I understand, I just wanted you to know, that's all."

"Why?"

Noor doesn't answer but instead hurries from the room. She bursts into her room and locks the door.

Why? Why did I feel it so necessary to tell him about my faith?

Because you wished he believed, a voice inside her says.

In Islam?

No, just in something.

But why?

Surely you don't need me to answer that.

Noor feels nauseous. She kneels down and begins to pray. She refuses to investigate the question any further.

THIRTY-FIVE

"YOU SHOULDN'T HAVE come," Charlie says.

The Pajero hits a pothole, and Wali bounces up and down in the passenger seat. Charlie glances at him and detects a poorly concealed wince.

"See what I mean."

"I assure you, Mr. Matthews, that your crazy mission would be an utter failure without my involvement."

"And with it?"

"The odds are only moderately improved."

Charlie steadies the wheel with his aching arm.

"Where did Aamir Khan say the girl lived?"

"Near the main mosque, I believe."

Charlie parks next to the concrete building and turns off the engine. Outside a one-legged man swings by on crutches, his asymmetrical shadow long in the morning sun. Charlie wonders if Wali is watching him with envy.

"So you think they'll be here?" Charlie says.

"The wedding always takes place at the bride's home."

Wali rolls down his window and lights a cigarette.

"If you do not mind me asking, why are you doing this, Mr. Matthews?"

"You want the bullshit answer or the real one?"

"No bullshit, thank you."

Charlie exhales.

"I'm in love with her, Wali."

Wali chuckles.

"I knew it from the moment you first mentioned her."

"That obvious?"

"You are a bigger fool than I am when you're around her."

"So what you think?"

"It's craziness, Mr. Matthews, even crazier than your venture today."

"You don't think she loves me?"

"No, she may very well. I've noticed when you're not looking that she cannot help but watch you, but this is a country where love stories don't end well. Think about it, most men only meet their wives at the wedding, and trust me most are deeply disappointed by their parents' choice."

"I'm guessing the women aren't so happy either."

"Undoubtedly, but what this means is that love cannot be allowed to grow. Its very existence is a threat—to the imams, to the parents, to the politicians, to those who are already married—and so when it does occur it must be snuffed out."

"Just like that couple in your village."

"Exactly."

Charlie takes the cigarette and inhales.

"Wali, I'm not going to get us killed today."

"Then may I be so bold as to enquire what your plan is?"

"Someone wise once told me an Afghan is like a lamb."

"So we are going to the depths of hell?"

Charlie smiles.

"Something like that."

Charlie flicks the cigarette away and retrieves Wali's wheelchair from the trunk. He lifts Wali into it.

"Okay, which tent do you think is theirs?"

Wali points at a shimmering spiral of smoke rising into the grey morning sky.

"It doesn't matter how poor the family is, if their daughter is getting married they must prepare food for their guests."

As they pass by, tent flaps open and refugees stare out at them; a young boy with a flap of skin over his right eye, a scraggly haired girl in a bright orange shalwar kameez, an old woman, so gnarled she no longer bothers to even cover her hair. Charlie feels like a gunslinger in the Old West entering a town where the inhabitants have fled for cover.

Problem is, I don't have a gun.

They come upon the source of the smoke; two rusted cauldrons sitting on a stack of burning wood. One is filled with bubbling rice while the other has chunks of meat boiling away in it. Yellowed fat bobs on its surface and flies circle. The cook, his shalwar kameez spotted with grease, stares up at them with a blank gaze. Charlie pushes Wali through the smoke, and they come upon a group of turbaned men sitting on the ground. One of the men notices them, and in an almost telepathic fashion the others turn their way.

"I don't see the girl," Charlie says.

"The women are behind there," Wali says, nodding at a long muslin sheet that's been strung between two posts.

Charlie sees a couple of Lee Enfield rifles propped up against one of them. He puts his right hand over his heart.

Stay calm.

"As-Salaam Alaykum," he says.

A smattering of salaams come back his way. Wali speaks up in Pashtu, and an emaciated man replies.

"That is the father, and the man to his right is the groom," Wali says.

Charlie looks at the groom. His ancient forehead has a thousand lines, his lips are so thin they barely exist, and his ear lobes dangle like overripe fruit on a tree.

"You're kidding?"

"The father says this is not a good time, that the ceremony is about to begin."

"Tell him we just need a couple of minutes, that I've brought him a prize."

"Mr. Matthews, I firmly advise—"

"Tell him it's a hundred dollars, but to give it to him we must speak alone."

Wali sighs and translates. The men murmur amongst themselves. The father gestures to a nearby tent.

"He says two minutes it is," Wali says.

Charlie bends down and picks up Wali. The father holds open the flap of a tent.

"This is our last chance to leave, Mr. Matthews," Wali says.

"Najib told me an old Pashtun saying the other day. 'The goat who flees from the wolf spends the night in the butcher's house.'"

"And how does that relate to our present situation?"

"Damned if I know."

Wali can't help but laugh, and Charlie carries him into the tent. Inside there is nothing more than a couple of sagging rope beds and a ragged pile of clothing. Charlie puts Wali down on the earthen floor. Wali leans back against one of the beds.

"Comfortable?" Charlie says.

"Absolutely," Wali says.

"Liar."

Charlie sits down on the rope bed, the father on the other. Charlie attempts a smile.

"Congratulations, this must be a very proud day for you."

Wali translates. The father says nothing.

"My colleague and I work for the organization that funds your daughter's school."

The father barks a reply before Wali's finished translating.

"He wants to know if we were the ones who sent that woman the other night," Wali says.

"Oh no, we'd never interfere in any decision you've made about Kamila's future."

Wali translates, and the father speaks.

"He asks why we are here then, and what is this prize? In fact that is something I am most intrigued to know myself."

Charlie pulls out a bundle of hundred dollar bills. He peels one off and hands it to the father.

"Your daughter was asked to write an essay in school this year, and it was submitted for a competition."

Wali translates. The father drags his gaze away from the hundred dollar bill.

"You should be very proud, over ten thousand girls her age competed, from countries all over the world, and Kamila's essay was judged to be the best."

Wali translates, and the father frowns. The father speaks.

"He asks when you say all the world if that includes America?" Wali says.

"Yes, she beat everyone."

The father's eyes well up. It takes him a moment to speak.

"He says his wife thinks there is no value in education. Not for a girl."

"Well tell him that there's a second part to the prize—a scholarship. For every year Kamila remains in school, his family will receive five hundred dollars, and if she goes to college that sum increases to a thousand. Unfortunately the only stipulation is that any recipient remain unmarried."

Wali stares at Charlie wide-eyed.

"That's way too much. I beg you, allow me to offer a lower amount."

"No, that's what I want to do."

Wali snorts and tells the man. Charlie watches the father closely. For a long time the father sits there stroking his patchy beard. The father glances out the flap at the wedding party who are all looking in their direction. Charlie stands.

"Tell him I understand that this is impossible given his situation but I felt obliged to let him know."

Wali translates, and Charlie goes to pick him up. The father speaks up.

"He says sit down: this wedding is not yet formalized."

Charlie returns to his rope bed. The father exits the tent.

"So what now?" Charlie says.

"It's up to the groom. Perhaps the father can offer him enough to call it off."

"Any chance the guy could take offense?"

"Of course, but if he does his relatives will shoot the father first before they shoot us."

"That's comforting to know."

Charlie peers out the tent. The father kneels beside the groom and speaks earnestly. The groom launches into a harsh invective, his hands gesticulating wildly. His relatives fling murderous glances in Charlie's direction. Charlie pulls his head back in.

"You think we should make a run for it?" he says.

Wali looks at his stumps and rolls his eyes.

"You know what I mean?" Charlie says.

Outside the voices become less vitriolic.

"You hear what they're saying?" Charlie says.

"It's good, they're arguing about money."

The tent flap opens and the now grim-faced father enters. He speaks to Wali.

"He says if this is to work he needs three hundred dollars more for the groom."

"That's it?"

"I suggest you pay him before the groom changes his mind."

Charlie reaches into his pocket and withdraws the roll. He peels off eight hundred dollars and hands them to the father.

"Three hundred for his cousin and five hundred for the first year," Charlie says.

The father stares at the bills as if they're a winning lottery ticket. This time he speaks directly to Charlie.

"He says he always hoped his daughter's education would lead to a better life, and now it has. He would be most honored if we joined him for some food," Wali says.

The father gestures for them to follow him. Charlie carries Wali outside to where the group are seated. Charlie looks at the gathered men. He receives respectful nods and even some smiles. No one is smiling more broadly than the ex-groom.

"Guess he did well out of the bargain?" Charlie says.

"Oh, extremely," Wali says. "Besides he'll find another bride soon enough."

A bunch of shoeless kids bring over bent metal trays laden with food and lay them in the middle of the rugs. Everyone turns towards Charlie. He places a sufficient quantity on his plate so as not to be considered an ungracious guest.

"Bismallah ar-Rahman, ar-Raheem," he says.

He rips off a piece of naan and uses it to grab some meat and rice. He shoves it in his mouth.

"Very good," he says.

The men all smile. Charlie glances at the muslin sheet and sees a girl staring at him through a tear in the material. All he can see are her piercing, intelligent eyes and her forehead with its distinctive birthmark.

Kamila.

She smiles at him and then just like that she's gone.

THIRTY-SIX

CHARLIE STANDS WITH Shamsurahman. The recruits are above them on the rocky hillside, their lanes marked by bright orange string. Some are swaying their detectors back and forth, others are on their bellies probing for mines while others are cutting back long grass so they can push their detection efforts further up the slope. Shamsurahman has been observing them for an hour now and hasn't said a word.

"I have seen enough," Shamsurahman says.

He heads down the hill. Charlie looks over at Mocam.

"What do you think that's all about?"

Mocam shrugs. The recruits look in Charlie's direction.

"Okay, that's it, we're done."

The recruits trudge down the hill towards the pick-ups.

"Hey, wait up," he shouts.

They turn back, their heads bowed.

"All I can say is I'm proud of you. If you were doing something wrong I couldn't tell, and when I find out what it was we'll fix it. Now go enjoy the rest of your day."

The recruits continue down the hill, and Charlie and Mocam spend the next half hour retrieving the dummy mines and reeling in the string.

"You good getting this back to base?" Charlie says.

Mocam nods. Charlie looks at his watch.

Only an hour late. They better still be serving.

If one thing's consumed his thoughts as much as Noor these last few days it's been the US Consulate's holiday barbecue. The idea of burgers and hotdogs is almost too good to be true. Charlie jogs down to his motorcycle and speeds towards town. Twenty minutes later he pulls up at the consulate's main gate. A spit-and-polish Marine checks him off the list, and Charlie parks his motorcycle at the end of a row of high-end cars. He runs past their chain smoking chauffeurs, through the consulate's marble floored atrium and out into the garden. Little paper American and Pakistani flags have been strung up between the trees, a tinny speaker set plays *Wouldn't It Be Nice*, and the aroma of barbecuing hot dogs and burgers laces the air with the familiarity of a long lost friend. Charlie makes a beeline for a billowing grill.

"Thought that was you," Jurgen says.

Charlie sees Jurgen standing with an unremarkable couple.

Shit, so close.

"These are my friends Josef and Angela from Stuttgart."

"Hi," Charlie says. "Good to meet you."

"Nothing like celebrating the pinnacles of American culture, is there? Hot dogs, the Beach Boys, Coca Cola."

"Yeah, suppose it's hard to beat bratwurst, Hitler and lederhosen."

Josef and Angela turn ashen. Jurgen laughs.

"I warned you this one was an acquired taste. Anyway I wanted to be the first to congratulate you. Shamsurahman told me your group passed. I want you in Afghanistan in a week, the village actually where your colleague lost his legs."

Charlie looks around, convinced this is some sort of practical joke. If it is, no one else seems to be in on it.

"I thought Kenneth took that one," Charlie says.

"Dear Kenneth had a nervous breakdown."

"Jesus."

"This country has the tendency to do a number on people."

"And Skeppar?"

"You let me deal with him. Just concentrate on getting your men ready."

Jurgen raises his Coke.

"To your glorious independence."

"To lederhosen," Charlie grins.

Jurgen laughs, and he and his friends drift away. Charlie remembers his original reason for coming and orders a hot dog and cheeseburger. He heads over to the condiment table: Heinz ketchup, French's mustard, and homemade relish.

Ah, it's almost too perfect.

He sees Ivor winding his way though the crowd.

Ah come on, not now.

Charlie bites into his hotdog. Ivor idles up next to him.

"How you doing kid?

"This is fricking amazing," Charlie says.

"All courtesy of the US government."

"I'll never complain about paying taxes ever again."

"You're an ex-pat, you don't."

"Oh yeah, forgot."

Ivor glances in Jurgen's direction.

"What that fag want?"

"You really know how to insult someone, don't you?"

Ivor shrugs.

"We're going into Afghanistan next week," Charlie says. "We just got our credentials."

"Well do me a favor, you see anything weird while you're out there, get word to me."

"I thought you said you weren't CIA."

"Just do it, okay."

"Chill, Ivor, just pulling your leg."

Ivor looks for someone better to talk to. Charlie couldn't care less. He finishes off his first hot dog.

"So did your guy make it?" Ivor says.

"Yeah, he's doing great, already out of hospital, actually I got him living with me."

Ivor nods at a couple of passing Pakistani officers.

"Tell me you're kidding," Ivor says.

"Don't see what's so funny."

Ivor drags his attention away from the party.

"Look, it's admirable you feel sorry for him, but there's three and a half million sad-as-shit refugees round here. You should stick to those who've got a future."

"Wali has a future."

"His legs were blown off, it's not like he can drive a cab."

"So I should just throw him to the curb?"

"No, but you could politely place him there."

"Sorry, just not that kind of guy."

Charlie starts away. Ivor grabs his arm.

"Hey, I'm just trying to impart some wisdom here. You forget, I've been around this shit longer than you. Life's a zero sum game, kid. You helping this guy, means you can't help someone else."

"I don't see it that way."

"Okay, you see an eighty year old man and a five year old kid drowning. You only have time to save one. Who do you haul out of the water?"

Charlie doesn't answer. It's the exact kind of scenario his father would throw at him. Ivor lets go of Charlie's arm.

"Don't get caught up in lost causes, Charlie. Too many people do—in dead-end marriages, boring jobs, shitty friendships, stupid-ass wars—fuck, ask the Soviets about Afghanistan, ask them how that went. Key in life is learning when to cut loose."

"Sure love to be in a foxhole with you, Ivor."

"That's the thing, I'd never get myself in one in the first place." .

Ivor slaps Charlie on the back and wanders into the fray. Charlie looks around. He sees Jurgen and his friends sitting on some wicker chairs laughing with other members of the UN aristocracy; Elma Kuyt by the fish pond chatting with an American diplomat; Mike and Dave propping up the bar. All he wants is to be with Noor. He starts for the door, the cheeseburger forgotten.

***

ELMA ONLY HEARS the odd word the consul is saying. He is none the wiser. Over the years she's perfected the nodding head and furrowed brow that makes anyone you're talking to believe you're listening intently.

Where is he?

She's certain Rod said he was flying back today. She feels a tingle in her stomach as if she were a teenager waiting for her crush to appear. These last two weeks without him have been excruciating. She's immersed herself in paperwork, visited as many projects as possible, taught Noor numerous Dutch lessons, yet everything has felt hollow. Just today she received both good and bad news in regard to the UNDP post, and yet neither seemed to affect her. The good news was that she was on the shortlist with two other candidates. The bad news was that one of those candidates was Andrea Engelson. She'd had no idea Engelson was interested in the position, and her inclusion has only lowered Elma's chance of being selected.

At any other time in her life, Elma would be crawling up the walls with anxiety. After all Engelson is in New York, no doubt schmoozing with UN decision makers while she couldn't be further away doing work that actually affects people's lives, yet work that she knows counts for nothing when it comes to scaling the developmental aid ladder. Yet all of a sudden the job doesn't seem that important. In fact Andrea Engelson can have it for all she cares.

I need to tell Rod. Everything.

If her relationship with Raymond taught her anything it's that relationships built on deceit inevitably founder. By now she knows Rod's character.

He'll understand. He'll probably love me even more for it.

In recent days she's even considered telling Isaac the truth.

My God, if anyone deserves to know it's him.

The next time she's in Holland they'll all sit down. Who knows perhaps Rod will be there too. She knows it'll be painful, but it is the right thing to do. In the long run they'll all be better off.

She looks once again towards the atrium doors and sees Rod at the top of the steps, his receding curly hair, his wide forehead, his heavy spectacles resting on the bridge of his stubby nose. In the past she'd never have given him a second glance, but this afternoon he might as well be the best looking man at the party. She excuses herself and works her way through the guests towards him. She wants to throw her arms around his neck but she doesn't. Not in this company, not with Ivor prowling in the vicinity.

"You made it," she says.

"Close run thing. The customs guys in Islamabad practically performed a strip search on me."

"Now that would've been something to witness."

Rod can't help but redden. She's glad her comment had an affect on him. She takes him by the arm.

"Come on, let's get you a drink."

They make their way over to the bar. He orders a whisky, and she joins him. Usually she never drinks spirits but today feels different.

Why the hell not?

"How was New York?" she says.

"Eventful."

He takes a hefty slug of his whisky.

"Well don't hold me in suspense."

"They offered me London."

Elma is dumbstruck. She takes a swig, and the whisky scalds her throat.

"You're kidding?" she says.

"Trust me, was the last thing I expected. Every old fart in that building has been lobbying for the gig."

"And what did you tell them?"

"I took it. I've been traveling from one hot spot to another for so long now, the idea of strawberries and cream at Wimbledon, the Queen, hell just somewhere normal to rest my head for a couple of years, how could I turn it down?"

"You couldn't, you'd have been mad to."

Rod smiles.

"I thought you might accuse me of selling out."

"You're a great reporter, Rod. Even the best need a break."

He reddens again and looks at his feet. She loves him all the more for his modesty. He brings his gaze back up.

"You're so beautiful," he says. "In so many ways."

It's now Elma's turn to blush. She can't remember the last time a compliment had such an effect on her.

"There's something else," he says.

Elma holds her breath.

He's going to ask me to come with him, she thinks.

They'll rent a cute apartment in Kensington, and she'll get a post with the European Community or a British NGO. They'll buy a dog, a small one they can travel with, have weekend trips to the Continent. And the sex, oh my God, plenty of amazing sex, in a grand antique bed with that constant British rain pattering outside.

Someone catches Rod's attention, and he stiffens. Elma sees Ivor winding his way towards them. She feels her stomach turn.

"Come on," she says, "let's get out of here. There's something I want to tell you too."

She grips Rod's arm and leads him out front where her SUV is parked. They drive away just as Ivor comes out its main doors. She decides that they'll fuck first. She knows there's no way she can wait, not anymore.

Then we can talk.

She feels her pulse quicken, closes her eyes a moment as she imagines him entering her. She hears a horn and sees a rickshaw cross in front of her. She swerves and misses the vehicle by an inch.

"Sorry," she says with a jittery laugh.

"Where are we going?" Rod says.

"My house, of course."

She places her hand on his thigh and runs her hand up his leg. She feels him harden.

"Elma—"

"Shhh, we're almost there."

By the side of the road a couple of men are pushing a cart stacked high with watermelons. She can't help but smile as she remembers the question that girl in Noor's class asked.

How long ago that seems.

She pulls into her driveway and comes to a halt outside the front door. She turns off the ignition, Rod's heavy breathing magnified by the silence. She glances at him. He's staring straight ahead.

"I need to tell you something," he says.

"Me too."

Elma places her hand on Rod's cheek and turns his face towards her.

"I love you," she says.

She closes her eyes and moves her lips towards his.

"I'm engaged," he says.

Elma pulls back and grips the wheel. She tries to take a breath but fails.

"I'm sorry," he says, "I shouldn't have let it get this far."

"Who?"

"Amanda, she works at the Times, we've been off again on again for years, but on this last visit something clicked, it just felt right."

"And you're sure?"

"As sure as I think I'll ever be."

Her whole body starts to tremble. He places his hand on her arm, and she drops it away.

Just get out, get out, get out.

"I had no idea you felt this way," he says, "if I had—"

"No, it's my fault. It was a fantasy that's all, stupid really."

"This won't effect the piece, I promise."

Elma begins to sob. She tries to stop herself but finds it impossible not to do so.

"Is there anything I can do?" he says.

She covers her face with her hands and starts rocking back and forth in her seat.

"I meant what I said, Elma. You really are a beautiful woman. You'll find someone way better than me, I promise."

She hears the passenger door open and close. His footsteps fade away, and now free of his presence, Elma collapses against the steering wheel and begins to bawl.

THIRTY-SEVEN

"DOES ANYONE KNOW what they'll be celebrating in America in two weeks?"

Noor looks out at her class. Half the girls have their hands raised. She nods at Yasmeen, a girl with wide brown eyes.

"Their new year, Miss."

"Well done. Now who knows what year it will be in their calendar?"

Eight hands go up this time. She's heartened to see one of them belongs to Hila. She nods at her.

"Nineteen ninety-two, Miss," Hila says.

"And why will it be nineteen ninety-two?"

"Because that's how long since the Jesus was born."

"Excellent. And what year is it in our calendar?"

Every hand goes up.

"Rashida?"

"Fourteen-twelve, Miss."

"And how many years is that since?"

Noor points at Zilla, a prim, studious type near the back.

"The hijra. The year the Prophet, peace be upon him, journeyed to Medina from Mecca."

Noor looks out at her students.

"I hope you know you're the smartest class in school."

The girls start clapping. Noor puts a finger to her lips.

"Shhh, that's our secret, we don't want the other girls to get jealous."

The girls giggle. Noor glances at Kamila's empty chair and feels a pang of sorrow. She wonders where Kamila is now; her husband's hut most likely, being harangued by his first wife while she waits in terror for him to return. She forces a smile.

"Now can anyone tell me what's the difference between the Islamic and Christian calendars?"

A host of hands go up.

"Mariam?"

"Ours is better, Miss."

"I was hoping for a more scientific answer. Hila?"

"They are not good Muslims, Miss."

"Hila, they aren't Muslims so they cannot be good or bad Muslims only good or bad Christians. Amina?"

"They celebrate their new year, Miss, and we don't."

"True but—"

"In New York City they set off fireworks and drop a glass ball and drink alcohol in the streets."

"I told you, Miss, they are not good Muslims," Hila says.

"I'm still looking for a scientific explanation. Anyone?"

"Our calendar is lunar and theirs is solar," a voice says.

Noor turns and sees Kamila standing in the doorway. The girls scream in delight and rush over to her. Noor takes a moment to compose herself. She tells the girls to sit down, and slowly they drift back to their desks. Noor walks over and touches Kamila's cheek.

You really are here.

Noor opens up her arms and hugs Kamila. She never wants to let her go. She does, however. She stares into Kamila's sparkling eyes.

"How?"

"I was saved by a knight in shining armor," Kamila says.

Noor dismisses the comment. Kamila's always had an overactive imagination.

"Well that's what knights are there for, aren't they?"

"I'm sorry for what my mother did to you. I tried to stop them, but they held me back."

"I survived."

"And so did I."

"Yes you did. Come, sit, we can talk more after class."

Noor leads Kamila to her desk. Kamila leans back in her chair with the confidence of a Captain who's returned to the bridge of his ship. Noor picks up her book and tries to remember where they were in the lesson.

"Do you think Allah sent my knight, Miss Noor?" Kamila says.

"I'm sure he did."

"Even if he's not a Muslim?"

Noor looks up, and the class leans forward as if they're about to hear the most fantastical of tales.

"The man who played tag with us in the courtyard came the day of the wedding with a man in a wheelchair. He told my father if I stayed unmarried he'd pay him money for every year I attended school. Right after, the wedding was called off."

Noor stands there, stunned.

Oh my Lord, he did this for me.

"Miss Noor, do you know this man?" Kamila says.

"No," she says, recovering, "but I've heard of men like him. They travel the country doing this sort of thing."

"Like Don Quixote and Sancho Panza?" Amina says.

"No, silly," Kamila says, "they were idiots. He's more like Saladin."

"Or maybe Salman Khan," Yasmeen says.

Noor allows the girls to squabble amongst themselves. She knows Charlie resembles none of these men, yet at this moment he's not only Kamila's hero, he's hers too.

That afternoon he never leaves her thoughts. He stands at the back of the class, sits beside her on the bus making fun of her burqa, walks her home, and opens the front door for her. He lifts the burqa over her head, his face inches from hers—

Noor hears a crash come from the kitchen. She shoves the burqa into the bottom of her bag and heads to the kitchen. Mukhtar is on his knees picking up the remnants of a shattered dish.

"I'm so sorry, Miss Noor."

"Don't worry, I did the exact same thing not so long ago."

Noor gets down and helps him.

"Where is everyone?" she says.

"Your father and Wali are at the hospital, and I believe your sister is washing some clothes."

"And Mr. Matthews?"

"Mr. Matthews?"

Noor feels her face burn up and turns away.

"It's of no concern," she says. "I was just curious if you expected him home anytime soon."

"I'm sorry, I have no idea."

Noor walks over to the sink and pours herself a glass of water. Through the window she sees Rasul hobble towards the hut. She lets the water slip down her throat, and feels her complexion return to normal.

"I prepared mourgh for dinner," Mukhtar says. "Is there anything else I can get you?"

"No, you can go," Noor says.

"Have a good night, Miss Noor."

"You too, Mukhtar."

Noor stands there a moment marveling at the absurdity of their final exchange.

When did I become a woman who dismisses servants.

She glances at the clock. It's quarter to six. It's time she went to Elma's. She retrieves her study books from the sitting room, and walks towards the hall. Outside she hears the roar of Charlie's motorcycle. She stands there unsure what to do. She hears the front door open, and Charlie fling his satchel down on the hall chair. He starts walking in her direction. Her breathing quickens. She looks around the room.

You can't just be standing here.

She spies the leather reading chair and hurries to it. His footsteps get closer. She drops the books on the floor and then retrieves the one on top. She opens it to a chapter on the passive voice. She might as well be reading a book in Sanskrit. The door opens.

"You're home," Charlie says.

Noor looks up. His shirt is wrinkled, his leather boots caked with dust.

"I'm studying before I go over to Elma's," she says.

"I just saw her at the consulate barbecue."

He spies the book in her hand. She has to remind herself to breathe.

"How's that going?" he says.

"One day at a time."

"Don't get all humble on me, I bet you're fluent by now."

"Hardly."

"Well say something then."

She thinks.

"Dank u," she says.

"Dank who?"

"It means thank you."

"For what?"

"Voor het redden Kamila."

"You got me on that one too."

"For saving Kamila."

Charlie smiles. He sits on the ottoman across from her. She can smell him from here; burnt charcoal, cigarettes, faint aftershave, the sweat that comes from having worked a full day under a relentless sun.

"Why did you save her?" she says.

He rubs the scar on his cheek.

"You want the fake reason or the real one?"

Don't answer that question.

She tries to stand and finds it impossible. His eyes stay fixed on her, and she can't help but look right back at him.

"To be fair the fake one's not entirely fake. I did it because I wanted Kamila to have a better life than Ameena."

Noor bites the inside of her lip.

"But the real reason?" she hears herself say.

His hands reach out and clasp the ends of her fingers.

"Because I'd do anything for you. Because I've fallen totally and utterly in love with you."

Charlie leans in, and touches his lips against hers. It's like no sensation she's ever felt before.

It's from heaven.

His lips part, and she finds hers parting also. Their tongues meet, and his hand reaches around her waist and pulls her closer. He runs his hand up her back and through her hair. Inexplicably, she reaches out her own and slips it under his shirt. His breathing becomes ragged. She runs her fingers along his smooth chest. His hand slips under her kameez and unclasps her bra so easily he might as well have designed it himself. He pulls the strap off her right shoulder and his hand caresses her breast. She moans and kisses him harder. She feels her groin moisten.

And then she hears a creak.

She pulls away, her hand ripping off one of his buttons as she extricates it. Bushra enters the room and looks their way.

No one says anything.

Noor breathes heavily; it's impossible not to. She spies the button lying on the floor. It seems as incriminatory as a bloody knife at a murder scene.

"You're getting better—" Charlie says.

She looks over. He's holding her Dutch books in his hands.

"Think Elma's going to be really impressed with the work you've done."

Charlie gives her a reassuring smile. Noor nods, and he hands her the books. She totters out of the room, her bra hanging loose, her underwear damp. She feels Bushra's eyes on her all the way. She stumbles outside and down the driveway. Once past the gate she leans back against the hedge. She is so lightheaded she thinks she might collapse. She draws her tongue over her lips; they no longer feel like hers but some appendage sown on. She hears the clip clop of an approaching donkey and opens her eyes. A teenage boy with the faintest of mustaches rides high on a cart stacked with tree branches. The boy stares down at her.

Does he know? Can he smell it on me?

She waits until the cart has moved on and fixes her bra. She starts walking the opposite direction.

"Oh Allah, what have I done?" she says.

She knows it was wrong. It went against everything she believes in. However when she closes her eyes her recriminations disappear, and all she wants to do is turn around and run back to Charlie.

Stop it. You're not thinking clearly.

She picks up her pace. SUVs speed past her delivering the aid worker elite back to their homes. She thinks about what Charlie did for Kamila, the danger he must have put himself in, and knows that at his core he's an honorable man.

He said he loved me, surely that means he wants to marry me.

But would you want to marry him? a voice asks.

She arrives at Elma's driveway with her very belief system under threat.

I don't need to answer that now.

She looks up the driveway and sees someone in the front seat of Elma's SUV. She approaches the side window. Elma's head is bent forward, her long hair covering her face. Noor leans in closer. Elma twists her face in Noor's direction. It is so sudden that Noor screams. Elma's make-up has run down her cheeks in dark rivulets, her eyes are hollow, her long hair all bedraggled. Noor opens the door.

"Elma? Are you okay?"

"It's been a bad day, that's all."

"I can come back tomorrow, when you feel better."

Elma takes a deep breath as if summoning all her will-power and steps out of the SUV.

"No, I could do with the company," she says. "Come on, it's cold out here."

They head inside, and Elma leaves Noor on the couch in her sitting room while she freshens up. Noor wishes she'd had the presence of mind to do the same.

She closes her eyes and once again imagines Charlie's lips on hers and his hand delving under her kameez. The foreign sensation she felt earlier returns, and her hand drifts towards her right breast. She hears Elma coming down the corridor and sits up straight. Elma enters the room. She has scrubbed her face clean and done her hair up in a simple ponytail.

"So how was your day?" Elma says.

Noor can't help but blush.

"It was ..."

Noor bites her lip. She can't think of a suitable lie. Elma sits opposite Noor and gives her a curious look.

"I need to tell you something," Noor says.

"Go on."

"For the last two months I've been living at Charlie Mat-thews' house."

Elma nods as if Noor's revelation comes as no surprise.

"He needed someone to look after his friend, Wali, and thought my father would be a good candidate. It meant naturally that our whole family had to move in."

"I am sure that pleased him no end."

"No, for a long time we didn't even see him. He's up early, home late, but the longer we've stayed the more I've come to

know him, and I'm not afraid to say that alongside my father
he's the best man I know. He's kind, brave, sensitive, more
intelligent than I ever thought possible, and most of all he
treats me as an equal. I don't think it matters to him whether
I'm a man or a woman."

"Yet he's not attracted to men, is he?"

Noor blushes. She imagines herself up on the scaffold like
Hester Prynne, her sin there for the whole world to see.

"Has anything happened?" Elma says.

"We kissed, just now... more than kissed—"

"Did you have sex?"

"No! We were interrupted by my sister—"

"But you could have?"

"No, never."

"You're certain of that?"

Noor looks towards the fireplace.

"Noor," Elma says, "Think back to that moment when
you were kissing him. Imagine what would've happened if
your sister hadn't come in."

Noor closes her eyes. She sees Charlie sweep her up in his
arms, their mouths searching each others as they make their
way up the stairs. He drops her on his bed, lifts her kameez
over her head and—

Her eyes flash open. Elma sits down beside her, and takes
Noor's hands in hers. Noor feels compelled to look at her.

"When I was seventeen, I fell in love with my politics
tutor. He was young, still in his twenties, passionate, he had a
way of speaking that made you want to fight for every one of
his causes. He was intelligent too, kind, sensitive, brave, he'd
been arrested a number of times taking part in all sorts of
protests, but it never deterred him even when the principal
threatened to sack him. At first I thought there was no hope,
that it would remain just some fevered fantasy of mine. He
was married to a beautiful woman, had a young child, and in
class he was no more attentive to me than he was to any of

the other girls. And then one day I spoke passionately about nuclear disarmament. It must have caught his attention because after class he called me over, told me about a march in the Hague that weekend, I could even drive with him if I wanted.

"That weekend was the first time we had sex, and over the next three months I don't think a day went by when we didn't. It was thrilling, romantic. There we were in crowds of thousands, linking arms, shouting slogans, running from the police, and afterwards we'd fuck until sleep finally took us. Then one day I missed my period. It's funny you'd think I'd have been distraught, but I wasn't. All I could think was that I was going to have this wonderful man's child, and when he heard the news he'd leave his wife, and we'd live this incredible life together.

"That night I cooked dinner for him at my mother's house; she was away visiting my grandmother. I spent hours slaving over it, but when I told him all I saw was shock. 'You have to have it aborted,' he said, and it was then I realized that he was never going to leave his wife. He handed me four hundred guilder as if I was some whore he'd fucked for the first and last time. 'Get it fixed,' he said. After that everything was a blur, that is until my mother returned and found me lying on our kitchen floor."

A thought worms its way into Noor's brain.

What if Bushra hadn't walked in? What if I had become pregnant. What would've been Charlie's reaction then?

"I tell you all this because I see a lot of you in me. The drive, the fierce independence but also a naïve innocence, especially when it comes to men. This Charlie Matthews, I promise you, he's no different than my politics tutor. All men want a fantasy and you a poor, beautiful refugee are like no other. He wants to save you, I dare say he may even want to marry you, but once he has, reality will set in, and the passion will fade. 'Men were deceivers ever,' that's what Shakespeare said, and it's as true today as it was then, and as a woman who wants to be independent and free you need to see what your 'love' for this man really is. Nothing more than a silly schoolgirl crush that threatens everything you've worked so hard to realize."

Noor knows Elma is right.

You have not only deceived yourself, you attempted to deceive Allah.

Noor collapses into Elma's arms and sobs.

"I promise you," Elma says, "six months from now you'll be in Holland, immersed in university life, and you won't feel a thing for him."

Elma holds Noor tight, and eventually her tears fade. Noor wipes her eyes with the sleeve of her kameez.

"I want you to come live with me," Elma says.

Noor looks at Elma in shock.

"I'll need to talk to my father first," she says.

"Then call him, the phone's over there."

"No, I couldn't do that to Baba. I need to tell him face to face."

"You're aware from the moment you step foot in that man's house that you're in danger of falling into his web again."

"That won't happen."

Elma looks at Noor with the air of a stern headmistress.

"You need to promise me you won't see him. If he attempts to talk to you, you must walk away. Lock your bedroom door if need be."

"I promise."

"And if you're not here tomorrow night, I'm coming to get you. You understand?"

Noor nods.

"Fine, I'll drive you to his place."

It takes no more than three minutes to get there, and before Noor gets out, Elma makes her promise one more time. Noor creeps up the driveway and opens the front door an inch. She hears Wali and Charlie having a boisterous conversation in the sitting room. She presumes her father is there too or on the verandah. She creeps upstairs to her room. She's relieved to find that Bushra is not there and heads into the bathroom. She stares at herself in the mirror.

Who are you?

She has no ready answer. She takes off her shalwar kameez and her yellowed bra and underwear. She catches a glimpse of her naked body; the curve of her right breast, the mound of hair between her legs.

To think how close he was to seeing it all, to possessing it.

To her shame, she feels a similar feeling as before infect her groin. She steps into the shower and lets the cold water blast her until her body is numb. She sniffs the water up her nose and grabs the bar of soap and scrubs her feet, her legs, her vagina, her breasts, her face, her hair, even the inside of her mouth. Only then does she turn off the shower. She dries herself and puts on her nighttime garments. She opens the door, and finds Bushra sitting on her bed. The two sisters stare at each other.

"Baba wanted to know if you were coming down for dinner," Bushra says.

"Please, tell him I have a headache."

For a moment it seems as if Bushra is going to say something, but then she stands and leaves the room.

Noor takes a deep breath and focuses on her prayers. She asks Allah for forgiveness, and by the end she feels a comforting heat envelop her body as blood returns to her skin.

I am forgiven.

THIRTY-EIGHT

NOOR LOOKS AT the clock for what feels like the hundredth time. It's five. Time to go. She slips out of bed and is shocked to see that Bushra is already up.

"What are you doing?" Noor whispers.

"I need to wash Wali's bandages, and then run his bath."

"You bathe him?"

Even in the dim light, Noor can see her sister is blushing.

"Who do you think I am?" Bushra says.

"I'm sorry, I'm just surprised that's all."

"It's a job, Noor. Someone must do it."

Without another word, Bushra leaves. Noor dresses and creeps down the corridor to her father's room. She kneels by his bed and looks at his peaceful face, his spindly body warm under a feather comforter, his reading glasses perched on the bedside table. His eyes open.

"Baba, we need to talk."

He gives her a befuddled look and sits up. She proceeds to tell him everything. He doesn't condemn her, if anything he blames himself for ever putting her in such a position, but she won't have any of it.

"It's no one's fault but mine," she says. "Not Charlie's, and certainly not yours."

She tells him about Elma's offer, and after that her father's mood revives. He tells her not to worry, he'll explain it all to Charlie.

"You should get going, my love," he says.

She spies his alarm clock. He's right. It's already five-thirty. She goes to leave when she realizes that tonight will be the first time in nine years that she's slept under a different roof than him. She tells him and he smiles.

"See it as preparation for when you go to Holland."

She tiptoes back to her bedroom. Outside her door she spies a gift wrapped in plain brown paper with a simple white envelope stuck to its front. It can only mean one thing.

Charlie's up.

She knows she must leave, but before she does, she picks up the gift.

All day it sits on her classroom desk, and now, with her class dismissed, she finds herself staring at it.

Don't open it. What good can come from it?

The shutters bang in the wind but she doesn't look up. It's as if the gift has magical powers.

It's fine, I'm stronger than any words he's written.

She peels the envelope off and opens it. The note is on a piece of paper he's torn from his sketch pad.

Dearest Noor:

Forgive me. I don't know what came over me yesterday. No, that's a lie - I do. I'm completely in love with you, and I let my passion get the better of me.

Perhaps you did only have a headache last night, and I'm stupid for worrying, but I'm petrified that I've scared you away. Please don't be - scared that is. I promise never to place you in a position like that again. Your honor means more than anything to me.

Please reply to this - even if it's just a one sentence answer. I'll be a nervous wreck all day if you don't.

I love you.

Forever,
Charlie

p.s. I got this for you a few day's back - as a Christmas present. I
hope it inspires you as you inspire me.

Noor trembles, all her previous feelings for Charlie come
tumbling back. She imagines him at home already waiting for
her, and her heart breaks.
Remember what Elma said.
But here in this moment, everything Elma said seems false.
Wasn't it Elma after all who'd once told her that she was
going to meet someone and fall in love with him without
even realizing it?
And I have found that man. I know I have.
She rips off the wrapping paper to find a black, leather
notebook. On the front cover there's an embossed quote:
'The reason one writes isn't the fact she wants to say something. She
writes because she has something to say.'
She recognizes it as one of F. Scott Fitzgerald's.
Except, of course, Fitzgerald wrote it in the masculine, and Charlie's
changed it to the feminine.
She feels an intense longing to see him; to kiss him; to
hold him; to tell him her love's as strong as his. She jumps up
from her chair and looks for her burqa only to realize that in
her earlier haste she must have left it at the house. She thinks
about finding another and discards the thought. The black
4x4 hasn't been back in weeks,.
Besides, I'm beginning to get much too comfortable in it anyway.
She picks up the notebook, makes certain her weekly wage
is secure, and strides out of the room. In the next door
classroom Miss Layla calls after her, but she ignores her. She
is too desperate to see Charlie to delay. She runs across the
courtyard and out the front entrance towards the main road.
She feels raindrops on her face and gasps. It's their first rain

in six months. She raises her face towards the sky and breathes in the fresh earthy smell. She smiles.

It's a sign. I'm absolved.

Up ahead a black SUV turns up the road. Her stomach turns.

It can't be.

She pulls her shawl tight around her face and stares at the ground. The SUV comes up upon her. She holds her breath. The tires crunch, and the hum lessens.

She breathes easier.

The SUV stops, and she hears an electric window descend.

"Ma'am," a man says in Pashtu.

She keeps on walking. The gears shift, and the SUV reverses.

"Ma'am, look this way please."

She quickens her pace. She hears doors open. She looks back and sees two bearded young zealots jumping out.

"It's her," one of them shouts.

Noor starts running. She reaches the bus stop and bowls into a woman. The woman screeches at her, and, like a flock of penguins, burqaed heads turn in her direction. One of the men grabs her arm and yanks her backwards. The leather notebook falls to the dirt. She twists around and sinks her teeth into the man's hand. The man screams.

Noor staggers on. She sees a bus pulling out. She sprints after it, and grabs a hold of the bar in its open doorway. Her feet drag along the road, mud splattering her face. She grits her teeth and pulls herself up.

"You mad?" the conductor says.

She cranes her head out the door. The SUV has stopped to pick up her pursuers. She knows it won't take long for them to catch up.

"Two rupees," the conductor says.

You can't stay on here.

"Two rupees, woman, or I'll throw you off."

"Fine," she says.

He looks at her as though she's insane.

"Let me off," she screams.

The conductor shouts at the bus driver to slow down and shoves her out the door. She lands on the side of the road. She cries out and rolls over and over until she comes to a rest by a stack of ghee cans.

Get up.

She clambers to her feet and sees nothing but mud huts. She realizes she's on the outskirts of Kacha Gari refugee camp.

She hears a vehicle skid to a halt and starts running.

Doors open behind her.

She plunges down a tight alley, turning right into one and left into another. She runs through the rubble of an abandoned hut and out into another alley. She sprints down it, and just before the corner looks over her shoulder. The men are nowhere to be seen.

Don't stop.

The alley ends, and she emerges onto a wider dirt road. Men with shawls wrapped tight around them are trudging towards evening prayers. She weaves in amongst them only to see shock sweep across their faces.

She looks over her shoulder.

The black SUV is careening down the road. The men dive to the side to avoid it.

She spies an alley and sprints towards it. The SUV skids to a halt beside her. Another door opens, and another man joins the chase. She hurls herself down the alley. The man is gaining on her.

Once more she makes a succession of quick turns.

She looks back. He's out of sight. She sees six curtained openings, three on either side of the alley.

Now or never.

She throws herself inside the second on the right. Everything is pitch black. Her eyes adjust. Two old women stare up at her, a couple of ancient sewing machines in front of them.

"Please," she says. "Please help me."

Outside she hears the man run past and not long after her two other pursuers. She scrambles for the door only to hear a fourth man come up the alley. He sounds slower than the others as if he's dragging one of his legs behind him. He stops.

"A woman's hiding around here," he yells out in Pashtu. "An adulteress. We're here to return her to her husband."

Noor shakes her head at the women. Outside she hears the other men return.

"I know your men are at the mosque, and you're probably afraid. Don't be, we won't enter your homes without their permission. All I ask is that if this woman's seeking shelter that you push her out. She's a whore and apostate, and Allah won't look kindly on anyone who harbors her."

One of the women sets aside her work and stands up.

"No," Noor pleads.

The woman ignores her and puts on a green burqa. She pulls back the hessian cloth and steps outside. Noor sees a sharp blade on top of an upturned box and grabs it.

"Just who do you think you are?" she hears the woman in the burqa say. "Frightening women like this. You should be ashamed of yourselves."

"Our apologies, ma'am," the man says, "but we can't leave until we've searched each of these huts."

"First you call them homes, now you call them huts, what makes you think our men would agree to such a thing?"

"We have money."

"It's always money with you people. How do you know I'm not this woman, eh?"

"Ma'am, it's clear that—"

Noor hears the woman lift up her burqa.

"Is that better," she says, "now you've seen my face and lost my dignity, does that help in your search? "

"Ma'am when your husband arrives—"

"When my husband arrives? To hell with that, I'll go get him now. Just let me get my shoes."

The woman slips back inside.

"There's no need, we can wait," the man shouts after her.

"Well I can't," the woman shouts back.

The woman takes off her burqa and shoves it into Noor's hands.

'Thank you," Noor mouths.

The woman gestures at Noor to hurry up. Noor throws the burqa over her head.

"You're bullies," the woman shouts, "here to liberate us, you say, while you treat us like dogs.

The woman snorts..

"I tell you, my husband will sort this out."

The woman pulls the burqa's sleeves over Noor's hands and pushes her out the door. Through the burqa's webbed mask Noor makes out the four men. Her legs wobble but she manages to steady herself. She heads down the alley.

"Ma'am," the older one says to her.

She stops.

"There's no need for your husband to rush; we have plenty of time."

Noor snorts with as much contempt as she can muster and continues on. When she comes to the dirt road she finds the black SUV sitting there with its high beams on. She carries on past it to the bus stop.

A solitary bus brakes to let off a passenger, and Noor stumbles aboard. She hands the conductor a bill from her payroll envelope and collapses to the floor. No one comes to her aid. She stares at the mud splattered shalwars of the men around her, and tries to muffle her sobs.

What were you thinking? You talk of signs. Well if this isn't one from Allah, what is?

The bus arrives at her stop, and she staggers off. She steps into traffic. Horns blare, rickshaw drivers curse, but they all somehow avoid her. Some time later she finds herself outside Elma's front door. Footsteps approach, and the door flies open.

"Welcome to your new ..."

Elma's voice trails off, her smile replaced with a frown.

"I'm sorry," Elma says, "can I help you?"

Noor realizes she's still wearing the burqa. She lifts the sodden cloth up until it rests on her head. Elma gasps. Noor collapses to the ground. This time she knows there's no way she'll be able to get up on her own.

THIRTY-NINE

CHARLIE SITS UNDER the front porch staring at the rain cascading down onto the driveway. Puddles have sprung up all the way down it, fallen leaves floating on top of them like the survivors of a defeated armada.

She may have gotten up earlier than me yesterday, but there's no way she could have done today.

He hears footsteps coming around the balustrade and turns only to see Aamir Khan at the top of the stairs.

"Ah, Charlie, how are you this morning?"

"Haven't seen rain in so long I almost forgot what it looked like."

"The best thing to do when it rains is to let it rain, isn't that what some wise fellow once said?"

Aamir Khan reaches the bottom of the staircase and plays with his sleeves.

"I was hoping to see you," he says. "It concerns Noor."

Charlie's throat tightens.

"This scholarship to the University of Amsterdam, it is of extreme importance to her, and this interview, well it seems it carries a lot of weight. She has to do the whole of it in Dutch, were you aware?"

Charlie nods.

"I suppose what I am trying to say is residing here has become a distraction for her. There are too many people, and Miss Kuyt, well she has kindly offered Noor lodging in her house, and from what Noor tells me they will only converse in Dutch. You can imagine how beneficial that is going to be for her."

Charlie knows that 'too many people' means him and that Aamir Khan knows that too.

"She there already?" Charlie says.

"She moved in last night."

"Just like that. No goodbye, nothing."

"You must understand this is the best chance she has of getting out of here. I suspect her only chance."

Charlie swallows.

How can you argue that?

He stands and grabs his satchel from the nearby chair. Aamir Khan holds the door open like a loyal butler.

"You are a good man, Charlie, one of the best I have had the privilege of knowing."

Charlie has never heard more hollow words. He climbs on his motorcycle and tears off towards Jamrud Road, his mind a whir, the rain lashing his face. A truck exits the driveway of a large mansion, and he swerves to avoid it. The motorcycle skids from under him, and he and the motorcycle careen down the side of the road. He hurtles past the truck, stones and grass ripping up his left side, misses a tree trunk by inches and tumbles into a rhododendron bush. He lies there in a daze.

The bearded face of the truck driver appears in front of him. The driver jabbers away in Pashtu and pulls Charlie from the bush. The pain hits Charlie; the searing scrapes down his leg and arm, the stinging lacerations on his face.

He hobbles towards his motorcycle. It's never been clearer what he needs to do. He lifts it up and climbs back on. The engine fires first time. He takes off past the astonished truck driver and heads back the way he came. He knows Elma's cottage is close. He goes up and down the quiet residential streets peering up each driveway for Elma's white Land Cruiser.

Just as he's about to give up, he sees it parked in front of a beige cottage nestled amidst a copse of drooping juniper trees. He does a one-eighty and roars up its driveway. He steps off and grimaces.

Jesus, I must be a sight.

The door opens, and Elma strides out wearing an embroidered shalwar kameez. In her haste, she hasn't even bothered to put a jacket on.

"What are you doing here?" she says.

"I'm here to see Noor."

"That's not happening."

"You can't stop me."

He skirts around her and limps towards the cottage.

"Enter my house and I'll have you deported by the end of the day."

He turns back.

"You couldn't," he says.

"You forget, I have friends in high places."

He glances at the house. He knows Noor's in there. Surely she must have heard him.

Why won't she come out?

He studies the windows hoping to see a curtain pulled back, but none of them are. Elma walks over. Her shalwar kameez has begun to stick to her skin, her full breasts there to admire.

To think that once might've turned me on.

"What were you thinking?" she says.

"I love her."

"You love the idea of being a knight in shining armor. That's why you helped Kamila."

"No."

"Really? If your cook had told you a similar story, would you have done the same for him?"

Charlie doesn't say anything. Elma holds out an envelope. The rain has smudged the ink, but he can still make out his name written in Noor's delicate handwriting. He rips it open.

Dear Charlie:

If you're reading this it means you have come by to see me. I apologize for not greeting you. It's not that I'm incapable of doing so, but it's important that I put into practice the decision I've made.

We can no longer have a relationship - of any sort. It's not that I don't respect you because I do, immensely. And it's not that I don't value your friendship. What you have done for me and my family I will never forget. But over the last couple of days, ever since that incident, I've had the opportunity to ponder my life and my feelings. I do not love you, Charlie. For a time I thought I did, but now I realize it was no more than an infatuation at best.

I have big dreams, Charlie. Dreams I'm desperate to fulfill. If you truly love me you will provide me the freedom to pursue them.

I wish you the best of luck in Afghanistan. What you are doing for my country is noble. You will be in my prayers. Always.

Noor

By now the words are beginning to run together as seamlessly as the tears and rain on Charlie's cheeks. He shoves the letter in his pocket.

"You'll get over this," Elma says. "In fact, one day you're going to look back and realize it was just as much of an infatuation on your part as it was on hers."

"Doubt that," he says. "I doubt that very much."

He hobbles to his motorcycle and starts the engine. He looks back at the house and sees a curtain snap shut.

Noor.

He waits, hoping she will run out the door and throw herself into his arms. But she never comes.

"Bye, Charlie," Elma says.

He wipes his eyes and turns the throttle. The bike lurches down the driveway. He has no clue where to go next.

Thank God, we're off to Afghanistan tomorrow.

He couldn't imagine spending another week in this city.

PART III

engage

FORTY

CHARLIE CLIMBS OUT, the biting wind searing his face, and gives the village a once over; no one seems to be there. He assumes the three families have moved on. He looks back. The recruits are clambering out of their motley collection of trucks.

"Gather round," he says.

They huddle up next to him.

"Good to be back in Afghanistan?" he says.

"Allah akbar," Yunus shouts, raising his fist in the air.

The others join in the same refrain.

"Allah akbar indeed," Charlie says with a broad smile.

The Afghans let out a cheer.

"Okay, Mocam's going to give each of you a map. You see this area in blue, that's safe for you guys to walk in. Everything in red is live so unless you want to share the same fate as Wali, keep out of it. Now we're going to split into three groups. Farooq, Zafar Khan, Ahmad Khan, Haamid, Qadir, Ali, Rahmat Saeed, go with Mocam and unload all the equipment. Bakri, Rahmahullah, Mohammad Khan, Abdul Nasser, Abdul Raouf, Habibullah, Yasir, Osman, Tarik, you're with Najib putting up the tents. Obaidullah, Yunus,

334 N. G. OSBORNE

Shafiq, Hamid, Omar, Wahed, Mohammad Farooq, Jameel and Qasim you're with me."

"And what are we doing, sir?" Obaidullah says.

"We're digging the shitter."

"I apologize, I am not familiar—"

"The toilet, Obaidullah."

Charlie winks at Obaidullah and grabs a shovel. He catches sight of the undergrowth and is drawn to its edge. He scans the area where Wali fell, and sees something white amongst the weeds. It's one of Wali's sneakers.

"I'm sorry, Wali," he says.

He gathers his group and chooses a sheltered spot behind one of the houses. It has a view of the river and the snow capped mountains beyond.

"Great place for it, don't you think?" he says.

"Pardon me, sir, but good view would not be first for me," Obaidullah says.

"What would?"

"Shelter."

"We're totally protected from the wind here."

"But not rain."

"Guess you got a point."

He turns to the rest of the men.

"Okay, let's dig three holes, four by four feet wide and to a six foot depth. Then we'll lay our planks down and put three tents over the top of them, that way if it's raining everyone can stay dry while I still have the option of opening up the front and admiring the view in the morning."

He picks up his shovel. The Afghans look at him as if there's a raving madman in their midst.

"Come on," he says, "no time to waste."

Two hours later the latrines are dug and their camp's in place. The sun that's hung above the mountains all afternoon disappears, and while Obaidullah leads the Afghans in prayer,

Charlie lies back against his tent and nurses his now aching shoulder.

He pulls out Noor's letter and reads it once again, its words stinging as harshly as the first time he read it. Obaidullah finishes the prayer and walks over. Charlie stuffs the letter back in his pocket.

"I feel terribly, Mr. Matthews, I forgot to wish you a most happy Christmas."

Charlie realizes he forgot himself.

"I trust you are aware we consider Jesus one of our great prophets."

"I didn't," Charlie says, "but that's good to know."

"You will be saying many prayers tonight, I am suspecting, in private as Christians do."

"I will, thanks."

"Then I hope Allah answers them."

That's unlikely, Obaidullah. Very unlikely indeed.

FORTY-ONE

TARIQ HEARS A burst of automatic gunfire and puts his pen down.

Perhaps a couple of mujahideen got into a dispute.

More and more guns start firing.

Oh no, we're being attacked.

He grabs his Beretta and wriggles out of his tent. Tracer fire lights up the night sky. He sprints past befuddled muja-hideen in the direction of the Prince's tent and cuts down the back of a row of tents until he sees it up ahead. The Prince's entire Saudi bodyguard rings it, firing their weapons into the sky. Tariq squints into the dark.

Is there a helicopter out there?

He can't see one and stumbles on. The flap opens, and the Prince strides out. He grabs an AK-47 from a guard and points it in Tariq's direction. Tariq flings himself to the ground just before the Prince unleashes a volley of rounds. Tariq lies there in disbelief.

The Prince lets off another clipload. The Saudi guard and some nearby mujahideen burst into roars of 'Allah akbar'. The Prince beams. Tariq sees Ashfaq, a mujahid who joined the group at the same time as him, dancing with his arms in the air. He staggers over to him.

"What's going on?" he shouts.

"We won," Ashfaq says.

Oh no, Kabul's fallen.

"When? Who?" Tariq says.

"The Soviet Union, it exists no more. We destroyed them."

Tariq wants to weep with relief. They won't be going back to Peshawar. Not yet at least.

"Allah akbar," Ashfaq shouts.

Yes He is.

The Prince shoots off one last burst and heads back inside. Tariq surveys the ever growing, grinning, dancing, gun firing mass of mujahideen and shakes his head.

You won't be celebrating in a year, you fools. Not once Afghanistan plunges into civil war, and the wolves descend on you with a vengeance.

Tariq traipses back towards his tent. There is a momentary lull in the gunfire, and he hears a distinctive snort. He freezes.

Iqbal.

He looks back. No one seems to be following him.

Maybe I imagined it.

He continues on and as he passes the next tent he glances right. One row over a man is keeping pace with him.

Could it be a coincidence?

He carries on. The gunfire starts up again as secondary celebrations break out across the camp. When he passes the next tent on his left he glances in its direction and sees another figure walking at a similar pace.

Nasir.

He stops and looks back. Ten yards away a man is facing him.

Salim Afridi.

Tariq's hand reaches for his Beretta and aims for the man's chest.

Go on. Do it.

He presses down on the trigger just as the camp is bathed

in phosphorescent light from an RPG shell exploding
overhead. He realizes that the man is nothing more than a
kameez hung out to dry.

Thank God. It's just the two of them.

He thinks of running back to the Prince's tent and seeking
sanctuary.

*You'll never make it. They'll shoot you in the back before you ever
get there.*

He forces himself to keep walking and tries to figure out
their strategy.

*It can't be to stab me in the back. If that was it they'd have surely
done it by now.*

He recalls Salim Afridi's words to him in – 'don't fear, I'll
be sure to make it as agonizing as possible'. He trembles as he
imagines how one will restrain him as the other cuts off his
balls. There's only one place they could do that.

My tent.

He picks up his pace. He sees it up ahead. The entrance
flap is open.

Did I leave it that way?

He knows he doesn't have time to ponder the question.
He nudges the cloth back with his gun and lunges inside. No
one's there.

Thank you, Allah.

He stumbles towards the back and kneels down facing the
entrance. He puts his Beretta on the floor and turns off the
lamp. He snatches the gun back up and waits in the darkness.
Outside the rat-a-tat-tat of gunfire intermixes with the boom
of RPG shells. He hears footsteps approaching.

Stay calm, stay calm.

He bites down on his hand to stop it from shaking.

Another RPG explodes, and he sees the outline of a man
outside his tent. The man pulls back the flap. Tariq wills
himself to wait.

Not yet.

Nasir's head pokes through. He looks at Tariq in shock.

Tariq unleashes a fusillade of bullets at Nasir's chest. Nasir tumbles face first in front of Tariq. Tariq fires over Nasir's body to where he presumes Iqbal is standing. His magazine empties, and in the fading light of the RPG burst he searches for his second.

Tariq hears a tearing sound behind him. He swivels around to see a gash opening up. Iqbal comes charging at him, a knife in his hand. The knife sinks into Tariq's left shoulder. Tariq screams in pain.

The two of them fall to the ground. Iqbal pulls the knife out, and Tariq twists away just before it can plunge into his stomach. Tariq drops his Beretta and grabs a hold of Iqbal's wrist. Iqbal uses his other hand to punch Tariq in the face.

If you let go now, you're dead.

The punches keep coming; blood pours from Tariq's nose. Tariq tries to knee Iqbal in the groin but it's to no effect. Tariq feels his grip weakening.

He jerks his head to the side just as the next punch rains down. For the briefest moment Iqbal is off balance. Tariq brings his head up and sinks his teeth into Iqbal's ear. Iqbal's roars are drowned out by a volley of gunfire from outside.

Tariq jerks his head and his teeth come away with a chunk of Iqbal's earlobe. He lets go of Iqbal's wrist and pulls himself towards the front of the tent.

He hears the whoosh of the knife. It barely misses his calf. He flips over and kicks out a leg. It catches Iqbal in the chest. Iqbal tumbles backwards.

Tariq's hand searches for his Beretta and the second magazine. He fails to find them and instead latches onto one of Yousef's grenades.

He brings the pin to his mouth and pulls it out. Iqbal is struggling to his feet. Tariq lets the grenade fall to the floor and barrels outside.

One, two, three, four, five—

He looks back.

Iqbal stumbles out after him only to catch his foot on a cord and go tumbling. Tariq keeps running.

Six, seven, eight, nine—

Tariq dives for the dirt and screws his eyes shut.

Ten.

Nothing.

He waits a moment longer.

Oh no, it's a dud.

He twists onto his back. Iqbal is on his feet, blood pouring down the side of his neck. Iqbal reaches inside his waistcoat and emerges with a pistol.

"O Allah," Tariq mumbles, "please help me in this moment of need—"

There's a blinding explosion. Tariq's head slams back against the ground and he lies there, his ears ringing. How long he stays there he doesn't know, but when he opens his eyes a light is shining in his face, and a group of mujahideen are bent over him. They sit him up and offer him a water canteen. He gulps down its contents. A large crowd has formed. They all nod at him as though he's just lost his two greatest friends in the world.

The mujahid says something, but Tariq doesn't catch it.

"You're lucky," the mujahid shouts. "Some fool fired an RPG into your tent."

Tariq stands and staggers over to what was once his tent. Iqbal and Nasir are on their bellies, their clothes shredded by hundreds of shrapnel wounds.

He hears frantic shouting, and the crowd parts. Salim Afridi emerges and runs to his two fallen sons. He twists them over, first Iqbal then Nasir. He lets out an anguished wail and slaps Nasir's cheeks in a forlorn attempt to wake him. When that fails he lifts his oldest son into a sitting position and holds him tight. He catches Tariq's gaze and stares up at him with unadulterated hatred.

"May Allah have Mercy on them," Tariq says.

Tariq walks away. He feels something lodged in his mouth and spits it out. It's the piece of Iqbal's ear.

FORTY-TWO

NOOR SITS IN front of the speakerphone, Elma across from her willing her on.

"We zijn bijna bij het einde," one of the interviewers says back in Amsterdam.

"We're almost done," Elma mouths to Noor.

Noor nods, relieved.

When they had woken Noor didn't think it was possible to feel any more nervous. Elma had decided they'd do the call at her office. That way she could listen in on a speakerphone and put it on mute if Noor needed a question translated.

Now an hour later they are almost done. Noor can hardly recall a question she's been asked or an answer she's given. Words had come out of her mouth but whether they were the correct ones or were in the right order is another matter.

"Verwacht je problemen met het aanpassen aan de Nederlandse samenleving?" the interviewer says.

Noor looks across at Elma; she doesn't know the word 'samenleving'. Elma hits mute.

"Do you think you'll have any problems adjusting to life in Holland?" Elma says.

Noor nods, and Elma unmutes the line.

"Een beetje," Noor says.

A little.

"In het verleden heb ik me vaker aan nieuwe omgevingen moeten aanpassen—daarom maak ik mij niet veel zorgen."

In the past I've had to often adjust to new situations —therefore I'm not too worried.

Elma gives her a thumbs up.

"Als laatste," another interviewer says, "zou je iets kunnen bedenken waardoor je zou afzien van het aanvaarden van deze studiebeurs?"

"Could you think of something which would prevent you from accepting this scholarship?" Elma mouths.

"No," Noor says. "I mean 'geen'."

At the other end someone laughs. After an hour, at last some human emotion from one of the interviewers.

"Dit zou een droom zijn," she says.

This would be a dream. It truly would.

Elma leans over the speakerphone and asks the main interviewer if he needs anything else from them. He says he doesn't.

"Then I just want to add," Elma says, "that I've yet to meet a more exceptional young woman than Noor. The University of Amsterdam would be lucky to have her."

"Coming from you, Elma, that means a lot," the interviewer says. "We'll be in touch."

Elma hangs up.

"Thank you for saying those kinds words," Noor says.

"I said it because I meant it. Gerben and I were at college together."

Elma lays her hand on Noor's.

"Trust me, you're so close to being out of this hellhole I can smell it."

Noor refuses to believe it.

Not until I am stepping onto a plane.

FORTY-THREE

THEY SIT CROSS legged on three sides of the vast Afghan rug. Forty men all looking in the Prince's direction. Behind the Prince stand his two most trusted bodyguards. Others dot the perimeter.

At least you're safe from Salim Afridi in here, Tariq thinks.

"Time is running out," the Prince says, his hands waving around as if he's conducting an orchestra. "I received word today that Massoud and Dostum have come to an agreement, and Hekmatyar and Sayyaf are now gearing up their forces. Even Rabbani has gotten off his fat ass."

Snorts of laughter breaks out. The Prince waits.

"Tomorrow we'll steal a march on them and claim Kabul in the name of Allah, the Beneficent, the Merciful. All that's left to discuss is the plan of attack. I want to thank Salim Afridi for being here in this trying time. His sons were true martyrs and are now enjoying the fruits of paradise."

The depths of hell more like, Tariq thinks.

Tariq knows his Quran, and it's explicit that paradise is reserved for men who die fighting for Allah, not for the petty plots of their father.

Salim Afridi starts his presentation, and Tariq feels his hopes slipping away. Earlier that day he'd received another letter from Yousef in which he'd relayed the news of their near miss. Along with the letter Yousef had sent the leather notebook that had slipped from Noor's grasp. It was a curious thing, the quote a perfect example of the fatuous nonsense his father and sister subscribed to.

Did Noor have it engraved herself? Or was it a present from Baba?

In either case he wonders how they could afford it.

At the end of the letter Yousef had quoted the twenty-third surah and remarked how he was sure Tariq would be rewarded if he too were patient. The problem is patience requires time, and Tariq knows he has little left. He grimaces from the pain in his crudely sewn up shoulder and focuses on what Salim Afridi is saying.

"This is not an enemy we need fear, brothers, this is an enemy we can dispose of with one lightning punch. We take the Jalalabad road at speed, in one column. A vanguard of two pick-ups, two hundred yards ahead, to draw fire and warn of any potential resistance. This will be no different than the Nazi blitzkrieg. We do not stop until our objective, and that objective is the capture of the Presidential Palace."

The assembled break out into shouts of 'Allah Akbar.'

Tariq rolls his eyes. Salim Afridi's acclaim as a military tactician comes from the guerrilla battles he's fought. He's no offensive genius, and in Tariq's mind to draw a comparison with the blitzkrieg is ridiculous. The Nazis had battalions of tanks. They, on the other hand, have four the Soviets lost in battle, manned by mujahideen who'd be hard pressed to hit a house at fifty feet.

"Any objections?" the Prince says.

The Prince looks around the assembled group. Tariq lowers his gaze.

"I sense hesitation on your part, Tariq," the Prince says.

Tariq looks up; the Prince is staring right at him. He wonders how he should play it. If he disagrees with Salim Afridi, and the plan succeeds, his reputation will be in tatters.

Yet so what?

If it does succeed the Prince will return to Saudi without him, and he'll be as good as dead.

However if it fails, I'll be the one prophet amidst this flock of fools.

"I remember Jalalabad," Tariq says.

"This is not Jalalabad," Salim Afridi snaps.

"I understand, and I mean to show you no disrespect."

Except of course he has.

"I'd just urge caution. It might take an extra week but why not use side roads, split the force in two so it's less concentrated, allow scouts to go further ahead so if there is actual resistance we have time to react in a proper manner."

Salim Afridi goes to say something, but the Prince waves him quiet.

"Your plan seems abundantly cautious," the Prince says.

"Even the Americans, your Highness, went into Kuwait in more than one column."

"Are you comparing our wondrous warriors to infidels?"

"Of course not."

The Prince stands and points his finger at Tariq as if he were some ancient doomsayer.

"Perhaps the real issue is you've no desire to be a martyr."

Everyone's eyes drop to the mat. In this company there's no worse insult.

"There'd be no greater glory than to die a martyr," Tariq says, "especially in the service of your Highness."

"Then you should lead the vanguard."

Tariq knows there's no way he can object.

"I'd be honored, your Highness."

A few of the men glance his way as if he's already dead. Tariq shivers.

How did this all go so wrong, so quickly?

FORTY-FOUR

CHARLIE SITS WITH a piece of paper in front of him. Next to him is a screwed up pile of failed attempts. He stares out the blown out hole in the wall at the moonlit mountains in the distance.

Come on, give me some inspiration.

He blows on his freezing hands and picks up his pen. Twenty minutes later he's done. He thinks about re-reading the letter but daren't in case it joins the pile beside him. He knows it's clumsy, but it's the truth.

"Never say I gave up on you," he says as if Noor were standing right there beside him.

He slides the letter into an envelope and licks it closed. Someone knocks, and he turns to find Najib at the door.

"Are you alright, Mr. Matthews?"

"Yeah, you just caught me daydreaming. What's up?"

"We were wondering if you were going to join us."

"Give me a minute, and I'll be right out."

Najib departs. Charlie takes another piece of paper and writes Wali a short note asking him to get the letter to Noor. He trusts Wali will; the man is nothing less than ingenious when it comes to such things.

He gathers up all the failed attempts, lays them on the earthen floor and sets fire to them. He walks outside and heads along a pitch black alley. In the distance he can hear the wailing of an Afghan song. He comes upon the village's steep lane. At the bottom of the hill the men are sitting around a blazing fire, a jukebox blasting away. Some are singing along, others smoking. Charlie makes his way down and plops next to Obaidullah, who's staring up at the stars.

"To think that God created all that above," Obaidullah says.

"Think there's any life out there?"

Obaidullah shakes his head.

"That against your religion?" Charlie says.

"To be honestly I do not know."

"There's like billions of stars and planets, you'd think there'd be life on one of them. I mean why else would God go to all that trouble?"

"Maybe to show us how special we are."

"Yet when I look at them I feel totally insignificant."

"That is the genius, no?"

Charlie has no answer. It's the most profound thing he's heard in a long time.

"Mr. Matthews," Obaidullah says, "I sincerely wish—"

"I know."

"You will pray very hard on this?"

"Every night, Obaidullah."

The music changes to a more upbeat track. Yunus and Bakri start dancing with their arms up in the air, circling each other, their bodies swaying from side to side like drunks on a boat. Everyone claps. When they finish Najib and Zahoor take a turn. Charlie turns to Obaidullah.

"Want to go next?"

"I couldn't," Obaidullah says.

"Come on."

"Really I am no good at such activities."

Charlie looks around and spots Mocam.

"What do you say?"

Mocam smiles, and when Najib and Zahoor sit down, he and Charlie spring up. A loud cheer goes up. Mocam stretches out his arm, and Charlie entwines his elbow with his. Round and round they twirl, whooping and hollering, the embers from the fire floating around them up towards the stars.

FORTY-FIVE

THE PRINCE SPEAKS to his six hundred men in the early morning gloom, green flags, with quotes from the Quran on them, flapping behind him. Every one of them is looking forward to the day ahead. Everyone of them that is but Tariq.

Tariq is well aware of what's promised him if he dies a martyr. Jeweled couches to recline on, youths waiting on him with bowls of fruit, seventy-two dark eyed virgins to whom he can make love for the rest of eternity. Yet he has no desire for it, not even with that pig of a wife he has now.

I don't want to leave this life, not yet at least.

He glances at Salim Afridi, standing beside the Prince with his chest puffed out.

Do you blame yourself? Do you blame Allah? Or have you rationalized your sons' deaths already? They can, after all, only add to your legend.

A final roar of 'Allah akbar' explodes from the men, and the mujahideen race to their assigned vehicles. Tariq watches the Prince and his bodyguards march to his Hummer. The rumor is that it's armored to the same specifications as the American president's limo.

You don't seem so keen on leaving this world either.

Tariq walks over to his pick-up and opens the passenger door. Three mujahideen are crammed up front. He suspects his father-in-law made certain of that. The only place left is the truck bed. He clambers into it and finds Ashfaq there.

"This is going to be a magnificent day," Ashfaq grins.

Tariq realizes the fool volunteered for this assignment. He looks behind him and is surprised to see his father-in-law standing in the bed of the next pick-up, his arms draped over a machine gun welded to its roof. Tariq shivers. Salim Afridi is in the perfect position to shoot him when the firing starts. Salim Afridi shouts an order, and Tariq's pick-up takes off. Tariq throws his hand out to steady himself, the icy wind blasting his face.

"O Allah," he mumbles, "forgive my sins of which You are aware, forgive the sins done by the action of my eyes, the negligence of my heart and the movement of my tongue. I beg you to keep me safe this day, spare me Salim Afridi's wrath and bring me back into the good graces of His Highness the Prince. Ameen."

Four hours later, Tariq is beginning to believe that Allah has answered his prayers. They have reached the outskirts of Kabul without a shot being fired. There seems to be no city to speak of, just hillocks of rubble from the pounding Hekmatyar's troops gave the area in the fall. The occasional building still stands, but none of them has a roof, and gaping holes dot their walls. They pass a burqaed woman wailing at the side of the road, her two small children lying beside her. There's no way to tell if they're alive or dead. Past her, sits the turret of a Soviet tank. Where the rest of it is, Tariq has no clue.

Is this what we've been fighting for all these years?

A young boy, no older than ten, runs into the road, and the driver is forced to slam on the brakes. The boy holds out his hands and starts babbling away.

"Get him off the road," Salim Afridi shouts.

Tariq looks warily at his father-in-law.

"Now," his father-in-law barks.

Tariq jumps down onto the asphalt.

Is this it?

Tariq braces for the barrage of bullets. They don't come. Not yet at least.

The convoy begins to bunch up behind them.

"Please, sir, please," the boy cries, "my mother is dying. Please, come help."

"There's nothing I can do," Tariq says.

The boy grabs a hold of Tariq's sleeve.

"Please, she's over there, she needs medicine, please."

"What's the hold-up?" Salim Afridi shouts.

Tariq ignores him. He hands the boy a twenty dollar bill.

"Here take this," he says.

The young boy cries harder. Tariq takes the boy's frozen hand in his, and walks him to the side of the road.

"She'll be fine," Tariq says. "I promise."

The boy uses his sleeve to wipe the tears from his eyes. Tariq hears a low rumble and looks up into the grey sky. A dot is making its way towards them.

A MIG.

He grabs the boy's hand.

"Run," he shouts.

The roar builds. The boy trips, and Tariq yanks him up. They stagger on another ten yards when an explosion lifts them off their feet. Tariq tumbles to the ground. His ears ring, and his mouth fills with dirt. He looks back and sees his pick-up is nothing but a burning shell while Salim Afridi's lies on its side. Tariq crawls around looking for the boy and finds him lying on his back. The boy's eyes stare blankly up at Tariq, his hand still gripping the twenty dollar bill.

There's another roar overhead followed by a second set of explosions further down the convoy. Tariq realizes there have to be two jets.

So much for the Communists not having fuel.

Tariq stumbles back to the road. Mujahideen are falling out of their vehicles and scrambling to safety. Further up, two tanks are billowing pitch black smoke while the remaining two turn their guns up to the sky in a futile gesture.

Tariq reaches the road. Nearby Ashfaq's head and torso are splayed on the road, his legs nowhere to be seen.

Tariq searches the sky. The jets' fiery engines are arcing around; they're making another run.

The Prince.

He hears groans coming from the overturned pick-up and sees his father-in-law lying there, his right foot trapped under the back end of his pick-up.

"Tariq, help me," he says.

There's an almighty roar, and the ground shakes as two more explosions rock the convoy. The other two tanks have sustained direct hits.

"Tariq," his father-in-law shouts.

Tariq ignores him and sprints down the road. He looks over his shoulder. The dots are coming closer once again.

Run.

He dives behind one of the burning tanks just before the first jet lets rip with its cannon. Chunks of road fly into the air, mujahideen are obliterated in a blink of an eye, vehicles are flipped on their side. The jet passes and the screams of the wounded and dying fill the air. Tariq waits. He feels the ground tremble, and the second jet unleashes a similar wave of destruction. He gets up and runs on. The road is a vision of hell, vehicles everywhere burning hot and bright.

Please Allah, don't let the Prince's Hummer be one of them.

A mujahid comes towards him, his eyes wild.

"Have you seen the Prince?" Tariq shouts.

The mujahid staggers on, and as he passes, Tariq sees blood streaming from the man's ears. Up ahead he spies the

Hummer ablaze next to an overturned supply truck. Boxes of ammunition and weaponry are scattered all over the road.

He scans the side of the road and spots the Prince crouching next to it, the bodies of his guard scattered around him.

Thank God.

The sole surviving guard tries to pull the Prince away, but the Prince resists, too frightened to move.

Tariq looks towards the horizon and sees the jets coming around again.

No.

He spots a metal box whose top has burst open. Inside it is a Stinger missile launcher. How many times had he and Yousef played with them back in the storeroom?

Tariq pulls the launcher out. He flicks on the switch. It beeps, and he realizes there's no way for him to hold the launcher and pull the trigger at the same time.

"Help me," he screams at the guard.

With his one arm he lifts the Stinger onto his shoulder and searches for the jets through the scope.

There. Just above the road.

"Help me, I said."

The Stinger beeps, its seeker now locked in on one. He feels a presence beside him. It's the guard.

"Pull the trigger," he shouts.

The guard leans in and yanks it. In a plume of white smoke the missile blasts out of the tube and winds its way above the road. A massive fireball bursts in front of them, and the jet tumbles into a nearby field. Moments later the second plane screeches over their heads, its guns silent. Tariq watches the plane's exhaust arc north towards Bagram airbase.

It's over.

He sees the Prince still cowering by the side of the road and scrambles over to him. He grabs him by the arm. The Prince resists.

"It's okay, I promise."

He leads him onto the road and places the launcher in his hand. The surviving mujahideen begin to stumble back onto the road. Tariq lifts the Prince's free hand.

"Allah Akbar," Tariq screams.

The mujahideen look his way.

"Allah Akbar," he screams over and over.

The survivors crowd around the Prince and hoist him up onto their shoulders. Color returns to the Prince's cheeks, and he punches the launcher into the air.

"Allah has brought us a great victory," the Prince says. "We return to Peshawar and regroup."

Tariq wanders back down the road past the burning vehicles and sprawled bodies. To his disappointment, he finds his father-in-law alive.

"Where the hell did you go?" Salim Afridi says.

"I shot the plane down."

Salim Afridi winces.

"Well come on, lift up the back so I can pull my foot out."

Tariq gets behind Salim Afridi and puts his arms around him.

"Not me, you fool, the truck."

Tariq slips his hand into Salim Afridi's shoulder holster and pulls out his pistol. Salim Afridi turns to grab it, but by then Tariq is out of harm's reach.

"I've always wanted to ask you a question," Tariq says. "When you killed your uncle was he surprised to see you there? Or was there a part of him that had always feared that day would come?"

Salim Afridi looks around for help only to see nothing but dead around him. He swallows.

"Those were different times, Tariq. All is forgiven, any bad blood between you and I is in the past."

"That's what your uncle thought, and while times may change, human nature doesn't. A son can never forgive the killer of his father, and likewise I see no way a father can ever forgive the killer of his sons."

Salim Afridi yanks on his foot.

"You bastard," he screams.

"May Allah have mercy on you."

Tariq fires, and Salim Afridi slumps back onto the road. Tariq checks his father-in-laws' pulse before putting the gun back in his holster.

He heads over to the body of the young boy and shifts it until it's lying on its right side and facing Mecca. He closes the boy's eyes with his fingertips and lifts his hands and face up to the sky.

"O Allah, raise this boy's soul towards You and direct Your guidance to him. O Allah, pardon us, pardon us."

He stands and takes one last look at Kabul.

Fuck this country.

He goes looking for a ride back to Peshawar.

FORTY-SIX

NOOR LIES ON her bed and reads *Bougainville,* a novel Elma's lent her. It's slow going but she'd read the Amsterdam phone book if she thought it'd make her Dutch better. She hears a knock and slides off the bed to find Nadeem, Elma's house-boy, at her door. Down the corridor, she can hear the hustle and bustle of the party being prepared. Nadeem thrusts a plain manila envelope into her hands.

"A cripple in a wheelchair approached me on the street," he says. "Offered me a hundred rupees if I'd give it to you."

Noor's pulse quickens. She glances at Elma's bedroom door.

"Please don't tell Miss Elma about this."

"Not likely. He said if I kept my mouth shut he'd give me another hundred next week."

Noor shuts her door and sits down at her vanity desk. She stares at the envelope.

Don't open it. This is the Devil tempting you.

She takes a box of matches out of the desk drawer and lights one. She puts it up against a corner of the envelope, and it bursts into flames.

No, I can't do this.

She waves the envelope in the air, but the flames only get brighter. She drops the envelope and stomps on it until the flames die out. A third of the envelope is gone.

She picks it up and extracts the letter. To her relief the letter was small enough to have escaped unscathed. She unfolds it and begins reading.

Dear Noor:

I thought I was over you, but I'm not.

The day after we arrived, a snowstorm hit us, and the temperature plummeted. The ground became so hard you'd think it was made of concrete - not something you want when you're trying to probe for mines. I threw it out there that we could wait out the bad weather, but no one was up for that. The guys were right, we hadn't come all this way to sit on our butts. So we set up a system where each team had a pot of boiling water near them at all times. Whenever a mine detector went off, we'd pour water on the ground to soften it up, and then one of the guys would get down and probe the soil. Our progress was slow, especially in the high frag areas, but we just kept going.

During those days if I thought about you it was only for the barest of moments. When it's that cold and wet, all your mind is concerned about is somehow getting through those frigid days.

Ten days in, it finally warmed up. It was so unexpected it felt like a miracle. By nine I was looking to take clothes off not put more on. And as the ground thawed so did my mind. That morning I saw brief flashes of you – sitting across from me at breakfast, near the back of the group as I was giving out the orders for the day. At one point I thought I saw you walking towards me across an uncleared field, and I shouted out your name. I wouldn't be surprised if everyone thought I was going crazy – I sure as hell did.

At lunch, Osman approached me – he'd unearthed a mine he didn't like the look of. Thank God he did. The guy who'd laid it had placed a couple of anti-tank mines underneath and linked them all together.

I ordered everyone back. The job wasn't that complicated (I'd worked on far harder set-ups in the army), but as I lay there on my stomach, I began shaking. I tried to work out why, and the only reason that made any sense was because now my life meant something – and it meant something because you're in it.

I should have pulled back, but my pride wouldn't let me - every man on the team had taken a break to watch me. And then something happened. I felt your touch on my arm, and my hands became steady. I felt your cheek next to mine, and my body relaxed. 'You can do this,' you whispered in my ear, and thirty minutes later I had. From then on, I have felt your presence everywhere – it's like you're my guardian angel.

At the top of the village, I created an office for myself in an abandoned hut. One of its walls has a massive hole in it and through it I can make out not only the guys at work but also the river below and the mountains in the distance. It has this rough, old table on which I've pinned a map of the surrounding area, and every night I color in blue the areas we demined that day. Slowly but surely the blue areas have kept extending – we're now down to the river to the west and across a field and irrigation channel to the north. Redrawing that map has been the most satisfying thing I've ever done in my life.

Last night I looked out the hole at the stars. I wanted to rename every one of them after you, and then I remembered how you'd prefer to have a shrub named after you than a galaxy. So the first shrub I saw today I named 'Noor'. I hate to say it's not much to look at, but come spring its flowers will bloom and it'll be worthy of your name.

I've thought a lot about whether I should send this letter or not. Please don't think I didn't take seriously your request to leave you alone. But I believe two things made it necessary.

First, I believe, despite everything you wrote, that you love me. I have gone over and over the moments we spent together, and I'm convinced that something incredible emerged from that initial antagonism. A true love. Something real and timeless.

Secondly, I believe, that our love won't hurt your dreams, if anything it will aid them. There's nothing I wouldn't do to help you achieve yours, and if you love me as much as I love you, there's nothing you wouldn't do to help me achieve mine.

I'm not a fool, I know there will be complications, things to work through, but after you've read this, all I want you to ask yourself is whether you love me too. If you do we will work it out. I promise. If you don't then I will respect your decision and never contact you again.

I thought I was over you, Noor, but now I realize I'll never be.

I'll love you forever.

Charlie.

Noor sits there, the letter shaking in her hands. She re-reads it once, then a second time, and then a third, and with each read, every word and phrase begins to take on greater resonance as if the letter were some holy text. There is a knock on the door. Noor slips the letter into her desk drawer. The door opens. Elma stands there in a tartan cocktail dress and a sleeveless black top.

"Everything okay?" she says, sniffing the air.

"I was playing with matches."

Elma smiles.

"You of all people. Come on, our guests will be here any moment, and I thought … well let me show you."

Elma leads Noor to her bedroom. Laid out on the bed is a long grey skirt and a simple white shirt.

"I thought you could wear something other than a shalwar kameez for once."

Noor stares at the clothes.

"Think of it as a practice run for Holland," Elma says.

Noor realizes that Elma wants her to put them on right there and then. She pulls her kameez up and over her head.

"My God," Elma says, "what a tatty old bra. We're about the same size, wouldn't you say?"

Noor blushes. Elma disappears into her closet and comes up behind Noor and unclasps her bra. Noor closes her eyes and imagines Charlie standing there. Her bra falls forward and she feels his hands on her breasts, the tips of his fingers encircling her nipples.

"Noor," Elma says.

Noor eyes snap open. Elma is holding out a lacy white bra. Noor places it over her breasts, and Elma clips it at the back.

Elma helps her into the shirt, and Noor buttons it all the way up to the top. Elma leans in and undoes a couple of buttons.

"Now the skirt."

Noor undoes her shalwar pants and grabs the skirt off the bed before Elma can suggest a new set of underwear. She wriggles into it. Elma tells her to sit on the bed and returns with a leather make-up case.

"When was the last time you wore make-up?" Elma says.

"I haven't."

"Well the secret is simplicity. You want to accentuate your beauty, but you never want a man to look at you and think you're trying to impress him."

Elma applies the foundation with her fingertips. Noor closes her eyes, and imagines Charlie caressing her face, standing in front of her as naked as the night she watched him from the tree. She breathes in sharply.

"Sorry, did I press too hard?" Elma says.

Noor shakes her head. She tries to think of something to say. Anything but think of Charlie right now.

The interview. How self-absorbed could I be?

"How did your interview go?" she says.

"How do you know with these things?" Elma says.

Elma applies powder with a brush. Her touch is gentle and sensuous.

"I think I impressed them. It was good to see our work out here doesn't go completely unrecognized—but I just got this sense that they've already made up their minds and decided to give the job to this other woman. It left me feeling so powerless."

Elma applies blush to Noor's cheeks.

"Maybe if you went to New York—" Noor says.

"I've thought about that, and if it'd make a difference I would—now open your eyes wide."

Elma extracts an eye pencil and lines Noor's eyes.

"Just before we escaped I asked my mother if she'd show me how to do all this," Noor says. "'Once we're in America,' she said. It was her answer to everything at the time."

"Well, if you let me, I'd love to teach you."

"You're too kind to me, Elma. I'll never be able to repay you."

"Trust me, having you here, it's been a blessing."

Elma stands back and takes in the job she's done.

"Good, now just the lips."

She rummages through the make-up box until she finds a color she likes.

"So there's nothing else that you can do?" Noor says.

"Who knows, maybe Rod's article will help."

"When will it be published?"

"In two weeks, I think. Pucker your lips—like this."

Elma pushes her lips out. Noor giggles. It looks so silly. Elma smiles.

"Go on."

Noor imitates her, and Elma applies her lipstick.

"Okay, go take a look."

Noor looks at herself in the floor mirror. She doesn't recognize the woman staring back at her.

"You're going to be the hit of the party," Elma says.

Elma finds Noor a pair of high heels, and Noor puts them on. She feels like a giraffe. They exit the bedroom, and she wobbles behind Elma to the kitchen. A team of Pakistani waiters are readying the drinks and appetizers. They stop what they're doing and gawk at Noor. Elma snaps at them to get back to work and gives instructions to their slick-haired supervisor. Noor wishes she could run back to her room and read Charlie's letter over again. The door bell rings.

"Our first guests," Elma says.

Elma guides Noor into the sitting room and introduces her to a burly man and his boisterous wife. From what Noor can gather he runs the United States aid effort in Pakistan. From then on the guests keep arriving at a rapid pace until there are close to thirty Westerners crowded into the room. Every few minutes Elma guides Noor from one group to the next as if Noor were her most prized possession. Noor meets the Australian consul and a Danish journalist, a tanned American academic and the German head of the UN's demining operation, a British charge d'affaires and a Canadian TV reporter. Everyone seems so interested in her, so eager to help. She remembers her father asking her how many Westerners they'd ever had the opportunity to interact with.

Oh, if only you could see me now, Baba.

She senses Elma stiffen, and turns in the direction she's looking. A short, beady eyed man in a suit jacket and jeans is worming his way towards them.

"I don't remember sending you an invitation," Elma says.

"Came as Jeremy's plus one," the man says.

The man catches Noor staring at him and smiles.

"Ivor Gardener," he says.

"Noor Khan."

The man sucks on his straw. Noor feels as if he is dredging the contents of her mind.

"It's funny, I feel like we've already met," he says.

"That's enough, Ivor," Elma says. "No games tonight."

Elma grabs Noor's arm and begins pulling her away.

"Of course," he says, "you're the girl from the article, you just look so different I didn't recognize you."

Elma turns back.

"What are you talking about?"

"Rod's article. It totally changed. Became about the plight of Afghan women. Noor, here, is a big part of it."

"Oh, how delightful," the English woman says.

Noor looks at Elma. Elma's lower lip is trembling.

"It's an amazing photo, really," the man says. "Noor stares right into the camera, as if her eyes contain all the pain of the Afghan people. Least that's what the blurb said. I can have someone at my office make you a copy if you want."

Elma turns to Noor and forces a smile.

"Would you mind seeing if the kroket are ready? They should have come out by now."

"Of course not," Noor says.

Noor scurries to the kitchen, and finds a cook already arranging the krokets on a silver platter. She looks around and wonders if she should go back to the party.

No, you've won yourself a reprieve.

She heads out into the garden. There by the leaf strewn pool, she sits on a recessed stone bench and slips her shoes off her aching feet.

What's going on? This article. That man back there. None of it makes any sense.

She shivers and wraps her arms around herself.

This is nothing to how cold it must be in Afghanistan.

Yet she would give anything to be there with Charlie right now.

You can't deny it, a voice within her says. *You love him. You know you do. You're going to love him forever.*

She laughs. It's true, and it's the greatest, craziest discovery she's made in her life.

FORTY-SEVEN

CHARLIE LOOKS AT the map—a solid swathe of blue surrounds the village He rolls it up. When they get back to
Peshawar he'll have it framed and hung in his office.

"Mr. Matthews."

In the dim morning light he makes out Najib at the door.

"We just finished our prayers."

Charlie nods at a couple of boxes on the earthen floor.

"Do you mind taking one?"

"It would be my pleasure."

Charlie picks up the other box, and they walk down the
alley towards the center of the village.

"I've never asked," Charlie says, "you married?"

"Ten years. I'm fortunate, my wife's most intelligent and
has blessed me with three beautiful children."

"Does she work?"

"She did, at a woman's health clinic, but it has closed
since. This job has been a gift from Allah to us."

"What'd you do before the war?"

"I was a lawyer in Kabul."

"Ever think then that you'd end up being a deminer?"

Najib laughs.

"Not in my wildest dreams."

They turn onto the main street. Down below the men are standing around smoking, their blankets wrapped tight around them, the vehicles exhaling exhaust fumes into the freezing dawn air.

"Najib, what'd you say if I put you in charge of these guys? It'd mean more responsibility but also more pay."

"What about you? Mocam?"

"We've got to concentrate on a fresh group of recruits."

"I'd be honored."

"Then the job's yours."

Najib smiles.

"Thank you, Mr. Matthews, thank you. I won't let you down."

"That's the point, Najib, you never have."

They come up to the Pajero. Bakri rushes over and opens the trunk. There's just enough room to shove the boxes in.

"Load everyone up," Charlie say to Najib.

Najib shouts out to the men, and without hesitating they scurry for their vehicles. Charlie smiles. He chose right.

FORTY-EIGHT

NOOR SQUATS IN front of her mother's grave and spies on the man sitting under the eucalyptus tree.

It's one of the few advantages of wearing a burqa.

She'd guessed Tariq would have someone watching their hut, yet she'd still come to an abrupt halt when she'd seen the effeminate young man sitting on the bench reading a Quran. She'd recognized him immediately; he was one of the men who'd chased her. He'd looked up and asked if he could help her. She had shaken her head and moved on.

Now to her relief, he was once again immersed in the holy book. From time to time he glances in the direction of their hut, but that's it. As far as he's concerned, she's just another war widow visiting her long dead husband. She closes her eyes and tries her best to forget him.

"Mamaan, are you there?" she says. "This is when I need you."

In the distance she hears the cries of children playing and dogs barking, a plane flying overhead and a dull explosion far, far away. But not her mother.

"I remember you telling me once how much you loved, Baba. It was after that day at Bamiyan when he'd taken us to see the Buddha statues. Just as we were leaving Baba had realized that he didn't have his keys on him, and for hours we scoured the paths looking for them. It was me, remember, who thought to go back to the car and look in his jacket. There they were. They'd dropped through a hole in his pocket and were nestled in its lining. The whole drive back— how long was it, three, four hours? —you harangued him. I sat in the backseat in tears. I knew Baba was forgetful, but this felt so unfair. That night you knelt by my bed and begged my forgiveness. It had nothing to do with Baba, you explained, you'd just had a miscarriage, and the real reason you were so angry was because the idea of having another child with this wonderful man had filled your heart with joy. 'We're harshest on the ones we love the most,' you said, 'one day you'll discover that, and though there's no excuse for it, if they love you too they'll weather it until your mood changes, and the sun shines on your relationship once more'.

"I was terrible to Charlie in the beginning, Mamaan. I couldn't have said uglier things, but he weathered it. That letter Elma gave him, I don't think I ever truly believed what I wrote, they were as much her words as mine, but he weathered that too. Is that true love, Mamaan? Elma says that all men move on, if not literally then in their hearts. But how does that explain Baba? You were forever putting him through the wringer, and yet he only loved you more."

Noor waits for a response but receives none. She opens her eyes. Over at the bench, there's a changing of the guard. She screws her eyes tight.

"Mamaan, why have you been so silent recently?"

I haven't, a voice says in her head.

Noor laughs out loud as she realizes that the voice, she hears on occasion, is her mother's.

Of course, I've forgotten what you sound like.

"What should I do, Mamaan?"

Noor waits, her body still.

"It's up to me decide, isn't it?"

Trust your feelings, never disown your instincts, the voice says.

Noor smiles.

"I won't, I promise."

She heads back towards the camp, this time taking a more circuitous route in order to avoid Tariq's snoops. Her legs feel strong, her head clear. She knows what she has to do.

As soon as she arrives at Elma's house, she goes to her room and writes a draft in her notebook. She needn't have bothered; the words flow effortlessly. She rereads it and feels her heart beat faster.

Once you send this, there's no turning back.

She pulls out a sheet of letter paper and transcribes it. She seals it in an envelope and writes Charlie's name on the front. She looks at the clock. Half past ten. She might as well drop it off now while she still has a chance. She hears a car roar up the driveway. Noor freezes.

"Noor—Noor, where are you?" she hears Elma shout.

Noor jumps up from her desk and runs out of the room. The front door flies open.

"Noor—Noor—"

Noor enters the kitchen at the same time Elma does. Elma's face is bright red.

"You got in."

"I got what?"

"You, Noor Jehan Khan, are officially a scholar at the University of Amsterdam."

Noor screams.

"They called me at the office; it's a full scholarship. That means everything—a living allowance, tuition, even your travel to Holland, and you know what the best part is?"

"I can't imagine."

"They want you to start this semester."

"That's good, right?"

"That's one week from now."

Noor lets out another scream. This one more in shock.

"But how?" Noor says. "I'll need a visa—"

"They can expedite it. Just please tell me you have a passport?"

"My father has it."

"Good, I'll go get it."

Noor hesitates.

"I can do it," she says. "In fact I'd prefer to, if that's okay. I'd love to tell Baba myself."

"But Charlie—"

"He's in Afghanistan."

"Of course. But hurry, I want to fax it over straight away."

Noor runs out of the house, and down the street. The mansions pass by her in a blur.

In a week, they'll be replaced with canals and barges, cafes and museums, bridges and bicycles.

She reaches Charlie's driveway and takes a moment to catch her breath. She studies his grand old house.

To think this was once my home.

She rings the door bell and waits. The door swings open to reveal Wali in his wheelchair.

"Ah, so you've returned to grace us with your presence," he grins.

"Only for a moment," she smiles.

"Well a moment's better than nothing."

Noor steps inside and remembers the first time she was here; Charlie standing there in his jeans and flip-flops, reeking of aftershave and cigarettes.

I couldn't have thought less of him.

"Is Baba around?" she says.

"That's it, no inquiry as to my own well-being, your sister's, Mr. Matthew's perhaps?"

"You've heard from him?" she says a little too quickly.

"Less than you."

Noor blushes.

"Thank you for getting his letter to me," she says.

"You should really thank your sister."

"She helped you?"

"Even I'm not strong enough to wheel myself all the way to that woman's house."

Noor stands there uncertain as to what to say. This is the last thing she'd have expected Bushra to do.

"I'm telling you, Miss Noor, your sister is a lot more open minded than you give her credit."

Noor smiles.

Maybe she is.

She takes the envelope out of her pocket.

"Well here's another letter for you."

"For me? Oh, you are too kind."

Noor gives Wali a stern look.

"Don't worry I'll see that Mr. Matthews gets it."

Wali deposits it in the side pocket of his chair.

"Now follow me."

Wali rolls through the house and out onto the verandah.

"Look who I found," he shouts.

Aamir Khan sees Noor, and jumps up from his rocking chair. Noor runs over and wraps her arms around him.

"Is everything all right?" Aamir Khan says.

"They gave me the scholarship, Baba. They want me there in a week."

Aamir Khan raises his arms and whoops.

"What's going on?" Wali says.

"This amazing young woman is going to Holland, Wali."

Aamir Khan grabs a hold of Wali's chair and twirls it around. He dances back to his daughter.

"Oh my dear, our prayers have finally been answered."

"My passport is still valid, isn't it?" she says.

Concern flashes across Aamir Khan's face.

"Hold on, let me go retrieve it."

Aamir Khan hurries away leaving Noor alone with Wali. In the garden Rasul is tilling a flower bed.

"I sat here with Charlie the night after your accident," Noor says. "I know there's a part of him who wishes it'd been him rather than you."

"I tell you, Miss Noor, I have never known a truer friend."

And I a truer man.

Noor hears someone approaching and turns expecting her father. Instead she finds Bushra there. She looks leaner, her complexion rosier.

"Congratulations," Bushra says. "I just heard."

"Thank you," Noor says.

"You've always worked so hard, Noor. It's why I respect you so much."

Noor blushes overwhelmed by her sister's words. Bushra looks down at Wali, and Noor can't help but notice that her sister's eyes are sparkling.

"It's time for your exercises," Bushra says.

Wali groans.

"I am telling you, Miss Noor, your sister may seem like a gentle woman but she is a taskmaster."

"Someone has to be," Bushra says.

Wali grins, and Bushra gets behind Wali's chair and pushes him down the ramp towards the parallel bars.

Noor hears Aamir Khan huffing and puffing back down the verandah.

"Here it is," Aamir Khan says.

He hands Noor a passport swaddled in cloth. She unwraps it with a reverence due a medieval text.

"O Lord," she says.

"Don't tell me."

"It expires in three weeks."

"Thank God for that."

Aamir Khan takes the passport and gazes at the photo of his nine-year old daughter, her mouth twisted up in a goofy smile. His eyes water over.

"Finally it can be put to good use."

The two of them sit down and watch Bushra help Wali out of his chair and up onto the bars.

"He's making real progress," Aamir Khan says.

"And so is Bushra, it seems."

"She has a project, may I even say a purpose once more. It's a marvelous thing to behold."

Aamir Khan gives Noor one of his sweet, gentle smiles, and she feels an overwhelming sadness. It takes everything not to cry.

"I don't know if I can leave without you," she says.

"After all these years, after all this effort, now you say this."

"It was never a reality before."

Aamir Khan clasps Noor's hands in his.

"I do not believe I have ever told you this, but in nineteen seventy-six I received an offer from my old professor at Duke. Over the years he had asked me to write some articles for the literary magazine, and from what he told me they were for the most part well received. In any event he was getting on in years, and wanted someone to take over the magazine's day-to-day running. He thought I was the ideal candidate."

"Why did you turn it down?"

"I didn't, I did something far more odious, I prevaricated. I had a young family, a sick father, responsibilities at Kabul University. I wrote to him and asked if his kind offer could wait until the end of the year. He wrote back and said it could. By the time January rolled around much had changed. Your grandfather had died, the political situation had deteriorated, and well, by now you will have forgotten, but the winters in Kabul are bitterly cold, and it had been an especially frigid one that year. All I could think about was my beautiful family ensconced in a cozy North Carolina home with rocking chairs much like these on its porch. So I wrote to him and said I gladly accepted his offer. January came and went, then February, and I began to wonder if he had received my letter. So one morning I went down to the post office and placed a call to his home. His wife answered and informed me that he had died on New Year's Eve. Whatever job there had been was no longer mine for the taking.

"Do not think I do not lie awake at night and wonder how things might have been if I had accepted his offer when I first received it. Your sweet mother would still be alive, your brother a different man, you and Bushra would have had such different upbringings, my word you would most likely be attending Duke right now. Do not make the same mistake I did, my love. By God, seize this opportunity Allah has granted you, seize it in a way I never did, if not for your sake then at least for mine."

Noor fights back tears.

"I'm going to be bereft without you."

"Rubbish, you are the strongest, most courageous woman I've ever known."

He pushes himself out of his chair.

"Now enough, we have a whole week for tears and fare-wells."

He hands the passport back to Noor.

"I love you, Baba," she says.

"And I you, more than life itself."

He kisses her, and she walks down the verandah. When she gets to the doors she looks back. She smiles. He has already settled into his chair and is reading his book.

On the way home, she wonders if Charlie will have re-turned by the time she leaves. She hopes so, more than hopes, she prays that he has.

But if he hasn't, it will be fine. To delay love is not to deny it.

She walks up the driveway. Elma's Land Cruiser is still parked out front. She steps into the entrance hall.

"Elma," she shouts. "You're not going to believe this. It expires in three weeks."

There's no reply.

"Elma?"

Noor heads down the corridor into the kitchen and opens the French doors. Elma isn't in the garden.

How strange.

She goes to her room, and decides to write her passport details in her notebook. She scans the desk. It's not there. She searches the vanity's drawer. It's not there either, and neither is Charlie's letter.

"Were you ever going to tell me?" Elma says.

Noor spins around to see Elma leaning against the door frame. She is holding the letter and notebook in her hand.

"Perhaps when I visited you in Amsterdam, once you had set up your love nest, one night at dinner, him bounding in with that ridiculous grin on his face. Or maybe you were always going to play me for a fool. 'Don't mention Charlie to Elma,' you'd tell your friends, and the only way I'd find out would be when you were featured in some sickening article about your fairytale love story."

Noor trembles. She doesn't recognize the woman standing in front of her. Elma rubs her eyes.

"I'm so tired of being played. I mean why do people do it? It's so destructive."

"I should have told you. I'm sorry, it just happened."

"Nothing just happens in this life, Noor."

Noor goes to protest, and Elma throws out a hand.

"No, don't patronize me and say it's God's will."

"But what if it is? You, yourself, told me that one day I'd meet someone and fall in love without realizing it."

"How many times do I have to tell you that this isn't love? I won't let you destroy your life, you hear me. You need to choose once and for all."

"I don't understand."

"It's either him or the scholarship. I won't allow both."

"But I've already been awarded the scholarship."

"You haven't accepted it yet."

"But I'm going to."

"Not if I call Gerben Janssen and tell him you're turning it down for a better offer from the United States."

Elma's gaze is unwavering. Tears spring in Noor's eyes.

"I could no more deny my love for Charlie than I could deny Allah is God and Mohammad his messenger."

"Then that is you decision."

Elma steps back from the door. The implication is clear. Noor should go. Noor tries to breathe but finds it impossible.

It's over. Just like that it's over.

She looks around the room. Apart from her passport there's nothing else in it that's hers. Elma holds out the notebook and letter.

"I wish you a wonderful life together," Elma says.

Noor takes them and continues on out of the house. She reaches the end of the driveway and feels as if the world has been turned on its end. She leans over and vomits.

FORTY-NINE

TARIQ ENTERS THE reception room to find the Prince sitting with Ivor.

"Ah, Tariq," the Prince says, "please come join us."

Tariq sits on the couch opposite Ivor.

"Mr. Gardener, was just commiserating with me over our setback."

"Hell, even we thought they'd run out of jet fuel," Ivor says. "No one could've foreseen it."

"Except Tariq did. It's to my great chagrin that I didn't take his advice."

Tariq sees Ivor glance his way as if he's measuring him in a whole new light. It's something he's grown accustomed to ever since they'd returned. It feels good.

"I still think they're laughing at me behind my back," the Prince says.

"No, they're relieved," Ivor says. "Hekmatyar, I know, was furious you stole a march on him. Supposedly when he heard you were on the move he grabbed his guard's AK-47 and fired it into his dining room ceiling. Chandelier fell smack into the middle of the table."

The Prince clutches his stomach and laughs.

"Fact is," Ivor says, "your legend's only gotten bigger. Shit, shooting down that MIG-21 took some guts."

"In battle you can only act on instinct," the Prince says. "I saw the Stinger lying there and Allah did the rest."

Ivor slurps his tea and leans forward.

"So you going back in?" he says.

"In three days," the Prince says.

"Anything I can help you with? I still got a couple of Stingers lying around if you need em."

"Well I suppose if you're offering."

"I'll have em sent over later today."

There's an awkward silence. Ivor shifts his position as if he can't get comfortable. Tariq watches him closely. There's something about this man; his damp brow, his pasty skin, his twitching eyes. He wonders why the Prince is so enamored by his company.

"What's bothering you, Mr. Gardener," the Prince says, "you seem unusually jittery today."

"Just things on my mind, you know how I am, always thinking. Did I tell you I'm out of here in a month?"

"No, I wasn't aware. Where are you headed?

"Cairo."

"Ah, a wonderful city. A buffoon for a President, but truly there's no place like it, you'll enjoy it there."

"You going back to Riyadh?"

"Once our mission's accomplished."

"You know, that's what I've always admired about you, your Highness, all those princes back in Saudi jumping up and down declaring their love for jihad, but when it came down to it none of them wanted to risk their lives. You know what we call people like that back in the States? Chickenhawks."

The Prince chuckles

"I like that, I must use that expression myself some time."

"Even bin Laden hasn't stayed to the bitter end," Ivor says.

"He became very upset by all the infighting amongst the mujahideen. You know how hard he tried to heal the rifts between the parties. He even had the humility to reach out to Massoud."

"I heard he left because Saudi intelligence had a bounty on his head."

The Prince snorts.

"They've no issue with him. No, I just think he needed some peace and quiet, a place to recharge his batteries."

"Before what?" Ivor says.

"I'm not following you."

"What's he going to do after his batteries are recharged?"

"Be a businessman like his father, I suspect. You must have heard he's bought some farms in Sudan, even a tannery; he's ready to settle down."

Ivor picks at the skin around his finger nails.

"I don't buy it, I hear rumors he's reached out to Hezbollah, wants to join forces."

"Oh come now, you're paranoid. How many years have we fought side by side to achieve this victory?"

"Means nothing. One year after the Second World War the Americans and Soviets were mortal enemies."

"So what are you saying, am I now your mortal enemy?"

"No, course not, but bin Laden ..."

Ivor works his fingers through his hair.

"All I ask is that you keep your ear to the ground; get in touch if you learn anything, however insignificant it may seem."

The Prince leans forward and takes Ivor's hand in his.

"You've been most helpful to me during your time here, Mr. Gardener, a friend even. And once you're my friend, you're always my friend."

"Appreciate that."

The Prince stands, and Ivor and Tariq follow suit.

"I suspect we won't be seeing each other again," the Prince says. "Not in Peshawar at least."

"Kick butt out there," Ivor says.

The Prince laughs

"And all the best in Cairo. Go with peace."

"Ma-salaam," Ivor says.

The Prince kisses Ivor on both cheeks. Ivor extends a hand to Tariq, and Tariq shakes it.

"Goodbye, Tariq."

"Goodbye, Mr. Gardener."

Tariq waits for the Prince to sit and takes Ivor's place. A servant comes over with a silver bowl, and the Prince washes his hands.

"He may be going to Cairo but I suspect he'll be spending most of his time in Khartoum," the Prince says. "We should let bin Laden's people know, send them some background on Gardener, that sort of thing."

"I'll make sure it's done right away," Tariq says.

"He's dangerous this one, most Americans couldn't care less about us anymore; they think we're going back to the hovels we crawled out of. But Gardener understands that now the genie's out of the bottle it can never be put back in."

"What do you mean?"

"Remember before we left for Afghanistan how you told me it was our duty to take the fight elsewhere. What did I say to you?"

"You told me a wise general fights one battle at a time."

"However an even wiser one is nevertheless preparing for the next."

Tariq feels a visceral thrill surge through him.

"It's America, isn't it?" he says.

"There's one true purpose in this life, Tariq: to lift the word of God and make his religion victorious."

"What will our role be?"

"To bamboozle the Americans so thoroughly that when bin Laden does strike they won't see it coming."

"I will do whatever you ask of me."

"Good. Now tell me, how's your sister?"

Tariq has been dreading this question.

"There has been a slight complication. She began menstruating this morning and won't be clean until the end of the week."

"That's a shame, I was eager to finally marry her."

Tariq maintains his composure.

Good. You just bought yourself a few more weeks.

"Trust me," Tariq says, "she's as eager to be married. But she is a patient woman, she can wait."

"Then I will wait also," the Prince says. "It's only two, three days more at most. We will postpone our departure."

Tariq forces a smile.

"She will be elated to hear that."

The Prince nods. It's time for Tariq to go. Tariq kisses the Prince on both cheeks and leaves. He heads through the building. Eager mujahideen recruits make way for him as he passes. He is too preoccupied to take any pleasure from their deference.

Where the hell are you?

He walks out the door. Ivor's SUV speeds past and a thought strikes him.

"Stop," he shouts.

The SUV picks up speed as it heads down the driveway. He runs after it in his lopsided manner.

"Stop that vehicle," he shouts at a group of mujahideen loading up a truck.

A couple sprint after it while another gets on his radio. The SUV's lights disappear around the bend.

Damn.

Tariq slows and continues to the bend. To his relief, he sees a couple of guards have barred the SUV from going any further. By the time he reaches the gate he's regained his breath.

"I can take it from here," he says to the guards.

He waits for them to retreat. Ivor winds down the window.

"Everything okay?" Ivor says.

"My sister, Noor Jehan Khan. She's gone missing."

Tariq reaches inside his waistcoat and pulls out his worn photo. Ivor scrutinizes it.

"She is older now, her face leaner—"

"How can I get a hold of you?" Ivor says.

"Through the Prince's office."

"Let me see what I can do."

"Thank you, I'd forever be in your debt."

Ivor rolls up his window, and Tariq nods at the guards. The massive gates swing open. Ivor drives away.

Who am I kidding? He's no more likely to find her than I am.

FIFTY

CHARLIE SKIDS TO a halt outside his house and grabs his backpack. He runs up the steps and pushes the heavy door open.

"I'm back," he shouts.

Down the corridor he hears Wali's creaking wheelchair pick up speed. Wali comes flying into the hall.

"As-Salaam Alaykum."

"And Wa'alaykum salaam to you," Charlie grins.

Wali pirouettes to a perfect stop.

"I see you're getting the hang of that thing," Charlie says.

"I call it my Lada. I trust you had a good trip."

"Greatest experience of my life."

"The village is clear?"

"The village, the fields, the riverbanks, and not a single scratch on one guy."

"That is most wonderful news."

Charlie unzips his backpack and pulls out Wali's tattered sneaker.

"Here I brought you back a memento. Thought it might remind you how you saved those kids."

He hands Wali the shoe. Wali stares at it for so long that Charlie questions whether he should have ever brought it back.

"I couldn't have asked for a finer gift," Wali smiles.

Wali reaches into his pouch and retrieves the envelope Noor gave him.

"Now I have something for you."

It's Charlie turn to stare dumbfounded at the object in his hands.

"Well open it," Wali says.

Charlie rips open the envelope and starts reading.

Dear Charlie:

From an early age my mother taught me that the last person you should try and fool is yourself. "Trust your feelings, never disown your instincts," she'd say, and whenever my father presented me with a marriage proposal it was easy to turn down because in every case I felt nothing.

And then you came along, and I felt something instantly. I despised you. In fact I don't think I've despised anyone more.

And yet somewhere along the way my feelings changed. I, of course, refused to admit it. Over the years I have assiduously cultivated this image of myself as an independent soul, someone who has no need of love, no need of even the slightest joy in their life. To admit that you made me happy, that I yearned to be with you, would mean that that artifice I had so carefully constructed would crumble to the ground.

So like a dictator whose people have turned against him, I retreated behind my walls, hoping to drown out their shouts. However a dictator can only do that for so long before the walls come crashing down, and in my case it was your letter that finally brought down mine.

From today on I am going to live by my mother's words.

I love you, Charlie. I love you like no man I've ever met. I'm not scared to admit it anymore, for now I understand I could only love a man who'd never want to constrain me and who'd provide me with the support to pursue my dreams.

Where we go from here I don't know, but as you said we'll work it out. There's my potential scholarship to the University of Amsterdam, your work here in Peshawar, the complications that are bound to emerge given our different backgrounds. We may even be apart for a while. However my instinct is that we'll sort all these things out.

Stay safe, my love, get word to me on your return, and soon enough, inshallah, we'll be together again.

I love you.

Forever.

Noor.

Charlie stares at the letter.

She loves me. She loves me. She loves me. She loves me.

He continues to say it over and over as if only by doing so will it truly sink in.

He hears someone coming down the stairs and looks up. It's Aamir Khan holding one of Wali's artificial limbs.

"Oh my word, is that you, Charlie?" Aamir Khan says.

It occurs to Charlie that he should probably get Aamir Khan's permission. After all when he sees Noor next he's determined to propose to her.

"I'd love to tell you all about my trip," Charlie says.

"And I'm eager to hear all about it, but unfortunately the workshop closes in half an hour."

"I'll take you."

"I do not want to put you out."

"No, I'd like to, that is if you don't mind sitting on the back of my bike."

"On the contrary, it sounds like fun."

They ride over to the hospital, Aamir Khan clutching the artificial leg with one arm while clinging tightly to Charlie with his other. Charlie pulls up outside the workshop. Aamir Khan climbs off.

"I should not be long," he says.

Charlie smokes a cigarette. And then a second. And the longer he waits the more jittery he gets. Finally Aamir Khan returns.

"They said it will take a couple of days to fix," he says.

"What's the problem?"

"The end is grating against Wali's leg."

An ambulance, its siren blaring, screeches up. Orderlies rush out to carry a groaning man inside.

This is ridiculous. I can't ask him outside a hospital.

"What you say we go for a walk?" he says.

Aamir Khan gives Charlie a curious look.

"You know that pink building off Jamrud Road, the one with all the domes?"

"You mean Islamia College?" Aamir Khan says.

"Hear it has really beautiful gardens."

"Why not? A walk would do me good."

Aamir Khan climbs back on, and Charlie takes off. All the way there Charlie rehearses what he's going to say. Nothing feels right. His attempts either sound stilted, self-serving, or facetious; in some cases all three.

He pulls up outside the college's main gates, and they walk up the driveway in silence. Islamia College looks like a palace from Mughal times, the gardens out front a maze of hedgerows, gurgling fountains and rose bushes. They pass under an archway and come upon a sports field where some students are playing cricket in the fading light. A couple of deck chairs sit unused at the edge of the field.

"Want to watch?" Charlie says.

"That sounds very pleasant."

They sit down and watch the game; the crack of bat on ball, the shouts of encouragement amongst the players, the cries of "how's that" whenever the fielding team appeals for an out.

"So, should we confer on the matter at hand?" Aamir Khan says.

Charlie snaps his head in Aamir Khan's direction. Aamir Khan smiles.

"A young man does not ask an elder one on a walk unless he wants something."

Charlie sits up as best he can.

"I'd like your permission to marry Noor."

Aamir Khan nods. Nothing more. Out on the field, a ball flies past the batsman and demolishes his stumps.

"Your permission's important to me," Charlie says.

"I am honored you would consider it so; however I cannot give it."

Charlie is stunned.

"What did I do?" he says.

"Nothing. I just find the whole custom to be an antiquated one. If there is one thing I have always strived for it is that my daughters be able to make their own decisions without interference from anyone, myself included. That said I am happy to bring your proposal to Noor like I have all the others."

Charlie can't help but laugh.

"Thank God, for a moment there, I thought you were going to stop us from getting married."

For the first time that day, Aamir Khan's unflustered manner falters.

"Do you mean to say she has already agreed?" he says.

"No, but I think she will."

"On what evidence?"

"We've been writing to each other."

"And she loves you?"

"That's what she says."

"Unbelievable," Aamir Khan says, shaking his head.

"You disapprove?" Charlie says.

"No, I am just astonished. When Noor makes a decision nothing can be done to change her mind. If what you say is true, it is a first, a miraculous first. It speaks to how deep her feelings are for you."

"And how do you feel about it all?"

"As I said my feelings are of no account."

"But still I'd like to know."

Aamir Khan looks off beyond the cricket field.

"When we first arrived in this city I was devastated, I was as much in love with Noor's mother as you profess to be with Noor, and to lose her the way we did, well it tore apart my heart, so much so that to this day it is still not mended. Of all of us it was Noor who stayed strong. She kept on smiling and telling jokes as if we were still in Kabul. I think she saw it as her vocation to lighten our spirits. Yet as the years passed, I could tell her smiles were increasingly forced, and about six months back I realized if I didn't do something drastic they would be gone forever. Trust me, under normal circumstances I would never have met you at the Pearl Continental. I am a coward by nature. But I did, and I thank Allah every day for giving me the courage to do so. You woke up her soul, Charlie. How could a father not be gladdened by that?"

Aamir Khan chuckles.

"I tell you," he says, "this has been a momentous day."

"What do you mean?"

"Of course, you're not aware. This morning Noor learnt that she had been awarded a scholarship to the University of Amsterdam."

"No way, that's awesome."

"They want her there by next week."

Charlie stares at Aamir Khan. It feels like a cruel joke.

"Is that an issue for you?" Aamir Khan says.

"It's soon, but no, it's fine."

"You do not sound fine."

"I love her, I want to be with her, but I'm happy, I promise."

"Are you still intent on seeing out your contract?"

"I'd like to. I think Noor would want me to."

"And after that?"

"I'll join her. Who knows maybe I can enroll in her college."

A spin bowler comes to the wicket and proceeds to bowl slow but confounding balls. Despite his assertions to Aamir Khan, Charlie feels as discombobulated as the batsman.

"I have always thought cricket and life have much in common," Aamir Khan says. "Both require enormous amounts of perseverance and patience."

"From the looks of that poor guy it seems like life just ties you up in knots."

Out on the field the batsman finally gets a read on the spin bowler's ball and smashes it in the air. Charlie and Aamir Khan lean back and watch it fly high over their heads.

"But then there are those glorious moments where everything goes right," Aamir Khan says. "And though they may be few and far between, let me tell you they are always worth the wait."

***

NOOR SITS ON the bough of the oak tree enshrouded in darkness. She desires nothing more than to stay where she is forever, like the tree, a mute witness to the world.

She hears voices and senses the lights in Charlie's room turn on and off. For some time her father and Charlie call out her name, and then someone walks along the verandah and across the lawn. They arrive at the tree and grapple their way up before making their way down the bough.

"Hi," she hears Charlie say.

She says nothing. He sits down beside her.

"Noor."

"Please go."

"Not until you tell me what's up."

Noor blinks back tears.

"Elma found out about us. She said I had to choose between you and the scholarship. I chose you."

"I'll go talk to her. She can't do that—"

"No, it's done."

"Nothing's ever done."

"You weren't there, Charlie, you didn't see the look in her eyes. It's over. Everything's over."

"What do you mean?"

"My family's cursed. I don't know what caused it, but the curse is real. We can't be together, Charlie, I'll just pass it on to you, and I love you too much to do that."

Charlie says nothing, and the longer he's silent the greater the tension. Noor fears what he's going to say yet yearns for him to say something. She starts to cry. He turns her face towards him.

"Your love," he says, "how can it be a curse? It's the greatest thing that's ever happened to me."

"But it's built on a lie. When we first came here it wasn't because I changed my mind, it was because my brother was after me."

"Tariq?"

"He's determined to marry me to his prince. He has men all across the city looking for me."

Noor can't make out, through her tears, whether Charlie's expression is one of worry or anger. She assumes it has to be the latter.

"Why didn't you tell me?" he says.

"There was nothing you could do."

"I could have gotten you out of here."

"How?"

"By marrying you. I still can."

"No."

"Why not?"

"The last thing I ever want is to force a proposal out of you."

"Are you crazy? I was going to propose to you tonight."

"I don't believe you."

"Then why would I have this on me."

Charlie pulls out a simple, diamond ring.

"My mother left it to me, and ever since I've kept it close, never believing that another woman could be worthy of it. That is until now."

Noor sits there paralyzed. Unlike most women she's never dreamed of this moment but now it's upon her she acts no different than any other.

Charlie rises until he's on one knee.

"Noor Jehan Khan would you do me the greatest honor I could imagine and be my wife?"

Charlie wobbles. Noor flings out a hand to steady him.

"Please get back down," she says.

"Only when you answer the question."

Noor looks up at him, at the hint of a smile on his lips, and knows that life without this man would be no life at all.

"Yes," she says.

He drops back down and she throws her arms around him. He holds her tight, and for the first time in her life she understands the words from the seventh surah:

'It is He who created you from a single soul, and made its mate of like nature in order that you might dwell with her in love.'

He takes her face in his hands, and their lips meet. This time his kiss is slow and tender, a reassurance of both his love and his respect.

"I love you," she says.

Nothing has ever sounded more true.

He pulls away and holds the ring out.

"You are aware that in Muslim culture there's no such thing as an engagement ring," she says.

He grins.

"That's what's so great about us, we're going to have the best of both worlds."

He slides the ring onto her finger. It fits so perfectly it's as if it was always meant to be there.

"Do you want to go in and tell the others?" he says.

"Baba's going to be shocked."

"He already knows."

Noor feels her old, indignant self return. It comforts her enormously.

"Well he doesn't know what my answer was," she says.

"I told him I was pretty sure it'd be a 'yes'."

"Oh you did, did you?"

Noor attempts to look peeved, but she can't keep the act up long. He makes a face at her and she laughs.

"Let's go," she says.

She takes his hand in hers, and together they make their way along the bough and down the tree. From inside the house, exclamations of joy can be heard, voices filled with hope and the possibility of better tomorrows.

Outside the tree stands a mute witness to it all.

PART IV

exit

FIFTY-ONE

CHARLIE ARRIVES AT the end of the line. The last of the new recruits is a serious, young man with a neat beard.

"A-salaam Alaykum, I'm Charlie, what's your name?"

"Ahmed Nader."

"And how did you find about the job?"

"Obaidullah is my cousin, sir. He says you are a fair man. He prays most fervently every night you become Muslim, that is how much he respects you."

"Well he's a good man, we're lucky to have him."

"I am most looking forward to learn from you, to be as good a deminer as he."

Charlie can't help but wince. He knows that while he might start Ahmed Nader's training, it's unlikely he'll finish it.

The previous night once all the excitement had died down, they'd turned to the subject of Tariq, and everyone had agreed that Noor needed to get out of the country as soon as possible. The only way she could do so was if she got a fiancée's visa. This morning Charlie had set out for the US consulate, however halfway there a thought had struck him. The last thing he needed was Ivor mixed up in his affairs. So instead he had turned around and driven to Mine Aware. There he had called the American embassy and spoken to an official in the visa section. Three months was how long it usually took for such a visa, she'd told him.

Three months. That's way too long.

There was one other stipulation. For Noor to be able to travel to the United States, Charlie would have to go with her. In effect he'd have to quit his job. It was okay. With Najib and Mocam at the helm, Mine Aware would be in safe hands until Stephen Adams arrived.

But three months.

He turns to Mocam.

"This is a good group," he says. "Let's get them kitted out."

Charlie heads for his office. In the middle of the compound, Najib has the original set of recruits cleaning their equipment. Najib waves, and Charlie waves back. It's going to be a quick turnaround. Jurgen had called him this morning. He wants them back in the field in a couple of weeks.

In his office, Charlie sits at his desk and stares at the phone. It will be six-thirty in New York; his father will be out of the shower by now. He takes a deep breath and dials. On the fourth ring a woman picks up.

"Hello," she says.

"Natalie?"

"Who's this?"

"It's Charlie."

There's no response. It's as if his stepmother's forgotten that her husband has another son. He hears a muffled conversation. The phone is passed over.

"Charlie? You in trouble?"

The hairs rise on the back of Charlie's neck.

"No, why would you say that?" Charlie says.

"It's just it's five-thirty in the morning."

"Oh shit, I'm sorry, I can call back later."

"No—don't go. My God, where are you calling from?"

"Pakistan. Peshawar to be precise."

"You there with the army?"

"No, I got out after the Gulf War. I'm working for an aid agency, we train refugees how to get mines out of the ground."

"That sounds like good work."

"Yeah, it's been really fulfilling."

There's an awkward silence. After five years there's so much to say but neither knows where to start.

"I'm calling because I met someone," Charlie says.

"American?"

"Afghan. We're going to get married."

There's another awkward silence. Charlie wonders if his father's put the phone on mute to talk to Natalie. He grips the receiver even tighter.

"Dad?"

"I'm here, I'm just shocked that's all."

"By her nationality?"

"No, nothing like that. It's just all so overwhelming. I had no clue you were in the Gulf War. Did you see action?"

"Some."

His father inhales. He doesn't sound like the man he once knew.

"Would your mother have liked her?" his father says.

"She'd have loved her."

"Then that's good enough for me."

Charlie relaxes his grip.

"Look, Dad, I need a favor. I need to get Noor a fiancée visa. Quick. It's nothing shady, I promise, we just need to get out of here that's all. I just thought, you know, with all your connections and everything—"

"Hold on while I get a pen."

Charlie waits for his father to return.

"Okay," his father says, "how can I reach you?"

Charlie gives him both his home and work number.

"I'll call you back when I have something," his father says.

"Thanks Dad, I really appreciate it."

There's silence. Charlie wonders if his father has hung up.

"I know you were angry, Charlie, I know I did many things to push you away, but I want you to know there's not been a day I haven't thought of you—I love you, Charlie."

Charlie swallows.

"I love you too, Dad."

Charlie replaces the receiver. He shakes his head.

Shit, maybe miracles can happen after all.

FIFTY-TWO

ELMA LIES ON her sitting room couch and nurses her third whisky of the night. The house is so quiet she can hear own breathing. She now regrets sending Nadeem away. At least with him here she had some form of company.

How pathetic. All alone. No career, no man, no friends.

She senses a fresh set of tears coming on, and downs the rest of her glass to quell them.

She heads down the corridor towards her bathroom. On the way she passes Noor's old bedroom. She looks at the bed that Noor made so neatly every morning, at the desk where she studied, at the prayer rug on the floor. She hates to admit it but she misses her.

What have I done? Who have I become?

In her bathroom, she squats over the toilet and pees. On the opposite wall is a print of an upset toddler being comforted by her elder sister. She always wished she'd had an older sibling, but she hadn't, and over the years she'd comforted herself with the knowledge that it had made her all the more self-sufficient. When she'd got knocked down it had been up to her to pick herself up.

And now's no different.

She flushes the toilet. She knows what she needs to do, or at least where to start. She grabs her car keys off the top of her bedroom dresser.

Thank God I never called Gerben.

She imagines Noor opening the door at Charlie's house. Elma will launch into her apology, and when she tells Noor that the scholarship is still hers, Noor will break out into a glorious smile, perhaps even scream with delight and throw her arms around her.

All will be forgiven.

Elma hears the doorbell ring. She smiles.

Well that saves me a trip.

She hurries down the corridor and flings the front door open to find Ivor standing there in a suit and a Houston Oilers baseball cap. Her heart sinks.

"Got a minute," he says.

"I'm sorry but—"

"Have news regarding that UNDP post. Good news."

Elma wavers.

Don't let him do this to you.

"Come in," she says.

She leads him into the sitting room.

"Want a drink?"

"Not much of a drinker."

"Right, I forgot."

Ivor settles himself on the arm of the couch. He smiles at her in that insincere way she's so come to despise.

"You don't look so good," he says.

"Let's cut the crap, Ivor, what do you want?"

"I want to tell you a story, two stories actually."

"I don't have time."

"Please, indulge me, you'll find it worth your while."

Elma goes over to the drinks cabinet. She pours herself a couple more fingers of Glenfiddich.

"The first's about a group called al Qaeda. Heard of em?"

Elma shakes her head.

"It's made up mainly of Arab mujahideen; men who came out here to fight the jihad and now find themselves at a loose end."

"Fine they can all go home. Afghanistan will be better off without them."

"And if only they could. Problem is their governments have no desire to see them return. You see these men are filled with a homicidal hatred of anyone they believe to be insufficiently Islamic, and if you're the King Fahd or President Mubarak, do you really want these battle hardened zealots training their sights on your philandering ass? No, you're much better off if they train them on someone else, the United States for instance."

"I don't see how any of this concerns me."

"I apologize, the second story. It concerns a woman named Andrea Engelson, I assume you've heard of her."

Elma nods.

"Great, then I can skip over her Peace Corps work in Peru and that celebrated memoir of hers, and get to the juicy part. You see while it's expected that most memoirs contain embellishments, even downright lies, it's what Andrea leaves out of hers that's most startling. Her relationship, a torrid one it'd appear from the photos, with a doctor called Rafael Ramirez, or as his compatriots in Shining Path like to call him, Comrade Vladimir."

Elma feels her pulse quicken.

"Now whether Andrea knew of Ramirez's association with Shining Path is open to question. Odds are she didn't, if anything he was most likely using her. However the fact that she went on a trip with him to Ayacucho, a rebel stronghold, and the day after they returned there was a deadly bombing in a Lima shopping mall, does raise suspicions, suspicions I'd suggest that need an immediate airing in the American media."

Elma finishes what's left in her glass and pours herself another.

"How are these two stories connected?" she says.

"It's simple really. I need an asset inside Al Qaeda, or at least close to it. You want that position at UNDP."

"You've lost me."

"The potential asset I've lined up is a young man named Tariq Khan, but to reel him in I'm going to have to deliver him something, and what he wants is his sister, Noor."

The full effect of the whisky finally hits Elma.

"No, never," she says.

"Why? What is she to you, Elma?"

"She's a friend."

"A friend it seems who's no longer living here."

Elma's face betrays her.

"Look," Ivor says, "you and me, we don't have a spouse or lifelong friends we hang out with every weekend. What we have is our careers, and the reason we give a shit about them is because, unlike most people, the work we do matters. Every day we make choices about whose life is worth bettering and whose isn't. What's your criteria, Elma? I sure as hell know what mine is. Whichever action saves the most lives that's the one I plump for every time, otherwise all I'm doing is playing favorites."

"If she marries this Prince her life will be miserable."

"What because no Afghan refugee would want to live in the lap of luxury?"

"She doesn't—she's in love."

It's clear this is a piece of information Ivor wasn't aware of. Elma's feels her hand shake. She puts her glass down and grabs a hold of the bookcase.

"So for this love of hers, you're prepared to allow thousands, perhaps tens of thousands of people to be condemned to a life of misery?"

"I don't understand"

"You're good at what you do, Elma. Hell, I've not run across someone who does your job better. But if Engelson gets that post, you know as well as I do she'll use it purely as a vehicle for her next gig, and like I said, thousands will suffer because of that."

"You could give the media this information without asking me to do this."

"I could, but then I'd be responsible for anyone who dies in an attack I could've averted. No, the only way this works is if you tell me where this Noor Khan is. It's the right thing to do, Elma. Hell, I'd go so far as to suggest it's the courageous thing to do."

FIFTY-THREE

IT IS THE greatest feast any of them can remember; to call it grand would be to do it a disservice. Mukhtar serves up shorwa soup, crispy samosas and buttery pakoorha before piling onto the table koubedah kebabs, qorma, lamb shanks and qabili pilau with copious bowls of yogurt and chutney to dip everything in. For dessert there are milky ferree puddings, coils of bright orange jalebi, stacks of laddous candy balls, and row upon row of barfi fudge in a panoply of garish colors. Speeches are made and dreams are discussed. It is a celebration filled with laughter and tears.

Afterwards as they drink endless rounds of tea a plan is formulated. Charlie will rent a house for Aamir Khan, Bushra and Wali close to the hospital, and then he and Noor will fly to the States as soon as her visa comes through.

"We'll go look at houses tomorrow," Charlie says to Wali. "I think it should just be one floor so you can get around, with three bedrooms obviously—"

"No, no," Wali grins, "two will be sufficient."

"What you talking about, you'll—"

Wali leans over and takes Bushra's hand in his. Noor shrieks in delight.

"When?" she says.

"Wali asked my permission this morning," Aamir Khan says.

From there chaos ensues. Hugs are given, more speeches are made, and even more tears are shed.

The phone rings, and Charlie excuses himself. It's his father.

"There's a man at the embassy in Islamabad," his father says. "Steve Farrell, he's in consular affairs, if you can get down there tomorrow he said he'd sort you out."

"Does Noor need to go too?"

"No. He said just to bring her passport and a photo, and he should be able to do a temporary visa on the spot."

Charlie stands there speechless.

"Look, I'm due in a meeting," his father says

"Dad, wait ... thank you."

"My pleasure. I can't wait to meet Noor."

Charlie runs to his room and grabs his camera. When he returns to the dining room everyone looks in his direction.

"We're going to have to postpone the house hunt."

"Why?" Noor says.

"My father's contact can get you a visa tomorrow."

"Come on, this is a joke."

Charlie shakes his head. Wali lets out a cheer.

"Now stand against that wall," Charlie says to Noor, "the lighting's good there."

Noor does as she's told. Charlie adjusts the zoom until Noor's head fills the frame.

"You're not meant to smile in passport photos," he says.

Noor tries to put on a serious expression only to crack up laughing.

"Noor," he says.

"I'm trying," she giggles.

Charlie clicks away.

FIFTY-FOUR

TARIQ SITS AT his father-in-law's desk eating a breakfast of eggs and naan. It's still dark outside, the Khyber mountains a ghostly black. He goes over the conversation he knows he must have with the Prince today. He's decided to stick with the story that Noor has hepatitis. It's simple, and something he can't be blamed for.

The Prince won't be happy, but, unlike before, I'll survive this.

He thinks about his father and sister with poisonous hatred. His father, especially; a weak, insidious man who's given him nothing in this life; a man who pretends to have the righteousness of a Sufi saint but who has the morals of a brothel owner; a spineless fraud who preferred to let his wife die surrounded by infidels rather than risk his own life trying to save her. His only comfort is his father's assured eternal damnation.

There's a knock on the door.

"Come in," Tariq says.

Badia steps into the room. She is wearing a black shalwar kameez. Tariq's mood brightens; he was hoping it was her. He gestures Badia over, and she comes and stands in front of the desk. Tariq's eyes travel up her teenage body, drinking in the curve of her hips, the thinness of her waist, the swell of her breasts, her full lips and lustrous hair.

"You can look at me," he says. "It's allowed."

She raises her chin, and looks him in the eye. He detects a spirit he hadn't sensed before.

What is it? Do you hate me?

"I'm sure you're aware that I'm head of this family now, at least until one of your other brothers comes of age, and so it's up to me to decide whom you should marry."

"I trust you will make the correct choice."

"I have. It's going to be me."

Badia's eyes flicker.

You weren't expecting that, now were you?

"It's forbidden for a man to be married to two sisters," Badia says.

"True, but since I divorced your sister last night it's no longer an issue."

Badia holds his gaze.

Were you holding out hope for the Prince? Not if you know his reputation. Are you sorry for your sister? Unlikely, you have different mothers. What is it?

"You're going to be a good wife, Badia, and I promise to be a good husband. This won't be your home for long, we'll be moving to Saudi Arabia soon. You'll dress in the finest clothes, shop in the best stores, have servants waiting on you."

"I will serve you faithfully," she says.

He detects a glint in Badia's eye.

No, you're happy, he rejoices. *Relieved to be marrying a man your age, a man of increasing stature and power.*

There's a knock on the door.

"What?" he shouts.

Sarosh, the young clerk from the Prince's office, sticks his head in. Badia turns away so Sarosh won't see her face.

"Can't you see I'm in the middle of something," Tariq says.

"I apologize, but you insisted I find you if the American called."

Sarosh holds out a piece of paper.

"He said you should meet him at this address."

Tariq walks over and snatches it from him.

"That's it?" Tariq says.

"Nothing more."

Tariq nods, and Sarosh retreats from the room. Tariq turns towards Badia, his interest in her over for now.

"Go and take off those dreadful clothes. No amount of mourning is going to bring back your father and brothers."

Badia hastens away.

Could Gardener really have found Noor? Why else would he call?

Tariq hurries out of the room and shouts for Yousef to join him. By the time he arrives at the front of the house his SUV is waiting for him. He surveys the courtyard with satisfaction; it's now devoid of its barnyard animals and rusting farm equipment. Yousef, his hair still wet from showering, hobbles out the front door.

"What's all the bother?" he says.

"He's found her."

Yousef grins. Tariq hands him the piece of paper.

"You know where this is?" Tariq says.

Yousef reads the address.

"Sure."

"Then let's go."

FIFTY-FIVE

NOOR LIES WIDE awake in bed.

Mrs. Matthews, Mrs. Noor Matthews.

It sounds so ridiculous yet so right at the same time that she can't help but laugh.

Down the corridor Noor hears Charlie's alarm go off. She slips out of bed and changes. When she reaches the kitchen she finds Mukhtar making an omelet.

"It's alright, Mukhtar. I can finish this. Why don't you take the day off."

"Are you sure?" he says.

"Absolutely."

Mukhtar smiles and leaves. Noor looks at the omelet bubbling away and realizes she's never made one before.

It can't be that hard.

She tries her best to flip it, and it breaks apart.

Unbelievable, I can't even do this.

"I didn't expect to see you up."

Noor turns to find Charlie standing in the doorway.

"Are you disappointed to see me?" she says.

"Are you crazy? You're the greatest thing I've ever laid eyes on this early in the morning."

Noor can't help but smile.

"Sit and eat," she says, "you've a long journey ahead of you."

"A hundred miles is hardly a long journey."

"Alright, you've an important journey ahead of you."

Charlie sits down at the kitchen table, and Noor places the broken omelet in front of him.

"So you always going to cook me breakfast?" he says.

"If you're fine with me being a stereotypical Afghan wife."

Charlie takes a bite.

"If you cook me an omelet this good maybe that won't be such a bad thing."

"So you want a fat, ignorant nag, is that it?"

Charlie takes another bite.

"It's a really good omelet," he grins.

"And you don't deserve it."

Noor goes to swipe the plate away. Charlie sweeps his arm around her waist and pulls her down onto his lap.

"Charlie," Noor shrieks.

"I'm not going to do anything, I promise."

"You already are."

"Fine, anything more."

Noor gives Charlie a searching look before allowing her body to relax into his. She gazes into his eyes and traces the scar on his cheek with her finger.

"You'll be safe, won't you?" she says.

"It's not like I'm going into Afghanistan."

"I know, but everyone says how dangerous that road is."

"I promise to be extra safe."

"I wish you'd drive Wali's car."

"The bike's quicker."

"That bike will make a widow of me before I'm married."

"Okay, I'll go by Mine Aware and pick it up."

"Promise?"

"Promise."

Charlie leans in and kisses her gently.

"I thought you said you weren't going to do anything?" she says.

"You bewitched me, what can I say?"

"So it's my fault is it?" she says kissing him back.

"Totally and utterly."

If only this could go on forever.

Noor hears someone in the hall and pulls away.

"Baba found a suitcase in the attic last night," she says. "I don't know what he was thinking, it's got far more space than I need."

"Then we'll have to get you some Western clothes at Heathrow. It's high time we got you in a pair of figure-hugging jeans."

Noor blushes and extricates herself from his arms.

"Go, before I report you to the local imam for indecency."

"Don't worry, he won't be shocked, he already has a file on me this thick."

"Away with you," she giggles.

Charlie leans in and gives her one final kiss.

"Back before you know it."

He winks at her and heads out the door. Noor looks at the clock. Quarter to seven. If everything goes to plan Charlie should be back by dinner. She goes out onto the verandah and prays, doing everything in her power to focus on God. Afterwards she sits down and allows thoughts of Charlie to overwhelm her. She senses someone and opens her eyes. Rasul is staring right at her from the lawn below. She's convinced he's read every one of her lurid thoughts. She scurries inside and finds her father engrossed in a book.

"I did not realize you were up so early," he says.

"I was seeing Charlie off. You?"

"I just returned from taking Wali to the hospital."

"This early?"

"I'm afraid you have to get there before seven if you want to salvage any hope of seeing a doctor. I told him I would wait but he was having none of it."

"Can I make you breakfast?"

"No thank you, I am most content."

Noor spies the cover of his book—*Anna Karenina*.

"Surely you've read that before?" she says.

"Of course, but when I was perusing the shelves just now I couldn't find anything I hadn't read."

"So you picked the longest book instead?"

"No, just the best," he smiles.

"Well I'll leave you to enjoy it."

Noor heads to go upstairs.

"Noor," her father says.

She turns back.

"Have I ever told you how much I love you?" he says.

"Every day of my life."

Aamir Khan smiles and returns to his book.

In her bedroom, Noor finds Bushra asleep. She begins packing her meager possessions into the case her father found; photos Charlie has taken of Aamir Khan and Bushra; her collection of threadbare shalwar kameez; her books; the essay her father made her write all those years earlier.

She hears a car drive up and wonders if Charlie's forgotten something.

Two more pull in behind it.

Doors open and men get out, calling out to each other in Pashtu and Arabic. A chill passes through her.

The front door crashes open; it is enough to wake Bushra.

Noor rushes out of the room and down the corridor. She hears her father say something followed by a sickening crunch. Aamir Khan falls silent.

"Find her," someone says.

She knows the voice well—it's Tariq's. The Devil's couldn't strike more dread in her.

A couple of men start up the staircase.

Noor sprints back towards her room. Bushra stands in their bedroom doorway, paralyzed.

"We've got to get out of here," Noor says.

Noor grabs Bushra's hand and pulls her down the corridor towards Charlie's room. The two of them slip inside it, and Noor locks the door behind them.

The men's booted feet come thundering down the corridor. They kick in her bedroom door and then Aamir Khan's.

"Come on," Noor says.

She flings open the balcony doors and climbs onto the ledge. The tree bough hangs three feet away. She hauls Bushra up beside her.

"We've got to jump," she says.

Bushra looks down at the drop and swallows. Back in the room, someone tries the door. When they discover it's locked, they start kicking it.

"You can make it," Noor says. "I promise."

Bushra closes her eyes and leaps. Her feet fall either side of the bough and her hands flail for something to grab on to.

Just as it looks like Bushra might tumble to the ground, her right hand grabs a hold of a branch and she steadies herself. She looks back at Noor.

"Go," Noor says.

Bushra crawls along the bough. Noor prepares to leap when she hears a clamor of voices below.

"You cannot do this," Aamir Khan shouts.

Two mujahideen drag Aamir Khan by his arms onto the lawn and toss him down. He struggles up onto his knees, blood seeping from a cut to his forehead.

"As your father, I beg you, these are your sisters."

One of the mujahideen kicks Aamir Khan over.

"Stop it," Noor shouts.

Aamir Khan looks up, and they hold each other's gaze. Another blow lands in the small of his back. He cries out.

"By the grace of Allah, leave him alone," she shouts.

Tariq comes out of the house and pulls out his pistol. Aamir Khan sees Tariq approaching.

"O Allah!" Aamir Khan says in a loud, clear voice, "Pardon my sins which are many and accept my deeds which—"

A shot rings out, and Aamir Khan's body relaxes into the ground.

"No," Noor screams.

The balcony doors fly open, and she twists around to see two mujahideen standing there. She recognizes them as two of the men from the camp.

Noor jumps only for a hand to grab a hold of the back of her pants. Her forward progress halts, and she finds herself hanging upside down. The younger of the two yanks her up and throws her over the ledge.

"Go easy," the older man says.

He wraps his thick arms around her. Noor kicks him, but her blows have no effect. Hobbling, he carries her out of the room and down the corridor. Noor tries to free her arms only for him to tighten his grip even more. They reach the top of the staircase. At the bottom, Tariq gives her a nod as if to suggest that Noor's now his.

Never.

Noor reaches between her legs and twists the older man's testicles. The man roars in pain. He loses his footing, and the two of them tumble down the staircase. She lands on top of him, the blow so stunning that for a moment Noor forgets where she is.

Then it all comes back. The one thing that doesn't is her breath. She can't get one out let alone take one in.

This is it, I'm dying.

"Yousef," she hears Tariq shout over and over.

She looks at her brother, bent over her assailant, the man's neck bent at an impossible angle. She closes her eyes and wills death to sweep her away too.

"You bitch," Tariq says.

He yanks her up by her hair only to let go. She falls back onto the tiles and looks towards the front door. Mukhtar stands there with his mouth agape, a grocery bag in either hand. Tariq grabs Mukhtar by the collar and drags him whimpering through the hall and out towards the garden.

Noor raises her head.

Get out, her mother's voice screams. *Get out while you can.*

Noor tries to stand, and her legs give way.

Now. You have to go now.

Noor crawls one strained elbow length at a time. The door gets ever closer, and as it does her lung capacity returns.

A gunshot rings out from the garden.

She stands and this time her legs hold. She staggers outside.

At the bottom of the driveway, she sees a rickshaw idling, the driver oblivious to what's going on.

Noor's pace quickens.

One of the Arab drivers' looks up.

"Stop," he shouts.

The rickshaw driver sees Noor coming and scrambles to put his rickshaw in gear. She grabs onto the rickshaw's door and throws herself into the passenger compartment.

"Go," she screams.

The rickshaw lurches forward. A hand reaches in and grasps her leg. She flails for something to hold on to.

She's too late.

Noor topples out, her knees scraping along the asphalt. The rickshaw flees down the street.

The mujahid driver drags her down the driveway and deposits her in front of Tariq.

"I won't have you dressed like a whore," Tariq says.

He throws a black burqa at Noor. She stumbles to her feet and looks for an escape route. Tariq's men encircle her.

"Help," she screams, "please, someone help me."

Two of Tariq's men come up behind her and grab each of her arms. The burqa comes down over her head. The two men pick Noor up and carry her to an SUV. Noor grabs a hold of the door, kicking out at anyone that comes within reach.

Through the burqa's gauze, she sees a couple of muja-hideen carry her father's body out of the house. They throw him in the back of a pick-up as if he were a bale of straw.

"No," she screams.

Something jabs her arm and she lets out a high-pitched howl. She twists around and the mujahideen take a step back. She tries to move but her legs won't comply. She notices one of the mujahideen is holding a depressed syringe in his hand.

Oh no. God, no.

She blacks out.

FIFTY-SIX

CHARLIE PARKS ON the street. He's glad no one picked up when he called from Islamabad.

It's only going to make it more of a surprise.

He still can't believe how easy it'd been. His father's contact had asked him four meatball questions and thirty minutes later had returned with the K-1 visa pasted into Noor's passport.

"You can leave tonight if you wish," he'd said.

Tonight, unlikely. But by the end of the week. Why not?

Charlie pulls Noor's passport from his pocket and flicks to her visa. She grins back at him. He feels an urgent desire to see that smile again. He walks up the driveway and finds the front door open. He closes it behind him and creeps through the house. No one's there. He goes out onto the verandah. Rasul is sitting on the steps in front of his hut. Charlie waves. Rasul doesn't bother to wave back.

Friendly as ever.

Charlie tiptoes up the staircase and along the corridor. He sees Noor's bedroom door open. He grins and sidles up to it. He jumps into the bedroom.

"I'm back," he says.

No one's there. Noor's suitcase sits open on her bed.

"Noor," he shouts.

There's no answer.

Could they have gone into town?

He heads to his bedroom and notices his shattered door. He pushes the door open and finds the balcony doors loose hanging off their hinges.

A cold sweat bathes his body. He runs out onto the balcony and shouts Noor's name over and over.

No. No. No. No. No.

He sprints out of the house to his SUV. He and drives like a man possessed. He prays there's another explanation.

Please God, let it not be this.

He pulls up to the front entrance of the hospital. Wali is waiting there in his wheelchair. Charlie jumps out.

"Ah, finally my ride's arrived," Wali says.

"Where's Aamir Khan?" Charlie says.

"He sent you, no?"

"He's not at the house, none of them are."

"Then they must have gone to the bazaar."

"They told you that?"

"No, but where else could they be?"

"Tariq's taken them."

Wali's smile falls away.

"We need to go back to the house," he says.

"Didn't you hear me? They're not there."

"But Rasul and Mukhtar are, no? Maybe they know something."

Charlie lifts Wali into the passenger seat. He slams the door shut and races to the driver's side.

"My wheelchair." Wali says.

"We'll get it later."

Charlie puts the SUV into first and tears away. The drive back is as crazed as the one there. Charlie lifts Wali out of the car and carries him through the house all the while shouting out Rasul's name. He finds Rasul sitting in the same position.

Charlie drops Wali into a rocking chair and runs over to the old man. He frog-marches him over to Wali.

"Ask him where they are," Charlie says.

Wali and Rasul go back and forth in Pashtu.

"He begs your pardon," Wali says, "but he wants to know why you're treating him this way?"

"I don't give a shit, where is everyone?"

Wali asks him. Charlie sees the blood drain from Wali's face.

"What is it?"

"He says he was in the garden when he heard noises coming from the house. Not good noises so he hid in the bushes—not long after some men come out dragging Aamir Khan with them. Aamir Khan pleads with them but they did not listen."

Rasul fills in more details.

"They threw him down, and their leader shot him—one of the woman was screaming on the balcony, and some men came and dragged her away."

Charlie clutches the railing to stop himself from collapsing.

"He says a few minutes later they dragged Mukhtar into the garden and shot him also."

"Where?" Charlie says.

Rasul points towards the lawn. Charlie staggers down the steps. The grass looks like someone has spilt a can of red paint on it. Charlie searches for air.

"Is it true?" Wali says.

Charlie nods, and Wali groans.

"What about the other woman?" Charlie says. "Where is she?"

Rasul points at the oak tree.

Oh thank God.

Charlie scrambles up the trunk. There in the nook he sees Bushra crawled up into a ball, a look of catatonic terror on her face. His heart sinks.

"It's okay," he says. "Hold my hand."

She takes it, and slowly but surely he guides her down the trunk. Bushra gets to the bottom and sees Wali sitting in the rocking chair. She runs over and wraps her arms around him. Charlie follows after her, everything a blur. He stumbles upstairs to his bedroom and flings open his desk drawer. There next to the pen gun he sees Ivor's business card. He grabs it and makes for the hall. Wali shouts out his name. He ignores him and calls the number scrawled on the back of the card. The phone at the other end rings.

Come on, goddamn it.

Someone picks up.

"Mr. Gardener's residence," a man says.

"I need to speak to Ivor, it's Charlie Matthews."

"I'm sorry Mr. Matthews but Mr. Gardener not here."

"Is he at the Consulate?"

"I believe he is at Miss Kuyt's house."

Charlie drops the phone and runs for the door.

"Mr. Matthews," Wali shouts from the verandah.

Charlie continues on and jumps in the Pajero.

Stay calm, stay calm.

He finds it impossible to. All the way there he makes ever more onerous bargains with God in return for Noor's safety. By the time he gets to Elma's cottage he's even promised never to see her again.

As long as she's safe.

He sees Ivor's dark blue Bronco parked out front and jumps out. He rings the doorbell.

"Ivor, Ivor, you there," he shouts.

He bangs on the door.

"Ivor, please, I need your help."

Charlie tries the door. It's locked. He runs around the front of the house to the garden gate. It's locked too. He pulls himself up and over the other side. He sees a set of

French doors and sprints towards them. He turns the handle. The door opens.

"Ivor," he shouts.

He hears voices down the corridor. He runs down it and throws open the door at the far end. Elma screams. She is sitting up, holding the sheets to her chest. Ivor stands naked by the bed, the bedside phone in his hand. Charlie stares at them, unsure what to say or do.

"What the fuck do you think you're doing?" Ivor says.

"He's taken her, Ivor, he's taken her."

Ivor comes round the side of the bed and struggles into a pair of pants.

"Who's her?"

"Noor—my fiancée."

Ivor stops midway through buttoning them up.

"You got engaged to an Afghan, are you out of your fucking mind?"

Charlie takes a step back, stunned by the ferocity of Ivor's tone.

"Elma knows her," Charlie says. "She lived here for a while."

Ivor looks at Elma.

"That true?"

Elma manages the slightest of nods.

"Please, Ivor, help me, you know these people, you can bargain with them."

Ivor grabs his shirt off the floor.

"Wish I could, buddy, but there's nothing I can do. This Tariq guy is the Prince's right hand man, he's untouchable."

Ivor slips into his shirt. Charlie stares at him in horror.

"How do you know his name?"

Ivor slides his feet into a pair of penny loafers.

"It's my job. I know every fucking mujahideen leader in this piss ant town."

"Yeah, but how'd you know Tariq took Noor?"

Charlie glances at Elma. She looks back at him with a mixture of dread and self-loathing. Charlie stalks towards the bed.

"You told him, didn't you?"

Elma cries out.

"You fucking told him where to find her?"

Ivor steps in front of Charlie. Charlie pushes past him. Elma scrambles off the bed.

"Help me," she screams.

Charlie advances on her, his fists clenched.

"He killed her father, my cook—you realize that."

Elma drops to the ground and raises her hands to protect herself.

"No," she cries.

Charlie stops.

Remember what's important.

Charlie hears someone come running down the corridor. A well built man bursts in. and points his gun at Charlie.

"Get on the floor," the man shouts.

Charlie doesn't flinch.

"It's okay, Jack," Ivor says, "Charlie was just leaving, weren't you, Charlie?"

Charlie walks towards the door.

"Forget about her, buddy," Ivor says, "She's not worth it."

Charlie continues on, not once looking back.

***

CHARLIE PULLS TO the side of the road just beyond the flickering street lamp and cuts his lights. He stares down the tree lined street; it looks like a tunnel heading straight to hell.

Remember stay calm, show him respect. If there's a peaceful way out of this, that's best.

Charlie get out and walks alongside a tall, brick wall, the pen gun in his right sneaker rubbing up against the side of his foot. Up ahead two black-turbaned guards stand outside a large wooden gate with AK-47s slung over their shoulders. One of them spots Charlie and says something to his compatriot. They aim their guns at Charlie.

"I'm here to see Tariq Khan," Charlie says.

The lead guard jabbers away and shakes his gun at Charlie.

"Tariq Khan, Tariq Khan. I need to see him."

The guards look at each other. After a lengthy exchange, one opens a door in the gate and disappears. The other continues to aim his gun at Charlie. A few minutes later, the guard returns with a young man.

"What are you doing here?" the young man says.

"My name's Charlie Matthews. I'm here to see Tariq Khan, I'm a close friend of his father's.

"That's not possible I'm afraid, it's late."

"If he knows I'm here he'll want to see me."

"Why would you think that?"

"I'm engaged to his sister, Noor."

The young man studies Charlie and steps back through the door. The two guards resume their staring contest. Charlie looks up at the top of the wall and sees two bands of concertina wire strung along its top. He realizes he has no plan B.

The man returns and says something to one of the guards. The guard comes over and pats Charlie down. His hands approach Charlie's ankles. Charlie shifts his right foot and the pen gun slips under it. The guard nods at the young man.

"Follow me," the man says.

They step through the door onto a driveway lined with massive oak trees. With the pen gun now under his foot it's impossible for Charlie not to walk with a limp. The young man glances back at him.

"Is there a problem?" he says.

"What do you mean?" Charlie says.

"You are walking strangely."

"I was wounded in the Gulf War."

The young man gives Charlie a contemptuous look and continues on. They come around the bend and Charlie sees a Victorian-era school with a floodlit sports field out front. Forty men are doing push-ups to the count of their shawled instructor. The young man leads Charlie down a path towards a two story house. An armed guard steps out of the shadows and subjects Charlie to another pat down. They carry on through a courtyard and the dim interior of the house into what Charlie assumes to be an office. It smells of incense.

"Wait here," the young man says.

Charlie glances around. There's a large writing desk at one end and a couch and two chairs centered around a coffee table at the other. The room has an impersonal feel; there are no family photos on the desk nor art on the walls. It's as if the place has been stripped bare.

Charlie looks up at the ceiling. He senses Noor is close. The urge to shout out her name is immense. He bends down and pulls off his shoe. The pen gun slips into his hand, and he pulls back its clip. He hears the door open and slips his shoe back on.

"I hear you came by to offer your condolences," a man says.

Charlie drops the pen gun into his pocket, and turns to see the shawled instructor by the door. He looks like a Roman statue that's lost an arm.

Tariq.

"Yes," he says. "I'm sorry for your loss."

Tariq walks over to the far chair and sits down. He lets his shawl fall away to reveal a pearl handled pistol and gestures for Charlie to sit across from him. A retainer enters with a tray and pours each of them a cup of tea. Tariq takes a sip.

"I'm afraid to say my father had few friends in these parts, in fact I wasn't aware until now that he had any."

"Your father was a good man."

"Oh, I wouldn't go that far. I appreciate your intentions in saying so at a time like this, but let's be frank, he was a fool and a heretic, two qualities I fear won't serve him well in the life to come."

"He prayed five times a day."

"To a god I'm unfamiliar with. His understanding of Islam was so warped he might as well have been a kafir."

Tariq plays with a set of prayer.

Stay calm.

"How's Afghanistan?" Charlie says.

"You tell me, I heard you were there recently."

What else has Ivor told you?

"It's a beautiful country," Charlie says.

"I'd say beautiful is a stretch; harsh would be a more appropriate description."

"Once the war's over there's going to be a lot of work to do."

"Yes, mines to be dug up, roads rebuilt, homes restored, just not by organizations like yours."

"We cleared a whole village."

"And I commend you for that, but Afghanistan's going to be an Islamic republic, inshallah, and it'll be Muslims who rebuild it not kafirs."

"We want to help."

"Of course you do, it keeps us weak and dependent."

Charlie fumbles for his cup unsure how the conversation has gotten so antagonistic so quickly. He searches for something conciliatory to say.

"I want you to know I respect Islam," he says.

"Ah, I had no idea you'd converted."

"You misunderstand—"

"Oh, then you must be considering doing so?"

"No, that's not what—"

"Because at its core Islam is very simple, it's most important tenet being that there's no God but Allah and Mohammad, peace be upon him, is his messenger. Now logically if you don't believe Mohammad, peace be upon him, is Allah's messenger then you must believe that he either lied about receiving the Quran or he was crazy. I trust you're someone who respects neither liars nor lunatics?"

Charlie stays quiet. Rather than heading to safer ground he's somehow walked straight into a minefield.

"So here we are," Tariq says, "two men, one a devout Muslim, the other someone who denigrates that which the other holds most dear. You must understand that leaves us with nothing to talk about."

Tariq puts his cup down and stands.

"Goodbye, Mr. Matthews."

"I will pay you," Charlie says.

"I assume you're talking about my sister."

"Your father gave me his blessing."

"Sarosh told me you'd said that."

"In Pashtun culture a father's word is—"

"Nothing if it contradicts the Quran; it's forbidden for a Muslim woman to marry a kafir."

"Just tell me how much money you want, and I'll get it."

Tariq shakes his head.

"Oh Mr. Matthews, even if I were so inclined, there's no sum you could give me. You see, my sister's already married."

Charlie tries to say something but finds it impossible.

"Did Noor ever tell you about her friend Ameena, how they used to fantasize about a couple of princes coming to the camp and whisking them away? Unfortunately for Ameena a fantasy is all it remained, but for Noor her fantasy's finally come true. It's a miracle, don't you think?"

Charlie's surprised to discover how calm he feels.

So it has come to this after all.

He stands up and whips out the pen gun.

"Take me to her now," he says.

Tariq laughs.

"Do you really think you'll hit me with that thing?"

Charlie sees Tariq's hand inch towards his gun.

"Touch that gun and you'll find out."

Tariq's hand wavers.

"You forget," Charlie says, "I'm the one who has nothing to lose here."

"Apart from your life."

"Without Noor my life means nothing."

Tariq's eyes flicker as if he's only now fully aware of the fanatic standing in front of him. Charlie edges closer.

"Where is she?"

Tariq hesitates and Charlie straightens his arm.

"Upstairs," Tariq says.

Charlie glances at the ceiling.

I was right.

"Turn around," he says.

Tariq complies, and Charlie edges up to him. With the pen gun up against the back of Tariq's head, he reaches around and withdraws Tariq's gun from its holster. He checks it's loaded and lets the pen gun drop to the floor. Tariq twists around, realizing the pen gun never was. Charlie points the gun at his forehead.

"Let's go," Charlie says.

Tariq's gaze switches ever so slightly. Charlie looks over his shoulder to see Sarosh, by the door, pointing a gun at him. A shot rings out, and he tumbles to the floor. Tariq's boot stomps down on his wrist, and the gun skitters away. Charlie tries to push himself up but it feels like a thousand knives are piercing his shoulder.

"You bastard," Tariq screams.

Charlie looks up. Tariq is pointing the trembling gun at his head.

So this is it.

He closes his eyes and does all he can to imagine Noor lying there beside him, cradling him in her arms.

I love you, she says.

"I love you too."

A phone rings. One ring, two rings, three. Sarosh answers it and says something in Pashtu. The only words Charlie can make out are 'Ivor Gardener'.

Everything goes quiet.

Am I dead yet?

He opens his eyes to see Tariq's boot arcing towards him.

It's the last thing he remembers.

FIFTY-SEVEN

NOOR AWAKES. HER head pounds, her throat is dry as sandpaper, and her hip throbs in pain. She keeps her eyes closed hoping what transpired the day before is but a dream. However deep down she knows it isn't. The pain's too real.

Keep it together, her mother's voice says. *You can outwit them, but only if you face reality.*

Noor opens her eyes and winces. The light streaming through the window only makes her headache worse.

Good, that's a start.

She looks past the bed. Tariq sits on a high-backed chair, one leg crossed over the other.

"Good morning," he says, "I trust you slept well."

Noor catches a glimpse of her top sheet. Halfway down blood spots it like an ugly tea stain.

"I won't marry him," she says.

"That's not your decision to make, dear sister."

"I've slept with many men, thirty, maybe forty. How else do you think we made ends meet? I'll tell the Prince that."

"Now that's a lie; you're still intact."

He indicates the blood stain on the sheet.

"The Prince had a woman check you."

Noor shivers. She sits up and sees the bedroom door is open. She suspects she could get past Tariq.

But from there where would you go?

All of a sudden she remembers her father.

"How could you?" she says, tears welling in her eyes.

"I assume you're referring to our father's recent demise."

"You murdered him."

"I did what had to be done; for you, for this family. Generations from now you'll be revered. A woman so beautiful she snagged a Prince."

"He never stopped loving you."

"He had a curious way of showing it."

"You of all people must know that the Quran states that 'if anyone kills a person, it will be as if he killed all the people.'"

"Except Baba wasn't a person, he was an apostate."

"He was the most religious man I've ever known."

Tariq laughs as if that statement's absurd.

Stop antagonizing him, the voice says. *Buy time.*

"I wanted to inform you," Tariq says, "that your marriage ceremony is scheduled for eleven o'clock."

Noor glances out the window; the sun is still low in the sky. She suspects that gives her two or three hours to find a way to escape.

"Are many people coming?" she says.

"You and Baba made it so hard to plan the joyous occasion that there's been no time to invite anyone."

"That's good, the best wedding is that upon which the least trouble and expense is bestowed'."

"I concur completely."

Keep going.

"And the Prince," she says, "is he a good man?"

"He is truly the most religious man I know."

"Then I will submit to your judgment."

Tariq wanders over to the window.

"Unfortunately past experience has taught me to doubt that," he says.

"Things have changed. Like you said, you're the head of the family now."

Tariq turns back.

"This Charlie Matthews came by and saw me last night. I was curious to meet the man, attempt to see what you saw in him, and frankly I'm baffled."

Noor feels the bed spin.

"You're lying," she says.

"He begged me to set you free, said he'd give me everything he had if I did, and when I told him you had alternate plans, he pulled a pen gun on me. It wasn't loaded, I could tell that immediately, but nonetheless in the heat of the moment I wanted to kill the bastard. Now I'm thankful I didn't, because now it's up to you whether he lives or dies."

Noor leans over the side and vomits. Tariq shouts out a command, and an old woman hobbles into the room.

"Clean it up," he says in Pashtu.

The woman hurries away.

"My patron, the Prince, is a deeply insecure man. So imagine how furious he'll be if a mere refugee, even one as beautiful as yourself, is anything but enamored with the idea of marrying him."

Noor vomits again, her throat burning from the bile.

"Sit up," Tariq says.

Noor stares at the remnants of the feast they ate thirty-six hours earlier.

"I said sit up."

The old woman returns.

"Should I wait?" the woman says.

"No, get on with it," Tariq says.

Tariq grabs a hold of Noor's hair and wrenches her into a sitting position.

"We return to the front today, and the Prince is eager to spend what little time he has left with you. Now if you please him, as a wife's meant to, and by that I mean you smile, you compliment him, are what they call a giving wife, then I'll let this Charlie Matthews go, unharmed—but if the Prince is in any way displeased, well you're an intelligent girl ..."

Tariq turns to the old woman.

"Get her ready," he says.

He leaves.

Tears stream down Noor's face as she realizes how close Charlie probably is. She imagines him, his face beaten, lying on a dirt floor, his hands and feet tied together, her brother dragging him outside into some desolate courtyard, putting a gun to his head and pulling the trigger.

This can't be happening.

The old woman comes back into the room. She hisses at Noor as though she were a barnyard animal. Noor edges off the bed. The old woman comes up behind her and pushes her. Noor staggers forward.

"That's it, move."

The old woman gives her another push, and Noor falls forward into the bathroom. The old woman hobbles in after her and starts running a bath. Noor sits on the toilet seat lost in her misery. She looks at her left hand and realizes the engagement ring is no longer on her finger.

Just one more thing that's gone forever.

A few minutes later the old woman returns. She rips Noor's nightgown off and leads her into the bath.

"I'll be back," the woman says.

Noor stares at the water and wonders how long it'd take to drown. Maybe a minute, two at the most. Didn't the Prophet say that anyone who takes their own life will be denied entry to heaven?

But surely nothing can compare to the hell you find yourself in now.

She edges her body down the tub. Her nose slips below the surface.

He won't have me.

Noor's throat constricts as her lungs beg for air.

And what about Charlie? If you love him, you'll do what Tariq asks.

Noor thrusts her head out of the water and sucks in a batch of desperate breaths. She realizes she was a fool for ever thinking her destiny would be any different from Ameena's.

For his sake I must embrace it.

The old woman comes back in. She gets on her knees and picks up a bar of soap. Noor lays a hand on her wrist.

"I'll do it," Noor says.

The woman hands Noor the soap and stands.

"I'll wait for you," the woman says.

Noor washes herself and gets out of the bath. She finds a toothbrush and some toothpaste and brushes her teeth. Up above the sink she sees an assortment of European perfumes. She picks one and sprays it on her neck and down her body. She feels like she's anointing a corpse. She walks into the bedroom and finds the old woman waiting for her with a younger, plumper woman. They take in her naked body.

"You'll need to take care of that," the old woman says pointing at Noor's groin. The plump woman nods.

They lead her to the bed, and Noor lies down and stares at the ceiling.

Is this why men don't run when they're led to the gallows? The fight has left them.

The older woman shaves the hair underneath Noor's arms while the plump one shaves between her legs. Noor thinks of Charlie, that final wink he gave her, so impetuous, so carefree, and a tear winds its way down her cheek.

Will I forget him the way I've forgotten Mamaan?

"Enough of that," the old woman says, wiping away the tear with a tissue.

They sit her up, and the old woman puts make-up on her face while the plump one draws intricate henna designs on her hands. They stand her up and wrestle her into an embroidered red dress.

"I need a moment to pray," Noor says.

The women retreat, locking the door behind them. Noor stands facing what she approximates to be the direction of Mecca and performs salat. Her breathing slows as she prostrates herself, and she focuses her thoughts on Allah and the belief that this life is but a trial for that to come. She almost finds peace. She hears the lock turn. She shivers.

"Ready?" Tariq says.

She stands and sees he's holding out some black garments. She takes the first and unfolds it. It's an abaya. She pulls the cloak over her head.

"And now this," he says.

She shakes her head. He frowns.

"Swear by Allah you will release Charlie today, unharmed, if I do as you ask."

"I swear," he says.

"Say it."

"I swear by Allah I will release Charlie Matthews today, unharmed, if you do as I ask."

Noor grabs the other garment from him, a niqab, and places it over her head. Tariq takes Noor by the arm and leads her out of the room. They walk outside and down a path towards a large stone building. On either side she sees mujahideen staring at her. Once inside they go up a set of back stairs, down a corridor smelling of fresh flowers and into a large room. At the far end, two gilt-edged chairs face each other. An elderly imam stands in between them. Tariq sits Noor down in one of the chairs, and soon after a man

makes himself comfortable opposite her. She recognizes him
from the Range Rover.

"Let's go," the Prince says.

"Praise be to Almighty Allah, the Sustainer of the Worlds
Whom we ask help and pardon," the imam says. "We seek
refuge in Allah from the evils within ourselves and from our
evil actions. He whom Allah guides no one can lead astray
and he who He leaves in error has no one to guide him. I
testify that there is no deity but Allah and that Mohammed is
His servant and His messenger."

The imam turns to Tariq.

"I presume you are this woman's wali."

"I am," Tariq says.

"Has this woman agreed to marry this man?" the imam
says.

"She has."

"Then go ahead."

Tariq turns to the Prince.

"In the name of Allah the Merciful, the Mercy giving,
Praise be to Allah, Lord of the worlds, and Prayer and Peace
be upon the Prophet Mohammed, his family and the com-
panions. I marry to you my sister, Noor Jehan Khan, whom I
represent, in accordance with Islamic Law and the tradition
of the Messenger of Allah, peace be upon him, and for the
Sadaq agreed between us."

The Prince starts on his lines, and when he's finished the
imam hands Tariq the marriage contract and a pen. Tariq
places it in his sister's lap.

"Do you accept this marriage contract?" the imam says.

Noor tries to speak but nothing comes out. Through the
slit in her niqab she sees the Prince's eyes tighten.

"She does," Tariq says.

"I must hear it from her," the imam says. "Noor Jehan
Khan, do you accept this marriage?"

"I accept," she says in little more than a whisper.

Tariq forces the pen into Noor's trembling hand. She scratches her name at the bottom. Tariq pries the pen away and presents it and the marriage contract to the Prince. The Prince signs it with a flourish.

"May Allah make it a blessing for you and a blessing to you together with all that is good," the imam says.

Tariq helps Noor to her feet.

"She's yours, your Highness."

The Prince takes Noor's hand and leads her out of the room and down the corridor. Noor sees a servant standing by an open door. She and the Prince enter a sumptuous bedroom. The Prince guides her to the center of the room. The door clicks shut, and she can't help but gasp.

The Prince takes off her niqab and abaya. He unzips her dress from behind, and it falls to the ground. The Prince steps back and appraises her naked body like a collector sizing up a work of art. She senses tears rising in her eyes and forces them back.

Remember Charlie. It's all about Charlie.

"How did you get those scrapes?" the Prince says.

"I fell," she says.

He steps forward, and crouches down as if his intent is to examine every inch of her body. She feels his warm breath on her skin and shivers.

"You truly are perfection," he says. "Now come, undress me."

Noor takes off the Prince's ghutra and undoes the buttons of his thobe. She pulls it up and over his arms and head. She takes the two items over to a nearby chair. When she turns back she sees him standing there, his chest matted with hair, his stomach protruding outward like a cow fattened for market, his penis straining against his boxer shorts.

"Hurry up," he says.

She walks back over and bends down. With her eyes closed she pulls his boxer shorts to the floor.

"Look at me," he says.

She straightens. His face has reddened, his breathing is quick.

"Do you like what you see?" he says.

Noor's never seen so hideous a sight. She tries to say 'yes' but can't. The Prince frowns.

"Bend over," he says.

She does as she's told.

"Our Lord!" she mumbles. "Grant us good in this world and good in the life to come and keep us safe from the torment of the Fire."

His hand strikes her buttocks, and she tumbles onto the floor. She lies there, her buttocks ablaze.

"Get up," he says.

Noor staggers to her feet.

"Again."

She bends over and once more his hand strikes her, this time with even greater ferocity. Somehow she manages to stay on her feet.

"Our Lord! Behold we have heard a voice calling us unto faith: 'Believe in your Lord' and we have believed."

The hand strikes her again. She bites the inside of her cheek until she tastes blood.

"Now stand up," he says.

The Prince stands before her.

"I will ask you again," he says, "do you like what you see?"

She forces a smile.

"Yes, very much."

The Prince takes her by the hand and leads her to his bed.

"Now, you'll do whatever I ask."

For the next hour and a half Noor complies with the Prince's every command. Not once does she cry or scream, and whenever he looks at her she somehow manages to smile. Finally, miraculously, it is over, the Prince spent, and Noor too numb to feel any pain.

"Draw me a bath," the Prince says.

She staggers into the bathroom and turns on the taps. She looks at herself in the gilded mirror; at the bite marks, the welts, the bruises. She notices a couple of bathrobes and puts one on. The Prince walks in. He steps into the bath and lies back, his eyes closed, a contented smile on his face. Noor kneels down beside him and starts washing his soft, pudgy hands. He opens his eyes and strokes her face. He has the touch of the Devil.

"So tell me about this American?" he says.

"Who?" she says.

He gives her a look.

"We lived with him for three months," she says.

Noor works on his legs.

"Why?"

"He and my father were friends."

"And did you like him?"

I love him. I love him enough to endure this a million times over.

"Well do you?"

Noor realizes she's stopped washing the Prince.

"No," she says. "He was uncouth and ignorant."

The Prince stands. Noor retrieves a towel, and the Prince lets her dry him.

"You know, he came here yesterday," he says, "declaring his love for you."

"My brother mentioned something along those lines."

"And what do you think about that?"

Noor holds out the bathrobe so the Prince can put his arms in it.

"It seems as if he was a little late, don't you think?" she says.

The Prince laughs.

"I was worried," he says. "I'd heard you were headstrong, but once we dealt with that early insolence, you were very giving. You're going to be a lovely gift, Noor, when I return to Riyadh."

Noor smiles and this time it is genuine.

You're saved my love.

The Prince heads into the bedroom.

"This Charlie Matthews," he says when he reaches the door. "Would you like to see him one last time?"

Noor almost says 'yes'. She catches herself just in time.

"No, I couldn't see anything useful coming from that," she says.

"I agree," the Prince says.

He takes a step closer to the door and as if by magic the door opens.

"Besides it's impossible, the man's dead already."

The door closes behind him. Noor crumples to the floor. She's too devastated to even make a sound.

FIFTY-EIGHT

"THE SLEEVE IS too short," Tariq snaps.

Badria, his ex-wife, trembles. Tariq straightens his arm.

"It should come down to the top of my thumb not my wrist."

Badria takes his camo jacket off making sure not to aggravate his stump.

"I will fix it immediately," she says.

"Well hurry, we're leaving any moment."

Badria scurries off. Outside Tariq can hear the Prince giving another of his interminable speeches. The Prince had given him special dispensation not to attend. After all Tariq had had to consummate his own marriage. He stirs as he recalls the delightful afternoon he's had. Badia was young and inexperienced, but she was eager to please and her body ...

He opens the door, and reenters his father-in-law's bedroom. Badia lies languidly under the sheets.

"I had to say one last goodbye," Tariq says.

"I hope I didn't disappoint you," she smiles.

"Far from it."

He stands over the bed.

"Now I'm your husband, you need not be shy."

She pulls the sheet away and turns her body towards him. He commits every inch of his new wife's body to memory.

If only I had another thirty minutes.

He hears a bestial snort and looks in the direction of the open door. Badria is standing there with his jacket.

Only one letter different, but they might as well be different species.

"I fixed the cuff," his ex-wife says.

"Well get in here."

Badria edges over trying her best not to look at her younger sister. Badia makes no attempt to cover herself. Tariq holds his arm out so Badria can slip the jacket on. He returns his attention to Badia.

"You leave for Saudi Arabia in the morning," he says.

"Where will we be staying?" Badia says.

"In the Prince's palace."

Badia can't help but grin. Her older sister does up the front of his jacket and begins pinning his loose sleeve.

"Your job is to keep an eye on Noor and report back to me."

"What exactly?"

"Everything. Her diet, the books she reads, the conversations she has. Do everything to become her confidante, even if that means speaking ill of me. You understand?"

Badria pricks him by mistake, and Tariq raises his arm..

"Good God, now can you see why I divorced you?"

Badria cowers.

"Get out."

Badria scurries away, and Badia comes over to him.

"Here let me finish that," she says.

She fixes his loose sleeve with the delicacy of a seamstress. Tariq nestles his nose in her hair and breathes in her scent. His hand wanders over her naked buttocks, and she leans up and licks his neck with her tongue. Outside a massive roar of "Allah akbar" goes up.

Damn.

He pulls away and extracts Noor's diamond ring from his pocket.

"Here. A small present to remember me by."

He takes Badia's hand and slips the ring on the middle finger of her right hand. Badia's eyes sparkle. She kisses him on the lips.

"I love you," she says.

"And I you."

He walks out the room, affording himself one last glance before closing the door behind him. Badria sits on a nearby chair rocking back and forth. He heads through the house and out into the courtyard. There Sarosh waits for him with a couple of mujahideen.

"I have something for you," Sarosh says.

He holds out a wrapped gift. Tariq tears off the paper to discover a green leather box. Inside is a gold Rolex and a simple white card.

Congratulations.
To a long and fruitful relationship.
Always,
Ivor.

Tariq slips the watch on.

"Who's it from?" Sarosh says.

"The Prince," Tariq says. "Now let's go."

At the front of the main building the vehicles wait, their engines idling. Tariq realizes they are waiting for him. Sarosh leads him to the Prince's new Hummer, and one of the Prince's bodyguards opens the door. Tariq looks up towards the windows of the Prince's quarters. He wonders if Noor is watching him. He hopes she is. He climbs in next to the Prince, and the convoy starts on its way.

FIFTY-NINE

CHARLIE WAKES TO the beeping of a heart monitor. He finds himself in a dark room. The only light comes from the glow of a monitor. He tries pushing himself up with his right hand and discovers that it's encased in plaster cast. He uses his left and winces. Every part of his body is in pain. He looks around. A soldier stands on the other side of a glass door.

What the hell am I doing here?

Memories begin to seep back; the trip to Islamabad, the meeting with his father's contact, getting back in the Pajero.

Was I in a car crash? Is that why I'm here?

He remembers his room in disarray, Wali outside the hospital, the blood speckled grass, Tariq staring across the coffee table at him.

Noor.

He shouts for help. A male nurse runs into the room.

"I've got to get out of here," Charlie shouts.

The monitors beep faster. The nurse grabs a syringe off a tray. Charlie thrashes his legs.

"No," he shouts.

The nurse cries out to the soldier, and the soldier runs in and pushes down on Charlie's arms. Charlie screams. The syringe jabs his arm, and soon after sleep overtakes him.

When he awakes the lights are on, and Jurgen is sitting in the chair beside him. Jurgen puts down his book.

"How do you feel?" Jurgen says.

"We have to find her."

"It's impossible, Charlie."

"No."

"The Pakistanis want you out of here. Actually they wanted you out of here yesterday, but I managed to get you a twenty-four reprieve."

Charlie tries to wrench himself up off the bed. He feels as if he's drunk ten tequila shots and collapses back onto his pillow. When he opens his eyes, Jurgen is standing over him.

"But what about Noor?" Charlie says. "What do I do?"

"You do what I did. You try and forget."

Jurgen places Charlie's duffel bag on the chair.

"I packed what I could from your house."

"I'm going to find her, Jurgen, I'm going to find her."

Jurgen gives him a sympathetic smile.

"You deserved better than this, Charlie."

Jurgen leaves, and two nurses come in. They dress him in a clean t-shirt and his now blood splattered jeans. Not long after three soldiers and an officer arrive. They put him in a wheelchair and take him down to a waiting ambulance. At the terminal, a burly soldier lifts Charlie into the wheelchair, and with the three other soldiers they enter the arrivals hall. The crowd falls silent, even the taxi drivers stop searching for prospective clients. They bypass immigration, pass through the departure lounge and trundle down a gangway to a waiting plane. The flight is packed. The burly soldier deposits Charlie in an empty seat in economy while another shoves his duffle bag into the overhead bin. Soon after the plane rolls away from the gate.

Charlie feels something poking out of his right pocket, and with the tips of his left hand he extracts Noor's passport. He turns to the back page and stares at her smiling face. The old man next to him gives him a curious look. Tears are rolling down Charlie's cheeks.

"I'm going to find you," Charlie says. "I'm going to find you, I'm going to find you, I'm going to find you."

SIXTY

NOOR STARES OUT the window. Through the slit of her niqab she sees a Pakistani International Airlines jet pulling away from its gate.

"You know, you can take off your niqab now," Badia says.

Badia lounges in the leather chair across from her. She has a childish grin on her face. A Filipina flight attendant approaches carrying two crystal glasses on a gold tray.

"Some orange juice?" the attendant says.

"Thank you," Badia says.

"Your Highness?"

Noor doesn't respond. The attendant places Badia's glass down on a mahogany side table and retreats to the galley.

"It's going to be fine, Noor," Badia says, "I promise you."

The engines whine, and the plane trundles down the runway.

Noor closes her eyes and finds herself back in the graveyard, running between the graves. A full moon shines above and perched on top of a mound is the rabbit, its glinting eyes following her as she rounds the bend. Up ahead she sees a warm orange glow. She runs faster, faster than she imagined was even possible. She realizes the glow is coming from the open door of her hut. Charlie, Baba, Mamaan, Wali and

Bushra are standing there. She shouts out to them, and they smile. She runs even faster, desperate to embrace them.

Then just before she gets to them she soars into the sky.

No.

She flies up over the flat, thatched roofs of the camp and looks over her shoulder. They wave at her with both hands.

"We love you," they shout.

"I love you too," she shouts back.

The higher she gets the smaller they become until the lights of Peshawar swallow them up.

She turns and looks towards the horizon. She braces herself for the journey ahead.

END OF BOOK ONE

ACKNOWLEDGEMENTS

First and foremost, incalculable thanks to Clarke, Harry and Frankie for allowing me to spend so many late nights writing *Refuge*, and to Clarke for being my first reader and constant and earliest supporter. I love you all utterly.

Thanks to all those who were my friends and co-workers in Pakistan twenty years ago. Dan Coulcher, my brother-in-arms, Paul Tzimas and Duncan Rourke, our fellow volunteers and intrepid explorers; all the staff and pupils at the Frontier Academy in Peshawar; Mocam, Shakoor, Wali, Syed and all the teachers and students of mine at International Rescue Committee; Pete and Jane Roffey and Annie who were such gracious hosts in Islamabad, and Nicholas Maclean-Bristol and all the staff at Project Trust, a truly wonderful organization that betters the lives of both its volunteers and the people they help.

Special thanks to Abid, our best friend and guide in Peshawar, who graciously proofed the manuscript for any cultural, geographical and historical discrepancies.

Thanks to the early believers and readers of the book. Trevor Engelson, my former business partner and now manager, his wife Meghan Markle, and everyone at Underground; Charlotte Boundy whose enthusiasm, feedback and perseverance on my behalf has, dare I say it, been boundless; Laura DiSanto, Brandon Dermer, Jason Ruscio, Jon Cassir, Katherine Cowles, Arthur Spector, Maria Kourtis for your early reads and peerless thoughts; George Lewis for allowing the use of his wonderful photo for the cover; Margo Murphy for the cover design; Dave Feldman, my lawyer, for being my tireless advocate; and to Jon Elek and everyone at A.P. Watt for their efforts on my behalf.

And, finally, enormous thanks to James and Georgie Osborne, my mother and father, who allowed me, at the age of eighteen, to go on such a crazy adventure and who have unfailingly encouraged my dreams throughout my life. I love you and feel so blessed to have you as my parents.

N.G.O

http://www.facebook.com/Refugenovel

http://refugenovel.tumblr.com/